SUZANNE'S LIFE CHANGED FOREVER THE DAY IAN CHANDLER LANDED IN HER ATTIC!

"We can't take a man who's been yanked from the year 1872 to Cherry Hill mall. You have got to be kidding!"

"You can bring the guy up to date." Suzanne's friend Leslie was starting to make sense. "Buy him some clothes, show him some video games, take him to a restaurant so he can get familiar with the new food of the nineties."

Suzanne had to admit that she felt safer knowing that she'd be in a crowded, familiar place rather than home alone with her unexpected guest.

"And how, pray tell, will Mr. Chandler buy a suit with money from the *eighteen hundreds?*"

Leslie covered her mouth to stifle a belly laugh. "Consider it your investment in your future."

Suzanne refused to join in the laughter. But the more Leslie howled with mirth, the harder it was to suppress the urge to giggle.

"Okay, one *cheap* suit. That's it."

"I never wear cheap suits, ladies." Ian stood in the doorway, wrapped in a makeshift blanket toga. Leslie took one look at him and howled.

Suzanne was not amused. "If my friend would stop laughing so hard, we could continue discussing how to get you some gentlemanly attire on my limited budget."

"I have never had a woman purchase my clothes," Ian said.

"Oh, really, you two are such spoilsports. A trip to the mall is going to be a real experience, Ian. Just stay close to Suzanne. Follow her lead, and you'll be fine."

"Follow her lead? I think I'm capable of conducting myself appropriately in an open air market and contracting with a tailor to make a suit of clothes." Ian stared at their amused faces. "Am I not?"

"No, Mr. Chandler." Suzanne managed to say. "You are definitely not." She wondered how Ian would handle the changes of the last hundred years— and she made a mental note. If he could learn to shop, he could learn to do dishes. Ian Stewart Chandler was about to earn his keep!

TURN THE PAGE FOR CRITICAL RAVES FOR THIS AUTHOR!

BEWITCHED

CONSTANCE O'DAY-FLANNERY

ZEBRA BOOKS
KENSINGTON PUBLISHING CORP.

ZEBRA BOOKS are published by

Kensington Publishing Corp.
850 Third Avenue
New York, NY 10022

First Printing: August, 1995

Printed in the United States of America

This one is for Leslie Esdaile . . . a fine woman,
a terrific mother, a wonderful friend
and a true character. The Ethel to my Lucy.
Thank you for "being there."

One

She knew she was in trouble when she started to fantasize about David Letterman. Okay, so it had been almost three years since she'd had intimate contact with a male . . . but there was something so damned sexy about his goofy grin. And then there were the eyebrows, getting lighter and growing by the month. She had a crazy urge to run her fingertips over them to bring them under control. It made no sense. The rest of America made jokes about his looks. Dave made jokes about his looks. Yet when he'd ask for a beverage, smack his lips and smile into the camera, the fantasy got really scary. She could actually imagine spending the day with him— and the night.

David Letterman!

It was beyond scary. It was sick!

Susanne Griffin was forty-one years old, considered successful, with everything in the world going for her except someone to share her life. She wasn't sure if she believed in love and happily ever after any longer. Sure there was infatuation with all those pheromones, endorfins and chemical changes taking place in the brain. But what happens when all that fades? When infatuation turns into reality? As hard as she tried, she couldn't think of one good marriage. Okay, there were marriages that had endured, but there wasn't one where she thought she would love to change places with the wife. Maybe she'd been alone too long, was too used to her own way. She was probably becoming like those men she'd heard about as a child. A *bachelor*. Someone too old to change their ways. The trouble was, she liked her ways . . .

She protected her independence like a futuristic warrior. Sometimes she thought she had been born too soon. In the next century women like her would be valued and accepted, and not be termed headstrong, bitchy or odd. She hoped reincarnation was true, because in her next incarnation she might fit right in with everyone. Not like now, when her friends worried that she might spend the rest of her life alone; when her mother was too polite to put into words her fear for a daughter that didn't like men.

It wasn't that she didn't like them. She did. She just didn't trust them. She had several great male friends, men who used her as a sounding board in their own relationships. She just knew that their minds operated on a different frequency than females.

She'd read all the books. She understood the "rubber band theory" about women. She respected men's right to hibernate in their dens and not communicate until ready. She knew all the reasons why men and women had problems

found my place. I'm happy to Zen ou
template the universe."

Susanne sighed, picturing her
in her mind. Leslie Peterson w
feet of love and intelligenc
hair framed a face of se
beauty. And her favorit
colorful sweaters, ga
pendants. That's w
thought of her
came into the
for Ramshe
"Sorry,
"May
you

"Hey, lady . . . did I wake you...
anything important?"

A soft giggle came through the wire. "Don't I wish? Mike is downstairs working on an energy report that has to be finished for his presentation tomorrow. I'm in bed reading this fascinating book on natural magic, and—"

"Oh God, I knew I'd regret sending you for that job," Susanne interrupted. "Leslie, just because you work in a bookstore that specializes in New Age material doesn't mean you have to turn into a metaphysical junkie."

"Now you sound like Mike," Les said, disappointment clear in her voice. "Why can't either one of you see this is really me? I feel like I've t and con-

dearest friend
as tall, almost six
e. Her black curly
rene, almost classical
outfits tended to be big
zy skirts and, yes, crystal
ny Suzanne had immediately
good friend when a job lead
agency for a part-time sales clerk
ad Books.

Les. Tell me about the book."
be later. First tell me why you called. Are
okay?"

Now that was the difference between men
and women, Suzanne thought. Women who
have bonded know that a telephone call late at
night spells emotional trouble and will put
aside anything, except the welfare of their children, to offer a sympathetic ear. It was sort of
a feminine code of honor.

"Promise you won't think I'm crazy?" Suzanne
first asked.

Again that affectionate giggle warmed her ear
as Leslie added, "Remember who you're talking
to, Suz. Mike thinks I'm having a quiet nervous
breakdown, but then again, what does a man
who works with math all day long know about
the big picture? Now what is it?"

Suzanne grinned. "You're right. You are the
only one I could tell this to without fear of being
slapped into a straight jacket."

"Sounds interesting. Spit it out."

She picked up the remote control, clicked the TV off, and then took a deep breath. "I'm fantasizing about David Letterman." It sounded so ridiculous.

There was a moment of silence.

"What?"

"You heard me." Suzanne refused to say it out loud again. Suddenly laughter filled her ear and she closed her eyes with embarrassment. "I know. It's sick. Maybe this is the way that stalker woman started, the one who breaks into his house and claims she's married to him."

"Stop it," Leslie chided in between giggles. "You're not sick. You're just lonely. You need a man."

"Oh, *please*. Great work, Sherlock." Susanne shook her head, while regretting calling. She should have waited until morning. "I know I need *something* in my life. I'm not so sure it's a man."

"Okay, I'm sorry for laughing," Leslie said, trying to sound serious. "Let's look at this intelligently. You're forty-one, attractive in a classic kind of way—"

"What's that supposed to mean?" Susanne interrupted. "Classic? Like I'm old, or something?"

"Oh, please, Suz. I just meant that you've got auburn hair, blue eyes, cheekbones that Elle McPherson would envy, and in those Donna Karan outfits, you look classic. It's that Main Line Philadelphia look, like Kate Hepburn."

Suzanne groaned. "Great comparison. Hepburn always played the spinster."

"Oh, c'mon. Even though you've never been married, you do own your own employment agency. And, may I remind you, you have had five fairly long-term relationships— "

"And they didn't work out, let me remind you," Suzanne again interrupted.

"They weren't right for you," Les countered.

"Oh, for God's sake, how does a woman ever know if it's the *right* man? It's a crap shoot, and I simply don't gamble well."

"Suzanne, you broke off with Richard three years ago because you felt smothered."

"May I remind you that Richard suddenly went country western on me and tried to get me to wear cowboys boots in bed because it turned him on? This from a dentist who lived all his life in New Jersey."

More giggles came from her friend. "He wasn't the right man."

"Obviously," Suzanne muttered, trying not to laugh at the memory. "Did you ever think that maybe there *isn't* a right man for me? He'd have to be one in a million. And even though I don't gamble well, I do know that's too much of a long shot. I'm getting older by the minute for this mating game and my window of opportunity may have been slammed shut by now."

"You just need some help."

Suzanne had heard that tone in her friend's voice many times over the last fifteen years. It had gotten them into such silly trouble that Mike had started to call them Lucy and Ethel.

"I don't want to hear this . . ."

"Listen," Leslie pleaded in that voice that clearly told Suzanne to hang up the phone before it was too late to save herself. "I have a plan."

Susanne clamped her eyes shut and whispered a prayer, "Oh, God help me. I should have never called you. Forget this. Forget I called. I'm just a middle-aged woman with an identity problem. Go back to reading your magic book and I'm going to sleep."

"Will you listen to me?" Leslie now demanded. "Mike is taking the girls on a camping trip this weekend. Tomorrow when he comes home from work he's picking up Jennie and Becca and heading for the Poconos. That means I'm free for two whole days and nights. Why don't I come over and spend the weekend with you? We'll come up with a solution, or at least have fun while trying."

Susanne thought it over for a few moments. Leslie had a heart of gold and it would be nice to have company for a change. "We could make it like the old days," she murmured into the phone. "Good food. Good wine. Good conversation . . . as long as we don't get back on this subject."

"Can only promise good food and good company. You get the wine."

"Done. But no more talk about finding a man, okay?"

"Hmm . . . Mike just came into the bedroom. Gotta run. See you tomorrow night?"

"Between seven and eight? That will give me time to get home from the office."

"Seven-thirty. Night, Suz."

"Good night, Leslie. And . . . thanks for the attempted rescue. Your intentions were good."

"Right. See you later."

Suzanne hung up the phone and turned off the light. Snuggling back into the covers, she sighed with contentment. Maybe she didn't have a husband and children and all that society said she should have by her age. But she did have one hell of a good friend.

She'd make it.

All day long Susanne found herself looking forward to Friday night. It had been too long since she had planned anything that wasn't related to business. Although it was only a girl-friend coming over to save her from her own loneliness, Suzanne knew she could count on a rarely experienced range of emotions when they got together. They'd laugh, they'd cry, they'd comfort each other and get angry at the world together . . . then they'd probably have more wine and get philosophical about the whole mess called her life. She could vent with some-one safe and trusted, wring it out of her system, and finally be done with it. Who needed a man when you had such a good friend?

Annoyed, and not quite sure why, Suzanne pulled into the store section of Ott's Tavern to pick up two bottles of white Zinfandel. Once inside, she ignored the sly smile that the old man behind the register cast in her direction. Yeah, that's right, she thought, I've got a hot date planned with my *girlfriend*. Why in the world did she suddenly feel so defensive? Why did she feel like everyone had some hidden knowledge of her lonely existence? It was pathetic.

Paying for the wine without looking at the clerk, Suzanne escaped from the store and back into her car. Now she was becoming paranoid, or like some sort of strange recluse that thought everyone was out to get her. It had to stop. Is this what happened when one's sexual needs were not tended to properly over an extended period of time? Is this what happened to the monks and nuns? Did they just become so odd and so paranoid that, they gave up and gradually faded away from society to live in gatherings amongst others like themselves?

Suzanne shook the feeling of dread that crept through her as she drove home. She refused to acknowledge the cute young lawn care guy with great buns as she passed him and turned into her driveway. Who gave a damn, anyway! She had a weekend planned with the girls. Just the girls. No Martians. No aliens. No fuss with makeup or hair. No perfumes. No panty hose. No games. Just plenty of laughs and fun.

She had a plan. She had a life.

As soon as Suzanne walked into the house, she kicked off her pumps and dropped her handbag on the foyer table. It felt good to relax. Making her way toward the kitchen, she pitched her suit jacket over the back of a chair. Yeah. It felt good. No one was coming over that she had to impress. Placing the wine bottles in the refrigerator, she pinched off a piece of American cheese and shut the door.

Turning to sort through the mountain of unopened mail on the counter, she noticed that the red light was blinking on her answering machine. Years of business experience had made her adept at doing two things at once. She ran back the tape while still sorting mail, and smiled as she listened to Leslie's chipper message.

"Hey, kiddo, are you ready for ladies' night? I'll be over shortly, as soon as I get my tribe out of here. Of course, I'll look sad and wave goodbye to my crew in the driveway and act like they've abandoned me. Then, I'll put on some makeup, my dancing shoes, and I'll be there in a flash! Presto changeo, we plan to party! Bye, hon."

Suzanne groaned. Party? Leslie must be out of her mind! Suddenly all of her plans for a quiet, uncomplicated evening at home began to evaporate. She knew her friend too well. There wasn't a soul alive who could say no to her. The woman should have gone into sales, she thought morbidly, rearranging the mail in a neat stack. Leslie's forte was merrily cajoling people into harebrained schemes of adventure. It happened every time they got together, and hadn't changed since they were in school. Suzanne could almost see it before her eyes as she grabbed up the most urgent bills and headed upstairs.

First, Leslie would probably whirl into the

room like a fireball of energy, then paint an irresistible picture of excitement and drama, using unparalleled humor, of course. Suzanne knew that she'd probably wind up laughing hard and trying to say no as Leslie ushered her out of the door with intensity. How does one combat a mischievous six-foot elf? How does one stop a roller coaster ride once you've boarded and the coach has begun to click up a steep incline?

Frustrated, Suzanne flung open her closet doors and began rummaging for something suitable to wear. Then it dawned on her . . . What does one wear to a *club*? She groaned again and sat down heavily on the bed. Going out meant shoes— correction, heels. It meant hose, refreshed makeup. She had to wash and redo her hair. It was too much, and that was just getting there. It had nothing to do with what she'd have to endure once they entered *The Inner Sanctum*. Christ.

The thought of doing the singles scene brought on more dread and melancholy than it was worth. Looking over at the digital clock on her nightstand, she realized that she only had twenty minutes to get ready. Twenty minutes. How the hell was she going to transform her face, body, and most importantly, her mind, in that short period of time? Although she didn't want to disappoint her friend, or want to deal with Leslie's effervescent coaching while she got dressed, tonight the task seemed insurmountable.

Okay, she rationalized to herself, it's fun for Leslie to get out once in a while— she has a nice, warm body to go home to later. That way it's easy for her to laugh at the strange men, the whole meat market scene, the Spandex Queens, and the lame pick-up lines when those aren't your options. But when you have to try to sort through that chaos in order to find companionship, and you know that, at forty-one, you probably don't even measure up to the dregs . . . Well, it was depressing. Beyond depressing.

The doorbell rang, and Suzanne looked over at the clock before standing to go downstairs. She hadn't moved in twenty minutes, but had chosen to sit there in her stocking feet, half dressed. She had abandoned her search for outfits and hadn't even considered washing her hair. She just couldn't. As the bell sounded again, tears found their way to her eyes. What was wrong with her?

Wiping at them angrily with the back of her hand, she hurried down the stairs and opened the door. As expected, Leslie greeted her with a wide grin that was full of mischief.

"Are you ready to *party?*"

Leslie rushed in the door and gave her a big hug. For a few seconds she enjoyed the nurturing security her friend offered.

"No," Suzanne murmured. "Not tonight. I just thought it would be the two of us. I— "

"Look at you!" Leslie exclaimed, holding her back from the embrace. "You're not even dressed yet. C'mon, or we're gonna miss happy hour."

"I can't," Suzanne pleaded, hoping that Leslie would relent. "I don't know what's the matter with me, but . . ." she trailed off almost with a sob. "Not tonight, okay? I'm sorry."

Leslie's expression changed immediately. Wrapping Suzanne in a motherly hug that made her want to cry harder, she whispered, "It's all right, honey. I know you've been upset, but I just didn't know how much. C'mon. Don't cry. We'll have fun tonight, and we can stay here for that. I just thought it might do you some good to get out."

Suzanne could only nod and whisper back, "Thank you." She was too choked up to elaborate on the feelings that she couldn't quite articulate now. At this point, she was just thankful that her friend understood without needing the words. She didn't have to go into a long justification about why she was feeling so blue, or why she wasn't wearing her dancing shoes. Leslie had accepted her unspoken emotions, and made her feel all right with them. It was enough that she simply didn't want to go out, and her best friend seemed to understand immediately.

As they crossed the foyer and went into the living room, Leslie's tone was gentle. "Listen, do you have any wine, or should I run around the corner and get some?"

"No, I have some in the fridge," Suzanne said quietly, while flopping on the couch. "I'm sorry to be such a party pooper."

"Hey, the party is only as good as the company," Leslie answered cheerfully as she hurried into the kitchen, returning with a bottle and two glasses. "Where's the opener?"

Suzanne shrugged. "In one of the drawers, I guess. Let me look for it. I haven't needed it in a while."

Leslie studied her carefully, and a slow smile crept out of hiding on her face. "I've got something in the car for you. I was going to save it until we got back. But no time like the present."

Skeptical, Suzanne eyed her friend who seemed to perk up just a little too much. "Oh, no, I'm almost afraid to ask."

"Just find that corkscrew while I run outside for a minute. Don't worry, it's not dangerous."

Suzanne had to laugh. "I'm not supposed to worry when you put a disclaimer on it? What am I in for?"

She could hear Leslie laughing as she bolted out of the front door. By the time she had located the corkscrew, her zany friend had returned with two small boxes and a book under her arm.

"Do you have a white candle and some sage?"

"What?"

"Oh, c'mon. A candle? A white candle? You do keep them in case the power goes out around here, don't you."

"I have a flashlight."

Leslie groaned. "Oh, please. Candles aren't just for romantic dinners with a man. You can use them when you take a bath, even if you are bathing alone. It's soothing. Humor me, and try to rummage in that junky kitchen drawer of yours to find one, will you?"

Giving up the fight against her friend's smile, Suzanne grudgingly went back into the kitchen to look for a candle. What in the world was she in for tonight? Shaking her head, she finally located a small, white votive left over from the holidays.

"And sage," Leslie called from the other room.

"Sage?"

"Oh, please. Don't you cook in here? Sage. Sage. Like turkey, chicken, poultry seasoning."

Suzanne peeped into the other room and watched Leslie pour two glasses of wine.

"I'll need an ashtray and some newspaper too. Oh, yeah, and some matches."

"For what?"

"Because, you silly goose, how will I light the candle without a match? And how will I light the fireplace without some newspaper to catch the fire. And how will I burn the sage without an ashtray?"

"I was following until the burn the sage part."

"Will you just get me an ashtray? God . . ."

"I don't smoke."

"Then a small saucer that you don't mind messing up will be fine," Leslie said calmly, her eyes still alight with mischief.

Collecting the items Leslie requested, Susanne returned to the living room. Her curiosity pulled at her as she sipped her wine and watched her friend build a fire.

"Why don't you run upstairs and put on some sweats and get comfortable?" Leslie asked, not looking at her as she worked on the embers. "It'll take me a minute to get ready."

It was a good idea. Picking up her glass of

wine, Suzanne rose without hesitation. She looked forward to taking off her straight skirt and hose. "I'll be down in a minute, but try not to get into any trouble while I'm gone. Okay?"

Leslie just laughed. "Bring back some notebook paper and a pen too. You'll want to keep a dated record of this."

She refused to ask. It seemed safer to run upstairs and change.

The room had been transformed into a rose-orange color when she returned. Leslie was working on her second glass of wine, and the fragrant scent of burning spice hung in the air. All of the lights had been turned off, and only the fireplace and candle provided illumination. It was beautiful, if not romantic. For a fleeting moment Suzanne wondered why there couldn't be a man relaxing on her floor before the fire, sipping wine, waiting for her return . . .

Banishing the thought that was sure to depress her, she entered the room and sat cross-legged on the floor near the coffee table.

"What are you doing, Les?" she murmured, not wanting to speak too loudly and break the tranquil mood that they had both lapsed into.

"I'm concentrating on your problem," Leslie said quietly, turning to look at her. "I've given it a lot of thought, you know?"

Susanne felt ashamed. Here her best friend was worrying about her, and there was really no problem, per se. Leslie was the one on a tight financial budget with two little ones to feed. She was the one that had to jockey school schedules, a husband whose company was downsizing, a dog, a new job. Given what her friend was coping with, what did she truly have to complain about? Loneliness? It seemed so trivial and selfish at the moment. How could she admit that because one little facet of her otherwise pretty good life wasn't right, she was near tears?

"I didn't mean to make you worry," Suzanne said quietly, while pouring another glass of Zinfandel. "I'm really okay. It just gets to me sometimes— you know the being without a life partner thing. It's stupid. We should've gone out."

"It's not stupid," Leslie said perking up, her voice full of authority. "Listen, first of all I'm not worrying. I'm thinking, or concentrating. There's a difference. Second of all, *it is important*. Who the hell wants to be alone without someone to share their life? It's the most fundamental pull in the universe, to find your other half, to find your soul mate, you know? Things and activities and great jobs only complete a portion of one's overall life. Those things are important, but it's not the whole enchilada!"

Susanne chuckled. "Well, I haven't had an enchilada in a mighty long time."

Leslie almost spit out her wine as she laughed. "Now, we're talking. I knew you just had to warm up. So, how long's it been?"

Suzanne groaned. "You don't want to know."

"*That* long?" Leslie stated, while frowning and clucking her tongue. "We definitely have to fix that."

"I don't want to seem desperate or anything," Suzanne offered in self defense. "I'm not a stupid woman. There are diseases out there, unscrupulous people. I'd rather live and be alone than end up with some jerk."

"Definitely," Leslie affirmed with confidence, leaning over to refill both of their glasses. "I never subscribed to that half-a-loaf-is-better-than-none theory. And I'd never suggest that you just settle for a total jerk. Out of the question!"

They both fell into a harmonious silence as they sipped their wine and pondered the problem. Finally, Suzanne's curiosity got the best of her.

"So, what do you do in the nineties to meet a nice guy? We're all so compartmentalized now, you know what I mean? We can order in food from great restaurants and eat alone. There are no more socials and house parties with eligible men. You can watch cable or rent a movie so you don't have to sit in a theater by yourself. God, Les . . . I mean, what-du-ya-do?"

"You ask the universe for a little help."

Suzanne laughed hard, feeling the wine begin to relax her brain. "Oh, yeah, I can see it now. I go to church, pray to God to send over this hunk tonight because I'm so lonely and so horny I can't stand it. Then I take communion to seal the deal, is that it?"

Leslie was giggling as she took a deep sip from her glass. "No, silly. Well, sort of. See, you've got to get beyond that old way of thinking and tap into the cosmic energy that's all around you."

Suzanne just groaned and poured the last of the bottle into her glass as she got up to get the second one in the refrigerator. "Cosmic energy, huh," she called over her shoulder. "I can just order one up, like I order a pizza?"

"Sort of like that," Leslie giggled, lifting her glass as Suzanne began to pour again. "If you had to make the perfect guy, what qualities would he have?"

"Are you serious?" Suzanne asked, sobering a little as she watched Leslie pick up the paper and pen.

"Yeah. Go ahead. Give me a shopping list."

Hesitant, Suzanne thought about the question for a moment before answering. "Depends on when you ask me— my order of priority that is."

Leslie smiled. "That bad, huh? The wine isn't helping, I'm sure."

Slightly embarrassed, Suzanne mentally changed her wish list. "Okay, okay, here goes . . ." she said, adjusting herself so that she could see what Leslie wrote. "He should be honorable, have integrity . . . he should be kind, and thoughtful, giving. He has to be intelligent and ambitious."

Leslie raised her glass. "If you're gonna order a guy from the cosmic pool, let's not go for a poor one."

They laughed.

"What else?" Leslie urged, thoroughly into the game.

"Oh, I don't know. I'd be happy with those

qualities," Suzanne said dreamily, taking another deep sip of Zinfandel.

"Gimme a break," Leslie broke in, giggling and almost spilling her glass. "Let's get real here. You can ask the universe for anything in a man you want, and all you request is this nice, kind, fairly well-to-do soul. How about some macho with that? A little testosterone?"

Susanne had to belly laugh at her friend's expression of mock disgust. "I was trying not to go there, Les."

"Trying not to go there?" Leslie seemed almost incensed. "If we're gonna do this thing, we're gonna do it right, or we're not doing it at all. Hell, I'm not trying to conjure up some sweet old man for you, lady.

"Wait, wait, wait a minute. What exactly are we doing?"

"We are making us a man, hon. Plain and simple. Just like the witches of Eastwick. If they can do it, we can do it. But we'll be sure to ask for a Heaven-sent one, not the devil."

Suzanne laid prostrate on the floor. "Save me. Somebody save me! My friend has lost her mind and I'm trapped in my house with her!"

Undaunted, Leslie picked up her pen and began writing despite Suzanne's protests. "Let's make us a *real* man. Okay, cosmos, he needs to be tall, say about six-two. Piercing blue eyes that draw you. He's gotta have that 'come hither' ability, you know? Dark hair. Suz, whadduya say to dark hair with blue eyes? Sort of Alec Baldwiny, don't cha' think?"

Rolling over on her side to stare at her friend, the idea began to have some appeal. "Yeah, I like men with dark hair. Say, can you really do this, Les?" She couldn't believe she had just said that. The wine had to be taking effect.

But quickly, worry began to replace Suzanne's mirth. Suddenly, she felt like her friend might actually be serious. When Leslie opened up a little book of magic, Suzanne put on the brakes. "Hold it. I knew it was a bad idea to send you for a job at that New Age place. You're really into this, aren't you?"

Leslie seemed to consider Suzanne's words, but her expression took on a strange brilliance. "Suz, I can't explain it to you, but it's changed my life. I now understand a lot of crazy coincidences, and my luck has absolutely changed for the better. It's as if all of the hardship makes sense. I see it as one big cosmic lesson, and I'm even grateful for the problems because I really learned something. My relationship with Mike seems better. The girls are happier. I'm happy. I don't know how else to explain it, Suz."

Suzanne began to relax again. Somehow, there was no denying the positive change in Leslie's attitude. If her friend was happy and centered, then she was happy. Whatever had caused the change, she was glad that it happened. But still *this*?

"Okay," Suzanne finally gave in. "So what do we do?"

Leslie beamed with excitement and leaned

forward expectantly. "Okay, let's get in the right mood and—"

"Am I going to regret this?"

"Not to worry, everything is in divine order. All right. Where were we? Now place your bets. He's gotta be hung, and—"

"Please, will you stop!"

"No, I may be married, but I am realistic. Size *does* matter, girlie. It can't have been that long for you. Or don't you remember?"

Suzanne waved her away. "I don't believe you are doing this. You're crazy. I'm getting some crackers and cheese. We're gonna get drunk."

"First of all, *we* are doing this. Second of all, I am writing down the fundamentals that you keep leaving out— this is a delicate equation and you gotta get it right. Third of all, I think we're already drunk."

Suzanne sat down again with an ungainly thud. "I think you're right."

For a moment both women looked at each other, then burst into peals of laughter.

"Let's do it!" They chimed simultaneously.

"Yes!" Leslie said with emphasis, pouring a new round and returning to the page. "He should be a *good* lover— tender, passionate, skilled . . . Oh God, I miss Mike right now."

Giggling and chatting over the various qualities that made up a good man, they eventually finished the list not long after the wine was gone.

"Let me raid your spice cabinet to really seal the deal," Leslie said standing on wobbly legs.

"Maybe I can run to my house and get some if you don't have what I need."

Catching up to her friend, Suzanne joined Leslie in the kitchen. "You must be mad if you think I'm going to let you drive home to get some stupid spices, half drunk. We haven't even had dinner, and it's pouring outside." As the words passed her lips, Suzanne gasped. "Oh, my God, I left all the windows open because there was such a nice breeze earlier. Don't go anywhere," she commanded as she bolted out of the room and began closing windows.

When Suzanne returned to the living room, Leslie had her entire spice rack on the coffee table, and she was putting little pinches of each jar onto the folded list of male qualities that they had made.

"What on earth, may I ask, are you doing?"

Looking up calmly with a smile, Leslie gave her a wink. "Just a little insurance, since this is the first time I've actually done a spell before."

"A *spell?*"

"Yes. A spell for love," her friend responded nonchalantly. "A little sage for wisdom, a little curry for his bedroom manner . . . spicy, hot, but subtle. Yeah, subtle. A little thyme for staying power . . . Hmmm," she said turning the bottles around in the candlelight, "How about some salt? As in, salt of the earth, for integrity . . . Mustard seed for strength . . . that's hot, and subtle, too. Ahh, yes. Allspice for machismo. Whoops! A bit too much there. Oh, well, we want a *man* right?"

Suzanne merely giggled and shook her head. "Do you have any idea what you're doing?"

"Sure. It's all natural, see? And, boy, this one's gonna be a doozey! Then let's add a little mint. He should be sweet, fresh— but I'm staying away from sugar because we don't want to make him gay, or anything."

Suzanne nearly howled with laughter. "You *have* lost your mind. I was right. I was absolutely right. And I'm crazy because I even entertained this madness for a second."

Leslie ignored her and continued matching spices to the qualities that appeared on the list. When she was done, she looked up with a satisfied grin. "Do you have a dollar?

"A dollar? For what?"

Leslie groaned this time and let out an impatient breath. "We did say we wanted him to have some financial acumen, did we not? Anyway, you can't burn silver or copper."

"You *are not* burning money in my fireplace. I won't allow it."

"Oh, stop being so cheap, Suz, and get me a bill. Just think of it as an investment in your future."

Suzanne could not understand why she was leaving her living room, going into her foyer, or digging in her purse to hand her girlfriend a dollar bill to burn. She was obviously having a nervous breakdown. No, they were both having wine induced, collective, nervous breakdowns. Maybe they should write down the store where they brought the wine, the manufacturer's name and the date of purchase. That way, when they finally flipped out, someone could find the note and trace the element that had caused their collective insanity. A virus in the grapes, perhaps?

Returning with the money, Suzanne grudgingly gave it to Leslie.

"Uh, uh. Give it to me with a free spirit, or he'll be a stingy man who only gives if he has to."

Snatching the dollar back from her friend, Suzanne waved the bill over her head, like the crazy woman she had become for even getting involved with this madness. "I give up! I've lost my mind! She's driven me past the point of no return! Let her have this bill freely, oh universe, so she'll get off my back and finish her spell!"

"That's the spirit," Leslie said, joining in the laughter. "Now, we must say a quiet little meditation. We must be serious," she said more calmly, ebbing Suzanne's laughter. "We want this to work for you, honey. Really we do. But you've got to really, really, really believe . . . if just for a few moments you have to act as though your very future depends on it. Once you've asked the universe for this good thing, which should only come from the highest good for the best purpose, then we burn it and agree not to worry about it any more. Okay?"

Suzanne had become quiet. There was something about Leslie's tone that told her the fun was over and that her friend truly wanted this to work. In truth, she did too . . . more than anything in the world at that moment. Closing her eyes, she put her full heart into their little ritual, which had now moved beyond a game. Silently, fervently, she prayed for a person like the one they had just imagined.

If only for a moment, she believed and hoped in magic.

Two

Suzanne stretched and yawned again as she pulled the pillows in closer to her chest. What a night! She and Leslie had laughed until their sides hurt, while berating the world for their fate as women. It was wonderful. It was what she had wanted the evening to be. It had been magical.

Too sleepy to move, and still too heady from the wine to care, she ignored her impulse to follow her normal routine of setting the alarm clock. It was two a.m. and for once she didn't have any pressing chores for the following day to worry about. Aw, live a little, she pleasantly told herself. This feeling of total contentment can't be beat.

Everything felt perfect. Maybe Leslie had been right. It would be okay. Just like the bedtime story that her mother used to read, she had been a good little mouse, had done all of her chores, then went out to play.

Allowing the peaceful cloak of sleep to engulf her, she listened to the rain and thunder outside. Flashes of lightning ripped across the sky, occasionally flickering an eerie, yet strangely beautiful blue light in her room. She felt safe and warm and secure. While Mother Nature wreaked havoc outdoors, she and Leslie were bundled in their beds after a great girls' night together. Who could ask for more? Tonight, she had decided she wouldn't, and tomorrow would be another day.

Suzanne let the last vestige of tension drain out of her body as each limb became heavier and heavier . . .

Then she heard it. A heavy thud brought her out of the drift and into clarity. Sitting up quickly, she craned her neck toward the bedroom door and tried to focus on the sound in the moonlight.

"Leslie, are you okay?" she called out, trying to stem instinctive panic.

"It wasn't me. I thought it was you," Leslie yelled back down the hall without masking her concern.

"Maybe the storm blew a tree limb over onto the house? Maybe that's all it was?"

There was a moment of silence. Suzanne swallowed down her terror. She was acting like a frightened child. She lived alone with a formidable security alarm system to protect her at night, and there was another adult in the house.

"Yeah, Suz, you're probably right," Leslie finally answered back. "I guess we're just spooking ourselves. The wine doesn't help."

"Sorry," Suzanne called again, thoroughly unconvinced as panic continued to ripple through her. "Now we're hearing things."

Leslie's nervous giggle did not make her feel better. She could tell from her friend's too-alert response that Leslie was also afraid.

Then there was a loud crash, and *footsteps*.

Both women simultaneously flung themselves out of bed and ran toward each other's rooms. Bumping into one another when they met in the hallway, they both screamed.

"Dear, God, you scared me!" Leslie whispered fervently.

"I know. I know. Did you hear it the second time?" Suzanne whispered back in a terrorized voice. "There's somebody in the house!"

"Oh, God, what do we do? Do you have a gun?"

"A gun, Les! A freakin' gun? Are you crazy? I would never keep a gun in the house! What happened to karma and Zen?"

"I don't think a prowler is into that shit, okay? If there's a rapist or a serial killer in here, then he's obviously karmically incorrect, and I say blow the bastard away then call the cops."

"Look," Suzanne said, trying to slow her own heartbeat and steady her breathing, "We'll go into my bedroom, lock the door, and call 911."

"But what if we're hearing things, and then the cops come and find two drunk women locked in a bedroom? What will— "

"Hey, I pay taxes," Suzanne nearly hissed, cutting her off. "I don't give a damn about what they might *think*. All I know is something is not right," she added, pulling Leslie by the elbow into the bedroom.

"Okay, but keep your voice down. We don't

want them to know that we know they're in the house."

Suzanne ignored her friend and reached for the phone. A tiny whimper escaped her lips, and her heartbeat now pounded in her head.

"Oh, my God," she gasped, clutching Leslie's arm for support. "The storm— the line's out."

Leslie pulled in closer to her. "Jesus. Maybe he cut the line?"

There were no words for a moment. Both women looked at each other in the dim moonlight as another flash of lightning flickered in the distance.

"We're trapped. We're gonna die," Leslie breathed heavily. "My children . . . I need some air."

Suzanne's gaze darted around the room furiously, searching for a makeshift weapon. The only instrument of death that she could come up with was shoe heels, hairspray, or a cordless phone. Leslie was right. They were going to die.

"We have to get to the kitchen. It's our only chance. I have knives down there and a flashlight," Suzanne commanded with false authority.

"What? Are you crazy, Suzanne? Try to use a knife on a deranged killer? Haven't you seen what happens to women who try to fend off an attacker? He could take the knife from us, then carve us up very slowly. Hell, I'd rather be shot or raped than be tortured for hours with a knife."

Suzanne stood stock still. The reality of Leslie's words caused a thin sheen of perspiration to form on Suzanne's brow. "Hey," she finally muttered, "I'm not going out like that. This is my home, and I'll fight that sonofabitch to the death."

"Let's just make it to the front door and out," Leslie's voice pleaded in the dark. "No heroics, okay?"

Leslie's plan did make sense, but there was no way to tell where the intruder was in the house. For all they knew, he could be lurking in the pitch black hallway now, waiting for them to unlock the door. Suzanne's mind carefully assessed their options, and her heart sank immediately when she realized that the panic remote for the alarm was sitting in full view on the dining-room table.

Another muffled sound drew the women into each other's arms.

"It's coming from upstairs," Suzanne squeaked. Fear was causing her heart to slam against her rib cage. "We can't take any more time, we gotta make a run for it."

"Don't you have a light in here? We can't even see where we're going! What if we bump into him in the hallway? What if there's more than one of them, and the others are downstairs?" Leslie demanded, her voice cracking with emotion.

"Let me out of this damnable dungeon, you bastards! God rot your hearts and souls for this abomination! I, as a gentleman and a citizen of the United States, demand to be released and remanded to my own country!"

Both women looked at each other with panic

and confusion. But somehow the crazy sounding request did dampen their fears.

"Did you hear that?" Leslie said in a more audible voice.

"Shhh!" Suzanne demanded. "He'll hear you!"

"But he didn't sound dangerous, just crazy," Leslie said, returning to a whisper again.

"Are you insane? You must still be drunk. Les, having a crazy person in my attic without protection, without a police escort, and without a clue as to how he got up there, doesn't exactly give me a warm and cozy feeling!"

"I don't know," Leslie murmured as her body relaxed and she slid out of Suzanne's hold. "His voice didn't sound scary. It's as though— "

"It's as though you must be out of your mind!" Suzanne interrupted, grabbing her friend's arm to pull her back. "Maybe he's a drug addict and freakin' hallucinating up there? What else would drive a person out into a stormy night to rob a house! Druggies are the most dangerous and the most violent criminals!"

Again, they stood still in the dark without speaking.

"I say we get a flashlight and go upstairs," Leslie said moving to the bedroom door and unlocking it. "Maybe he got into the house earlier, hid in the attic, passed out from the drugs, and just woke up. He could die, or need medical attention."

"Do you hear yourself? Do you absolutely

hear yourself?" Suzanne shouted, unable to control her voice.

"And now you rogues have incorporated women into your dastardly schemes. What cowards! The whole lot of you! At least be men and release me from my prison! Let me out of this infernal ship's hull!"

"He's a lunatic," Suzanne shivered. "Ship's hull?"

"Yeah, but at least we know there's only one of them in the house now. I'm going to get the flashlight from the kitchen, then I'm going upstairs to check this vagrant out. He sounds like a drunk or something, not a serial killer. 'Side's, you can tell from his voice that he's not a young punk teenager. The two of us can take him if we have to."

Suzanne was floored. She watched her friend of long standing open the bedroom door and enter a dark hallway with a lunatic raving in the attic! There were just no words that could form in her brain to escape from her mouth. Quickly catching up to Leslie's side, they negotiated past the furniture, and made their way to the kitchen.

"Where do you keep it?" Leslie motioned with her hand in the shadows.

"Bottom drawer on the left." Suzanne heard her own voice mutter the response. She felt her vocal cords move in her throat. But her brain refused to process what was happening.

"Got it!" Leslie exclaimed, after noisily rummaging for the instrument. "Now, let's go see who's paid us a visit."

Without thinking about it, Suzanne drew the

largest carving knife that her hand connected with out of the butcher block.

Cheap insurance.

Finally creeping up the stairs and stopping before the attic door, both women held their breaths.

"I don't want to die. Are you sure about this?" Suzanne whispered urgently when her voice returned, trying to avoid eminent harm.

"Not really," Leslie answered a little too calmly. "I just have a feeling about this, is all."

"Oh, great!" Suzanne groaned.

A loud bang against the door startled them both and they screamed, almost tumbling down the stairs as they held onto each other.

"And now you send women to do a man's job! What cowards! What total cowards! How dare you! I will not rest until this is righted in the eyes of the courts! As an attorney, this is an outrage, and you will have a fight on your hands! Believe my oath! I will not rest until it's over!"

Suzanne and Leslie looked at each other in the eerie flashlight illumination.

"He thinks he's an attorney? Jesus!" Suzanne whispered. "Don't open the door."

"Hey, fella," Leslie called out as Suzanne cringed. "How the hell did you get up there? You know you're trespassing, and we've called the police?"

"You, Madame, have the unmitigated gall to inform the authorities on *me*?" the male voice boomed back. "I will prosecute you to the fullest extent of the law, Madame, if you have in any-way been an accomplice to this outrage!"

"If anybody's going to jail, it will be you, buster!" Suzanne yelled back, finding courage behind the impenetrable attic door. "You can't just break into somebody's home, take a little nap, then wake up and scare the shit out of them! It's against the law!"

There was an unexpected silence, and Suzanne and Leslie looked at each other warily.

"Are you drunk, Madame?" the voice called from behind the barricade. It was a low baritone, cultured, and trying to sound patient. "I have a boarding pass in my breast pocket for the Mary Celeste to transport me to Liverpool, England. My papers are in due order, I assure you. What is not in order is the fact that your so-called captain, and his crew, are little more than highwaymen. My personage has been assailed. My dignity and honor affronted. I have been the unwarranted victim of an attempted murder— all because I had the integrity to love and want to marry a woman. And now I sit here, soaked to the gills and freezing, about to catch my death of cold. From your inane responses, and your unnecessarily shrill screams, I would have to surmise that you were unaware of the circumstances. But I have no problem taking a female to court if you elect to participate in the debacle by refusing to free me. Do I make myself clear, Madame?

Again, Suzanne and Leslie looked at each other. It was surreal.

"Although obviously insane, this guy sounds fairly intelligent," Leslie said in a curious whisper.

Suzanne found herself nodding in agreement. "You think maybe some frustrated professor from the community college took a bad acid trip, or one of his students slipped him something?"

"Well, the poor guy is freezing, which means he had to get in here during the storm. Maybe the storm knocked the alarm out for a few seconds while we were in the living room and he climbed through the window."

Suzanne could see the wheels turning in her friend's mind.

"And, Suz, regardless, this is about some kind of unrequited love thing . . . Who knows? Maybe, the spell?"

Before Suzanne could stop her, Leslie had turned the latch and flung open the door. Suzanne's heart actually skipped a few beats and a deep, hot dread spread through her torso. Somehow she knew her life would never again be the same.

Standing before them was a very wet, very angry, tall man, with an aristocratic arrogance that couldn't be denied.

"Well, I thank you for using your better judgment, ladies," the man said with irritation, as he pushed his damp hair away from his forehead.

To their surprise, he didn't move toward them nor away from them. He just stood there and looked them over with obvious disdain.

"Upon my return to my country, you will be well compensated for your assistance. Unlike the rest of your shipboard clients, I do not require any other service you might deem to render."

"What?" Suzanne asked, her brain absorbing too much data at once. "Are you implying that we're prostitutes, or something?"

"Well," the man answered nonchalantly, adjusting his soaked cravat, "no decent woman would be roaming around shipboard in a silk nightgown that exposes half her body, clutching a dagger, I might add. But I do suppose that your profession does pose certain dangers. The knife I thoroughly understand," he added, surveying her body closely. "Thoroughly."

Leslie chuckled, and Suzanne shot her a dirty look.

"Well, sir, frankly I'm flattered. I didn't think this old girl still had that certain charm. However," Leslie pressed on, ignoring Suzanne, "you are indeed on private property, disoriented, and most certainly going to catch your death of cold. Suz, do you have some sweats we can give this guy until we can get a call out to the paramedics?"

"What?" Suzanne snapped, refusing to hide her shock as she held the knife out in front of them. "This lunatic has got to go! I'm not running a homeless shelter here. We don't know if he's dangerous in addition to crazy. He's outta here!"

Leslie giggled as the man drew himself up even more.

"Insane? Did I hear you suggest that I am insane? And worse, did you accuse me of ungentlemanly conduct? I have never laid my hands on a woman without first being invited to do so. Do not be so ridiculous as to suggest that I might take my liberties with such common women as yourselves, at least not without paying in advance. As I said, I have no need of your services."

For some odd reason, this crazy man's tone grated Suzanne. Insane or not, she had been insulted.

"Look, mister, it's bad enough that you broke into my house, woke us out of a sound sleep and scared the living daylights out of my friend and I, banged and yelled like a trapped animal in my attic, then when we open the door, we find a kook dressed like he's going to a Halloween party . . . Then you stand here babbling like a madman about some lost freakin' love. You really have lost your mind if you think that I'm going to also stand here and let you call me a prostitute in my own home! Go to hell, Mister Whoever-you-are!" Suzanne nearly yelled. "C'mon, Leslie, lock the door, to hell with karma, Zen, and spells. We'll go to a neighbor's and wait for the police."

For the first time since they opened the door, the man's face registered an emotion other than anger, and he stepped back from them immediately.

"Spells. Did I hear you correctly? Spells? And that strange torch that throws light without benefit of fire or gas . . ."

"Aw, Suz, see? You went and scared the poor guy. Most people don't understand how harmless this stuff is. You can't just go around explaining the love ritual to people. They just don't understand how powerful the cosmos really is," Leslie said in a motherly chiding voice. "Hey, we're sorry, Mister. We didn't mean to scare you. It's okay. We'll bring you up some sweats, and you can get out of those wet clothes. We'll throw your costume in the dryer and get somebody who knows how to handle your situation to help you. Does that sound fair?" Leslie's voice had become patient and calm, as though coaxing a frightened child out of the corner.

"This . . . this is not a ship?" He looked to the unfinished attic wall and touched the rough planks of wood.

"It's the attic of my home," Suzanne answered, seeing the fear intensify in the man's eyes.

She felt herself relax a little. Something really weird was going on, but this time it was in their favor. The poor man seemed absolutely terrified and, for a moment, she felt guilty for yelling at him. How would she have reacted if she were having a nervous breakdown and found herself in a strange place, totally disoriented? She let her shoulders slump with resignation and lowered the knife a little.

"Hey, look, we didn't mean to scare you, but you really scared us, too. Les is right. You need to put on some warm things while your clothes dry. We can make you some hot tea and bring it up, but I'm afraid we have to lock the door. We simply can't let you out. We don't know you, or what you'll do," she added, looking at Leslie for a nod of support. "Then it's settled."

Still standing back in the shadows, the man's response was only a whisper of fear.

"Dear Mother of God, save me, for I have landed in a witches' lair."

Three

Ian Stewart Chandler stared at the attic door as the two women slowly shut it behind them. What in God's sweet name had happened in the brief moments where he'd felt a stinging blow to the head, followed by the suffocating sensation of water filling his lungs?

Had he died? Was that it? Were those women his keepers in Hell?

Everything seemed so eerily confusing. His head throbbed, and he winced as he brought his hand up to touch the source of his pain. Inspecting his hand in the semi-lit room, he saw there was blood and relief washed through him.

He was obviously not dead, nor was he dreaming. But where was he?

Fear had made it impossible for him to move. He could only stare at the door and wonder when the two strange beings would return. It took every shred of his reason not to spiral into believing the old wives' tales he had heard as a child. Damn superstition, he thought irritably as he paced for the women to return. He was wet, tired, and had a massive headache. What's more, he had to get back to Philadelphia and find out what had happened. And Marissa . . . God, where was she?

He couldn't think of her now.

Wrestling with his logic, there was only one rational conclusion. If his two jailers were not prostitutes or witches, they were most likely a part of that damned suffragette movement. What else could account for their odd manner of dress, or their quite obvious disregard for a gentleman in their presence?

Relaxing a little, Ian almost smiled. After all, Virginia Woodhill and Tennessee Claflin were two batty sisters who travelled extensively without a male escort. They had even started the International Working Men's Association. Much like his captors, they were self-proclaimed clairvoyants, and professed a belief system that included women's equality and free love. Those two were so shameless that they even committed their brazen ideas to print in a weekly. And so persistent were they in such socialist concepts that, even though they had been ousted from the organization by more conservative, right-thinking male factions, they'd then had the gall to try to run a woman for president of the United States in seventy-two!

Yes. His two captors were definitely women of questionable ethics. The one named Suzanne certainly exhibited qualities that bordered on fanatical. She most certainly could have been a high ranking official in that ill-formed Equal Rights Party, despite her beautiful face.

Suddenly, his jailers didn't seem nearly as formidable, and Ian could feel the tension drain from his shoulders. Besides, it was only four years until the Centennial, and the strange torch that the women brandished might well have been a new invention. Those kinds of people were always in the company of the eccentric. Witches. Ha! Was he mad? The blow to his head must have made that ridiculous conclusion take root in his mind. Maybe he was already in Philadelphia, or New York? Perhaps he had been ironically saved by members of the Woodhill-Claflin gang. He almost chuckled.

As he heard his hostesses' noisy approach to the door, Ian stood back.

"We could only find some sweat pants and an oversized T-shirt that might fit you," the one named Leslie offered with a smile, as she adjusted another of the strange torches under her arm.

Ian took the garments without hesitation, and began to inspect the strange items. "I've never seen clothes fashioned in this way before. But, at least they're dry, and I thank you, madame."

The one named Suzanne stood back a pace, holding a small tray containing a teapot, a crude china cup without a saucer, a bowl of sugar and a spoon. While eyeing him suspiciously before she spoke, the woman nudged her female companion with her elbow. "Okay, Les. Let's just let him change. When he's done, he can knock on the door and we'll take away the wet things."

Both women nodded and looked in his direction.

" 'I deeply appreciate your efforts, ladies," he said stifling a smile. "I will give you the signal in a moment, then you can collect my wet and tattered laundry."

The comment seemed to make Suzanne bristle, and she set the tray down heavily on the floor. "Fine, don't take all night."

Once he was alone again, Ian studied the garments. The pants seemed to be some type of fleecy gray cloth that felt warm and soft, but didn't resemble anything he'd ever seen before. And the shirt . . . it was a massive man's size, yet covered with a bright floral print. Somehow, the manufacturer had intricately woven a saying onto the front of it. Squinting in shadows cast from the tiny lamp provided, he could make out the word: *A Woman Needs A Man Like A Fish Needs A Bicycle.*

If it were not for the persistent chill that swept through him from the damp clothes, he would have hurled the shirt across the room. They were definitely suffragettes. Pulling off the wet items and leaving them in a pile near the door, Ian slipped on the strange pants and turned the annoying shirt inside out. At least the women would not have the satisfaction of seeing a man emblazon their rhetoric across his chest.

Suzanne and Leslie stood side by side facing the dryer while inspecting the strange costume. It positively reeked with a salty odor reminiscent of the Jersey shore. Suzanne shuddered. How in the world had she gotten herself into this mess?

At Leslie's insistence, of course.

Holding the sopping pile away from her, she was prepared to throw the whole disgusting bundle into the dryer barrel when Leslie stopped her.

"Hey, wait a minute, Suzanne," her friend said excitedly. "What if he left his wallet or ID in there? Maybe we can find out who he is, or where he lives. When the phones come back on, we can at least give that to the authorities."

Suzanne shrugged. "I don't know what we were thinking anyway, Les. How are we going to dry clothes without power? Hmm?"

Leslie laughed. "Oh, gee, I hadn't thought of that! I guess with the excitement of it all . . . Well, maybe we can put them on a line in the basement, and give them to him when they're dry."

Suzanne was incredulous. "Feel the weight of these clothes. It'll take two days of hot sunny weather to fully dry them. I say we throw them in a green garbage bag, run over to the neighbors, and wait for the paramedics to come get him. Once they have him in a hospital, or in an insane asylum, they can dry his stuff there."

Leslie looked defeated. "Okay, okay. But let's find out who he is first."

It was amazing to watch her friend in action. Without fear or trepidation about what she might catch from a vagrant, Leslie began rummaging through the pockets of the man's suit.

"Don't you want some rubber gloves? We don't know what this guy might be carrying."

"Oh, relax, Suz," Leslie chuckled. "He doesn't seem like he's a street person or anything. Just a little disoriented, that's all."

There was no way to argue with crazy people, Suzanne thought, peering over her friend's shoulder. But something about the way the costume was made drew out her curiosity. Each stitch was tiny and irregular. If she didn't know better, she'd swear that it almost had a handmade quality to it.

"Can an industrial machine do that?" she asked her friend.

Leslie stared at her in the flashlight's glow. "Do what?"

"Make that kind of handmade-looking stitch. And check out the label," Suzanne added with growing interest. "It almost looks embroidered, but it's from John Wanamaker. That doesn't make sense. I didn't know they had a costume division."

Wringing out the suit jacket in the laundry room tub, Leslie grunted with the effort and then opened up the garment and laid it flat on the surface of the dryer. "Looks almost real, huh?"

"Oh, don't start!" Suzanne snapped, derailing her friend's obvious consideration of the fantastic. "It's a damned costume, just a well-made one. Okay?"

"But, Suz," Leslie persisted. "How do you account for this?"

Both women squinted as Leslie carefully

opened a tri-folded document that appeared to be made of a heavy rag content paper. Although the script on it had run considerably, some of the words could be made out and the seal was still embossed.

"It's a boarding pass for the S.S. Mary Celeste . . ." Leslie whispered. "Dated the year of our Lord, eighteen hundred and seventy two, for the admission of one Mr. Ian Stewart Chandler, Esquire."

"You have got to be kidding me!" Suzanne nearly shouted, snatching the document from her friend's hand to inspect it more closely.

"Read it for yourself, Suz."

"Oh, please, Leslie," she scoffed, tossing the document on top of the wet jacket. "Either this is an elaborate scam, and this guy decided to stake out someone in advance with this story and act crazy, or this guy was truly insane enough to go to these lengths to spend a lot of money to have this stuff all made up to authenticate his craziness. Or—"

"Or," Leslie said with a smile, cutting her off. "We just pulled someone through a vortex in the universe with our little spell, and he really is who he claims to be. If so, we're responsible for him."

"What!

"I'm afraid so, Suz. What if this guy is really from eighteen seventy-two, and we conjured him up at the exact time he thinks he's been cast overboard to drown? And somehow, we did something in conjunction with the storm at just the right time, place, and energy pull, to jettison him across the time-space continuum, or parallel reality, to us?"

Suzanne simply stared at her friend for a moment. "When we go to the neighbors, I want you to lie down for a while and give me Mike's number in the Poconos, okay?"

"I'm not making this stuff up, Suz," her friend protested. "Don't you see what we could be onto here?"

"What I see is the fact that you have been under a lot of stress for a long time. I just didn't know how much pain you were in, honey," she whispered quietly, her voice cracking with emotion as she reached to hug Leslie. "It'll be all right. You'll see. We just have to get over to the McAlister's now."

Suzanne could feel her friend stiffen in her embrace.

"Why do people always jump to conclusions and assume you have to be mad if your definition of the world isn't in a neat little black and white package? Suzanne, there are wonderful colors, shades of gray, and a million things that we still don't understand, despite our technological arrogance. Yes, I've been under financial stress for a few years now. But I most certainly haven't lost my mind."

Abruptly reaching into the trouser pockets of the wet suit, Leslie pulled her fist out with triumph. "I'm not even going to look at what's in my hand. You inspect it, first."

Suzanne gingerly opened her hands to receive Leslie's fistful of so-called proof. Anything to humor her friend who was obviously having a nervous breakdown. Who wouldn't? It was a crazy night, and she supposed she was having one herself. As she felt the cold coins and soggy paper hit her palms, she blinked back tears and stared at Leslie's face. How, or what, was she going to tell Mike? What was going to happen to her friend's children? The poor, confused vagrant in her attic took on less importance. His presence was almost surreal and definitely coincidental. But what was happening before Suzanne's eyes, the unraveling of her dearest friend, made her heart ache.

"Stop it, Les," she whispered, not looking down at her hands. "It's gone too far now, and you have to make the break between wishful thinking and reality."

"Look at the money," Leslie said sternly. "Look at every single coin and bill tangled up with seaweed in your hand."

Again, Suzanne held her breath. What if the money was clearly marked with current dates? How would her friend react? What if Leslie was so caught up in her dream-state that she could no longer read the minting on the coins and bills correctly? Fear for her friend's fragile condition congealed at the bottom of her stomach. "Okay," she gave in quietly. "Let's see what we have here."

Turning over each coin with a triumphant squeal, and throwing the seaweed over her head, Leslie pressed her for an answer.

"How do you explain this, Suzanne! How? Look at the dates. Not a one later than eighteen seventy-two! And he doesn't just have American money. Look, these are Italian coins mixed in, like he was either planning to go abroad or just coming back from that country! Before you lock us up, Suz, at least wait till you can go to an antique dealer and have this stuff authenticated."

Suzanne stared at the contents overflowing her palms, and lowered her nose to the jacket.

"It smells like seawater, doesn't it? Admit it, Suzanne. We can't explain this."

Dropping the money on top of the dryer, Suzanne left the room and headed for the kitchen in the dark.

"Do you want some tea?" Leslie asked, catching alongside of her and touching her shoulder. "This stuff takes a minute to sink in, and you've just been given a crash course."

In a few short moments the tables had turned again. Now *she* felt like the one who was having a nervous breakdown.

"C'mon, I'll put on some water," Leslie said, suddenly sounding more concerned, more in control of the situation.

"No," Suzanne answered quietly. "The pot's upstairs with our guest, and I need something a little stronger than tea at the moment anyway."

Leslie just stared at her.

"What I need is the morning to come, you to be in the guest bedroom asleep, our guest to be gone, and for this to all be a very, very, realistic dream."

Tears ran down Suzanne's face and she didn't wipe them away. Her reality was being altered right before her eyes, and every available explanation was too frightening to digest. Either they were being stalked by a professional con-man, or they had a truly eccentric lunatic housed in her attic. Worse, her best friend was losing her mind. And, probably, she was having a private nervous breakdown of her own.

What was supposed to be a fun-filled ladies-only gathering of two friends evening, had been suddenly transformed into a night of the living dead with spells, ghosts, and crazies!

Heaven help her.

All she had wanted was a man.

Four

It had taken Suzanne forever to get her eyes to close and her body to relax enough to sleep with a strange person still in her attic. The only way she had agreed to give in to Leslie's insane request was to make her best friend sleep in the same bed, only one pillow away from her.

Stretching and painfully uncoiling her muscles, she looked over to her friend who was peacefully resting beside her. That's when she knew it all hadn't been a bizarre dream. In the cold light of day, reality hit. There was a lunatic in her attic, and possibly one sleeping beside her.

What the hell were they going to do now?

Suzanne slipped from the comfort of the warm sheets and blankets that surrounded them, and reached for the phone. "Thank God!" she murmured to herself. The dial tone was back.

Now, all she had to do was dial 911, give her address, and let the authorities haul this nightmare out of her house. This time, she was not about to give in to Leslie's ranting and raving about the cosmos.

As she sat looking at the receiver, trying to

come up with an opening line that didn't sound like a crank call, she heard Leslie stir.

"Hi, lady. What a night, huh?"

Suzanne refused to dignify the comment.

"What?" she finally sighed, looking at Leslie's forlorn face. "What are we supposed to do, keep him locked in the attic, or pen him in the kitchen like a new puppy? Leslie, c'mon, we've got a six foot tall, two-hundred-pound crazy person sleeping on my third floor."

Leslie's shoulders slumped with resignation. "I know, I know, Suz. But, if you give him over right away, we won't have a chance to really talk to him. He seems so fascinating— even assuming that he's crazy. Don't you want to know how he came to believe what he believes? Wouldn't you just love to find out what made this person lose touch? Seriously, wouldn't you always wonder whether or not he was just a poor deranged soul, or a person who had actually slipped through a tear in the fabric of the universe?"

Suzanne looked at her friend for a moment. "Frankly, no."

"Aw, Suz, at least we could feed the guy first."

"If you feed him, he'll never go home. Didn't your mother ever tell you about the first rule of handling strays?"

Leslie laughed. "I've had a wounded sparrow, a pigeon, two cats who were sooo sweet, a hound with a broken leg . . . Pepper must've gotten hit by a car before we found him, a— "

"I remember, and that's *just* what I'm talking about."

"But what about all the unanswered questions, Suz?"

Suzanne stared at her friend, trying to ward off her wacky charm. "See, people like you are the same ones who run behind the police with a video camera, or do foreign correspondence in Kuwait . . . just to see for themselves. Let's just say that you and I have a different threshold for curiosity."

Leslie's eyes sparkled with expectant mischief as Suzanne continued to hold the phone without dialing. Somehow, Suzanne was sure that her madcap friend had broken down the invisible stone wall that had been built up over night. How did the woman do it?

"Okay, so we feed this guy, then I slip out of the room to make the call. After that, it's finished. Do you understand me? Over. Finité. Done. No more stall tactics. So, you'd better get your interview in fast."

Leslie hugged her and nearly squealed with delight. "Oh, Suz, this'll be sooo wild! I knew you wanted to know about this guy. And, have you looked at him? Hey, he was cute last night in the dark, let's see what he looks like in the daylight. This is so *interesting* you'll see. Just wait."

Suzanne let out another exasperated breath before standing. "Why do I allow you to do this stuff to me? Maybe we're all having a collective nervous breakdown or something. And with you around, why am I not surprised?"

* * *

He'd been awake for hours, as soon as he could make out daylight coming in through the slats of his cell. The headache and stiff muscles that cloaked him made him realize that, indeed, it had not been a fantastic dream. And his clothes . . . dear Lord.

Pulling the blankets around him more snugly, and fashioning a makeshift toga robe, Ian paced. How was he going to convince his captors to free him? How was he going to get decent clothes in order to walk the streets and hunt for Marissa? Certainly he couldn't go about in this sorry uniform. If anyone saw him, they'd surely believe him to be mad. And money? Was he in Italy, or another American state? His captors were American, but in the late nineteenth century Americans could be found in just about every country. He was lost, in the truest sense of the word. Where could he go without resources or his passport? What if they'd robbed him?

Hundreds of questions bombarded him, making his head throb. That, combined with his rekindling anger at the Hamiltons for snatching their daughter away and trying to send her away before they could legally wed, was enough to make him question his sanity. After all he'd done for them. After being their family attorney for years. After treating them with decency, honor . . . keeping all of their dirty little family secrets, he was not good enough to marry their daughter. All because he wasn't one of the landed wealthy, and didn't have their millions to hedge against the financial panic. Yet he wasn't a pauper. He'd managed to amass a sizable portfolio of his own, and had thus far protected it. Even if he were to lose everything, did they question his integrity? Did they think so little of him as to imagine that he'd allow their daughter to become a bereft vagrant, begging the streets for money, or worse? Didn't they know that he'd guard her security with his very life?

A new wave of resentment made his stomach muscles clench. Marissa's father had actually had the gall to laugh at him when he'd asked for her hand in marriage. Ian closed his eyes, remembering the humiliation, remembering the way her mother had smiled and said calmly, "Oh, Ian, don't be silly." It was then that he realized they had never considered him a friend of their family, nor was he even considered a valuable asset to them. He was merely hired help. Pleasant, affable, hired help. Much like the invisible servants that moved about their world . . .

Hearing footsteps, he leaned his head back against the angular wall and took a deep breath. This morning he was in no mood for idle chatter, long explanations, or even anger. He was tired and could no longer muster the enthusiasm to be sarcastic. He just wanted to go home, possibly with or without Marissa. Maybe they had won. He'd been defeated, and a sensible person would have given up long before now. It was just that he needed to see her again. To look into her eyes . . . to finally know how she felt about him before he could let it all go. If they reflected the same smug contempt that he'd seen in her par-

ents' instead of the vibrant fire that had drawn
him to her in the first place, then he'd know she
was never really his from the start, and that he'd
been a fool.

Maybe that was the crux of it. He'd been a fool
on a fool's journey to nowhere.

When he heard the latch turn he didn't move
or open his eyes. What did it matter? Marissa
already held his heart prisoner, and his body
was now simply the ransom.

Finally opening his eyes as the door was flung
wide, he stared at the woman who called herself
Suzanne. Dressed in a laborer's britches of work
denim and a fisherman's sweater, she stood in
the arch of the attic entrance with her arms
folded across her chest, and her amiable friend
peering over her shoulder. Annoyance seemed
to have replaced her earlier fear, and fatigue,
much the way it affected him, had probably congealed her emotions to something quite close to
indifference. He doubted whether any of them
had slept well last night.

"Okay, Mr. Chandler," the bold one sighed
with exasperation, "My friend thinks that we can
all have a cup of tea and some breakfast in the
kitchen without incident. Do you think we can
manage a civil morning, and then let you go on
your way?"

Ian considered her words briefly, and decided
that it was indeed a hospitable offer. At this
point, the lure of freedom was too compelling

to challenge her with a sarcastic response. "May I begin our civil morning with an apology?"

The dark-haired woman behind the one named Suzanne positively beamed, but said nothing. He liked her. Immediately. She had a friendly, open, almost child-like curiosity that he was sure had saved him from a more horrible fate than breakfast. The other one . . . well, he'd have to work harder on making amends with that shrew.

Straightening his posture a little, he stared directly at the short, red-haired, combative woman who still had her arms neatly folded before her. "By now I've gathered that you ladies were not involved in my unfortunate incarceration, and in my state of distress I may have said some things that were uncalled for. Thus, please allow me to make amends, so that a civil morning is possible."

The small woman tilted her chin up a little higher and drew a deep breath. "Do you eat eggs and bacon, or do you have any dietary restrictions about cholesterol, red meat, etc.?"

He just stared at her. What the hell was she talking about? Breakfast was breakfast, was it not? "Surely, if I am your guest, I will be pleased with whatever you serve. Thank you."

She seemed to relax a little, while the woman behind her looked like she might do a small gleeful pirouette. It just didn't make sense.

"A true gentleman, Suz," the other woman said with a giggle. "We conjured us up a true, honest-to-God, gentleman."

The comment seemed to make the bolder of

the two ladies more annoyed. "I said drop it, Les. I don't want to hear any more about that business last night. Can we at least eat in peace?"

Nodding rapidly, the more friendly of his two captors stepped forward and extended her hand. "The name's Leslie Peterson, Mr. Chandler. Forgive my friend, Suz. She's always a bit skeptical of everything. A real hard case. But I find you positively intriguing, and if you're not too tired, I'd love to hear all about your quest over breakfast. Maybe we can even help?"

He found himself smiling despite his mood and circumstances. Truly, the tall woman that shook his hand had an elfin, almost magical sparkle in her eyes. Whereas the other one was more mysterious, and when he looked into her smoldering, angry gaze . . . there was just something there that he couldn't quite articulate, something that didn't make him comfortable.

Hoisting up his blankets which covered the ridiculous outfit that he donned, Ian followed his hosts down two flights of stairs to what he assumed to be the first level of the house. Immediately, he was struck by the strange furnishings and metallic objects that he passed on his way to where they would prepare a meal. Yet, when he reached the doorway of the so-called kitchen, he stopped in his tracks.

"What's wrong?" the one called Leslie said quietly, appearing concerned.

He could not move, let alone blink, as his eyes scanned the bizarre surroundings. Without wood or coal, a controlled fire blazed up from little circles on a square object which stood in the middle of the room. Obviously it was a stove of some sort, heating a kettle of water, but it had no chimney, and no place to furnish a flame. The blonde moved about it with ease, touching the sides of it, even leaning against it without burning herself! And he could smell bacon cooking . . . the smell seemed to be coming from a white metal box that was built into the wall. On closer inspection, there was a platter of the meat turning around under some sort of lamp that lit the inside of the enclosure . . . and dear God in heaven, there were blue glowing numbers counting backward on the side of it!

Yet, there was also a window. In fact, there were several large-paned glass windows open with a gentle breeze coming into the room. Thinking of an immediate escape, he moved toward freedom, wondering all the while whether or not guards or dogs patrolled the grounds. "Where am I?" he asked stoically, taking in a cleansing breath. "Are we in the Americas?"

The woman didn't answer, but shook her head and walked over to another large white cabinet. He watched her with deep fascination as she opened it, and another lamp flicked on. Inside the pantry were a number of items that should have required ice to keep them from spoiling. Curiosity overtook his fear, and he hurried over to where she stood, trying to understand.

Placing his hand in the chamber that contained the eggs, he was astonished. It was cold. Everything was cold, but there was no ice. Opening the other side of the large cabinet, his jaw went slack. Everything was frozen solid, but still no ice.

Backing away from the contraption, and moving closer to the window, he restated his question with more urgency. "I'll ask you two ladies, again. Where am I?"

"This is worse than I thought, Suz," the friendly one responded quietly. "Listen . . . haven't you seen a microwave, or a refrigerator before?"

He didn't answer. He didn't know how to.

"Oh, give me a break!" the surly one broke in, while cracking an egg in a pan. "You're in Mt. Laurel, New Jersey, okay? How do you want your eggs? Scrambled, over easy, or what? This isn't a diner, so let's not be too picky, either."

Ian just stared at them both. "Mt. Laurel, New Jersey? Couldn't be."

She let out a little snort, and walked over to the kitchen table and picked up what looked like a weekly. Throwing it toward him, she then turned on her heel as he caught the paper and moved toward a little glass box that sat on the counter. "The Courier Post. Check out the date and the location. Give him a magazine, Les, and let him read the label in the corner with my name and address on it. This *Back to the Future* game is really getting on my nerves! Listen to the news," she said flicking a small switch on a black box containing a square of glass on the front of it.

Ian felt his heart pound wildly within his chest.

From a pinpoint of light that began within a black orb, a light grew until it consumed the whole front of the box. Once it did, his horror increased as miniature people began speaking and showing scenes of violence and mayhem around the world. It was too fantastic to comprehend. It was as though these two women could view the events around the world from one tiny crystal square.

A witches window.

Traumatized, he held onto the newspaper for stability. But when he glanced down to inspect it, his revelation made him weak. The headline date read, *April 12th, 1995!*

"Nineteen ninety-five? How? When? How could this be? It was April 12th, in the year of our Lord eighteen seventy-two, when I was attacked on shipboard. I was on the Mary Celeste, trying to find Marissa Hamilton. They had taken her from me," he nearly yelled, becoming increasingly more hysterical. "How could you take me like this? How did you two conjure me across an ocean to you? At least grant me a last wish of knowledge before you poison me."

He felt hot tears of confusion sting his eyes, and he wiped at them fiercely, trying to regain his composure.

"Hey, listen, it'll be all right," the brown-haired one said, approaching him slowly. "Why don't you sit down. We're all confused, and not quite sure of where you came from either."

The other woman just stood still, watching him take a seat from her position by the fire circles.

"Suz, I really think he doesn't know where he is. I don't think this is a game. I'm going to call my teacher. I've never seen anything like this in my life."

"Your teacher? What kind of teacher?" the other woman asked, seeming to grow more wary as she made the fires go out with a flick of her wrist. "We don't need to get any one else involved in this madness, except to turn him over to people who can help him."

"And what if we did do this, Suz? Huh, what then? You give over a perfectly sane man to the authorities, let him tell this story, then what? They'll lock him up forever! It's not fair. Not until I'm convinced that we didn't do this."

"I don't care what you—"

"Please," Ian interjected, cutting off the woman named Suzanne. "Please, help me understand. What did you do last night? Obviously something fantastic has happened here, and we're all overwrought. How about if I tell you what I remember, then you can do the same? Perhaps we're all losing our minds."

"That sounds fair and reasonable," the brown-haired woman said, taking a seat beside him as she scowled at her friend who remained standing. "What happened?"

Ian took a moment to collect himself, calling back his years of litigation for support. Only this time he wasn't negotiating with a fellow attorney, investors, a judge, or even foreign barristers. This time, he had to remain calm to negotiate his freedom from two witches.

Witches! Nothing else could explain the things he had seen.

"The reason I was on the ship," he began slowly, "was because I had fallen in love with Marissa Hamilton. Her family is wealthy, and unfortunately, I am only an attorney, not an aristocrat. While I was away on business, they abducted her. I believe they sent her to Rome on an extended vacation until our love waned. So I followed on the next ship headed for the region, hence my pass on the cargo vessel Mary Celeste."

The two women just looked at him, not uttering a word. Yet, the brown-haired one was clearly interested in hearing him out. He could tell by the way she frowned and leaned forward, nodding occasionally as he made a point. The other one leaned away, her head tilted slightly and her glare unwavering. She reminded him of Marissa, who had that same penetrating gaze when she sensed fraud.

"How were you sure that she went to Italy, and that they weren't hiding her in the States some place?"

He leaned in, pleased to have some dialogue with at least one of his captors. "Miss Peterson, I have considered that very possibility myself. When I first learned of her abduction, I rode to Philadelphia to her parents' home in Radnor township."

"Hamiltons? Radnor? What's their address?" the shorter one asked suddenly, becoming very animated.

"Suz, you don't think that—"

"Quiet!" she commanded to Miss Peterson, apparently hiding something. "The address where you went. Describe the house."

It seemed like an odd request, but then again, what about the last twenty-four hours hadn't been strange?

"The house number is eighty-four twenty-two Monroe Street. The house sits at the end of a lane and occupies three acres. The front of it has two sapling oak trees that were newly planted last season, and the perimeter is framed by newly planted pines. There's an apple tree, two old dogwoods, and azaleas that rim the back stone patio and white wrought-iron gazebo, but the front of the home is quite magnificent. Large white balustrades greet you before you enter the house. It's painted a soft, pale yellow and has a large sitting room with six ten-foot windows that face south in a grand semi circle—"

"Oh, God . . . Suz?"

He observed Miss Peterson's shocked expression as she stared at her cohort.

"Be quiet, Leslie," his reluctant hostess warned in a voice that immediately let him know he had said something of importance. "Let the man finish."

"Yes . . . well, let's see. There is a great deal of furniture in the room. Medallion and serpentine sofas and settees. Dozens of parlor chairs. Oh, and yes— a grand circular marble table and a fine spinet piano that Marissa loved to play. She was quite accomplished and had a fine voice that could—"

"Suzanne?" Again, Miss Peterson stared across the room, as though demanding a reaction from her friend.

None was forthcoming. Miss Suzanne Griffith merely shook her head as if the very act might deny his words.

Not wanting her to succeed, he hurried to add, "As you can see, ladies, I have been on the property and in the Hamiltons' company on several occasions. I am also more than some vagrant, although this is how they have treated me. I am surely their attorney of record. You have but to pull up any family document that I've filed for them and you will see my name."

Becoming more confident, he turned to Miss Peterson. "Have you a piece of parchment and a quill? I can give you my signature which you can match against those records if you like. I have none before me, and most forgers must have the intended victim's signature before them in order to copy it. Go and visit the Hamiltons' estate, if you will. Correspond with them and say that you are from a renowned New Jersey family, and have heard about one Ian Stewart Chandler. Tell them that you wish to check his references. While I'm sure they do not want me to marry their daughter, I would be hard pressed to believe that they would also damage my career and livelihood as well."

The one named Suzanne merely stared at him for a moment, then whispered quietly, "Leslie, get the man a piece of paper."

He knew he had her. Something he said had

captured Miss Suzanne and held her at bay with the truth. And although he was convinced that they were witches of some sort, it appeared that they weren't of a malevolent nature. Perhaps they were just troublesome fairies, not real cauldron stirrers. But whatever they were, they had caused him a great deal of inconvenience.

When Miss Peterson returned, she slipped a piece of smooth linen paper before him. He had never felt such a weight before, and the writing instrument didn't require dipping! Hiding his awe, Ian picked up the pen and scrawled his full Christian name, then slid the paper back to the two women to inspect.

"Who attacked you?" Miss Suzanne asked warily, inspecting his expression and the signature at the same time.

"I'm not quite sure how this came about, but I began asking the captain about other ships that had departed to the same destination within the last few days. He assured me that there had been none bound for Italy, and his vessel was the only planned departure from the region for months. Then, as we shared several brandies, I began to speculate about where Marissa could have been hidden. As long as I spoke of Italy, our conversation remained civil. Then it began to storm, and as he hoisted himself up to gather the crew, a strange sensation came over me. I don't know quite how to describe it. But, in an instant, I felt sure that she had never gone abroad. I told him that the Hamiltons had just acquired a large parcel of farmland in southern New Jersey, and perhaps they had sequestered her there. He then became unnecessarily bellicose, and I have to admit that my demeanor became coarse, and a fight ensued. Yet the ferocity in which he attacked me was truly unwarranted— even with too much brandy under his belt."

Both women looked incredulous.

"Electricity."

"What?" he asked, confused and questioning Miss Peterson.

"They tried to kill you?" the other one asked, appearing distraught. "What happened next . . . what time was it?"

"Well," he began slowly, testing for their continued tolerance. "The last time I looked at my pocket watch it was about eleven-thirty in the evening. But with the argument, then the fight . . .

"Would you guess a little after midnight?" the brown-haired woman asked just above a whisper, running her hands through her curly mane. Looking at Miss Suzanne, and virtually ignoring him, she added, "I knew it. He couldn't have known about the timing, we never spoke to him about it."

"Yes," he replied, searching both women's faces as they conferred without speaking out loud to each other. "I would say about ten after the hour, perhaps."

"Suz, that's when we threw the spell into the fire. I looked at the small clock on your mantel over the fireplace. Remember, it had just started storming— you had shut all the windows in the house and had come back— then it took about twenty minutes to do the spell. That would have put it at about five or ten after twelve. Jesus!''

Ian sat back in his chair and rubbed his face with two hands. "I had received a blow to the head which nearly flattened me. I felt my body lift and hurl toward the rushing water, and as I hit it, it seemed like lightning had struck me at the same time."

Sensing that they could not comprehend, he continued. "My body felt like tiny fish were biting me all over, especially down my spine. I gulped in water once, and sensed that I was under the waves, but yet I was coughing a mixture of water and air. It was black and almost hollow undersea, but there was a light, almost as though I was in a long tunnel. I thought perhaps another ship was passing, so I struggled toward the light. Then I felt myself lose consciousness. The next thing I remember was my body colliding against the wooden floor of your cell."

"Absolutely incredible. Electricity, then a pull through a vortex . . ."

The other woman moved over to the table, collected the paper containing his signature, and shoved it into her shirt pocket as she returned to her remote vantage point. She was dressed like a farm boy, and stood against the cupboards near a basin. After a moment she pushed a metal lever which was attached to the tub. To his amazement, crystal clear water poured from it into her hands. Splashing her face and drying it on a towel, she leaned against the metal basin as though for support. Her face had gone white.

Swallowing hard, she reached into the opposite shirt pocket, and produced his timepiece.

She clicked open the front of his gold watch, and handed it to Miss Peterson. "Twelve ten, Les. Like the man said." Then she carefully returned his money and his identification to the center of the table and retreated to a far corner of the room without a word.

"I have to call Grandma. You have to call your teacher, Les. I don't know what to believe any more."

"I know," the more affable woman said quietly. "This *is* our fault. We did it, didn't we, Suz?"

The other woman shook her head slowly. "I don't know. I hope not. But if we did, we have to send this poor guy back. Didn't they teach you how to do that part?"

"No, I told you this was my first spell. Suzanne, I had no idea that we'd bring some poor, lovelorn guy out of the past. I was just trying to draw a decent nineties kind of guy to you. I swear. That's all, really."

Ian stood and paced toward the window, fury quickly overcoming his calm negotiating facade. "You mean to tell me that you've never done this particular 'spell' or incantation as you call it, before! How irresponsible! Even witches ought to have some sort of apprenticeship, shouldn't they? Don't you have to study carefully like Merlin before you snatch someone from their reality? I cannot believe this. First I cannot believe that I, as a rational, educated person, am having a discussion about witch conduct. Number two, I cannot believe that you two were afraid of me! Number three, how dare you question me like a vagrant, when I can readily prove my identity, and you, madames, have yet to tell me who in the *hell* you are! And four— "

"Look," Miss Suzanne said, stopping his excited litany as he ducked when she held up her hand. "If we did do this, it was not with you in mind. And you're right. It was both irresponsible and unintentional," she added, casting a heated glance in Miss Peterson's direction. "I am also a disbeliever in such things as magic, spells, or anything I can't see, feel, or touch. So you have my good friend, Leslie, to thank for your situation. That is, assuming we aren't all mad."

Resting his forehead against the window he closed his eyes, breathing heavily as he tried to take it all in. "Please," he murmured, "haven't I been tortured enough? If you want to kill me, then be swift about it."

He felt a hand against his back. A woman's touch. When he looked up, the brown-haired one stood next to him with tears in her eyes.

"I am so sorry. Oh, God, we didn't mean to hurt anybody. But maybe we saved you from drowning, you know? If we send you back— if we knew how to send you back— maybe you'd go back to exactly where we pulled you from. In that case, from what you've said, you'd be overboard in the middle of an ocean, during a storm, and with no help in sight. You'll die. We've gotta find a way to get you back, but to a safer place."

He considered her words carefully before he spoke. In an insane sort of way, her convoluted logic made sense. "Then," he began hesitantly, "I suppose I should thank you for saving me."

"We'll do whatever we can to get you to where you're supposed to be," the other one said unexpectedly from across the room. Her eyes now contained the same level of confused concern that Miss Peterson's held and, for the first time since they'd met, he sensed compassion.

"Listen, I can't just let you roam my home freely before we get more information. You have a choice. We can let you stay in the attic for a day or so, with the door locked. We'll feed you, give you some warm blankets and stuff, and let you take a shower, whatever, while we try to figure this out. Or you're free to go now, and we won't call the police. But before you do either thing, at least have some breakfast."

Both women waited quietly for him to respond. Weighing the options, he moved over to the table and sat down heavily. "I am indeed hungry, and tired. I don't want to trouble you further, and hate the idea of incarceration, but I have no idea of how to return without you."

It was a compromise.

Clearly these two weren't about to harm him. And there was something undefinable in their eyes that made him know that they also knew the Hamiltons. True, they were eccentric, yet hospitable amateurs . . .

Besides, where else was he going to go?

Five

Leslie returned the phone to the wall jack and sat down at the kitchen table. "How's our guest doing?" she muttered, as Suzanne stood in the doorway expectantly.

"He went back upstairs with no problem after he showered and changed into some more of my sweats. Oh, and you should have see *that*. He acted like he'd never been in a shower before. I had to show him. And now I know I must be crazy. I'm doing a man's laundry, feeding him, and for what? To find out if he's slipped through the fourth dimension or something?"

Weary, Suzanne joined Leslie at the table. "So, did you catch up with your instructor or psychic counselor? What's the proper designation for him or her, anyway?"

"Teacher is fine," Leslie sighed. "How about your grandmother? Was she home?"

"Frankly, I haven't had a chance to call her yet. She's eighty-four, for God's sake. I don't want to upset her, or make her think that something strange is going on. What do I say? 'Hey, Granny, I got horny one night so my girlfriend and I did a magic spell and brought a man back from the past. Not my past. *The* past. Does he look familiar to you?' Oh, Les, this is really insane."

"Call her. The sooner we get some evidence one way or the other, the better we'll all feel."

Suzanne was horrified. "Don't tell me you're getting second thoughts now? Oh, no you don't. You can't just scare the life out of me, convince a vagrant that he's blown in from the past, then go home to your safe little love nest with Mike. If you go, he goes. You wanted adventure? Well, darlin', you're in it for the whole ride."

"That's why we have to know for sure. Mike and the kids will be home on Sunday morning. That means we have exactly twenty-four more hours to figure out what to do. My teacher will be here in a couple of hours. Maybe we should take a nap. I don't know about you, but for some reason I'm exhausted."

It was the first suggestion that made sense.

Lolling the kinks out of her neck, Suzanne winced. "I'm beat too. I feel like a week has passed, but I'm too keyed up to really rest."

"Well, how about if we just cat nap on the sofa and love seat until Rahmin gets here. I don't think I can keep my head up, Suz. It's like somebody hooked up a siphon to my internal battery and just sucked all of the energy out of me."

Suzanne went still. "I know what you mean. Ever since last night I've been weary beyond words. I can barely stand up, yet I can't really sleep. What's going on?"

"Maybe he feeds off of our energy while he's in this trapped state."

"Like a vampire," Suzanne whispered, feeling a new wave of terror engulf her.

"Not in the classic sense of the word, but all of us are a wreck. Perhaps all of our lifeforce is escaping through the hemorrhage that was created in the vortex. We're sapping his, he's sapping ours . . . it's not good, whatever it is."

"Oh, great," Suzanne mumbled, forcing herself to stand and walk into the living room. "Just what we need. A vampire."

Suzanne couldn't tell how long the doorbell had been ringing. Everything around her seemed hazy, and it was difficult to gauge her whereabouts for a few moments. Thrusting her body into a sitting position, she wasn't sure if she had the energy to move. Leslie seemed equally as paralyzed, as she placed her feet gingerly on the floor.

"Hey, Suz, you want me to get that?"

Suzanne blinked the sleep away from her eyes. "Yeah, I don't know if I can," she murmured before lying back down. "I'm just so drained . . ."

Leslie looked like she was moving in slow motion, and it took all of Suzanne's strength to focus on her as she left to answer the door. When she returned, a small Pakistani man followed her into the room, donning a slow, easy, smile.

"Very tired?" he said in a clipped accent. "This is a good sign."

"A good sign?" Suzanne responded curtly, her ire being the only emotion strong enough to propel her to a sitting position.

"Oh, most definitely," the man replied in a charming voice. "This lets me know that there has indeed been a significant energy transfer. This is very real. It's like a fingerprint. Unique. Very interesting."

As the man dragged a chair across the room and sat before her on the sofa, Leslie took a seat next to her as well. "Suzanne, this is Rahmin. My teacher."

Suz looked again at her six foot friend and the tiny foreign-sounding man. "Your teacher?" Nothing made sense any longer.

"Leslie has explained what you did last night," the man said in a low voice. "Very courageous, indeed. I'm glad that she had the good sense to ask for this as a gift from the highest realm for the highest purposes, because . . ." he added, clicking his tongue in admonishment, "you could have done yourselves great harm."

Suzanne and Leslie looked at one another and a silent gasp passed between them.

"Like what?" Suzanne questioned, despite her fears. "What could be worse?"

"Well, from what I am sensing, this is a good soul. A kind man. It didn't have to be such a benign presence, if you understand my meaning."

Both women looked at each other again, and Suzanne could tell that Leslie was ignoring her silent warning glare.

"We could have brought an evil presence?" Leslie asked in a shaky voice.

"Precisely."

This time Suzanne did gasp.

"How do we know what this is? How do we know that we don't have a confused serial killer upstairs who'll snap out of his gentlemanly conduct and take us out? How do we know that we aren't harboring a fugitive from justice, or a con artist, or whatever? I'm tired," she nearly wailed. "I want my house and my life back to normal. I'm drained, can't function, don't know what to think . . . I'm having these screwy dreams! If you can work some mumbo jumbo and be done with this, I'd appreciate it."

"Ahh. Patience," Rahmin scoffed lightly. His voice was like an easy breeze that just flowed over her, making her relax despite her resolve to remain tense. "First things first."

Sitting up straighter, Suzanne hung on his every word. For some reason, this petite, wiry fellow had an air of such confidence that it made one want to hear him out. In that moment, she could understand why Leslie had been drawn to him. Within the depth of his eyes she saw calm, patience . . . wisdom.

He spoke slowly and in an easy tenor, and never lost eye contact with her. And as he did so, he brought his hands to the outer edges of her body, yet never touched her as he arched around her silhouette.

"Ahh . . . Your aura has been disrupted for a long time, I see."

Suzanne didn't question his methodology, but sat still, and waited for instructions.

"There is some unfinished business. Many,

many, many, loose ends that dangle in this lifetime like threads from a fine cloth. You and your
friend simply picked up one of those threads and
pulled. The one you picked up is unraveling your
current energy, as well as that of another being's,
because they were inextricably entwined from the
beginning. You see?''

Suzanne just shook her head no, and for a moment she felt like the slow kid in a class. Leslie
was obviously getting it, since her head was bob-
bing wildly in affirmation and her smile had returned.

"Ah. Let me better state it. When there is a
significant issue, something very important that
is left undone, we carry that problem into each
incarnation until it is resolved. In your case, the
dangling thread was in the area of your romantic
liaison with someone special. It will be the same
thread for him. Yet, if you are not psychically in
tune with yourself, you do not know how or
where to pick up the thread. This is where the
universe tries to intervene to help you. She is
kind, and it pains her to see her children stumble
and bumble through their lessons. But, she can
only teach by example . . . and she cannot do
your homework for you. She can only put stimuli
in your path, hoping that you will respond. Do
you see?''

Slowly, Suzanne absorbed the analogy and tried
to make it merge with her reality. Not an easy
task. "So you mean that because something trau-
matic happened in my past life, as it were, in the

area of romance, I can't establish a solid relationship in this life until I fix that old problem?"

"Exactly!" The old man clapped his hands and his expression became almost brilliant. "Yes, yes, you have it! This is what was affecting your aura. Other beings who would come into your life shied away because of the blocked energy in that field. It could have been a career issue, a childbearing issue, conflicts with your current mother or father . . . whatever. But, if it was an issue before, it will always resurface again, until it is corrected. That is why a vibrant, warm, intelligent, beautiful woman such as yourself is lonely. Under any other circumstance, it makes no sense."

"Wow! Now that's deep," Leslie sighed in awe, allowing herself to fall back on the pillows. "It just blows me away."

"Oh, shut up!" Suzanne snapped while glaring at her pleased friend.

Turning her attention back to the man before her, she asked, "So how do I fix this aura-slash-past-life problem? And what do I do with the misplaced lunatic in my attic?" Feeling defensive, Suzanne stood and paced away from the small group. She needed space. Her entire love life was under a microscope, and with a stranger, no less. It was weird. It was beyond weird. And she was a normal person!

"The universe, in her infinite wisdom, has already begun the process," he exclaimed, appearing quite pleased with himself.

"Say, what?" Suzanne nearly shouted from

across the room. "This is supposed to be corrective surgery for my past life?" She didn't know if she felt more appalled, disgusted, or should have laughed. Yet, oddly, her energy did seem to be returning.

Ignoring her outburst, Rahmin continued in a controlled voice, his smile broadening as she sat down in front of him.

"Coincidences, child of the stars. Mere coincidences are your guide posts."

At the risk of being rude, Suzanne waved her hands suddenly to stop his airy rhetoric. "Oh, please."

"I want you to think about this calmly," he said in a matter- of-fact tone. "Now, I will begin without any interruption."

Suzanne restrained herself, as the man closed his eyes and Leslie followed suit. It was like sitting in church and wanting to laugh at an inappropriate time. Feeling suddenly mischievous, she kept peeping over to her friend, hoping to get her attention, hoping to draw her in without the teacher knowing it.

"Please, you must take this seriously," he said in a pleasant voice, never opening his eyes.

Caught, her face burned with shame. She was being silly. This whole exercise was silly. And what did this have to do with Ian Stewart Chandler, as the man upstairs called himself?

"That's it, focus on his name. Let me feel him through you."

Suzanne went still. The hair stood up on the

back of her neck. How the hell did this person know what she was thinking!

"You must go to a calm place. Visualize his face. Think of a childhood scene that brought you great comfort. Many times, places, scenarios, names, even physical structures will repeat themselves . . ."

The only calm place that Suzanne could recall was playing in her grandmother's garden while Grandma Hamilton clipped her roses. She was an eccentric old woman who would have been shunned by mainline Philadelphia society had she not been so wealthy. She sat on every charity board in the city. Suzanne loved Granny's house. It was big enough to explore for hours, without ever seeing the same knickknack twice. Yet, with all of the expensive antiques that it housed, she never made children feel like it was a roped off museum. No, that was more like her parents. Their home was sterile, uncomfortable . . . they would be the ones to yell at Granny when she allowed dirty shoes to cross her threshold . . . they—

"There is more than one thread here," the old man whispered, opening his eyes abruptly. "Two or more threads that tie you to your past. Hmmm . . . it will take time."

"But what do we do in the meanwhile? What do I do about this guy up in my attic?" Suzanne's questions were more like a lament than anything designed for an answer. As absurd as it was . . . she was actually buying it!

"You said you had dreams, correct?"

She nodded slowly, hanging on the teacher's every word.

"I want you to keep a journal of them. I also want this other person to do the same. Each morning, before you are fully awake, write what you feel . . . even if you cannot remember what you dreamed. Capture the emotion on the page—sadness, desire, happiness, peacefulness—even if you cannot remember the actual events. Can you do that?"

Again, Suzanne nodded in the affirmative.

"Then, I want you to begin going back to these places. Visit the place that I saw where there is a child laughing in a garden. Take the other soul with you."

Suzanne gasped and covered her mouth. Tears welled in her eyes and ran down her face without censure while Leslie reached over and hugged her. "How did you see it?" she whispered, "Nobody knows where that is."

The old man stood and rolled his shoulders. "There is so much energy here that I must go now. I am old and must unfortunately rest. But will you allow me to visit again? Next time with this other soul?"

Suzanne found herself nodding yes again, even without being sure when the old man could return.

"Show him the signature, Suz.," Leslie interjected hastily.

The man stopped his advance to the door and waited, while Suzanne numbly searched her pockets. When she handed the paper to him, he gingerly unfolded it as though it were a rare and fragile document from antiquity. Then, as he focused upon the signature, he allowed his fingers to graze the letters before closing his eyes.

"You have been given a rare gift," he murmured as tears stained his deeply lined face. "Oh, my child, She has been so kind to you both. Do not miss this opportunity. Take him to the garden. I must meet him when I have the strength."

Both women stood in the doorway stunned, as the old man returned the paper to Suzanne. Giving Leslie's face a little pat, he smiled broadly, exposing a few yellowed teeth.

"You have done so well, even in your amateur state. You will be blessed for what you have shared with your friends." Turning to Suzanne as he opened the door, his expression became gentle. "Understand that there are no coincidences, only stones in your path to mark your way. Some are wonderful gems to collect and add to your spiritual wealth along the journey. Others are markers too high to go over, and too wide to pass. Those are placed in front of you by the Goddess to force you to take another direction. Your good friend is a gem. For she has pointed the way to a large obstacle that you can no longer ignore. You will have to change directions, and you have her to thank. Rest now, for the new journey will be arduous. Your soul knows that this is the source of your fatigue."

Suzanne and Leslie looked at each other as the old gentleman made his way down the front steps toward his car. A silent understanding passed between them as they turned their focus to the foyer stairs and looked up. Somehow, they now understood they'd have to go for the ride.

"Absolutely not!" he bellowed. "There is no way in God's name that I will agree to meet with an East Indian warlock! Have you both gone completely mad?"

Leslie and Suzanne sat down on the attic floor, ignoring Ian Stewart's protests.

"Remember, Suz, you felt the same way at first."

"I know, I know. Until you've experienced it, you can't begin to comprehend."

"If he just spoke to Rahmin, you know. He has such a gentle way . . . he's such a meek soul . . ."

"You two are carrying on as though I have no voice in this matter. As though I'm not even in the same room with you!" he announced again, seeming agitated from the sudden interruption to his sleep.

"And what about when he saw the signature, Les?" Suzanne went on, continuing to ignore her distraught guest.

"I know. Wasn't that *deep?*"

"You showed him my signature?" Ian asked, obviously losing the battle with his curiosity. "He knows my name?"

"He knows your energy," Leslie interjected. "It's like a fingerprint."

All three fell silent for a moment.

"Then, he could verify my identity? He could vouch for my legitimacy?"

"In a matter of speaking," Suzanne admitted slowly. "At least we don't exactly fear you any more. But, we still have to be sure . . . we need something more to go on."

Ian walked over to the far corner of the room and banged his fist on the wall in frustration. "So, how long does that mean I'll have to remain captive in your attic, ladies? If I have been cleared as a potential criminal, why must I be detained like a common thief!"

"He has a point, you know, Suz. It isn't exactly fair. After all, he didn't ask to come here, really.

For the first time since this entire fiasco began, Suzanne had to agree with her friend. "That's true. And, I guess he can't do too much damage . . . I hope," she said looking at Ian Chandler's face with skepticism.

Again, the threesome fell silent, while awaiting Suzanne's disposition.

"Okay. He can stay for the weekend. But, Les, you've got to make up some cockamamie excuse to tell Mike so that you can sleep in the room with me. And we lock my bedroom door at night."

"I beg your pardon, madam. Are you assuming that your virtue is in jeopardy?" Ian huffed, pacing to a new corner. "I am insulted."

"Hey, I think Suzanne is being pretty lenient. If you've watched the news . . . Oh, I guess things weren't so dangerous in your day. But, regardless," Leslie continued with conviction, "we're *all* new to this stuff . . . maybe you can understand it said this way. It isn't exactly proper for a strange man to board with a single woman. Okay?"

The information seemed to sink in, as Ian Stewart Chandler turned around slowly. "I truly had been so wrapped up in my own concerns that I had never considered your reputation."

It was Suzanne's turn to take offense. From some deep reservoir within, his words felt like a stinging slap in her face. "Never considered my reputation, Mr. Chandler? How presumptuous of you. As though to say that I had no reputation to protect?" Her voice had become more shrill than she had intended. She wanted to throw him out on his ear.

"I do owe you an apology, Miss Suzanne. I— "

"There are no words for your conduct, sir!" she yelled, cutting him off as she stood. "You have come to my house unannounced, by whatever method. I have clothed you, fed you, and listened to your very long and difficult-to-substantiate story. And in return for my hospitality, you have yelled, pounded on my walls, scared my friend and I to death, called us prostitutes, and regarded us as whores because of the way we dress. As I told you on the very first night, you may go to hell, Mr. Chandler. Straight to hell!"

Her face felt flushed, and her ears began to ring as she hastened toward the door. She wanted to slap him.

"Wait, Suzanne," he said quickly, stepping forward to grab her arm. "I'm sorry. You're right.

I have behaved badly, and I owe both you and Miss Peterson much better than that."

"Leslie will be fine," her friend said smiling.

Ignoring Leslie's comment, Ian continued staring at her face as he spoke slowly. Maybe it was the urgency in his voice, or the way his gaze penetrated her . . . perhaps it was the way he said, "Suzanne," that had halted her retreat. But the exchange with him standing so close, seemed so very, very, familiar.

"I only ask that you allow for our mutual distress. We have all had our worlds turned upside down. I think had we met under different circumstances, perhaps we would have begun on a more civil note. Forgive me, dear lady. My apology is sincere."

Suzanne stared back at the tall man before her, trying to adjust her focus to see what was unfathomable. She allowed her gaze to scour his face and, for an insane instant, she wanted to reach up and touch the barely visible black stubble along his square jaw line. Quickly censuring herself, she lowered her eyes from his penetrating gaze on her. Whatever drew her for that moment had to stop. It was both inappropriate and dangerous. She didn't even really know who the hell he was!

"Apology accepted," she murmured. "No more dramatics, though."

"None," he said in a low even voice that went through her while revealing a perfect smile that made her look away again.

God, he was handsome . . .

"Rahmin said that you need to begin keeping a journal of your thoughts. Every time you fall asleep you should record the dreams, or even the feelings if you can't remember the dream."

Leslie's voice seemed very far away, and Ian didn't respond immediately.

"If it will please the lady, consider it done."

"Umph, umph, umph . . ." Leslie sighed with obvious appreciation of their guest.

"Oh, Leslie, stop it," Suzanne protested, stepping onto the landing and away from Ian Stewart's hold. "The man has been through enough. Is anybody hungry? It's four o'clock."

Suzanne refused to look at either of them as she descended the stairs. She had to get away from them, away from herself . . . away from the feelings that had suddenly swept through her. Anything but that. How could she feel such a primal urge toward a disoriented lunatic? Letterman was one thing, but this?

It was sick.

She tried to escape the amiable voices that followed her. As Leslie droned on about Ian's visit to a garden somewhere, she almost froze. She had to call granny, and take a lunatic via automobile across state lines to go visit this so-called special place. What if he freaked out on the drive over, looking at bridges and cars and trucks? What if he flipped at her grandmother's house, and gave her a heart attack? What if he accused them of kidnapping him? They would have to cross over into Pennsylvania. Or worse, what if Rahmin was just a flake, and this person who boarded in her home was dangerous? What if he came back later and robbed a little old eccentric lady in her mid-eighties? She'd never forgive herself. She could picture it now, explaining how stupid she and her friend had been to the police, the reporters for "Hard Copy" and "America's Most Wanted."

Suzanne groaned as she crossed the threshold into the kitchen and flicked on the Sony for the news. Somehow, hearing about the day-to-day realities of the nineties felt like a ground wire—something to root her to the present. Too much had happened too soon. Looking over at her two house guests, Suzanne was forced to smile. They were perfectly happy, chatting away about the cosmic possibilities, and here she was tied to the stove like a scullery maid. If Leslie was her gem, and Ian was her boulder, she couldn't imagine what lay in her path next!

Six

They had argued about what to do with Ian
Chandler all morning, and the question was s
unresolved. It was clear that Leslie eventually h..
to go home to Mike and the kids. Grandma Hamilton was unreachable by phone, and Suzanne
could only pray that she hadn't gone on a cruise,
or something. There were a lot of areas she could
research, but it was Sunday and the libraries
weren't opened. Besides, that would mean leaving him in her home unattended— out of the
question. And she didn't exactly feel comfortable
walking around the house with a complete
stranger that she didn't fully trust.

"Okay, Suz, I've got it," Leslie said in a con-
spiratorial whisper, looking up the stairs in the
direction of the guest bedroom. "We'll take him
to the mall.

"The what!" Suzanne gasped in astonishment.
"You have got to be kidding."

"Hold your voice down. No, seriously. It's the
only safe answer. I'll follow you by car. If he
tries to abduct you, or something, I can go for
help. Once the two of you are safely in the
Cherry Hill Mall, you can bring the guy up to

date. Fast. You can buy him some clothes, show him video games, the lingo, etc. . . . take him to Houlihan's so he can get familiar with the new food in the nineties. He's real flexible these days, you know? He wants to learn," Leslie went on with excitement. "That way I don't have to worry about you. It'll give me time to make up an excuse to Mike that you're really depressed . . . suicidal— "

"I am," Suzanne muttered in a surly tone.

"Feed the kids and stuff like that," Leslie pressed on, ignoring the comment. "Then I can scoot back over and meet you guys in the parking lot and tail you home and spend the night. It's perfect."

"And what if he freaks out in the mall?" Suzanne shook her head as they entered the kitchen to begin breakfast.

"Then, we walk away from the nut and call mall security."

They both laughed.

"And what do we tell 'em?" Suzanne asked, not able to keep the sarcasm out of her voice. "Especially when he says he spent the night?"

"That he's out of his flippin' mind and we don't know him. And we tell him that's just what we'll do if he tries anything funny. Trust me, Suz, the guy will be so freaked out when he hits the mall and sees the teenagers, that you won't have to worry about him straying. If anything, you won't be able to shake him."

Suzanne had to admit that she felt safer know-

ing that she'd be in a crowded, familiar place
than home alone with her unexpected guest.

"Okay. But what if he won't go?"

Leslie ran her fingers through her hair. "I've
got it. Tell him that he has to buy a suit. That
gentlemen don't walk around looking the way
he does, in too-tight sweats. That'll get him."

Suzanne looked at her friend in amazement.
"And how, pray tell, will Mr. Chandler buy a
suit with money from the *eighteen hundreds*?"

Leslie covered her mouth to stifle a belly laugh.
"Consider it an investment in your future."

"An investment! An investment? That's what
you said when I handed you a dollar and you
burned it in my fireplace!"

By now Leslie was doubled over and holding
onto the edge of the kitchen table. Wiping at
her eyes, she could barely speak. "I know, I
know," she laughed, waving her hand. "But this
time, trust me."

"Trust *you*?"

"Okay, poor choice of words But Rahmin said
I was your jewel."

Suzanne refused to look at her. She refused
to laugh. No, this time Leslie's antics wouldn't
work. But the more Leslie howled with laughter,
the harder it was to suppress the urge to giggle.
"Okay, one *cheap* suit. That's it."

"I never wear cheap suits, ladies."

The sudden male voice brought their discussion to a halt. Leslie immediately took one look
at Ian Chandler standing in the doorway with
his makeshift blanket toga, then back at Suzanne,

and began fighting the renewed urge to scream with laughter. "No," she managed between deep breaths, "I guess, sir, you wouldn't! Better take him to Boyds then!"

Suzanne was not amused.

"If my friend would stop laughing so hard, we could continue discussing how to get you some gentlemanly attire on my limited budget."

The man moved into the room and took a seat at the head of the table. Her seat. The spot where *she* always began her morning and had *her* meals. It grated on her.

"I have never had a woman purchase my clothes, nor have I ever had to— "

"Oh, give it a rest, Ian," Leslie said still giggling. "This is the nineties, okay? Right now you don't have a pot to p— "

"Leslie! C'mon. Let's not start this mess first thing in the morning." Turning to Ian Chandler, she tried to explain, rationalizing that his shopping expedition was a security precaution. "In truth, Ian, you cannot go around trying to find Marissa in that attire. It just can't be done. People won't take you seriously. How about if we call this a loan— an investment of sorts."

She ignored Leslie when her friend nearly spit out her tea.

"Besides," she continued undaunted by his surly expression, "We may have to travel a bit, in order to research Marissa's whereabouts."

Ian nodded grudgingly, and he looked down at his outfit. "As much as it pains me to admit, you do have a point, madame. But I can only accept new attire if it will be considered a loan."

"Noooo problem," Leslie laughed.

When they both turned a serious glare in her direction, Leslie seemed to become more amused. "Oh, really, you two are such spoil-sports. A trip to the mall is going to be a *real* experience, Ian. Just stay close to Suzanne. Follow her lead, and you'll be fine."

"Follow *her* lead? I think I'm capable of conducting myself in an open air market and contracting a tailor to make a suit of men's clothes. Am I not?"

Suzanne and Leslie caught and held each other's gaze, and within seconds, Leslie was doubled over again with peals of laughter.

"Ahh . . . not!" she managed to say. "Definitely not."

The look of sheer annoyance that crossed Ian's face made Suzanne smile. "No, Mr. Chandler," she began. "This is a new age market. There will be devices, contraptions, all manner of technology that you've never seen before. But in order not to draw significant attention to yourself, you will have to learn how to blend in. And the *only* way to do that will be to *follow my lead.*"

Both women watched as Ian Stewart Chandler stiffened his already perfect posture at the mere mention of following a woman's lead. It both amused and infuriated Suzanne at the same time. How odd, she thought, to be caught in a time warp with a true, down-to-the-bone chauvinist. As she broke the eggs and began serving the meal, Suzanne wondered how he would handle the changes that had happened in society during the last hundred years.

She made a mental note. Today her house guest could earn his keep. Today, Ian Stewart Chandler would do the dishes!

"I do believe you are enjoying this."

Suzanne looked at him from the corner of her eye, before quickly returning her gaze to the road. "I beg your pardon?"

"I said I believe you are enjoying my discomfort. First you instruct me in washing dishes, and now you have me harnessed inside this contraption. I told you that if you'd show me how it operates, I will take over and you can be the passenger."

Suzanne again looked into the rearview and saw Leslie's Pontiac keeping pace behind her. "You're a real piece of work, Ian. You know that? *It* is a car, and you can't operate it without a license. You have to pass a test given by the state police. A car isn't just a means of transportation. Look at how many there are on the road, and the speed we're traveling. It can also kill."

"I am a very careful driver. I also— "

"Ian," she interrupted with impatience, "You're talking about driving a horse and buggy. This is an Infinity J30. V6. 3.0 liter engine and 210 horsepower. That means I'm controlling the power of two hundred and ten horses under me. Believe me. It takes practice."

"You cannot be serious. No human being could do that."

She tried to control the grin from appearing, but failed. "I can," she said with satisfaction. And then, because she felt so perverse and ticked off at the bizarre intrusion into her life, she added, "Hang on. I'll prove it to you."

They were on a deserted back road, doing a lazy thirty-five miles an hour, and she quickly pressed down on the accelerator. The car immediately responded by jumping to life and leaving Leslie far behind. Suzanne observed her passenger clutch the dashboard, as if preparing for a crash. At seventy miles an hour, she pressed in the CD button and almost laughed at Ian's startled expression as the car filled with Elton John's voice.

"Convinced?" she yelled over the music and felt positively exhilarated as Mr. Macho nodded. Immediately, her foot lifted and the car gradually slowed to its former pace. "Now will you stop arguing and listen to me?" she asked, turning down the volume of the CD.

Lifting his hand to wipe the sweat from his forehead, he managed to say, "You have demonstrated your point well. It appears I have no alternative but to take your lead."

This time her smile was automatic. "Thank you," she said quietly. It was a small victory, but a victory nonetheless.

When they arrived at the mall and said goodbye to Leslie, Suzanne led Ian inside the huge structure. She found herself tugging at the sleeve of his sweatshirt to stop him from gaping. She supposed if someone had transported her a hundred and twenty years into the future and she was confronted with a Star Trek-like world, she too would be seized with awe and bewilderment.

"Here," she said, and pulled him over to the ATM. "I need to get some money."

"There is a bank inside this?" he asked, while staring at a group of racially mixed teenagers, all wearing their jeans almost off their backsides and topped with the mark of youth— Grunge flannel.

Suzanne grinned at his expression. "Look, see this machine? It's connected by a computer to my bank. Ahh . . . a computer is a . . .well, think of it as a super intelligent machine. I insert my card and punch in my secret code, like this. See? It asks questions and you just answer. Very simple."

"Amazing," he whispered, as twenty dollar bills spat out of the machine. "A machine that thinks. How is that possible?"

"I don't know," she answered honestly. "Something to do with microchips and wiring, I think. And electricity. Nothing you'll see today would be possible without it. It's energy."

She put the money in her purse and led him into the interior of the mall. When he saw all the people, he stopped and stared at what looked like mass confusion.

"Where do they all come from? Why are they all shopping? Is it a holiday?"

Suzanne gazed at the normal Sunday crowd.

She sighed. "I never really gave it much thought. New Jersey is a small but highly populated state. This really isn't unusual. It's just a protected place to shop."

"But the sun is shining. And most don't even have packages."

She saw that his observation was correct. Suddenly it occurred to her how much society had changed, even from her childhood. The mall was much more than a place to shop. It had become a safe place to spend the afternoon. People came for social reasons. The elderly were proficient mall-walkers. The kids met each other and hung out. And middle-aged couples strolled the shops, forced away from the house and the TV. It was a cultural mecca for suburban Americans where, on weekends, they came and paid homage to the god of materialism.

"C'mon," she urged, not wanting to comment on his remark. "We've got to get some clothes for you. Leslie's sweats are starting to look a bit strange, don't you think?"

She watched as he looked down to his costume and then around him. "I am dressed in women's clothes," he muttered. "I would deeply appreciate visiting a tailor. The sooner the better."

She started walking and he kept pace at her side, weaving in and out of the crowd. "There are no tailors here. Everything is ready-made. Off the rack, so to speak. Follow me. Let's try this place."

In the brief span of letting Ian wander through the shop, she saw a look of total confusion cross his face and immediately took over. Suzanne cornered a salesmen and told him to measure Ian and then picked out two pairs of jeans, two shirts— one white, one chambray. An off-white cable-knit sweater followed by underwear and socks were added to their purchases. She could see how upset Ian was, and presumed that he thought she was being condescending.

She knocked on the dressing room door. "Ian?"

"Excuse me, madame, but I am in a state of undress."

She looked around her to see if anyone overheard his formal statement. "No, listen," she whispered through the slats in the door. "I think it would be a good idea to get dressed in jeans and a shirt. And I have underwear here for you."

He immediately opened the door and stared at her. Suzanne was taken back by his appearance. Dressed in jeans and the soft chambray shirt, he looked modern and . . . positively handsome. It was so unexpected that she couldn't think beyond the revelation.

"As you can see, I have already changed." He stared at the package in her hand with distaste. "And I am wearing my own undergarments, thank you. It is totally improper for you to purchase such personal items."

Feeling as if she were a child being chastised by her parent, Suzanne straightened her shoulders and lifted her chin in defense. She didn't care how good looking he was. "I think you forget, Mr. Chandler, that you may be here for some time. Therefore you *might* need a change of underwear. I certainly hope you don't think I was being indiscreet. Besides,'' she added for emphasis, ''you aren't my type.''

He stared at her for a few timeless seconds, before saying, ''I wouldn't think so. I can't imagine what kind of man would be comfortable having a woman choose his clothing and— ''

''Excuse me, but didn't we agree that you would take my lead?'' she interrupted. ''Since I live in this time *and* am paying for these clothes, I would think you could be grateful enough to shut up and say thank you.''

It was a war of wills, a testimony to the age-old fight for dominance. Or, at least equality.

He straightened his shoulders and muttered, ''Thank you, but this is merely a loan. Once I have the proper clothing, I shall seek employment.''

Now was not the time to tell him that he would have a hard time finding employment even within this mall, let alone at his profession. It was her job to know the market and, without a social security card and some verifiable background, he didn't stand a chance. That was something else she and Leslie hadn't thought about. If Ian Chandler remained in this time, how would they ever make him legal?

''Fine,'' she said. ''Let's pay for these and then find you a suit.''

The matter seemed settled.

Macys' proved to almost overload Ian's brain as they walked through the immense store to the

men's department, and Suzanne constantly had
to pull him away from displays. He was either
in awe by the abundance of choices or scandal-
ized by the state of women's fashions. Finally,
surrounded by suits, Suzanne found that there
really wasn't such a thing as a cheap suit, at least
not in Macy's. For a few moments, she pondered
taking Ian to another store, but her compassion
won over and, since they had brought the man
to this time without his consent, she decided to
just charge this purchase and worry about it
later.

It was sick. She knew it, yet allowed it for some
odd reason. When Ian came out of the dressing
room in a dark gray suit with a white shirt and
a colorful print tie, Suzanne found herself groan-
ing deep in her throat.

She was attracted to the man!

He belonged to someone else, was dedicated
to this Marissa woman, and yet she felt a sudden,
wild surge of appreciation for the man. And she
wasn't alone. She had noticed the attention he
received from other women as they had walked
through the mall.

As Ian stood in front of the three-way mirror
and was measured by the salesman, Suzanne bit
her bottom lip to keep from grinning. She had
to give Leslie credit. If all this was real, as it
seemed, then her best friend had pulled from
the space-time continuum one heck of an attractive man. Face it. Leslie was a true novice, and
she herself could be here in Macy's trying to
dress a nineteenth century version of Rush Lim-

baugh. If nothing else, someone or something had decided to smile on them by sending Ian Stewart Chandler— a Timothy Dalton look alike with an attitude.

Not bad. Not bad at all.

When they once more rejoined the throng in the mall, Suzanne allowed Ian to window shop and people watch. They visited Sam Goodys and she bought him some classical CD's. Ian wandered into The Bombay Company and was seized by nostalgia of a time long past. She spent two *long* hours in Houlihan's, arguing over lunch about women's rights and then dragged him to the Food Court and bought him an ice cream cone. Sitting at a table, she answered all his questions about society and fashion trends. He really was a chauvinist. She realized that he was also very intelligent, albeit puritanical, and then, to lighten the mood, she took him into Woolworth's so they could take a strip of pictures to remember the day.

"We cannot both fit into this booth," Ian stated while holding back the curtain.

"Sure we can," Suzanne answered with a giggle. "You go in first and I'll squeeze in."

"Suzanne . . ."

"Oh, just do it, Ian. You'll see. It'll be fun. And, no matter what happens, we'll both have proof that this really took place. Face it. No one, not from your time or mine, will believe this unless it happens to them. C'mon. Let's do it."

He shook his head, as though indulging a

child, and sat down on the small seat. "You will never fit in here," he again proclaimed.

She inserted the proper coins and hurried into the booth, trying to find a comfortable position. "Move over," she whispered.

"There is nowhere to move," Ian whispered back, while pressing himself against the wall.

"Okay," Suzanne decided, while half standing in the cramped quarters. "I'll have to sit on your lap. Nothing personal. Right?"

"Madame . . . I do not think that would be proper."

"Oh, please. Knock off the 'madame' title. Remember, Ian I just bought you your underwear," she said while plopping down on his lap. "We know each other well enough for this." To stop any further objections, she pressed the start button and added, "Okay . . . here we go. Smile!"

"Not yet," Ian protested. "I'm not ready. You're sitting on my— "

The light flashed and Suzanne braced herself with her hand against the wall as Ian moved.

"Stop it," she said, while looking at him shifting underneath her. "It's going to take another . . . Damn!"

The light flashed again, capturing their clumsy movements, and Suzanne once more cursed. "Shit!"

"Your colorful vocabulary is quite unsuitable, you know."

"Yeah. Right. Because I'm a woman? Just shut up and smile."

They stared ahead and forced smiles as the camera flashed its last picture.

Both of them let out their breaths with impatience, and Suzanne immediately jumped off his lap and out of the booth. Ian quickly followed.

"Now what?" he asked, adjusting his jeans and looking extremely prudish.

"We wait for the pictures to be developed. A couple of minutes."

He gazed about the store and then muttered, "I don't think what we just did was proper. To have it immortalized for all to see is just—"

"Ian?" she interrupted, and he looked down to her.

"Yes?"

"Stuff it."

Good Lord, she thought while checking her watch, wasn't it time to meet Leslie? Gorgeous man or not, Ian Stewart Chandler was wearing on her nerves. And no man was worth that. It was one lesson she had already learned well.

Seven

"Are you sure you're going to be all right?" Leslie questioned nervously, fiddling with her crystal pendant as she spoke. "I hate to just abandon you like this, but you know our financial situation . . . and I haven't built up any vacation time yet."

Suzanne knew that she should be handling this better, but at the moment, all she could think of was walking back into her home to find vacant space when she returned from work. She'd heard about this too many times on the news, seen too many incidents of how trusting, foolish people had been taken advantage of. Now she was faced with having to leave a stranger in her home all day long without supervision. What if he snooped in her personal effects? What if he had a gang, and they came back while she was gone and cleaned her out? Worse, what if they were waiting for her when she returned home from work? What if this had all been, a well-planned scheme on his part?

"I know, Les," she finally said, slipping her feet into her pumps. "You have to go. So do I. This morning I have a meeting with the vice president of personnel at Blue Cross, and there are a lot of opportunities to place temporary help there. I can't miss that meeting, especially as a small firm. He's probably only seeing me because I qualify as a female-owned disadvantaged business. Anyway, how do we know for sure that you did this spell thing, really? Maybe we're just fooling ourselves."

Leslie looked so upset that she wanted to do or say something to comfort her, but nothing came to mind.

"Maybe I can ask Mike to check on the house during the day? He's a sales rep, and can sometimes steal a few hours of flex time."

"No," Suzanne said quickly, feeling a sudden rush of protectiveness toward her strange guest. "He just wouldn't understand any of this anyway. Besides, you two have already been arguing over me, I'm sure."

Leslie turned away, looking embarrassed. "Yeah," she sighed. "He really has a bug up his butt about the amount of time I've been spending over here away from him and the kids. He almost had a coronary when I came back on Sunday night . . . and the kids have after-school activities that I have to chauffeur them to, then dinner, and lunches . . . I haven't done the food shopping or laundry yet, and . . . oh, Suz, it's so hard to juggle everyone's needs and still find room to manage your own."

Suzanne walked over to her friend and gave her a supportive squeeze. "You know, Les, I've been so caught up in my own problems that I haven't really considered your life. I'm sorry," she murmured into her friend's hairline. "I was the one you were trying so hard to help. I was the one who really started this whole mess if you think about it. And now I got *you* into trouble."

Leslie returned her embrace, and the two stood holding each other not saying anything for a moment.

"I just wanted you to be happy, Suz. To have the same boring but comfortable, loving life that I did . . . because you seemed to want it so much. It broke my heart to see you lonely, and I'd give anything for you to be married, and loved the way you deserve, but, God, if anything bad ever happened to you . . ." Leslie's voice broke as she buried her face in Suzanne's shoulder.

"Hey, listen, it's not all that bad. I'm a big girl, really, and can take care of myself. We're just at different life cycles, is all. I'll have my turn. Besides, we did have one hell of a weekend, didn't we?"

Her attempt to cheer Leslie seemed to work a little. When her friend lifted her face, she gave her a quick kiss on the cheek and wiped a stray tear from her face. At that moment, all she wanted was to see Leslie's old effervescent smile again. To see that devilish grin that was always up to no good.

"C'mon, Les. Cheer up. One day when we're old ladies, sitting on a porch somewhere chewing snuff, we'll laugh and tell the kids about our foray into magic how we conjured us up a man.

A good-looking, sexy chauvinist who turned out to be a disoriented law professor or something."

The comment made a smile come out of hiding on Leslie's face. "Yeah, and we'll tell them how we didn't just find any ole nut. We had an authenticated one, and even brought in a psychic from Pakistan to corroborate his story."

Her smile warmed Suzanne's heart, and as the sparkle returned to Leslie's eyes so did Suzanne's sense of peace. "It'll be okay, Kiddo. Listen, if you want, I'll call you when I get home at five-thirty. Then you can call me at eight-thirty, when the kids are in bed."

"How about if I sneak out and say I'm going to Seven-eleven and stop by, just to check. That way, I'll feel better. I mean, what if he's holding you hostage or something?"

The thought had actually occurred to Suzanne, but she had decided to put it out of her mind for the moment. Yet the reference sent a sudden chill down her spine, and Leslie seemed to pick up on her fears immediately.

"I'll drive over with Mike . . . my neighbor can house sit with the kids for a few hours. Let's have the two of them meet. Mike might be a pain in the butt, but he's an excellent judge of character. If he sniffs out anything fishy, at least we'll have some brawn right there on the spot."

The suggestion made her feel better, and she sat down on the bed slowly. "Are you sure you wouldn't mind, Les? I hate to be so silly."

"What? Are you kidding? This'll kill two birds with one stone. Mike won't think I'm crazy for

worrying that you have a man in your house—
you know you're like a sister to him. It'll give him
a chance to sort of help without really knowing
the whole deal. You'll feel better. And Mr. Chandler will know that a big strapping guy who loves
you like a sister lives just around the corner. That
oughtta keep him on his peas and ques."

"You think so?"

"Didn't I tell you to trust me? I've always got
a plan."

They both laughed as Suzanne stood to collect
her purse and briefcase. "So I've noticed. Well,
okay. I have to admit that your plans are improv-
ing since the first wild one on Saturday night."

"I know. I'm never going to live that one
down," Leslie laughed again, opening the bedroom door.

"No, definitely not." Suzanne followed her
friend into the hall, surveying her bedroom one
last time before she shut the door, trying to remember where every item had been placed. "Oh,
wait." Dashing back into the room, she picked
up her journal. "I'd die if he found this."

"What is it?" Leslie asked curiously, trying to
peer over her shoulder.

"My journal. You know—the dream entries
that your teacher said to keep. It's sort of personal."

"That hot?" Leslie asked, then laughed with
a wink. "Well, I've been keeping one too."

"You have?"

"Yeah, but mine is more for a chronicled history of events. I thought, if anything happens

to either of us . . . like we get murdered, or we slip into the other side of the void, at least Mike can have an idea of who we were abducted by, or how to contact Rahmin to get us back."

Suzanne just looked at her friend. As crazy as it was, it did make sense, but it was the last thing she wanted to think about on her way out the door. "Well, on that pleasant note, I feel so much better."

Leslie tweaked her nose and headed down the stairs. "I even taped his photo in the book, so the police don't have to work from a composite sketch."

Frozen, Suzanne stood at the top of her landing. "I'm not going to work. I can't. I'll have to just lose the Blue Cross account. I— "

"Come on, come on, it's all decided. If he cleans you out, you've got homeowners. But you are physically getting out of here. Where's our guest this morning, anyway? Did you prep him last night for your departure?"

"Yes," Suzanne replied flatly, allowing her friend to usher her down the stairs. "I showed him how to make tea and coffee. How to make bacon and eggs and a sandwich, and how to turn on the television and the lights. Can you believe it? I even had to show him how to flush the toilet."

Leslie laughed and stopped at the bottom of the landing. "I've got news for you. When you get married, you still have to show them how to do that. Men haven't gotten that concept since the caveman days. And if he can make breakfast and a sandwich, and flush a toilet, then kiss that frog, girl, 'cause you've got a prince! So don't be too hard on our Mr. Chandler."

Suzanne had to smile. Her friend was a character, but the more she thought about it, Leslie was also right.

"Feeling better?" Leslie asked again, her mirth masking her nervousness.

"Yeah, I suppose so."

"Well, let's both walk out together, okay? But first let's see what he's up to."

Hesitating to encroach upon Ian Chandler's space for some odd reason, Suzanne stopped her return up the stairs. "I'm not sure if I want to wake him up."

"I am fully awake and normally rise at dawn."

The deep male voice made both women jump. There was no way to get used to another person in the house. Especially not a male person.

"Jesus! You gave us a start!" Growing annoyed, Suzanne paced quickly into the kitchen. "What are you doing up?"

"Am I under specific orders not to rise until a certain appointed hour also?"

Leslie was right on her heels, and they both stood in the doorway marveling at the *new* Mr. Chandler. If one didn't know better, she'd swear he was a nineties-sort-of-guy, sitting at the table, reading a newspaper and wearing denims and a tee shirt. The only strange thing was that he was drinking his tea and reading his paper by the early morning sun but had neglected to turn on the kitchen light.

"You'll go blind like that," Leslie said with a wink in Suzanne's direction as she flipped on the light. "Isn't that better?"

"Hardly," he retorted, seeming annoyed at the intrusion. "I was just capturing a moment of peace and solitude before I begin my household keep. Hence my farm-hand attire."

"Ah . . . just like Mike," Leslie whispered with a giggle. "He gets all ticked off when it's Saturday, house chore day, and he wakes up like a bear. Get used to it, girlie, this is the married life you pine for."

Suzanne had to turn away from Leslie to stifle a groan. "Are you going to be all right in here alone all day? Do you need anything before I leave for work?"

Ian looked over the top of the newspaper briefly regarding them, then returned to the print. "I think I can bear to manage for a few hours without constant hovering and tutoring. Perhaps if I just sit on the sofa and look out the window like a small child, I won't wreak too much havoc while you're gone."

"Ooooh, boy!" Leslie said under her breath, giving Suzanne's side a little pinch. "Are we in a bad mood this morning? What did you do to the guy at the mall, Suz?"

"Shhh," she admonished quickly. "We just had a difference of opinion about the roles of men and women."

"Same fight, different era. Why am I not surprised."

"Pardon?" Ian looked over his paper again,

but this time holding both women in a steely gaze.

"I said," Leslie began to Suzanne's horror, "that I'm not surprised."

Ian let out a noise that was something between a grunt and a snort, then went back to his paper. "Well, I am glad that one of you is not surprised by my capabilities."

Leslie covered her mouth, and Suzanne knew that she had to get away from her before they both laughed out loud.

"See, Suz," she whispered, "you have to learn to talk morning code to them. Just repeat the last part of your sentences— sort of like pig Latin."

"I think it would be rude to converse in Latin, since I am not completely fluent in the language. If you two are keeping little secrets, then it would be far more courteous to simply save the dialogue until you were out of the room."

Ian hadn't even lowered the paper this time, and Suzanne hustled Leslie out of the kitchen on that note.

"I'll be back at five-thirty," she called over her shoulder, swallowing down the giggles.

"Bye, Ian," Leslie added, unnecessarily drawing out the syllables in his name.

It was terrible, but it felt like high school again. Two teenage girls tittering over the cute guy sitting at the cafeteria table. Suzanne cringed. It had come to this.

* * *

Her concentration could only be described as mush. Rather like oatmeal in her brain— sticky, heavy, and slow moving. Instead of her normal fluent sales responses to her potential client's questions, she was just a lap behind the conversation. Finally, when the client had risen and thanked her for her time, she had blinked twice, smiled politely and left. She hadn't even tried to close them, or make them commit! But the worst part was the fatigue. It was all she could do to keep her head up during the day.

A sense of defeat loomed over her as she sat at her desk, internally kicking herself for being so foolish. Even her frantic phone call to Leslie didn't make her feel any better. As expected, her jubilant, carefree friend had told her that the universe would provide! She was really getting sick of Ms. Universe, or Mother Nature, and her wicked sense of humor. If Leslie and Rahmin were right, and there was this large female presence out there called the universe, well . . . she'd sure like to give her a piece of her mind!

She had tried hard all day to ignore her dread, using the incessant phone calls and follow up scheduling problems to shield her from the six-foot-tall issue that was waiting for her at home. But the closer it came to quitting time, the more anxious she felt. Nerves. Just nerves, she told herself, chewing on another TUMS. Les was right. She was fully covered by insurance. In fact, she'd make out financially if someone did trash her house. But that wasn't the point. It was the sense of possible violation of her home, her person, and her life, that bothered her. Besides, she really wasn't afraid of Ian Chandler, per se. He didn't seem to be a violent person. Arogant, yes. A pain, absolutely. A chauvinist, without question. But a thief and a killer? No.

So why was she so nervous around him? The question had haunted her since they left the mall. It had been both the worse and the best time she'd spent with a man in ages. So, what was the big deal? Perhaps it was the way he had described her grandmother's home so accurately. There was no explanation for it, at least not one that she was ready to accept.

Clicking open her briefcase, Suzanne shoved a pile of job requisitions into the side pocket. Trying to ignore the small floral journal that sat precisely in the middle of the open case, she cast her gaze around her desk for some additional work to take home. Her plan would be to try to call her grandmother again, then go home, eat, visit with Mike and Leslie, do work on her sofa until she passed out, then go to bed. Hopefully she could get Ian over to her grandmother's within a day or so, go to the library, and ask Rahmin to return for more divination. Then she could put her guest out without any guilt. She'd done enough already. Way too much, in fact.

All she wanted was her normal, boring life back.

Yet, as she tried to force herself to close the case, she couldn't resist the temptation to reach for the journal. Carefully opening the pages, she allowed her gaze to fall on the first entry.

Can't remember the dream. Just feelings of, incredible sadness. Tears. Anger. Loss. Suzanne closed her eyes briefly, recalling the feelings that she remembered from Saturday night, and just prior to the scare of Ian's arrival. Turning to the second page, she opened her eyes and stared down at her own handwriting. It didn't even look like her normal signature, but was tighter, more defined . . . more decorative. *An argument of some sort . . . A young woman and a man dressed in turn-of-the-century clothes. They were out in a garden, she followed behind him angrily, his back was to her. I couldn't understand what they were saying, but I could tell they were arguing. I couldn't really see their faces. He turned quickly, and pulled her into his arms and kissed her hard. I felt the kiss. I felt the desire. As she melted, so did I . . . God, it's been so long since I've made love. I really want to.*

Suzanne's cheeks burned with embarrassment. The urgency had come back, just by reading the entry. Fighting her bottled-up emotions, she cursed her body for responding and betraying her. Here, of all places! She'd just die if anyone found her book. Slamming the briefcase shut, she spun the combination locks on either side. How in the world was she supposed to show *this* to an old Pakistani man? She wouldn't even show this to her best friend, or to a good therapist for that matter.

Taking several deep breaths, she tried to make her heartbeat slow down. Every inch of her skin tingled . . . and a dull central ache had begun to consume her. Unable to stop the sensations,

Suzanne stood and paced. She couldn't go home in this condition! What if Chandler sensed her vulnerability? What if he tried to . . . She immediately stopped the thought, but it came back with a vengeance. And, what about when Mike and Leslie left? For a split second, she was sorry that they were coming over! What was wrong with her? She actually wanted to spend time alone with a lunatic . . . No, more specifically, she had envisioned herself making love to a lunatic! That was even scarier.

The phone seemed to provide the only bridge to her sanity. If she could connect with her grandmother, set up this ridiculous meeting, the sooner Ian Chandler could be on his way. Reaching for the life-saving device, she dialed the familiar number again. Mercifully, on the fourth ring, it picked up.

"Grandma? Oh, I've been so worried about you," she lied, relief washing over her.

"My, Suzanne!" the old woman exclaimed. "What a wonderful surprise. How are you, darling?"

"I'm okay, I guess . . . I was trying you over the weekend, but— "

"Oh, yes, yes, of course, my dear," the elderly woman interrupted, "but you know my commitments. I had a charity ball on Saturday morning to plan for, after brunch with my friends from the Women's Guild, an antique auction on Sunday morning for The Homeless Children's Defense Fund, and I must confess to a date with a rather handsome chap that evening . . . He's a widower, you know."

Suzanne was speechless. Her grandmother was eighty-four and dating? "A date, really?"

"Oh, now, Suzanne. Don't be such a prude. I am well above the age of majority, and although he's a younger man in his seventies . . . we still enjoy each other's company, if you understand what I mean."

Shock was the only response Suzanne could muster. "You don't mean that you two still . . ."

Her grandmother laughed, almost sounding like a young girl again. "We met on a cruise after he lost his wife. He said I took years off his life. I just hope that I don't kill the poor man," she chuckled. "Oh, the sunsets in the Barbados . . ." the old woman crooned wistfully. "Suzanne, there is nothing like romance. He simply makes me feel fantastic. And young, at least younger. But that reminds me. We must do something about the sad state of affairs for your love life, though, darling. You're much too young not to have a gentleman caller. It isn't healthy, and will ruin that beautiful complexion of yours. After all, what you don't use, you loose, I've always said— much to my family's chagrin. So what's new with you, my pet? Hmmmm?"

Suzanne had almost forgotten the purpose of her call, and now felt more tired and depressed than ever before. Her life was pathetic. Even her eighty-four-year-old grandmother was at it! Maybe Rahmin was right. Maybe she did have some sort of serious electro-magnetic damage to her aura that drove men away. Something sure was wrong!

"Suzanne, are you there?"

"Uh, oh, yes, I'm sorry. Someone came into my office and distracted me for a second," she lied, stalling to collect her thoughts. "I was thinking of coming over, as soon as you had the time. I'd like you to meet a couple of my friends."

"That would be marvelous," her grandmother said with a laugh. "Oh, Suzie, I have missed you so. You are absolutely my most favorite grand-daughter in the whole wide world. A visit from you would be pure heaven. And any friends of yours are most certainly welcomed in this big old dusty house of mine. Ah, but I must get rid of it soon. I was thinking of a condo on the south of France. Does that seem like a reasonable idea to you? However, I told James that it felt so far away from this side of the world and his family."

Again, Suzanne was speechless. Her grand-mother living with a younger senior citizen in a condo in the south of France? Had everyone around her flipped out?

"Maybe we should go somewhere more tropi-cal?" the old woman went on, as though weigh-ing the possibilities while she talked to Suzanne. "But I do hate the hot weather of those places. And Florida, with all of those sickly old people, crashing about in cars that they can no longer drive, is absolutely out of the question."

"Grandma, I'm glad you're happy," Suzanne interjected quietly, a smile forming as she got used to the idea.

"I'm truly ecstatic. Suzie, life is so short, and when you're near the end of it, you realize how much time you've wasted along the way. But, I have been blessed for the better part of mine—and have to admit that I didn't allow too much grass to grow under my feet. So don't waste time, dear."

They both laughed hard now, as Suzanne vividly remembered how her grandmother was always the scandalous one in the family, causing her parents to virtually pull out their hair at her antics.

"You remember my friend, Leslie, right? She'll be coming. You two share the same *joie d' vivre*, and quest for adventure. My other friend is a tad more sedate, however."

"The strong, mysterious silent type? Hmmm? I love him already. When do I get to meet this handsome young gentleman?"

Her grandmother's insight made her blush, and she couldn't answer immediately as she grappled for the words.

"Oh, now, he must really be handsome. I haven't heard you at such a loss for words in years. Well, this will be a treat. Now, unfortunately I have already planned a bridge party tonight with James. But, tomorrow afternoon, around four o'clock, we could have a bit of tea and supper in the garden. Wouldn't that be lovely?"

"Perfect," Suzanne said with a sigh of relief. As always, if one waited long enough, her grandmother would ask, then answer, her own questions.

"Then it's settled. Tomorrow at four then, darling. But, I must run to get ready for my evening. Loved chatting with you. Big kisses and hugs until then. Love you."

"Love you too, Grandma," she whispered as she put the receiver back in the cradle. "Love you, too."

Suzanne stood in her foyer and held her breath. Peering around cautiously, she kept her briefcase clenched tightly in one hand, her purse over her shoulder, and the pepper spray on her key chain poised in the other. If she had to make a break for it, she would. Yet, the string of curses that rang from the kitchen made her hasten her entry to further inspect her surroundings. Wide-eyed, she stopped short in the hall, then followed the male voice that bellowed from the room before her.

"Oh, my God," she screamed, dropping her purse and briefcase and rushing toward the microwave. Blue and yellow sparks were coming from everywhere as the unit sputtered and blinked. Pressing the clear button, she flung open the door, and searched for a towel. "What were you doing?"

Ian stood beside her, obviously at a loss and quite annoyed. "I was trying to prepare a meal of meat, carrots and potatoes for dinner," he retorted, taking the hot pan from her and setting it down hard on the counter. "But the blasted thing nearly blew up and began spinning fireworks instead of cooking the meal."

She wanted to smile but didn't dare.

"That's because you set it in a metal pan."

He just stared at her without comprehending.

"It was a nice gesture, and I should have explained about metal in a microwave. Aluminum foil will do the same thing," she added matter-of-factly, trying to use the sound of her voice to calm his frayed nerves. "I just never thought about it."

"I suppose even a fool would know that," he said curtly, turning from her to look into the pan.

For a moment she felt sorry for him. He seemed so forlorn, so out of place . . . Then she surveyed the room, and wanted to die. The man had set the table, placed flowers in a vase in the center of it, and the dishes were done. Her heart hurt.

"Oh, Ian," she said softly, touching his shoulder. "You tried, don't worry. I wouldn't have done so well in your time either. And you must have been bored to death in here all day."

"Don't be silly," he scoffed, obviously not wanting her to sense his disappointment. "Actually, I had a fascinating day. I managed to get the black box to work. The things I saw, Suzanne. People have virtually lost their minds."

His comment made her chuckle. "What time of day did you begin watching?"

"From late in the morning, say about, nine o'clock. There were these plays where journalists asked the most intimate questions. And in front of, what I presume to be hordes of strangers, people revealed the most candid details of their lives. It was the most fascinating thing I have ever seen. Were these some sort of staged theatrical events?"

This time she had to laugh. "No, I wish they were. They were real people telling about their very real lives."

The look on his face was priceless.

"No. You are teasing me."

"Truth."

"No. At the risk of sounding crude . . . well, they talked about their liaisons. Mostly that's what it was about. Then, there were these little vignettes that lasted about thirty seconds and told one about different products."

"Commercials. Advertisements."

"Merchants use the box to sell their wares? Even women's bodies?"

Suzanne shook her head and poked at the half gray meat in the pan. "Well, they aren't selling the bodies exactly, but they're using the bodies to get your attention so that you'll pay attention long enough to remember the product."

Ian tilted his head to one side in consideration. "That is very strange logic. I found the bodies quiet distracting, and could not for the life of me recall the product in the least if my life depended upon it."

Stifling another giggle, Suzanne left the mess on the counter and walked over to the table. "These are beautiful," she said quietly, lowering her nose to the fragrant blossoms. "Where did you get them?"

Without looking at her, Ian tried to make his voice sound nonchalant. "From the garden. I walked out through the servants exit into the garden. But I didn't realize that the door was magical as well, and would lock behind me. I was therefore forced to return through the kitchen window."

Suzanne covered her mouth to hide another inappropriate smile. Turning away from him she smelled the flowers again. "Thank you, it was a very kind thing to do. I'm so sorry that you had such an eventful day."

He didn't answer for a moment, and his expression held the insecure look of a young boy trying to please his girlfriend. She was flattered, and glad that he'd tried to do something nice.

"I just thought . . ." he stammered, "that after all the burden I've been, and how well you have taken my misdirected snipes . . . I wanted to say thank you. But I have totally spoiled the meal, and probably cost you even more money."

She wanted to walk over and give him a big hug. There was no way that she could make him understand that it was his effort, not the result, that made her happy. Opting for a compliment, she tried to allay his concerns. "You have truly outdone yourself in here, and I must admit that I'm impressed. Don't worry about dinner. I'll tell you what— we can order out."

"Go to another restaurant? I don't think I

could manage it," he began shakily, obviously referring to the mall and his dread of crowds.

"No, we don't have to go anywhere. They'll bring the food to us. I'll just call Food Taxi and order up a steak and baked potatoes and a salad. How's that?"

Ian stood before her, astonished. "You mean to tell me that one can get a servant at this late hour to shop for meat, bring it to your home, and cook it? The expense, Suzanne. I couldn't ask you to—"

"No, no, no. See," she said producing a menu from her kitchen junk drawer. "Look, all the major restaurants in the area are represented. I just call on the phone, they cook it in their kitchens, and, voila! They bring it in one half hour to an hour."

"Call on the phone?" Ian took the menu from her hands and perused the information. "Any of this fare? What's a phone?"

It had never occurred to her to show him the device. "Did you hear a ringing at all today while you were home?"

"Yes," he said, still appearing confused. "But I thought it was someone trying to gain entry at the door, so I hid myself as to not cause complications or speculation. Then they would talk for a while and leave."

Smiling, she took his hand and motioned toward the stairs. "Welcome to the world of technology." When they reached her bedroom door, she hesitated a moment, then banished the slight fear. It was safe, she hoped. Opening the door she ushered him in, and wound back her answering machine tape. "This is the phone," she declared triumphantly. "People call this device, and each person has their own personal number," she added, calling the Food Taxi. "When the party on the other end responds, you give your message."

"Incredible."

Chandler stood before her, mouth agape.

"When they answer, say Hello, and tell them what you would like to eat, then give it back to me so that I can give them my address for the delivery."

She watched in amusement as he held the instrument away from his face and cringed when the order taker answered.

"I would like to have two medium rare steaks, two baked potatoes, and two salads for dinner, madame." Once he made his pronouncement, he shoved the telephone back into her hands as though it were alive. And supposed that it was.

". . . No, I'll have dressing, thank you," she added, finishing the order and giving her address. "Now, Mr. Chandler, all we have to do is wait for it to arrive."

Speechless, he touched the phone and pressed one of the buttons. When a tone sounded, he dropped it. "Lord! But this is remarkable! I actually spoke to a person somewhere far away from this house!"

"Yup," she said matter-of-factly, returning the receiver to the holder. "And, when you're not home, you can let them leave a message on this little box." Playing back her messages, she watched his face with delight. It was like witnessing a child discovering ice cream.

"These are the voices I heard earlier!"

"Yup," she said again, allowing herself the freedom to giggle. "And when I have the time, I'll return these calls and chat awhile with my friends."

Leading him back downstairs, she had to admit that for the first time since he arrived, Ian Chandler's company was becoming fun. It would be nice to have someone interesting to talk to over a meal. Usually, her kitchen was silent, save the drone of the television. But, Chandler was much better entertainment. He was so hungry for knowledge, so eager to learn, so interested in what she had to say.

Somehow, they had lost track of the time when the doorbell rang again. Over dinner, she had completely forgotten about Leslie and Mike, and truthfully, their visit now felt more like an intrusion than a rescue mission. Standing quickly, she hurried down the hallway to open the lock and invite them in.

Mike looked tired and totally coerced into the visit. Leslie looked harried and nervous, and as though she had been through an emotional wrangle with her husband. Suzanne immediately felt guilty, because she and Ian had laughed and talked the hours away without incident.

"You okay, kiddo?" Leslie asked in a low voice, dragging Mike behind her.

"I'm fine," Suzanne added quickly, trying to keep herself from smiling too much. "Hi, Mike. Haven't seen you in awhile, stranger."

Mike gave her a quick reassuring hug. "Just working hard, lady. You know the drill. So, are you okay? Is this guy giving you any trouble?"

Leslie elbowed her husband hard in the ribs. "Mike, for God's sake! Pay him no mind, Suz. He's not the diplomat in the family."

"Pleased to make your acquaintance. The name is Ian Stewart Chandler."

Suzanne drew an audible breath. She hadn't realized that Ian had followed her down the hall, and she prayed that he hadn't heard Mike's comment.

"Mike Peterson." Leslie's husband extended his hand, and shook Ian's hard.

Both Suzanne and Leslie stood by quietly, watching the timeless male ritual of sizing up the other guy. After they pumped each other's hands with extra, unnecessary pressure, sort of puffed up their chests and sucked in their stomachs, albeit Mike had more to suck in, and made themselves seem taller, while deepening their voices, it could be assumed that they were ready to speak to each other civilly.

"How about if we all go into the living room? Would anyone care for something to drink?"

"Brought some beer," Mike said in a deeper than normal voice, handing over the bag to Suzanne. "How about a brew, man?"

"Thank you," Ian responded in a baritone that she hadn't heard before.

"I think they'll get along fine," Leslie whispered as the men headed for the living room and they made their way to the kitchen. "So what happened today?"

Her friend stopped short when they entered the room and looked at the table. "Flowers?"

"He locked himself out of the house and had to crawl back in through the kitchen window," Suzanne admitted, feeling giddy. "I couldn't believe it."

Walking over to the sink as Suzanne brought down some glasses, Leslie inspected the pan of gray meat. "What the hell happened here?"

"He tried to make me dinner, but didn't understand about metal in a microwave."

Leslie held her arm and turned her around. "He's turning into a prince, isn't he? This frog is turning into a prince. I can feel it."

Shrugging out of her friend's hold, Suzanne headed out of the room. "He just wanted to say thank you for all the time, money, and food. That's all."

"That's all?" Leslie whispered quickly, trying to get in another comment before they joined the men.

Sensing a series of probing questions, Suzanne slipped into the living room to forestall any further comments. "Here we are, gentlemen. But, I guess I'm too late."

Upon entering the room, they found the men laughing heartily, drinking from cans, and slapping each other on the back. They were talking about the most recent, gruesome murder that

Ian had watched on the five o'clock news, and he was giving Mike his legal opinion.

"I think they should hang the bastards too, if they catch 'em. I'm all for capital punishment. That's what's wrong with society today, you know? Everybody gets away with murder."

"I wholeheartedly agree," Ian said with authority, reaching for another beer, and deftly popping the top of the can open. "An eye for an eye."

Suzanne stood still in amazement. In less than five minutes two different men, from two different eras, had bonded over a beer. They shared the same political views. It was incredible. Looking over to her friend, she whispered, "Are you thinking what I'm thinking?"

"Wild, ain't it?"

"Never seen anything like it in my life."

It was true. Her grandmother's old adage that, the more things changed, the more they stayed the same, had been right. Thank Heaven, for once she'd been correct.

Two hours later, Suzanne and Ian stood at the top of the porch stairs waving as she watched her friends leave.

"Hey, Suz, thanks for inviting us over. Haven't had a time like this in a long while. Ian, maybe you can play baseball with the guys on Friday. Some of us ex-jocks get together and have a league. Since you're new in town, I'll introduce ya around. Saturday night's poker night too, that is, if Suz'll let you come out to play."

Ian looked at Suzanne and smiled, ignoring

her alarm as he slipped his arm around her waist. "Thanks for the kind offer, I'd love to. Safe journey!" he called behind Mike.

"Yeah, good thing we live just around the corner. Two six packs'll do it to you."

Leslie just shrugged and waved to her.

They were crocked. Absolutely, positively, crocked. Tugging at his arm, she got Ian inside of the house. "And just what do you think you're doing?" she asked.

"I like that fellow, Mike. Affable chap. I think he and I could be friends. He also has a fine mind for business. He reminds me of my old school chum, Roger. He could sell anything, and he certainly didn't need a female body to do it."

Suzanne ignored him as she helped him up the stairs. "Well, tomorrow, Mr. Chandler, we have a four o'clock supper with my grandmother."

"Very good," he pronounced and laughed, brushing her forehead with a kiss before staggering down the hall toward the guest bedroom. "And, thank you for a most enjoyable evening with your friends, Suzanne."

Suzanne stood in the hall until she heard his door close and his body thud on the bed. She now had a half drunk, still disoriented crazy person from the past who fit right in.

And he had kissed her, actually kissed her. Tried to make up for his sarcasm by cleaning the kitchen. Tried to make dinner, and had even climbed through the window with a bouquet to bring her flowers.

Truly, Madame Universe had a wicked sense of humor. Maybe she would just have to kiss this frog again before he really turned into a prince. Not bad. But the sad irony was, just like all of her past relationships, she'd do all the work, only to have the man leave and be the perfect match for someone else. After all, Ian Stewart Chandler was desperately in love with another woman from the last century. A young, petite little Miss Perfect. Suddenly Suzanne felt tired. She was tired of fixing men. Tired of sending them off once they were honed and tempered, only to have the next woman benefit. Isn't that why she had pulled out of the dating game? She went into her bedroom, not bothering to turn on her light. All she could wonder was, when would it be her turn?

Eight

As they crossed the Betsy Ross Bridge into Pennsylvania, Suzanne monitored Ian's expression in the rear-view mirror. Both she and Leslie had talked privately at length about his possible reactions when he began to see real Philadelphia landmarks. There was no way to judge the possible shock of it all. She knew that had the situation been reversed, had she been the one to see her world in the year two thousand ninety-six, no question, she would have seriously freaked out.

"Hey, Ian, how are we doing?" Leslie asked quietly, turning around from her front passenger seat to face him.

Suzanne craned her neck to look at him in the mirror when he didn't respond immediately. The expression on his face made her eyes moist with emotion. Swallowing hard, she tried to ignore the way his hand trembled as he placed it to the back passenger window and traced the skyline with his fingers. She could see tears brimming in his eyes, and she watched his Adam's apple move as he forced down emotion with hard swallows.

"You okay?" she asked again quietly, glancing at Leslie and sharing her worried expression.

"Tell me this is Philadelphia . . . and they've honored one of the most brilliant men I've ever heard of. He predicted this . . . he was a visionary . . . he saw all of this and they thought him mad . . . eccentric."

"Who?" Leslie questioned gently. "Ian, we don't understand."

"Ben Franklin," he said, stopping to collect himself. "He, and many of his friends were inventors, artists, people who dreamed of great things. I wish I could go back to his time and laugh and raise an ale with him. I wish I could say, 'Ben old man, you were right. In the future, you'll stand atop one of the tallest structures in the entire city.' "

"Yes," Suzanne said, sharing Ian's enthusiasm. "You could tell them that he stands on top of City Hall."

A noise came from the back seat that almost sounded like a sob, and she knew that Ian was fighting a difficult battle with his emotions. Honoring his privacy, and his sense of male dignity, neither she nor Leslie turned around. It was sort of an unspoken agreement that both of them picked up on, not needing to talk to one another in order to understand.

"It's just so beautiful," Ian said after awhile. "I almost can't bear it."

"You should see the University of Pennsylvania campus now, or, Suz, lets go past the East River Drive on the expressway. We have to show him the Art Museum and Boathouse Row."

"I don't know if that's a good idea," Suzanne

hedged, not wanting to totally overwhelm Ian before they reached her grandmother's house.

The plea in his expression dissolved her heart. When he reached his hand across the seat and touched her shoulder, she covered his fingers with hers and he closed his eyes. Again, no words were exchanged for a moment, only a silent understanding that crossed all dimensions.

"Thank you, kind soul . . . Even if I die here, I'll never forget this day." Ian opened his eyes after he spoke. The look on his face made her want to reach out and touch his cheek. He was in so much awe, it was as though he had glimpsed heaven, and he was thanking her for it.

Silly thought. But she looked for the next exit.

Pulling off the expressway at University Avenue, Susanne wound around the University of Pennsylvania Hospital, Civic Center, and Penn Towers Hotel, toward the University Museum. Her turn-of-the-century passenger sat spellbound as they passed each monument, but when she turned down Thirty-fourth toward Walnut Street and he looked at the beginnings of the campus, tears ran down his face without censure.

"We must stop. Please. May I get out for just a moment to walk the length of it?"

Assessing the dubious parking situation, Suzanne hesitated a moment.

"Go ahead. Just put your flashers on, and I'll wait in the car," Leslie motioned quietly. "He needs to understand."

Double parking along a strip of stores on Walnut, Suzanne and Ian hopped out.

"We'll go just up to the center of the campus, then come back. Campus police and the Parking Authority are diligent in this area. Okay?"

Ian simply nodded his compliance, and she held his hand firmly as they crossed the street. All she needed was for him to get hit by a Septa bus and have to go into the hospital as a John Doe. His face lit up like a small child's as they passed the expansive lawn that virtually led the way into another world. On the outer side of the old structure lie a city in urban blight, inside the ivy walls was an era untouched by a hundred years of city decay.

"Look at them," he whispered. "Look at all of these students."

"Twenty-five thousand every four years come through these gates," she said, suddenly feeling like a tour guide, and enjoying his company.

"No," he said, his face turning ruddy in the late afternoon sun. "Look at all of the colors. Black children, white children, Asian children, Indian children, both boys and girls alike . . . different languages being spoken . . . it is what they said it could be. Learning . . ." he added, motioning to the massive library before them. "Pure intellectual pursuit, devoid of war, and slavery, and hatred. People all coming together to learn about this world and to create, and invent, and discuss . . . I am now more convinced than ever before, that there is a God in Heaven who surpasses all understanding." Turning in each of the four directions, Ian opened his arms and flung them wide, laughing and almost hopping about. "When I left my time, there were young men broken by a war that ripped our country in half. There were diseases, and . . . It takes my breath away!"

Grabbing his hand again, they paced up the cobblestone walkway. "These are the Dean's offices, and here, if you look further up, is The Wharton building. Over here is The Annenberg School of Communications."

They went along the path, Ian stopping every few feet to gape. When they reached the arched bridge that rose above Thirty-eighth Street, Ian stopped in the center and let his head fall back to look at the sky.

"Thank you," he murmured. "Thank you, dear Suzanne, for giving me a second chance at life. Perhaps I have died, and this is Heaven. For what more could I have prayed for, than to be plunked down in the middle of a bastion of learning to live out eternity?"

While she didn't think he was suicidal, Ian's comments made her nervous. "Ian, it's not all like this. There is poverty, and violence, and war going on as we speak. There are new diseases that have come about with no known cure." Again, her grandmother's adage came to mind. "Ian, I have been told that the more things changed, the more they stayed the same."

"I know. I have watched your news journalists, Suzanne. Just allow me this moment to take it all in. The beauty of what I see before me now.

You must learn to capture those moments, and to be thankful for each second of awe and happiness that you grasp."

They stood on the bridge for a while, saying nothing but soaking in their surroundings. His words had pulled at some deep reservoir of emotion at the very core of her that she could not define. Ian was right. When had she ever simply basked in the moment? When had she ever been able to see beauty amongst the blight, wonder amongst the profane? If she had been alone and looked over the edge of that bridge, she would have seen street people, and noisy dirty traffic, and extreme wealth amid extreme poverty. She would not have seen new faces marching off to learn. Nor would she have seen future doctors who might find the cure for Aids, future chemists, teachers, business people who might find a solution other than war to fix this declining economy.

Then it hit her. Hope. What Ian Chandler was soaking in. He saw and clung to hope as a life-sustaining force. Hope had pulled him through the void, as much as she and Leslie's spell had. That was the thread that he held and pulled, and it brought him to the other side of the universe. Tears filled her eyes suddenly, and threatened her composure. Hope was what Leslie had when she proposed the crazy idea of conjuring up a man. Hope was the magic, not their incantation. And for the briefest second, for that infinitesimal moment, when she allowed herself to dream, something unexpected and magical had happened.

"We have to get back to the car," she said nervously, pulling at his sleeve. "Leslie will worry, and we'll be late for my grandmother's supper."

Ian followed her without resistance, chuckling to himself, and pacing with the energy of a teenager. She had to push herself to keep up with his long strides, and several times she almost ran to stay along side him. When they returned to the car Leslie handed her a parking ticket.

"They started writing it before I could move it. Sorry, Suz."

Suzanne accepted the ticket without emotion, and put the car into drive. Winding her way back to I 76, she took the scenic route, to show Ian Chandler the other side of the world. Yet, as they passed the decay, she didn't comment. This time she merely watched his expression from the mirror.

"We are on Spring Garden Street," she said dryly, jockeying for position to go down the Parkway before looping back onto the expressway. "And that," she added with triumph, "is the Art Museum."

It was beautiful, there was no question about it. Ian opened his window and leaned his head out, taking in every inch of the structure's spectacular wonder.

"Did you know that a black man architected this?" Suzanne added with enthusiasm, becoming swept up in Ian's amazement.

"My, God!" he exclaimed, rubbing his eyes. "If

it were not for my quest . . ." then he trailed off, becoming somber. "I wish Marissa could see this, see how the world has changed. I may be ruined forever, now. I don't even know if I'd want to go back."

Leslie looked over at her, and she turned to glimpse her friend before focusing on the traffic again. From some remote place within her, the mention of Marissa had spoiled the moment. She knew it was ridiculous to be jealous of a ghost, but Marissa had intruded on their adventure. The ghost of a woman still held him in her grasp, and a sad silence engulfed all passengers as they wound past the monument and entered the expressway. Ian sat quietly, nodding with appreciation as Leslie pointed out Boathouse Row, but somehow his earlier enthusiasm had waned. It was as though each spectacle made him sadder than the last, and by the time they passed Villanova University, he was positively morose.

"A few days ago, you couldn't have paid me to believe I'd feel this way," he said quietly, as they pulled into her grandmother's driveway. "I would have thought you daft, and told you not for love nor money would I want to stay here."

Suzanne turned off the ignition, and the three of them sat for a moment before speaking.

"Do you recognize it?" Leslie asked, unable to contain her excitement. "Look at the front of the house."

Ian's facial expression changed subtly, while each deeper emotion burned in his gaze as his eyes scanned the new terrain. "The trees . . .

the oaks . . ." he whispered, lowering his face to his hands.

"Are you going to be able to handle this?" Suzanne questioned nervously, now unsure whether a meeting was a good idea or not.

"Just give me a minute . . . please. I apologize. It's all like a dream. I was just here a week ago, yet a hundred or more years ago. If Marissa walks through the door, I don't know if my heart could stand the shock."

"It's okay," Leslie crooned softly. "It's okay. You've been through a lot. But I assure you, Marissa isn't here now."

Her comment seemed to make him relax a little and, for once, Suzanne was glad that her chatty friend had found the right words. The entire experience was a strain on them all, and yet, felt so very necessary now.

"My grandmother will make you feel comfortable," Suzanne added, trying to relax him even more. "She's a hoot, and loves eccentric company, being a tad eccentric herself. Let's go inside and at least say hello. If you feel overwhelmed, we can leave."

"Yes, that is the appropriate thing. Perhaps she can intervene with the Hamiltons and give us more clues. I'll be fine, and will act accordingly. It is not my intention to startle an elderly lady."

Suzanne and Leslie looked at each other for reassurance as they opened the car door.

"He still doesn't understand, does he?" Leslie asked in a low whisper.

All Suzanne could do was shake her head

sadly as they approached the front stairs and rang the bell.

"Oh, my goodness sakes alive," her grandmother exclaimed, flinging the door open wide and rushing out to give Suzanne a hug. "I was wondering if you all were ever going to get out of that car. I was waiting by the window, you know."

Suzanne returned the hug and soaked in the elderly woman's warmth. There was something so special about being held in her grandmother's arms. It was a safe haven that she had discovered as a small child, a feeling of security that even her mother could not reproduce.

"Gran," she murmured. "Oh, how I have missed you so." At that moment she just wanted to stay in her arms, swaying and hiding her face in that frail shoulder, away from the complex world that bombarded her.

Holding Suzanne back, the old woman clucked her tongue. "Look at you! Pretty as a picture, and oh, my goodness, come here, Leslie Peterson!" Opening her arms, she invited Leslie into her embrace, and the three stood hugging and giggling, reversing time on the porch.

"Now, now, girls, we must remember our formal manners in the presence of a gentleman," her grandmother said with a wink, stepping away from the fond embraces. Walking toward Ian, she extended her hand and almost batted her eyes in the most demure, coquettish fashion. "And, please introduce me to this handsome young man."

Suzanne and Leslie looked at each other and stifled their smiles. It was incredible. If she didn't know better, she'd swear her grandmother was flirting!

"Grandma, allow me to introduce Ian Stewart Chandler."

Taking the old woman's hand, Ian half bowed before her. "I am very pleased to meet you, madame. I have heard so many wonderful things about you."

Suzanne watched proudly as her grandmother beamed with approval.

"Oh, Suzanne, I like him already," she exclaimed. "Such wonderful manners. You don't always find that today. What a shame . . . Oh, my, please come in everyone. I have iced tea in the parlor, and supper should be ready in about fifteen minutes. I thought we could take our meal in the garden, but it's really too cool for me, my darlings. However, we could take a short stroll, then eat in the parlor. How does that sound?" Without waiting for Suzanne or Leslie's reply, she looped her arm through Ian's and waltzed into the house.

Looking at each other in utter amazement, Leslie and Suzanne laughed.

"She's a character, Suz. I love her. She hasn't changed at all."

"Nope. Not old age. Not infirmity. Not the turn-of-the-century. Grandma is still an outrage . . . and that's all there is to it."

Entering the large Victorian parlor, Suzanne hung back from the group. She had been in her grandmother's home hundreds of times, but today, for some odd reason, the visit seemed surreal. Although every piece of furniture was still in its original placement since she was a child, Suzanne touched the edges of sofa, chairs, tables, and lamps as she passed, as if trying to be sure they were real.

Leslie had left her side, and had caught up to Ian and her grandmother. From the large bay window that faced the garden, she could see them walking about, chatting and smiling. It was as though the threesome belonged together, and had been that way since . . . forever. Unconsciously running her hand down her right side, she had oddly expected to feel the soft fabric of a dress instead of the coarseness of denim.

Looking down, Suzanne rubbed her eyes and quickly pulled her fingers through her hair. What was happening? The texture of the jeans provided a jolt to her senses, and now felt strange . . . and her hair. When she'd reached up, she hadn't expected to feel her customary, loose bob. For some reason, her fingers were expecting to make contact with a smooth chignon. It was becoming eerie, and she rushed to join the group before the walls of the parlor closed in on her.

What in God's name was happening?

"Ian was admiring my roses, and I told him how you used to play about, chasing the birds while I pruned them, when you were a little girl."

Still shaken, Suzanne could only smile at her grandmother.

"Now I will really embarrass her. When Diane calls us in for supper, I will show you some family albums. Our Suzie was so cute as a child. All chubby, and rosie, and always adventurous."

Suzanne groaned. "Oh, Gran, I'm sure he doesn't want to see those mug shots. He'll just be bored to—"

"I insist," Ian cut in, his energy seeming to be restored. "I can't wait to see all of your family pictures. I just love old ones. I have an affinity for turn-of-the-century artifacts and photos." Ian cast a knowing glance in Suzanne's direction.

"I'd love to see them, too, Mrs. Hamilton," Leslie added quickly, keeping her gaze steady on Suzanne. "I love antiques too, but old documents are my bag."

"Oh, goodness me. Had I known, I would have brought down all of those old letters and such. The script work on some of them is quite lovely, especially how they made out deeds and penned their diaries."

"If it wouldn't be too much trouble," Ian persisted, "I find all such matter simply riveting."

"Well, then, it's settled," her grandmother said excitedly. "Some of it is up in my old hope chest. What I was hoping for, I have yet to determine. However, my darlings, if you'd like to amuse yourselves while I go hunting about, perhaps I can produce a few goodies before we have our meal. Now," she exclaimed with authority, "be sure to have Diane summon me when supper is served. I'll only be a few moments. Oh, this is such a wonderful visit! I knew we'd all get on famously."

Both Ian and Leslie focused on Suzanne as they headed back to the house. She didn't feel well. Drained was a better word. It was all she could do to keep from passing out. Feeling Ian's arm around her waist, she stopped and leaned on him to catch her balance.

"You look pale," he said in a low voice, obviously trying to keep her grandmother from being aware of any problem.

"Let her sit down outside on the bench," Leslie added, motioning toward the long stone seat. "Maybe she just needs some air."

Suzanne couldn't answer, and she allowed her head to fall forward in her hands. Her brow was moist, and she felt disoriented. Alarm coursed through her body, making her feverish and short of breath.

"I don't know what's wrong," she panted, nervously looking at her grandmother's form disappear through the parlor window. "I don't want to worry her. I don't want her to see me like this," she said, now shivering, as a cool breeze chilled her to the bone.

"When did you start feeling this way?"

Leslie had taken a seat beside her on the bench, placing her hand to Suzanne's forehead.

"As soon as I entered the parlor, and saw you two through the window with Gran. I feel like I have the flu, or something. I don't know how I'll be able to keep supper down."

Ian squatted before her, his face contorted

with fear. "Dear God, let's get her into the house. It could be influenza. That scourge has killed thousands. We have to call a doctor and quarantine her immediately."

Leslie reached forward and placed her hand on Ian's shoulder. "Flu only kills the very sick and the elderly these days. We have a vaccine for that. No, the way this happened suddenly, seems like more than a physical ailment. It's probably a link . . . part of the thread, Ian. Something happened here that's zapping her. When we get to the root of it, it'll pass."

Ian's gaze darted from Leslie to Suzanne, but he nodded in affirmation as though accepting a physician's diagnosis.

"I don't want her to go through any undue discomfort because of my quest— I couldn't bear it. We will have to leave if her condition doesn't improve rapidly."

Suzanne lifted her head, swallowing hard as her throat began to close with pain. "It really feels like the flu. I'll be all right. But, Les, you may have to drive us home. I don't know what's doing this, but it sure feels real."

Standing on shaky legs, she propelled herself toward the house. "I'll be okay. Let's not upset Gran. She's having such a good time."

Her two friends filed into the house behind her, and Suzanne flopped down on the large brocade settee by the window. "Can you throw me that afghan, Les. It's so cold in here."

Ian and Leslie looked at each other, as Leslie brought the blanket to her. Rubbing her chin,

Leslie regarded her for a moment. "Just before you came outside, you were in the house alone. Did you see anything strange, or feel anything? I'm not sure what I'm digging for here, but I just feel like there's a link."

Suzanne cloaked herself in the warm crocheted folds, snuggled down, and closed her eyes. Her head hurt, and her eyes hurt. For that matter, her entire body ached, making it difficult to think. "I dunno," she said, fighting the soreness in her throat. "It's weird. Hard to describe . . . and it only flashed in my head for a second. But, you know how they say when amputees lose a limb, they can still feel the arm or leg even though it's gone? Well that's how it felt. I automatically reached down to smooth my skirt . . . but that was so bizarre, because I'm obviously not wearing a skirt. Especially not floor length taffeta. Then, for a second, my hair felt different. I just don't know."

The smile on Leslie's face was like that of a detective who had found an essential clue. She paced about in excitement, almost unable to speak. "I knew it! I knew it!" she nearly yelled, stopping to grasp Ian's arm. "She's channeling the energy somehow. She's *feeling* the events that took place here in the past."

Ian's expression remained perplexed, if not a bit fearful. "Can this *channeling* hurt her?" he asked warily, looking at Suzanne as he spoke.

"I don't think so," Leslie shrugged, still seeming pleased. "I never discussed it in depth with Rahmin."

Shaking his head, Ian walked back toward Suzanne and sat down beside her. "This whole thing is making me uncomfortable. Especially, since you don't exactly have full knowledge about what might happen. Maybe we should leave?"

"Don't be silly," Suzanne muttered, unable to stop a sudden cough. "Look, when Gran comes back, we'll act normal and entertain her for a while, then we'll tell her that you guys have other commitments."

"Suzanne, Leslie, how are you!" Bustling into the room, Mrs. Hamilton's elderly British housekeeper swept the two younger women into a meaty embrace. "Goodness, it's been ages, girls. I was so busy in the kitchen, I hadn't come out to give you two a big hug. And I must be introduced to this young man. The name's Diane McDonnell, and it's a pleasure to meet you." The older woman could never be classified as a stuffy Brit.

Exchanging greetings and receiving a few lively slaps on the back from Mrs. McDonnell, Suzanne rose and went to fetch her grandmother. Although chilled to the bone, she left the afghan, and ascended the wide spiral staircase, calling for Gran along the way. When she reached the top, her grandmother poked her head out of the master bedroom doorway while smiling and brandishing a large shopping bag.

"Suzie, be a dear and get the albums from my bed. I don't think I can manage to carry all of this rubbish at once."

Suzanne took the overstuffed department store

bag from her grandmother, amid protests, and scooped up the heavy photo albums from the bed in the process. "Gran," she said, feeling winded from the effort. "Diane has supper, and our guests are already seated. We're just waiting for you."

Looking at her skeptically, her grandmother touched her face. "Why, you're freezing cold. But, your cheeks are flushed. Are you feeling well, my dear?"

Her grandmother's wisdom almost penetrated her facade. Avoiding more probing questions, Suzanne slipped past her and began down the stairs. "Oh, I'm just a little excited about how well you all are getting along. I'm fine. Now, come have some supper, and you can embarrass me in front of Ian and Leslie with your collection of baby mug shots."

Laughing, her grandmother followed her into the parlor, giving directions the entire time. Suzanne just sighed as her grandmother insisted on being seated next to Ian, and began pulling out the most horrific photos she could find.

"Gran, please," Suzanne groaned in self-defense. "Let the poor man eat."

Ian hadn't touched his plate, and was thoroughly captivated by the photos. Suzanne didn't manage as well. The food made her want to wretch, and she merely pushed small portions around to make it appear that she was engrossed in the meal. Gran took demure little bites amid editorial comments, while Leslie ate and laughed heartily, interjecting her memories of their child-hood antics along the way.

Finally relenting, Mrs. Hamilton begged Ian for his patience. "I am so sorry. I have gotten carried away, haven't I? It's a blasted sign of old age. Absolutely appalling." Ignoring his polite protests, she called for Diane to reheat his plate, sneaking in the opportunity to show him one more picture. "Now, this one is my favorite. Suzanne at seventeen on her senior prom."

Suzanne dropped her head into her hands and groaned again. "Oh, no, Gran. Not that hideous picture with me in a lavender taffeta dress, and my date in a matching tuxedo! Don't show him that."

Chuckling deeply, Ian took the photo from Mrs. Hamilton, making a show of it as he waved the eight-by-ten in front of the little group. "If you hate it that much, then I must see it," he said still laughing, ignoring Suzanne's second groan.

"I have got to see this, too," Leslie said, join-ing in the mirth and rising to come around to Ian's side. "I remember that prom. I wore pink satin . . . Mike wore a white tux with a pink shirt and red bow tie. Those were the days!"

But soon all the laughter quickly dissipated, as Ian's face turned ashen. Standing and hold-ing the photo under the light, he cast his gaze from Suzanne to the photo, then back again. "It's remarkable," he whispered, reaching across the table to touch Suzanne's jawline. "I never realized it before."

Becoming alarmed, Mrs. Hamilton searched the faces in the group. "All right. What's going on here?" she said flatly, holding Suzanne in an authoritative stare. "I wasn't born yesterday. Literally, I wasn't. But something is amiss, and I demand to know what it is."

Turning to her abruptly before Suzanne could answer, Ian confronted Mrs. Hamilton's stare. "She looks like Marissa . . . with her hair pulled back and wearing an appropriate gown. Although the hair is more red . . . Marissa's was a dark brunette. And Suzanne's eyes are a dark hazel . . . Marissa's were crystal blue. But here, in this photo, I can see it clearly," he said steadying himself by holding onto the edge of the table.

Suzanne held her breath, and Leslie twisted her cloth napkin nervously in her lap.

"Is that all?" Mrs. Hamilton scoffed, tossing her linen napkin on the table. "Why of course it's quite possible for there to be a resemblance. Marissa Hamilton is a relative, after all. And if genetics bear out, Suzanne could have some likeness to her." Reaching down into her sweater pocket, Gran pulled out a pair of half-moon reading glasses. "Now, I know I have a picture of her in one of these dusty old books. Poor girl," she went on, not looking up. "Died so young. It was influenza I believe. You know, in those days, people didn't have the modern inventions to protect against even simple infection."

Leslie hadn't moved, but put her arm around Ian's shoulder. "Mrs. H, do you know anything else about her?"

Clicking her tongue as she routed through the books, and then not finding the photo she wanted, Mrs. Hamilton rose to get the shopping bag.

"John Wanamakers," Ian said quietly, as he read the names across the bag. "Does that clothier still exist?"

"Of course. Don't be silly. I only go to the older establishments that know how to give superb service," Gran said in an annoyed voice, dumping the contents on the settee. "Oh, I get so angry with myself. I should have compiled and organized all this years ago."

"Show her the signature," Leslie whispered. "I'll bet she can recognize it."

Still shaken, Suzanne rose and went to her grandmother's side by the settee. Reaching into her purse, she produced the small slip of paper. "Gran, I found this in the house. It looked like something that would have been in one of your boxes or bags. Do you recognize it, or should I throw it away?"

"Hmmm, how strange. Ian Stewart Chandler . . . was the old Hamilton's attorney for years. He's probably responsible for the solid condition of our family wealth, you know. For a few years his name appears on almost everything financial or legal."

Leslie covered her mouth, and Suzanne could feel the blood rush from her head.

"Gran, do you recognize the signature?"

"Oh, it's his, all right. It's on deeds— debenture, original stock certificates, and I think, the old mortgage to this house. But what it could be doing on a piece of paper alone, without a lot of legal mumbo jumbo before it, is very odd. Now, his story was even worse than that poor child Marissa's."

"What happened to him, madame, if you please?" Ian moved to the old woman's side, wiping his forehead with the back of his hand nervously.

"Well," she said with a wink, still fussing over the pile of papers. "We Hamiltons have a few skeletons in the closet . . . Like all wealthy families I suppose. We did come by some of our assets with a little skullduggery."

Chuckling to herself, Mrs. Hamilton continued her search without looking up. "He was courting the same young girl you've asked me about. My mother used to say I'd wind up just like her, since I was so willful, and that I gave the entire family apoplexy. Anyway, those are stories for another time." Appearing to give up, she straightened herself slowly and took off her glasses. "It's in here somewhere, just let me think."

"About their relationship, we may have interrupted you," Ian said politely, trying to steer Mrs. Hamilton back to the subject.

"Oh, that, yes, well . . . Quite a scandal, I'm told. My mother was absolutely shocked by the behavior of her mother's mother's sister's daughter, especially in those days. What does that make her? My great aunt's daughter? I can never figure these things out . . ."

"Why?" Leslie blurted out, obviously unable to contain herself. "Why were they shocked?"

"Well, at seventeen, she had a fairly blatant and torrid affair with an older man— the family's attorney. When she got pregnant, he wanted to marry her, but nobody in the family even knew about it until they took her away. I think they sent her to their country house, but told all the servants she was going to Rome or London? I can't remember now. The problem was that she had been transported during a bad week of constant rain. That's when she caught the flu. Once the doctor examined her, they also found out that she was carrying more than the flu! Well, Great Uncle Milton threw a hissy fit, and swore that his barrister would pay dearly for the affront. So he robbed the poor chap blind, while he sent him on an ill-fated, wild goose chase, to look for the girl across the Atlantic. He never returned. At least not to Philadelphia."

Ian sat down and let his head drop in his hands. Suzanne and Leslie could only stare at each other as Mrs. Hamilton routed through albums and puttered about searching for the obscure photo.

"She was such a beauty, too. Never made it to twenty-one. Such a pity. The poor thing died one stormy night, and her parents were heartbroken. They even had to ship her body back here to bury her. And, of course, my dear mother used that story to scare me senseless until I settled down and married in my thirties. Thought I'd be a spinster!" she laughed with a clap of her hands. "Mother would say, 'Cecelia, this is what happens to wanton girls. Don't be foolish, or too promiscuous. *Try* your best to conduct yourself like a lady of the manor born, if you please!' Well, little did she know that I idolized the stormy romance. That's why I'm so disturbed by not being able to find the photo. I used to press it, with his steamy letters to her, in my diary. I was so young and silly in those days. Hoped for a dashing young cad like him to whisk me away and curl my toes," she chuckled, adjusting her sweater. "And, yes," she added sighing, "I did go through a lot of beaus trying to find him. But, Lord knows, I haven't kept a diary since I was in finishing school. Now, you can just imagine how long ago that was!"

"And, no one ever heard from the attorney?" Leslie asked quietly, her eyes misting over.

"I'm not sure, but I don't think so," Mrs. Hamilton remarked, still extremely distracted. "This is going to worry me all night, now. Hmmm. Maybe it's in my vanity . . . or perhaps in my first wedding trousseau . . . probably not. After Roger, I threw that away when I married Alan, or was it Todd . . . ? Now, he was one of my *favorite* husbands." Semi-indignant with herself, Mrs. Hamilton left the room. "I'll be just a moment, darlings. Ask Diane to bring the tea and dessert. Let me check one more spot."

Suzanne and Leslie stood still as Ian rose and faced the window.

"The grave markers at the outer edge of the

property, under the pines . . . I would like to go outside for a while. Alone. Please."

They didn't follow him as he straightened his carriage and walked out the door. Tears brimmed in their eyes, and neither woman spoke. Yet Suzanne immediately felt the physical discomfort pass when he left the room. She no longer had flu symptoms, or felt chills and fever. Just a sad malaise had settled over her, and she finally allowed the tears to course down her face.

"Oh, Jesus, Suz. What are we going to do? He'll die of a broken heart."

Suzanne just shook her head, wiping at her cheeks. "I don't know what any of us can do. I never thought we'd hear this. The whole story is so tragic."

"Ah, ha!" they heard Mrs. Hamilton exclaim from the foyer. "I may be senior, but I'm not senile! I've found it. Of course, I would have put it where it belongs. In the old antique desk in the study!"

Trying to force a smile, Suzanne took the diary from her grandmother's hands. She held the object with reverence, and kissed her grandmother's cheek warmly. "May I?"

"Oh, dearheart, of course you may have it. Now that I've buried three husbands, and countless lovers, and you're over twenty-one, I suppose there wouldn't be any harm in your reading these wickedly sexy accounts of my daydreams," she laughed, patting Suzanne's cheek. "I hope your Mr. Chandler can— "

Suddenly the old woman stopped in the middle of her banter and looked at both Leslie and Suzanne hard.

"What a strange coincidence . . . He has the same name, Suzie. Exactly the same name. It hadn't dawned on me before."

"I know, Gran. That's why we brought him here."

The elderly woman tilted her head to the side and studied them both with a smile. "Hmmm. And you look like her. Marissa." Walking into the parlor, the elderly woman stopped to gaze at Ian's form through the window before sitting down. "Girls, that man is pining away for something lost, that he doesn't even understand. I can feel it, but can't put my finger on it exactly. Such a pity."

Mrs. Hamilton shook her head sadly and rang the small silver bell for Diane McDonnell, dispensing instructions when she came into the room. Once they were alone again, she bade both Suzanne and Leslie to sit down. "I've been told by an exquisite Oriental gentleman friend of mine . . . well, a lover actually, that there is no such thing as coincidence. And, in the last portion of one's life, what greater pleasure could I find than to have my favorite grandchild stow away with my fantasy. Oh," she laughed, clapping her hands. "What a vicarious thrill! I knew God had a wonderful sense of humor. I can't wait to meet that dear, old gentleman. Really, I can't."

Suzanne and Leslie sipped their tea quietly, allowing Grandmother Hamilton to entertain

them with her outrageous stories. Suzanne was
thankful that all they had to do was nod and
smile, for the old lady virtually carried the conversation alone.

As much as humanly possible, Suzanne tried
to interject comments and seem involved in what
her grandmother had to say. But, her attention
stayed at the window, watching Ian's shoulders
shake from the emotions that he could never
reveal before any of them. It tore at her soul to
watch him kneel and touch the headstone, then
lovingly caress and trace each letter with his fingers. She watched him bow his head, cross himself, and walk out toward the trees. And as the
sun dropped, casting a rose-orange haze over his
shoulders, she said her own silent prayer for his
peace.

Nine

"He's been up there since last night," Suzanne said in a low voice, cradling the phone in her hand. "I don't know what to do, Les. He went back up into the attic, and won't come down, not even to eat."

She heard her friend sigh, and prayed that Leslie had a plan. For once she'd go along with any crazy scheme that Leslie came up with, as long as it would help dissolve Ian's pain.

"I don't know, Suz. I'm really at a loss."

Defeat made Suzanne's shoulders slump. "I can't bear to see him like this. He looks so beaten . . . I actually miss his old sarcastic, chauvinistic ways. At least he had some fight in him then. Now, Les, he's just sitting up there waiting to die. It's so pitiful to watch. Yet I don't know why I feel so involved in this. We solved his puzzle, so maybe we should just leave it be now?"

"Aw, Suz, you can't be serious? We can't just turn the man out into the streets in this condition."

Suzanne let out an exasperated breath: "I know. I know. I couldn't do that. But, what are we supposed to do with him now? Did the cosmos give you any more clues?"

She was being half serious and half sarcastic when she made the comment. How was she to proceed? Let him turn into dust in her attic and simply blow away?

"Can't you keep him until Rahmin can meet with us on Friday?" Leslie said, as though talking about caring for a stray puppy.

"This situation is going from bad to worse. C'mon, Les," she pleaded, dragging out the syllables of her words. "What the hell are we supposed to do?"

"Can't you entice him downstairs?"

"How? With what? Food doesn't work. He won't talk to me. What should I do, drag him downstairs and force-feed him?"

Leslie sighed again. "Well, there is something he really wants . . . but it's gonna be embarrassing."

"Have you lost your mind!" Suzanne nearly shrieked. "You don't expect me to go to bed with this man, do you? He's not that depressed. Or, if he is, too bad!"

"Calm down, Suz. Calm down. No, I'm not suggesting anything that extreme. But, you know, he hasn't seen the diary or Marissa's picture yet. He doesn't know what your grandmother gave you, does he? Or about your journal . . ."

"I could possibly see giving him the diary, but wouldn't that make him more depressed?"

"That's why you should show him the journal, too."

"Oh, no," Suzanne said feeling dread course through her body. "It's so personal, so crazy . . . I just couldn't."

"Tell him you'll show him yours if he'll show you his. What could hurt? You'll both be mutually exposed."

"You have lost your mind," Suzanne stammered, hating Leslie's analogy.

"Suz, it's like getting naked together. Nobody can hide or laugh at the other— "

"I know what it's like, and I'm not doing it. Okay? Case closed."

"Then start off with the diary, and see what happens. But if it makes him go into a deep funk, then you should give him a little more to go on. You know?" Leslie said with a sigh of resignation. "You've gotta give him hope . . . something to consider as a possibility, is all I'm saying."

The word "hope" rang in Suzanne's mind. It registered as soon as her friend said it.

"Let me consider it, Les. All I know is, I have to do something. And I'm not sure what."

"Maybe, we could try to get him to go out to a club or something?" Leslie added, obviously fishing for an answer. "I don't know, Suz. It's all so sad."

Letting out a deep breath, Suzanne agreed. "It is sad, Les. So terribly sad, and I hate the fact that we brought this man here to break his heart. What was the cosmic purpose of that? Where's the lesson in it, or is this just eternal hell for Ian Chandler?"

Both women fell silent for a while, neither

speaking as they weighed the possibilities. Finally, Leslie broke the stalemate with another deep sigh.

"Look," she said in a firm voice. "With all this poop, there's gotta be a pony in here somewhere. So, let's keep shovelin' till we find it. In the meanwhile, give the poor guy a little hope to cling to until we can pull together a plan. Okay? That's our plan for the next two days. To stall until we have a plan."

Suzanne had to smile despite herself. "Okay, Captain This is your show. But, if it backfires, I'm telling you . . ."

"What could go wrong?" Leslie asked in an upbeat voice, her normal mirth returning. "Didn't I tell you to trust me? We haven't done so bad, so far."

Suzanne let out a snort. "Oh, yeah, right. We haven't done bad at all."

"Well at least we know that he's not a killer, or a thief. And, by now, we're pretty sure that he isn't crazy. The trip to your grandmother's proved that."

"I'm not sure what that visit proved," Suzanne said, feeling unsure. "Really, Les. These last few days have felt like a dream. But, you're right. He's not dangerous or evil. And that stuff at Gran's was too real to ignore."

Leslie laughed with triumph. "Then you admit it! We did it! We actually brought somebody back from the past. A lover, no less. Granny H. said so. Isn't it exciting?"

"Frightening is more the word."

"Incredible, isn't it?"

"Go to work," Suzanne said quietly. "And, don't rush off to 'Hard Copy' with the story yet, okay?"

"I promise," Leslie chuckled. "Boy, I can't believe I did it! My first spell, and it worked."

Suzanne refused to laugh as she hustled her madcap friend off the phone. Shaking her head at the irony, Suzanne ran her fingers through her hair. She was actually best friends with an honest to goodness New Age screwball. One with bad aim, who cast a spell and hit a target that was over a hundred years old. "It figures," Suzanne mumbled to herself, as she returned the phone to the wall jack and moved toward the stairs. Now all she had to do was to get up enough nerve to leave Ian the diary. But giving him her journal was absolutely out of the question!

"I suppose I have caused enough trouble, and should take my leave now."

Suzanne spun around, and clutched her chest. "Ian, please! You have got to stop creeping up on me like— "

"Like a ghost, Suzanne? For all intentional purposes, that's what I am. I have no records, no life here, no way to earn my keep or contribute . . . but I'm sadly trapped between two worlds. One where I fit in, but can't get back to, and this."

His words tugged at her insides, for she understood the emotions of isolation and loneliness all too well. It broke her heart to see him bravely stand before her, dressed in his old tattered suit, apparently ready to go out into the hostile foreign world.

"Look," she said in a low voice, trying to calm him. "You haven't been much trouble, really. We all just needed to get adjusted to this situation. A couple of more days wouldn't hurt, at least until Rahmin can try to help you."

Ian just shook his head sadly. "No, Suzanne. Unless he can raise the dead, what's the purpose?"

She had no answer for him. What could she say to make him accept Marissa's death? She wasn't a psychic, or a therapist. All she was, was human. A lost human, just like Ian Stewart Chandler. A person who didn't fit in.

"Look," she whispered, nearing him and tentatively placing her hand on his shoulder. "I cannot imagine what it must be like to lose someone that you've loved as deeply as you loved Marissa. I suppose it's a two-edged sword . . . a blessing to have loved, with the curse of this kind of pain when you've lost that person. No one has ever cared for me that way. She was very fortunate to have had you while she did."

She watched him swallow hard, and say nothing, able to only nod his understanding.

Searching her mind for a way to stop him, she settled on her grandmother's diary. "I have a gift for you. I wanted to be sure that it wouldn't upset you, though . . . It's just sort of a remembrance before you leave."

Ian covered her hand with his own. "Dear Suzanne. You have been too kind to me already. You were right, all along. I've crashed into your life, upset things terribly, have cost you enough . . . I cannot accept a gift."

Smiling, she clasped his hand and lead him to the stove. "Humor me with a little tea and toast, first. Okay? I'll be back in a moment."

Without waiting for his response, she slipped out of the kitchen and dashed up the stairs. Searching her nightstand drawer, she found the beautiful silver covered book and sat down on the bed. Each flower along its border was delicately etched in the fine metal, and in the very center of the decorative scrollwork, she traced the inscription with her fingers . . . *"To C.M.H., with all my love, and may your dreams come true. Mother."*

Suzanne closed her eyes and said a quiet prayer. *Dear God, Let it work.* What better person to have this, than her grandmother's crush? She was sure that the pages contained the unconditional freedom of a sixteen-year-old girl's dreams, loves, and hopes. She only prayed that would be enough. And Marissa's letters . . . Maybe they would help Ian finally bring the loss to closure.

When Suzanne entered the kitchen she found Ian standing by the counter, absently buttering a plate of toast. He didn't even turn around as he layered the bread and cut it into neat triangles. She had been there before . . . using a mindless task to staunch the pain. Watching him only made her chest feel heavier, and she sidled up next to him to peek around his shoulder.

"Thanks, Ian," she said, trying not to startle

him with the intrusion. "C'mon, and sit down for a moment, so I can give you something very special."

This time he didn't object, but his expression held a level of defeat that pained her as they slid into their chairs. Producing the diary, she gently pushed it across the table toward him. "This was my grandmother's. She gave it to me while you were in the garden yesterday . . . and I thought you'd like to have it?"

Ian studied the small silver book carefully, then looked up at her. "It's a diary?"

"Yes," she said with a smile, feeling encouraged for some odd reason. "She kept it from the time she was sixteen years old."

"But this is so personal," he stammered, looking away shyly, then standing to walk over to the window. "It might contain very intimate things that she wouldn't want anyone else to know . . . especially not a stranger."

Suzanne chuckled. "You met my grandmother, right? Did she strike you as the shy type?"

As Ian turned away from the window to face her, a slight trace of a smile graced his mouth. "No. Shy would not exactly be my depiction of your grandmother. However," he added, as his smile broadened, "her memoirs are still very personal, I would think."

Suzanne rose and turned off the kettle, pouring hot water into two mugs, then came back to the table. "I'll tell you a secret," she said still smiling. She wanted to hold onto his interest, and could tell that it had been peaked. Anything to lift the dark cloud from his shoulders.

Although Ian didn't answer, he didn't turn away again. His intense expression seemed to beg for an answer, even though she knew he was too much of a gentleman to give into his curiosity without a little nudge.

"You're not a stranger to Gran."

Successfully baiting him, she watched Ian's brow furrow in an attempt to understand without asking for more clarification. Men! "Tea?" she asked nonchalantly, adding one sugar and a drop of milk into his mug, just the way she knew he liked it.

"Thank you," he said grudgingly, as the sway of his interest pulled him toward the table and into a chair beside her. "Not a stranger," he finally repeated, taking a sip and losing the battle with himself.

"No. Not at all. She's followed you from her youth."

Suzanne almost giggled as Ian's eyes widened.

"Oh, I can't play poker!" she fussed at herself. "I'm just dying to tell you. C'mon, c'mon, ask me."

Ian chuckled despite his obvious plan to remain stoic. Excitement made her laugh. After all, Leslie had shown her how to wear down the toughest customers. This time, by golly, it had worked.

"All right. If it's driving you mad, then you may tell me."

Leaning in to him in a confidential manner,

Suzanne nearly giggled again. "Ian. Gran has had this fantasy all of her life to be with a man like you. She's saved all of your correspondence . . . don't ask me how she came by it. And, I would imagine, she took great care to save everything she got her hands on. So, it's all there. All of the letters, all of the notes, pictures . . . everything. And with her editorial comments, to boot."

Immediately sitting back in his chair, Ian nearly gasped. "You do not mean to say that she has collected the correspondence between Marissa and I?"

"Yup," Suzanne said with a satisfied grin. "But I haven't opened this. I felt that since I knew you, it would be a violation. It must have been really hot, though," she added teasing him, "since it kept Gran going for over sixty years."

If she didn't know better, she would have sworn Ian Stewart Chandler had blushed. The thought made her chuckle as she studied his face for a response.

"All of them?" he repeated again in amazement, as he fiddled with the salt and pepper shakers nervously. "But your grandmother was only sixteen, and, well . . . err, uh . . . some of the content was definitely not for a young girl. I mean, surely . . ."

"Marissa was only one year older, seventeen. Right?"

Ian coughed and took a sip of tea, apparently trying to steady himself before answering. Why was she needling him so? Suzanne shook her head. It didn't make sense. Here she was, getting whipped up into a jealous snit over a seventeen-year-old girl who had been dead for a hundred and fifty years. It simply didn't make sense.

"Well?" she went on, unable to contain herself. "What's one year?"

"That was different," Ian protested. "Marissa had a maturity about her, a certain older presence."

The comment made her seethe. All of her efforts to remain detached and just give the man the damned diary were quickly eroding. "Perhaps you were drawn to her openness, her willingness to explore, or the fact that she hung on your every word without question. Or was it her high-spirited, rebellious nature that drew your passion to the fore?"

Ian blanched, and sat his cup down on the table. She knew she had gone too far. Thoroughly expecting him to leave, Suzanne steeled herself for that possibility.

"I never thought of it that way, Suzanne. You may be right . . . It's so odd, you speak of her as though you've known her." Leaning forward he held her in his gaze. "Marissa was both open and intemperate."

They said nothing for a brief moment, yet neither seemed to be able to look away. There was a current that bound them, and slowly, she again became aware of the charge that had awakened her at night. A physical ache consumed her, almost making it impossible for her to speak.

Fighting against it, she straightened her carriage, determined to make her point.

"So, you wanted to have your cake, and eat it too," she declared, shaking off the discomfort. "Marissa was young enough to be naive, and rebellious enough to be passionate. My question is, however, how long does it take for someone who is plunged into an adult relationship to grow up? I doubt she would have stayed naive forever— not with the way you two were carrying on."

Suzanne's hand flew to cover her mouth, as shame washed over her. The errant comment had made it's way to her surface before she could stop it. But, much to her surprise, Ian laughed.

"Let me stop your apology before you issue it," he chuckled. "You, dear lady, would have made an excellent attorney were women allowed to bar. Perhaps you're right."

"Women can now, you know," she countered, thankful for the diversion he offered. "And one of these days, maybe tonight or tomorrow evening," she added, stalling for time, "Les and I will take you for a night on the town. Just so you can see why *modern women* aren't so naive. Dare I use the word, pristine."

Ian nodded, still smiling. "Touché. I don't suppose, after having read your grandmother's memoirs, or my letters, that you would even call Marissa pristine. I have been exposed. Now you know that I am not quite the staid gentleman I professed to be. But, I assure you, my intentions were honorable."

Her gaze narrowed on him. "I told you. I haven't read it."

Ian just smiled. "Whatever you say, Madame."

"I didn't. I wouldn't do that! Not with you in the house."

"Why not?" he asked, his gaze still holding amusement. "I might have been tempted, were I in your position. I'm just glad that you haven't gained access to my current journal."

"And what position is that?" she countered angrily, still grappling with the strong emotions within her, and ignoring the second part of his comment.

It was his turn to look embarrassed. Casting his gaze down to his tea, Ian reached for it and took another long sip. "I am behaving badly in the company of my beautiful, intelligent hostess. I apologize."

There were no words. He had openly complimented her, obviously feeling the same immediate pull to something indescribable that she had felt. She was both flattered and frightened at the same time. How long would it take, she wondered, before something happened? Before one of them went further than appropriate, said something intractable . . .

He wanted her. Or, at least to know about her intimate life. He had just admitted that he would have read her diary, had it been laying around. And his journal? Nah, couldn't be. She would not allow herself to believe that he had written anything about her . . . not something positive, or steamy, anyway. Conflicted, her thoughts went to her own journal. She'd just die.

"I give you this gift," she added more gently, pushing the book toward him, "with no strings attached. Really, I didn't read it. You have more right to it than I. Please. It's the least I can do."

Bypassing the diary, Ian surprised her by suddenly covering her hand with his own as his eyes misted with tears. "Suzanne," he whispered with raw emotion, "you have given me something so precious . . . so important. How can I ever repay you?"

Caught in his gaze, she fought the urge to look away. There was something so familiar that it defied definition. "For some gifts, Ian, there is no repayment required. Just to see your face light up like this, to get you to laugh a little, to see how much you would treasure it, is all the payment in the world. Just stay long enough for Leslie and I to right this terrible wrong. If you leave now, you'll never know why any of this happened."

She could tell that he would stay, at least for another day or so. As he removed his hand from hers, and touched the filigreed cover of the diary, she knew.

"How in the world did you get him to agree to go out with us?" Leslie stood in the foyer shaking her head.

"I gave him Gran's diary, then I went to work. I guess he's been up there all day reading it. In any event, he didn't leave or slash his wrists. When I came home, he was here. And when I mentioned going out on the town, he said he would, then made me show him which items to wear. Can you believe it?"

Leslie seemed speechless for a moment, and ran her fingers through her hair as though the action would help her think. "Is he gonna be okay, Suz? I mean, do you think he can handle a drink at The Mulberry Inn . . . in public?"

Suzanne laughed. "What, you, nervous? C'mon, Les. Where's your sense of adventure? Trust me."

Leslie joined in with her laughter, although her expression still seemed to question the viability of the plan. "I don't know what's happening to you, lady. It's like, over the last few days, you're becoming the wild one, and me— I'm just trying to live the quiet life."

Still smiling, Suzanne considered Leslie's words. Something had happened. For the first time in years there was someone to come home to, someone whom she cared about, some untold adventure to look forward to. Oddly, work seemed laborious, and her personal life seemed so much more exciting than drab, old contracts, client problems, sales . . . For once she had a secret, a big one, that lived in her attic. When Mondays rolled around, she could come in with a Cheshire cat smile on her face, and let others wonder. For the first time, in too long, she had another dimension to her life.

The feeling was exhilarating.

"Oh, come on. Listen," she giggled, ushering Leslie into the living room by the elbow. "What could happen? If he starts talking about the past, or says something inappropriate, people will just think he's had one too many. What better place to showcase him than in a bar? It sure beats the mall. I did that with him, remember?"

Again, Leslie just shook her head and flopped down on the sofa. "If you're sure, he—"

"Oh, my, God . . ." Suzanne barely whispered, assessing Ian from head to toe as he came through the door.

"Humph, humph, humph— Lady, you did a good job at the mall!" Leslie exclaimed.

Seeming a little shy, Ian walked into the room, and stopped a few feet before them. "Are you sure this is correct?" he asked tentatively. "I haven't gotten used to the new cravats yet."

Ian stood before them quietly, appearing like a prom date waiting for their approval. He seemed to relax only when Suzanne walked up to him, adjusted the knot in his tie, and brushed the non-existent lint from his lapels.

Stepping back to gaze at him again, she smiled broadly. "Ian Stewart Chandler, you look like a million dollars."

His bashful expression made her want to kiss him, but she checked herself. He seemed so much younger, so unsure . . . and so endearing. Where had her arrogant, self-assured, chauvinist gone during the day?

"You really look great, Ian," Leslie said with

genuine appreciation. "You'll be the best looking bachelor in the place. So, you'll have to behave yourself. The women will die, Suz, won't they?"

Suzanne answered her friend with a wink.

"But what made you decide to go?" Leslie pressed on, still gaping.

Ian shrugged, and looked down at his feet before he returned his gaze to Suzanne. "I realized that Marissa was so full of life and love, that she wouldn't want me to give up on either. I know, having loved deeply, that I wouldn't want that for anyone whom I cared about. Suzanne made me see that clearly this morning."

Ignoring Leslie's raised eyebrows, she looped her arms around both of her friends' waists. "C'mon gang. The night is young, and we'll banish sad thoughts for a little while. Good wine, good music, maybe even a dance or two. What do you say?"

As the threesome gathered coats, and Ian held them in his old world manner, Suzanne's mind leaped away from the room. They all seemed as though they had been friends since . . . forever. It was a comfortable place to be. Oddly, a safe and reassuring feeling that knit the little group together like a warm sweater. She had wanted to feel this way for so long, without pretense, without the customary nervousness, just friends—true friends, with someone who cared about her. And, somehow, in that moment, she was sure that Ian Stewart Chandler did.

Ten

"As I told you last evening, I have never been so completely appalled in all of my life as by the behavior of your so-called, modern gentlemen." Ian straightened himself in the chair as he dug into his plate of eggs. "And to think, Suzanne, that they would not even offer to buy a woman a drink without expecting something in return."

Stifling a smile, she nodded while sipping her orange juice.

"Suzanne, tell me, how much do the drinks cost again?"

"Anywhere from two to about five dollars," she said, hiding her smile with her glass. "Why?"

"Well, even in my day, even if one perceived that the woman was, shall we say, for hire . . . To expect her to keep you company on that relative pittance?"

She almost spit out her juice, coughing in the process as she tried to keep him from seeing her chuckle.

"I'm sorry," he said hotly, "I don't mean to bring indelicate subjects to the breakfast table, especially issues that we have fully discussed at length last night. But I am still amazed."

Baiting him, she joined in with his disgust. "Yes, and would you believe that if a woman doesn't succumb on the first night, often the cad won't even call her again? She must at least give him the illusion that she's willing, just undecided about when."

"No!" Ian threw down his napkin, and, pushed back his chair. Examining her facial expression, he rubbed his chin. "You are teasing me again, are you not?"

"Not," she said evenly, digging her nails into her palms to keep from laughing. "I know it seems strange, but things have gone pretty awry between men and women since the last century. I'm not sure which was better. Being put on a pedestal, but not being allowed to do anything interesting or being slung into the mud, and being expected to do everything, and like it."

Raking his hands through his hair, Ian's brow knit in its familiar pattern when he was deep in thought. "I know when we entered the establishment, you and Leslie tried to make me understand this need for liberation. After our lengthy debate, you ladies forced me to concede that perhaps the roles for women had been too narrowly defined in my century. But, when I saw their scantily clad bodies, and the way the women were disrespecting themselves, and worse, being disrespected by men, I wasn't sure."

Suzanne pondered his comment for a moment. "You weren't sure about what, Ian? That a woman can do any job that a man can do? I thought we settled that argument in the mall."

"No," he muttered, appearing to be still deep in thought. "I have been astounded by what you have shown me of your capabilities, and of the things I've seen on the black box. I have also read a great deal while I was home . . . Capability doesn't quite sum up my meaning."

"Well, if we can do anything you men can do, what's the problem?"

Hesitating a moment, Ian looked at her before speaking. "If a woman can do a certain job with the same proficiency as a man, then true, she should get the same pay. That's not where I have difficulty."

Perplexed, she stared at him. For some reason, this time she truly wanted to understand his position, if not to argue her own point better. "Okay . . ."

"Well, it's just that, why would any woman want to be treated this way, even if she had the freedom to do what she wanted? Why, in this era, did she elect to get equal pay, open new career options, have legal rights and protection under the law from violence and abuse, only to act in the same brutish manner as men? This is what I don't understand, Suzanne. And, why, pray tell, would any man worth his salt treat the object of his affection in such a *common* manner? Where is the romance of it all? The mystery . . . the excitement?"

Suzanne had to smile, yet she could only shake her head in wonder as she stared at Ian Chandler's intense, perplexed expression. He really didn't understand. He was a naive man-child in this awful world, and she didn't have the heart to ruin his fresh perspective.

Taking a deep breath, she sighed. "Ian, you have asked the question that every woman I know has asked in this century. If you can figure out why women can't be respected for their intelligence and their ability, and, at the same time, be treated with respect in their personal relationships, then you can do the talk show circuit. I'll represent you, and be your agent."

Still appearing confused, he shook his head. "It doesn't make sense, Suzanne. It's as though the world has gone mad. Why can't a man say to himself, she's smart, she's witty, she's intelligent . . . *and* she's beautiful, and fragrant, and wondrously female? Why is that so wrong? And why is that what they call, sexual harassment? What I saw at the Inn, in my estimation, was the worse form of harassment I've ever witnessed. Both ways, to boot."

Shrugging, she took a bite of toast. "It's only wrong when the man says, I want you to put out, or you won't get promoted. Or, he puts his hands on a woman, when she doesn't want him to, then threatens her sense of well being at work. Or— "

"But that's just common courtesy, gentlemanly conduct! That cannot be legislated! No decent man would assume that just because a woman was in his employ, or his colleague, or having a toddy with a group of her friends, that he should have the right to impugn her personage. And for a mere two dollars, at that! Would he?"

Suzanne smiled again. "That's why we have the laws. Because some knuckleheads did just that, to one too many females. Before that, women had no protection."

"Then, I forbid you to go to work or to these Inns. These are intolerable conditions. You cannot go out of here each day and suffer such abuse. I won't have it."

Despite his tone, Suzanne smiled. "You forbid it?"

"Absolutely."

"See, this is just what we're talking about. You have no right to forbid me to do anything."

She watched him smolder in his chair and dig into his eggs again silently, although she had to admit that his sudden burst of protectiveness was sort of sweet.

"Anyway," she said mildly, continuing to eat her breakfast, "That's why I don't do the singles scene. I can't stand the meat rack any more than you can. And I own my own company. So if anyone were to be so foolish as to harass the boss, they'd be fired on the spot."

He didn't look up, but she did notice that his shoulder's relaxed by two inches.

"Then, as the boss, you could perhaps agree to show me the countryside during the day? That is, if your schedule permits?"

He hadn't looked at her when he'd asked the question. Somehow, she knew he couldn't. Based on the way Ian was pushing his food around on his plate without devouring it, she could tell that he was expectantly waiting for her answer.

"Perhaps," she said evenly, enjoying his invitation. "Let me see what I can do."

When Ian finally looked up, he was smiling. Something was happening to the old, strident dynamic that had existed between them when they'd met. It was as though time spent away from him felt like it dragged on, while time spent with him fled quickly. She had noticed the phenomenon earlier the night before. She was sure he felt it too. Because, even after they'd left the club Ian had suggested that they continue their debate, practically begging them to allow him to experience a cup of coffee in a diner. He had seen a diner on a television commercial, and all Leslie had to do was mention that they were close to one.

And when they had arrived home, she was no longer afraid to be left alone at night with him. The awkwardness had vanished. They had stayed up until the wee hours, discussing philosophy, lifestyles, practically everything. He even slept in the guest room, claiming to be too tired to suffer the attic floor. It had been a glorious evening. Just the way she had hoped it would be.

"I'm really tired from last night, I have to admit. A drive in the country could be therapeutic."

"I can make a lunch . . . we could spend the day," he exclaimed, jumping to his feet and taking away their plates. "It will do you good to get away from the smoke-filled factories for a while."

Suzanne chuckled, as she helped him clear the

table. "Remind me to tell you about the environ-
mentalists, and the new ecologically correct so-
cieties. No more factories in the center of town."

Ian cocked his head to one side, but waved
her away with his hand before she could explain.
"We have all day for you to tell me about the
new American industries. There's just so much
to learn, Suzanne."

She had to agree with him. There was a lot
to absorb. Even though she was from this era,
she still didn't understand it all herself. How
could she explain world wars, trips to the moon
and outlying planets, Star Wars, Star Trek . . .
modern medicine, Save The Whales, gay rights,
Nelson Mandela, "Wheel of Fortune," NJ State
Lotto, Columbian drug cartels, oil cartels . . .
crack, AIDS, flight, Amtrak— all in two more
short days? She'd need a lifetime with Ian Chandler to make him understand.

Somehow, in the quiet recesses of her mind,
she had begun to hope that would be possible.
Now *that* was crazy.

Suzanne let her elbow dangle out the window,
enjoying the sensation of the wind whipping
through her hair as she drove. Ian had been
right. This was too glorious a day to spend
hunched over files and handling complaints. It
was a day to cling to, like new life.

Inhaling deeply, she breathed in spring. It had
been so long since she could face this season
without a twinge of resentment. But today she

was one with the elements. She felt as purposeful
as the birds who hopped from branch to branch
building nests . . . as warm as the sun that
beamed down on her face. She had someone special to share her life, even though they were just
friends.

"Want to stop and get some wine to go with
lunch?"

Ian smiled at her, and nodded. "That sounds
like a perfect idea."

"And there's this little place in Medford Lakes.
They have genuine, old fashioned, hand-rolled
pretzels."

"With mustard?"

The look on his face made her laugh. "They
ate pretzels with mustard in your day?"

Ian mocked offense. "Any real Philadelphian
knows that the genuine article requires mustard.
Please do not offend me, madame."

Laughing and chatting as they drove along the
quiet country roads, occasionally she would point
out town borders that dotted the landscape. It
was amazing that not much had changed over the
years, save the paved roads and cars, and many
of the old farmhouses still held their ground
against would-be developers. Hearing the deep
lowing of cows in the distance, they had managed
to stop for a while to sit and watch them casually
graze before continuing their journey. Even Ian
was surprised by the amount of wilderness still
left in the Pine Barrens. After seeing Center City,
he had assumed that everything had been wiped
out to make way for glass and chrome.

"Wait. Stop. Pull over," he shouted, scaring her nearly to death. "Look at the sign, Suzanne. Look at the sign!"

Suzanne squinted, and tried to focus on which sign Ian was referring to. The sudden hysteria had momentarily disoriented her, and she negotiated the car to a stop on the shoulder to avoid blocking the lane.

"Where? You can't just scream at a driver. I've got to keep my eyes on the road, Ian."

"I'm sorry, I know," he said quickly, hopping out from the passenger's side and nearing a post. "But, look. The township of Mount Laurel, New Jersey, established in eighteen hundred and seventy-two. Amazing."

Catching along side of him, she tugged at his elbow. "What? Okay. But, I'm not following."

Spinning her around, almost in a Maypole dance, Ian threw his head back and laughed. "Don't you see? This is part of the land that the Hamiltons purchased. Just like when they annexed three hundred acres of Blockley."

"Blockley?"

"Yes, Blockley. That was the name of the city before it became Philadelphia, and way, way before my time. Sixteen hundreds. I believe. But, in the seventeen hundreds, the family had invested in a three-hundred-acre section of Philadelphia, where the University of Pennsylvania now stands. That was Hamilton Village."

"Now it's called University City," she murmured, still fuzzy about where he was going with this useless information.

"Precisely."

"But what has that got to do with anything?" She was confused, if not a little disgruntled, that their outing was being spoiled by the past again.

"I don't know. I just think it's remarkable that, without knowing about these things, you're taking me to every place that she would have been familiar with. Even here— this must have been where they took her to hide her from me."

For an instant Suzanne wanted to vomit. They were still being haunted by the ghost of a girl who hadn't even lived long enough to . . . to what? Love? Suzanne forced reason back into her brain. After all, she had no right. What was wrong with her?

"Amazing," she intoned flatly, turning toward the car. Try as she might, she couldn't hide the disappointment in her voice, nor banish the confusion in her brain. She wanted to cry, scream, yell.

But by what right did she assume those emotions? Steadying herself, she quietly admitted that she was getting too attached to her guest. She tried to focus on the fact that he'd be leaving soon, one way or another, and wasn't that best? How long could she keep a time traveler in her attic, anyway? It wasn't practical.

Ian touched her arm as he slid back into the passenger's seat. His smile had faded, and his intense expression had returned. Immediately feeling guilty for ruining his discovery, she turned on the ignition and pulled onto the road, trying to force a smile.

"So, where to next?" she asked lightly, blinking back the tears.

"Someplace where we can spread a blanket, and you can have a well deserved cry."

She looked at him, immediately stunned and somewhat ashamed.

"Keep your eyes on the road," he said while patting her hand. "We'll talk when we get there."

Terror gripped her as she passed up convenient road turn-offs near lakes and streams. She didn't want to have a discussion about anything too deep, especially not about how she was feeling at the moment. If he'd asked her directly, she wouldn't have known what to tell him. Opting for procrastination, she pulled up in front of the pretzel stand.

"Look, Ian. They have shops in here, an old water wheel, benches where we can sit and eat before we go home. Isn't it lovely?"

He didn't answer her, but just covered her hand. "Let's go get the pretzels, then find a place to talk. No stalling, agreed?"

Panic made her heart pound in her ears, and as she sat in the car trying to decide how to evade Ian's suggestion, an old couple strolled by. They were holding hands and seemed to be leaning on each other for support. Yet, when they entered the small shop area, the elderly man held the door, and his companion smiled prettily, accepting his gesture with demure grace. The sight made tears form in Suzanne's eyes, and she immediately looked down. The floor blurred as tears washed her vision. She needed air.

"I'll get them. Don't bother, wait here," she gasped.

Dashing from the car, Suzanne rounded the little pretzel shed, and closed the screen behind her. Just space. A little distance. Fresh air. She'd be all right. Ignoring the stares of the people in line, she quickly wiped at her eyes with the back of her sleeve and placed her order.

Thankful that the pace of the two old women who ran the shop was slow, she counted on their leisurely service. She needed that time to pull herself together. There was no way she was going to face Ian with tears running down her face. Never. It didn't make sense. She had no right. She'd ruin the comfort level that they had established, making things awkward. Then he'd leave for sure.

"I thought you might need a hand carrying those."

The deep voice that came from behind gave her a start.

"Oh, no problem. I can manage." At that moment, she hated the sound of her own voice. It was shaky, and the words splashed out just a bit too quickly.

"I know you can manage on your own, but you don't have to. I'm not forcing my help, just offering it. Is that all right?"

Suzanne closed her eyes and tried to shut out the sensation that Ian's words created. "Yes," she said quietly. "Thanks."

Again she ignored the kindly nods and stares they received in the pretzel shop, as she paced to the car at breakneck speed. They probably thought that we'd had a lovers' quarrel, she thought, cringing as she hopped into the car. If they only knew . . .

"How about that bottle of wine now, madame? I think we could both use a splash, don't you?"

It was the best suggestion she had heard all day and, for once, Ian Chandler's sense of propriety was welcomed. He hadn't forced the discussion, made her feel small or stupid for not wanting to have it, or gotten angry because she wanted to be quiet for a while. He had respected her wishes. Oddly, this man-out-of-time allowed her to exert the feminine side of herself. She didn't have to explain her whims. She didn't have to be practical, or have a logical explanation. Nor did she have to endure any pop psychology explanation for her craziness. She was a woman. That was enough.

Finding a clearing by a lake, they lugged Ian's food stores and two bottles of wine over to a peaceful spot. As they opened the blanket, standing apart and fluffing it several times, she couldn't help but imagine them chatting away on a Saturday morning . . . making a bed together, having meals together, growing old together . . . like that couple. But it had to stop. The daydreaming was insane, and making her unnecessarily blue. Yet, she couldn't help wonder why the thoughts had intensified so. It seemed that ever since she handed the diary over to Ian, she couldn't pull herself together. It was frightening.

Once they settled in, Suzanne immediately reached for the basket, trying to avoid any eye contact with Ian. When she finally looked up, he was staring at her.

"You haven't taken one bite of your pretzel, and you left it in the car. Now I see you rearranging food that you probably won't eat. I'm not hungry yet, either. How about if we start with wine?"

His smile soothed her, even though his insightful comments had embarrassed her. She felt like a stumbling teenager.

"Oh, my God. That's it. That's why I'm being so crazy. I'm picking it up, just like in Gran's house!"

Ian stopped pouring the wine for a moment, then smiled. "Not influenza again, I hope."

"No, no, no," she murmured, feeling her body relax with the discovery. "Whatever is going on between us, I mean, this connection, gets echoed somehow. I wish Leslie were here so that she could explain this cosmic stuff."

"You seem to be doing all right on your own. Please, give it a try." Handing her a glass, he clinked his against hers, and leaned back on the trunk of a tree. "Here's to discoveries, dear lady."

Raising her glass to him, she took a sip and cleared her throat, allowing her gaze to take in the view of the lake before speaking. "Look at it, Ian," she nearly whispered, motioning toward the water and the ducks. "It's so simple. I mean, it sits right before our eyes, and yet we can't explain how it got there. Does that make sense?"

"Perfectly."

"Then what the hell are you doing here out of time, Ian Stewart Chandler? Why aren't I afraid of you anymore? Why do we fight so well, and get along so well together? Why am I feeling like I'm seventeen again, and on the verge of tears? It's right before my face, but I don't know how it got there."

Ian nodded and took a careful sip of his wine, staring into the glass when he had finished. "You know," he said quietly, changing his gaze to encompass the water. "When I came here, I was on a mission to find Marissa. I was angry, hurt, betrayed . . . so many things that I can barely describe. Then I found out that she had died, and I wanted to crawl into that grave with her." Stopping himself to collect his emotions, Ian took another sip, turning the glass by its stem in the bright afternoon sun.

"You don't have to," she stammered, feeling as though she were invading a part of him that was far too private for her to enter. "It's already painful enough."

"No," he said, surprisingly. "No. You need to hear this. It's my gift back to you. Agreed?"

Suzanne just stared at the man.

"Well, it's an inexpensive gift, really. But wisdom is priceless, or so I've been told," he added, smiling as he refilled her glass. "Will you accept?"

"I suppose so," she hedged nervously. "I guess."

"I'll take your conditional response as a yes, for now."

Ian's smile gave the sun competition as she watched his eyes sparkle with enthusiasm. By now, she had learned to tell when his brain was formulating an idea, a hypothesis, a premise . . . and the results were always remarkable. Indeed, she liked this strange being. His intensity and mercurial temperament, oddly reminded her of her own. Perhaps that's why they felt like two well-fitted gears. Equally matched, with equal force and torque . . . equally able to grind the other down when they got out of sync.

"Well," he began slowly, "you made me explore my own thinking when you gave me your grandmother's diary as a gift."

"I thought you should have it," she shrugged, trying to ward off the effects of the wine and his presence. "I just wanted you to have something to remember Marissa by."

"I know," he whispered, looking at her steadily. "That's why it meant so much. It was a gift to a virtual stranger, yet one given without expectation for payment in kind. A true gift of the heart."

She lowered her eyes, and took a quick sip of wine. Looking at him was almost impossible now. Too many feelings swept through her.

"But the real gift was the comment you made before you gave it to me." Ignoring her perplexed look, he went on. "Suzanne, you said that perhaps I had loved her, or more correctly, was infatuated with her, for the breath of fresh air that she gave me. Her youthful *joi de vivre*. And at first I was truly insulted. My first reaction was to leave your presence and dare you to minimize our relationship that way."

Guilt almost strangled her, and she tried to rush in an apology, but he stopped her with his hand.

"No. To some degree you were right, Suzanne. When I read your grandmother's diary, I saw our relationship from the perspective of a sixteen-year-old girl, and was frankly embarrassed. When I met Marissa, formally, she was only sixteen. And, thinking back on it clearly now, I enjoyed the way she looked up to me. Oh, Lord. This is so difficult to admit."

"You don't have to justify your relationship with her to me. I had no right to say those things."

"Please. Let me finish," he said firmly, leaning forward in earnest. "I re-read every letter, and cringed at the sound of them. It was like a slap of reality. We had a torrid, three-month affair, just after her seventeenth birthday. Fact. I loved her dearly, and she loved me. Fact. But I also deified the relationship. Fact. When she was abruptly taken from me, I can't tell you how much of my mission was longing for my lost love, or how much of it was a vendetta. A matter of principle. That fact kept me up nights, and was something that I couldn't deal with until you made me face it with the diary."

Suzanne was speechless. She had never meant to spoil his dream, never wanted to take away his memories. All she could do was close her eyes against the horror of his words. "Oh, Ian. I am so sorry. That was never my intention, you must believe me. I wanted you to have something to hold on to. Something to give you hope. Not to destroy what had given you joy."

"No. Don't. Let me explain what you did give me."

His hand made contact with her jawline, and she held her breath.

"Look at me," he said in a low voice. "You were right, Suzanne. I enjoyed having the consuming attention of a young girl. She enjoyed being cloaked in the romance that an older man could offer. But were we friends? Were we mental equals? Could this relationship stand up under the real pressures of everyday life? No. We had created a secret garden of happiness, an island to escape to. And, in that Eden, I could be all things . . . creator, consummate lover, teacher, protector, mentor. It fed my ego and my arrogance. And she could be the bright, shining, passionate student. It fed her fantasies, and flattered her beyond words. She deified me, and I immortalized her. I finally understood it from the woman-child's perspective, by reading your grandmother's fantasies. And by reading the letters I had written to Marissa, I saw myself."

Suzanne covered his hand, trying to absorb the pain that echoed in his voice and in his eyes. "But had she not died tragically, if she had had the chance to age with you, and marry you . . ."

"Perhaps," he sighed, removing his hand and taking up his glass again. "But, more than likely, the fire would have died along the way, once the catalysts had changed. Yes, she would have aged, and gained the wisdom of a grown woman. But probably not before becoming disillusioned with me. Not before finding out that the world was larger than her parents' Radnor estate, or her first lover's arms. And I would have become bored with being her teacher during that process, or perhaps begun to feel confined by the strain of having to remain her deity, instead of a mere mortal. It was wondrous. It was breathtaking. But it wasn't real."

"I don't know whether I gave you a gift or a curse," she said quietly, in awe of the man who sat only inches away from her.

"It was a gift, Suzanne. A release from bondage, so that I could accept our parting, and live again. Had I not read the diary, I would probably have taken my life."

A new wave of fear confronted her, and she sat up to pour herself more wine. "Listen," she said, stricken by the thought. "Please, I couldn't have that on my conscience."

Ian chuckled, making her frown with confusion.

"Far too melodramatic, my lady. I just wanted to thank you for making me understand. But what of you? Still waters run deep, and your face has said it all these past few days."

Somehow, she had forgotten that Ian had picked up on her inner turmoil. She had hoped that they wouldn't have to discuss it, especially since the mood seemed to be fading on it's own.

"I don't know," she shrugged, looking at the sky. "My life has been fairly uneventful— that is, until you dropped in."

Laughing, he began to open the second bottle, and spoke without looking at her. "While I may have been fairly consumed with my own quest and grief, I have never been accused of being oblivious to my surroundings."

"The mark of a good attorney?" she asked, becoming evasive again.

"Touché! But, let me proffer a guess. The way I understand it is that you and your friend were trying to conjure up a mate for you."

Suzanne groaned. "Oh, that."

"Yes, that. And during my stay, I have yet to notice even one gentleman caller to come to check on your well-being."

"And?" Defensiveness coursed through her, making her hungry. Bread and cheese. She could rummage in the picnic basket and deflect this interrogation. "Proceed."

"And," he said slowly, dragging out his words as he took another sip. "And, I saw the barbaric conditions under which mate selection is done in your era. If my hunch proves correct, this is why a gentle, giving soul, such as yourself, has opted to give up the search. I would have."

Again, Suzanne stared at him, looking up from her task of finding something to munch. "It's depressing," she finally admitted, pulling out a block of Longhorn cheese and the box of Triscuits.

"It has to be," he said quietly, leaning forward and searching for a knife. "Here, this might work."

Suzanne studied the cheese knife, and whacked off a wedge before handing a hunk to Ian. "It's too dull," she said flatly.

"Too dull?"

"Yeah, to slash my wrists with it."

His startled expression made her laugh.

"Don't worry. I'm well past my initial grieving phase. I'm where you are, firmly planted in reality. See, Ian, you are correct. There are phases to this. First, you panic, and run around trying to force yourself to endure the humiliation of the meat racks. Then you get angry. You don super feminist's banners and say, 'to hell with the bastards. Off with their heads!' Then you dive into your career, and refuse to look at family shows, walk in the park on Sundays, make up excuses for why you can't be a bridesmaid, and send a gift via UPS to baby showers. Then, you cry . . . until your heart breaks. And you hurt, until your soul breaks. Then you give up, cut your hair, buy a small dog or some fish, and have cable installed. That's how you get to become eccentric Auntie Suzanne— the one who never . . ."

She had to stop. Her voice was betraying her, and her eyes were filling again against her will. The subject had been banished from her psyche long ago. It was just that her crazy friend, Leslie, had unearthed it, and brought it back to life.

Now, it was sitting before her, sipping wine on a perfecting spring day, flashing perfect white teeth, and a perfect set of pecs under his argyle sweater. That's all it was. A hormonal jolt to her otherwise pragmatic system. Once the focal point left her house, and went back through his vortex, or wherever he came from, her system would normalize. Her head would clear.

"I don't think it's possible," he said after a while, munching on a section of apple with his cheese. "Not for a loving person like yourself."

"What? To slash my wrists?"

"No. I wasn't referring to high drama. I just don't believe that you can stop feeling at will. It isn't a mental function, it's a function of a dumb muscle called the heart. That organ doesn't think, you know. It just responds to stimuli. Plus, you cannot bury what isn't dead. Look at me, for example."

If she weren't so close to tears, she would have laughed. "Easy for you to say, Ian. You'll fit right in here, and sweep some beautiful young thing off her feet. Then you'll have a family and live happily ever after. That's not how it's going to go for me. You saw the dregs out there. I haven't the energy to sift through that morass any more."

Her comment seemed to still him, and he reached for her hand, clasping it tightly. "Suzanne, don't give up on the world yet. Please."

Tears coursed down her face, and she didn't turn away. "I'm forty-one years old. Okay! I have my own business, and my own home— a nice one.

Which either makes me an easy target for a gig-
olo, or frightens men away. I have a brain in my
head, and a Wilkinson's stainless steel blade for
a tongue, which terrifies them. And, no, I can't
pretend to be stupid without losing respect for
them or me! I don't have a seventeen-year-old's
body, either. So, let's be really real here. You've
seen the magazines, and that's not what's under
these covers. Okay? Your reality, even zapped out
of time, is much different than mine. And it's
not fair!"

"No. It isn't," he said quietly, wiping her face.
"But, maybe if they saw what I've seen, they
would know how to treat you."

She didn't answer him. Nor, did she want to
go where he was headed. She was suddenly
tired, and just wanted to go home.

"Suzanne," he said swiftly, not allowing her to
pack up the food. "If they saw the dynamic
woman, who was interesting beyond all imagination . . . If they saw your warm heart, and
your willingness to give, even under duress . . .
If they saw your wry humor, which makes the
brain have to function in order to appreciate the
intelligent wit . . . If they could see the passion
in you, often disguised by anger . . . And if they
could watch the sun in your hair, and the smile
in your eyes, they'd know better."

Reaching for her, Ian pulled her into his arms,
and held her against his chest, and she allowed
all the years of pain to pour forth with her tears.

"We men are such fools," he whispered into
her hair. "In any era imaginable. And some-

times we take for granted that which has been placed right under our very noses."

Suzanne allowed his warmth to sustain her, until the sobs had ebbed. She felt so foolish, so vulnerable, yet so safe. Somehow, in that tiny expanse of time, she knew that Ian would not prey on her because of what she had allowed him to see. It was as though a sacred trust had been established, even without the promise of sex, a relationship, or gain. Her friend simply held her, and rubbed the pain away from her body. She had needed a hug for so long. Just the caring contact of another human who cared enough to understand. Enough to just let her be.

They sat that way for what seemed like a long time, until her breathing calmed. And when she pulled back from him, and wiped her nose, he just smiled and began packing up their belongings. No words were necessary. No awkward, "What's next?" to contend with. Just a refreshing ride home, and probably a quiet, contemplative evening to enjoy.

Wouldn't that be a welcomed change?

Eleven

"We've been over this a hundred times, Ian. You cannot get a decent job on your own without papers to prove who you are." Suzanne sat down on the sofa and looked at him squarely. She hated to deliver this bad news as much as he probably hated to hear it. But, the fact was, there was no way that an uncertified, uncredentialed, illegal alien could practice law in the U.S. Even the mob went to *bona fide* attorneys. "Just give me some time to pull in a few markers. Maybe a friend can find something for you to do."

"I don't want someone to *give* me a job. You mean to say that with all my years of experience, the references, the—"

"Stop, right there." Suzanne stood and walked over to him, placing her hand on his shoulder. "Listen, your knowledge of law stops with legislation passed in eighteen seventy-two. First of all, you could go to jail for masquerading as an attorney. You can't teach law, or even matriculate in a law school without proper documentation—transcripts from your undergraduate university. I don't think they'll accept one from Penn in the eighteen fifties."

Shrugging out of her hold, he paced the floor. "Then a manual job will do. I have no problem doing honest labor."

Her heart hurt.

"Oh, Ian. What can you do? You just saw a car about four days ago. So, auto repair is out. To be a delivery boy for pizzas, you need a driver's license. We've had that discussion about your learning how to drive. Besides, you have to produce a birth certificate for Motor Vehicles to even issue the license. To become a carpenter, you have to know at least how to hold a Black & Decker saw without cutting off your fingers. Skilled construction workers have to be apprenticed and licensed . . . haven't you seen the skyscrapers? You have to have a fundamental understanding of electricity, and they didn't have AC/DC, or two hundred twenty volt lines in your day. Either you'll fry yourself or cause a fire. Plumbing? Did they have indoor plumbing with fiberglass tubing, rubber hosing, and pressure meters or sprinkler systems in the eighteen hundreds? You can't just go out on a construction job site, and try to rebuild the Roman aqueducts by hand. They use jackhammers now to dig ditches."

"Then I could work the cash register of any well-known establishment, and do just fine, thank you."

Suzanne shook her head. "Afraid not. Even at McDonald's the register's are computerized, the fries are dropped on a hot oil timer, burger buns are microwaved, and you have to be able to drive to get there."

He spun on her, his eyes narrowing to an intense glare. "Then, I could be a lawn boy, grounds keeper—a farm hand."

She wanted to cry. "Ian, please, I'm so sorry that this has happened to you. I wish there was a way. Look, to work on a modern farm, you've got to be able to work the tractors, and the cows are milked, at the big dairies, using milk-letting equipment. Small farms hire family members, and can barely afford to pay them. And landscapers have to drive trucks, and know about fertilizers . . . they don't use cow dung anymore, they use chemical products manufactured by large companies like DuPont and Dow. Mulch isn't a bunch of crushed up leaves and rotting vegetables."

"Then I can become a merchant. I can at least make pretzels."

"Not legally."

He stared at her for a moment. "And why not? There are hundreds of little shops in and around town. We saw them yesterday."

"You need money to rent a store front and buy inventory. And I'm not about to sink my—"

"I didn't ask you to fund my enterprise, did I?"

Letting her breath out slowly, she slipped on her pumps and prepared to leave for work. "You also need a mercantile license for tax purposes. If you open up a store front, you have to have that registration clearly visible to the public and inspectors. To sell food products, you need a battery more of said same licenses. It all gets back to the first issue. No birth certificate, no social security number. Without a social security number, you don't exist. You can't even join the army without one."

She could tell he would not be moved, and she waited patiently for his voracious mind to absorb her information before coming up with a new series of challenges.

"All right, then. What do these so-called illegal aliens do?"

"Oh," she groaned. "You don't want to know."

When he didn't step out of her way, she leaned against the wall for support. "Okay. They work in sweatshops under the table. But, you have to know how to use a power sewing machine. So, that's out. They wash dishes, or bartend, under the table. So, you'd have to work for less money, and find an unscrupulous business person to affiliate yourself with, in order to get such a job. They clean people's houses for under the table cash, or watch their children. Or they get abused in migrant farm worker camps— where a bus picks them up on the side of a country road at dawn, makes them pick vegetables for pennies, and then drops them off at night. Satisfied?"

"I could do that. Pick fruits and vegetables."

"You'd last a day before the attorney in you came out. You'd be organizing a strike, and wanting to take a class action suit to the Supreme Court. I know you better than that, Ian Chandler."

He was silent for a moment, and she hoped

that she had closed the discussion once and for all.

"Suzanne, how do these people— poor people— live in such an expensive society where there's no work? What about the chaps who have no education or skills?"

The question made her sit down again. It was valid, it was asked without ill humor, and he had the stunned expression of a child on his face when he'd asked it.

"Ian, remember I told you that if you stayed here long enough, you'd start to see the ugliness? The unnecessary waste in such a flourishing society? Well, all of the skyscrapers, technological advances, modern medicines, and food production that fills vast supermarkets with out of season produce has its price. The price of modernization means that a poor little carpenter cannot compete with a big chain store that sells ready-made products, like cabinetry and furniture. Nor can the independent seamstress or shoemaker compete with ready-made wear manufactured offshore in Taiwan, and sold here for a few bucks in gigantic department stores. It means that the caterer has been replaced by fast food take-out services, and dishwashers, microwave ovens, and vacuum cleaners make housekeeping a more stream-lined process. So who needs servants? And who needs cow dung when chemicals can do the trick? Or hand-bottled milk, when you can get a gallon for a dollar, twenty-four hours a day at Seven-eleven, and know that it's always available and shipped to the supermarket by the eighteen wheeler truck? Exit, the local farmer."

She was becoming weary, but held firm to her point. "And, think about it, Ian. Who needs somebody to wash your car when you can drive it through an automated service station, or some kid to shovel your snow, or cut your grass, when you can buy a snow blower and riding lawn mower? Get the picture? Those jobs just don't exist any more. At least not like they did in your time."

Relentless, he went on, walking back toward the windows. "But, in heaven's name, Suzanne, how do these people survive? The ones on the edge of things, the ones without degrees, and skills? Are those the vagrants, the street people? And their children . . ."

"I know that beggars are not new to the nineties, Ian. C'mon."

"No, they're not," he retorted angrily. "But, in this country, there was always honest work to be had for those willing to do it. Even for *illegal aliens,* which made up *most* of the population. That's what the Founding Fathers fought for. London had beggars! Not America! Have you forgotten your history? The street people of my era could sell rags, brooms, shovel coal, make deliveries . . . invent some new device. There was work, Suzanne! There was work!"

His gaze held an intensity that threatened to make her weep. She knew his struggle all too well, and how being gainfully employed was very much a part of a person's self-esteem. She had

seen modern day executives come into her placement office, shut the door, and get choked up
when she had to tell them that their chances of
a management position were slim. She had witnessed the stunned expressions of men laid off
from area factories, and had tried to calm them
when she had to explain that their skills were
now obsolete. She had seen the deflated faces of
the single mothers who didn't have a G.E.D. or
a secretarial certificate. Worse, the older women
who were great on a typewriter in their heyday,
but who had never learned to use a word pro-
cessor. How did a sixty-year-old woman learn to
use a high-tech AT&T switchboard, when she
was pulling wires and connecting them to a wall-
board in her nineteen-fifty receptionist's job?
What could she tell Ian, but the truth?

"Some go on transitional welfare. Others stay
on it for a lifetime. But, again, not without a social security number, or an address that the State
can verify. They sometimes work when they can
find a little niche or cubbyhole of opportunity,
and get fired when they can't take the abusive
environment any longer. Other's wind up shut-
tling from homeless shelter to homeless shelter,
with their children in tow. Many resort to crime,
and go to jail for three square meals, a dry roof
over their heads, with dental and medical benefits. And the ones who give up hope go to substance abuse. Alcohol, drugs, anything to numb
the pain. Which starts a spiral of crime. The men
rob, the women sell their bodies. It's ugly, Ian.
It's the subculture of America in a sluggish,

technology-laden economy. The results are the mayhem that you see on the six o'clock news."

There. She had said it. Case closed. She would not send him out into that chaos, no matter how angry he got. Surely, she could find something for him to do behind the scenes of some establishment— just like she had for her friend, Leslie. But for now, she couldn't think of where or what. Maybe, if she got to a neutral place, her office, and had time to think. She needed the time to peruse her Rolodex. She did, after all, have favors out there.

There was no way to make her understand. No way around it. As he watched Suzanne collect her work paraphernalia and close the door, he felt trapped. Never in his life had his pride been so assailed, his sense of self-worth been so shattered. To know that adolescents and vagrants, with their precious social security numbers, could command more income than an attorney. Damn. His initial assessment was correct.

This new world had gone mad.

Pacing into the kitchen, he stopped to look at the modern conveniences that surrounded him. Her maid. He was simply her live-in maid. And in his heart he knew that she would never respect him unless he were gainfully employed. He'd never respect himself, for that matter.

Ignoring the breakfast dishes, he decided to set out on his own. While he was sure that Suzanne had told him the truth about her world, he wasn't sure whether or not she was being a tad too dramatic about it. Women! There *had* to be something he could do. What did the old merchants of his day do when they didn't have business start-up capital? Work hard and earn it. What sparked their ingenuity? Necessity.

Then it hit him. Trash. They restored people's rubbish and turned it into something useful . . . Hmmm . . . But, what would a modern, streamlined society throw away?

Ian rushed upstairs and rummaged in his makeshift cardboard box for a sweater. Donning it quickly, he descended the stairs two at a time and headed out the door. He'd use his old research abilities. Surely the American language hadn't changed in the last century. If he could read, then he could enter the public library. Thank God, that was still free. But where was it?

Since there were schools nearby, he assumed that he could follow the road until he reached the center of town. Perhaps, if a yellow carriage passed, he could wave down the driver, and ask the fellow if he was going in the right direction? Perhaps a kindly passerby would give him a lift, if they were going in the same direction? The particulars of his new mission didn't matter. The important thing was action. Not sitting around and waiting for some woman to unfold his destiny for him.

Ian ignored the traffic as it whirred by. His mind was singularly focused on unraveling his current problem. Trash. He would make something out of trash. But what? There were already companies that hauled away old bottles, tin cans, and plastics. He'd seen that on the black box gadget. What was it called? Recycling? Okay, some ingenious person had already taken over that particular business. No, that wasn't it. And, resources. Who did he know? As he walked, his mind scrambled for an answer. Mike Peterson. A likeable fellow. His new friend might show him how to use the power tools that Suzanne had mentioned. Maybe he'd even allow him to borrow one or two, for some service that he could offer Mike in return. That would be fair. Bartering. He could barter for help.

But that still didn't solve the dilemma of proper licensure. Ian ran his fingers through his hair as he half walked, and half jogged along. He was so impatient about getting to his destination, that a comfortable stride seemed intolerable.

Partnership! A silent partnership.

Almost running now, his thoughts became clearer. Who said *he* had to bear his name on any license? He had been an attorney too long to forget how that was done. His wealthy clients did it all the time. There was always a loophole in the grand design of the American legal system. The rich called it justice. After all, they had invented it. Now, all he had to do was understand the new laws regarding that process. Ian practically laughed. If he could just figure out what his product would be! What in the world could he sell that people would throw away, that could be

restored with sweat equity and a pittance, then
resold at a reasonable price? He'd have to think
about that.

As he kept to the shoulder of the road, looking up occasionally to see whether anyone would
slow down to pick him up, he continued walking
until he hit a little strip of stores. Pressing his
face to the deli window, he hailed the proprietor.
"My good man, can you tell me how far the
local library is?"

The man looked up from his sweeping, and
yawned. "We don't open till ten. Closed. Don't
you see the sign, bud?"

"Just need directions," Ian yelled back, refusing to give up. "The free library, good sir."

Unlocking the door with disgust, the man
leaned on his broom and yawned again. "They
don't open for another hour, till nine, Buddy."

"I like to be early," Ian said cheerfully, "and
I thank you for your inconvenience. I'm new to
this area, and don't know my way around yet."

Moving away from the door, and stepping into
the small establishment, the man scratched his
head. "I hear ya. I've got to be up early myself
to get anything done. Let me think? That's at
least five miles down the road. Go to the second
light, then make a right. Then go down . . . no,
that road's closed for repair, you'll have to detour, and drive down— "

Ian held up his hand. "I'm not driving, so the
fastest route will be sufficient."

The man just smiled. "Getting your daily walk
in, huh? I need to get back to a routine. Used

to work out, but with the wife, the kids, and this killer business, hell, I'm lucky if I sweep the floor in the mornings."

Trying his best to stifle a grin, Ian calmed himself. "Well, sir, if you ever need someone to help you, just let me know."

The man seemed shocked. "You know, the kids today aren't dependable. Can't come in early, cause they've been out partying. Can't stay late, cause they've got somewhere hot to go. Don't want to get their hands dirty, and can't count change to save their lives, unless you've got one of those fancy registers that'll do it for 'em. Then they want to call in sick every five minutes."

"I know what you mean," Ian said sheepishly, running his hand along the greasy counter. "Why, in my day, we'd be glad to put in an honest day's work for an honest day's pay. Gladly."

Standing his broom in the corner, the man wiped his hands on his apron front and extended one. "The name's Jim. I own this deli and take-out."

Returning the handshake, Ian smiled broadly. "Ian Chandler. I'm new to this country . . . don't have my papers yet, but looking for some honest work."

"You drive?" the man asked excitedly.

Ian shook his head slowly, his heart sinking in the process. "No, can't get used to it here."

"Guess they drive on the wrong side of the road where you come from?"

Ian smiled. "Exactly. Like I said, I can't get used to it."

"Well, no sense in killin' yourself, now is there?"

Ian just nodded, walking to the far edge of the counter and picking up the broom. "But, even without a car, I'll bet I could be here earlier than any one of those modern youngsters. Tell you what," he said, as he started to sweep. "How about if I give you a free half day of work to show you what I can do? Just let me watch you prepare the dishes, and show me your system. I can clean up, wash pots, pans . . . serve customers and count change without a computer. You can do your inventory, watch me, or take a nap, and there will be no theft. I assure you, I'm an honest man."

The man's expression was incredulous. "For no pay? C'mon, what's the hitch, Buddy?"

Ian rubbed his chin and considered his options. "You can have the best in-store clerk, who'll open up every morning, and work as late as you want. But you'll have to pay me under the table. Like I said, I don't have my papers, and I don't want any trouble from the government."

"Damn the Feds!" the man exclaimed. "Who needs tax problems? They're running small businesses into the ground, while the rich boys get fatter and happier."

"Precisely," Ian said with an even voice. "So, do we have a deal?"

"And you don't expect any pay for today?" the man asked cautiously.

"How about, when— if— your delivery boy finally comes in, he gives me a lift to the library in the afternoon? That seems like a fair swap for apprenticeship. I don't mind paying my dues in advance."

"Mister, I like your style," he said, slapping Ian's back. "We have a deal. God must have sent you my way today, 'cause heaven knows, I'm tired."

It took all of Ian's resolve not to jump for joy. Instead, he offered the man a hearty handshake and returned his slap on the back. He couldn't wait to get home to tell Suzanne where he'd been. She'd see that there were *always* possibilities, and that as a man, he needed to find them for himself. And when he got to the library, there was no telling what he'd find buried in the stacks! Before long he'd have a thriving enterprise. One that could support them both. He'd show her. Necessity was always the mother of invention . . . and the early bird always caught the worm. She'd learn.

"What do you mean, he's at your house?" Suzanne paced the floor as she clutched the phone. "I've been frantic for over an hour. We had this big blow-up about him working this morning, but I thought it was settled. Then, when I got home, he was gone."

She could hear her friend's children in the background, and the distraction rattled her.

"Suz, don't worry. He's been out in the garage

with Mike since he got here. He said he took a
detour today, and wanted to learn how to use
some power tools. Well, of course you know
Mike is in his glory. This gives him a chance to
blow the dust off of some of his boy-toys and
show them off to someone who stands in awe
of all their glory."

Suzanne forced her voice to remain even.
"Leslie, I want him back immediately, before
he says or does something that'll tip Mike off.
We're playing with dynamite here. What if he
lops off a finger, huh? How do we get this
time traveler medical attention, with no I.D.?
Send him home. No. Better yet, I'm coming to
get him."

Before her friend could answer, she had hung
up, snatched her purse and headed out the door.
By the time she had gotten to Leslie and Mike's
house, she was furious. Of all the hair-brained,
inconsiderate, stupid things. She'd kill him.

Not even bothering to enter through the house,
she pulled her car up in the driveway and stared
at the open garage door. She'd definitely kill
him. Male laughter and hoots assaulted her
senses when she hopped out of the car, and as
she approached, there they were, Millers in hand.

"Man, isn't she a beaut? Now, if you want to
sand down a nice piece of wood, or redo your
floors, this baby has four speeds . . . and you can
buy the different grade sandpaper to go on her."

"Amazing," Ian said, as Mike demonstrated
the equipment, touching the handle as though
it were made of gold.

She had to yell over the running motors of several machines, since Mike was in full sales demonstration mode. When they finally recognized her, they didn't even switch off the units.

"Impressive," Ian yelled over the noise. "Look, Suz. Mike's got everything in here."

Mike waved, holding up the sander like a trophy fish. "Yo, Suz! How ya been?"

Ignoring her evil eye, the two men went back to the workbench. Were it not for Leslie's entrance, she might have body slammed Ian against the wall.

"Hey, Suz, I thought I heard your car pull up. C'mon in the house while I get dinner on. There's enough spaghetti for everybody."

Suzanne shook her head. "Not tonight. Les. We'll—"

"We'd love to," Ian cut in over the noise, as Mike turned on another power tool and waved again.

"You girls go ahead. We'll be inside in a minute. Right, partner?" Mike chimed in enthusiastically.

"Right!"

Suzanne stared at Mike. Girls? The word almost produced a growl low in her throat, but she forced herself to remain civil. Besides, what the heck was going on? "Partner?"

"Yeah," Mike exclaimed, grinning and lifting his goggles. "Ian's my kind of guy. Real smart when it comes to business. Boy, the two of us can make a mint!"

Leslie tugged at her arm before she could

speak, "That's *why* I want you to help me with dinner, Suz. Better you hear it from me first."

Stumbling next to her friend, nearly blind with rage, Suzanne entered the kitchen and immediately spun on her. "Les," she whispered through her teeth, "have you all lost your minds? A business partner from another time zone, era, whatever! Tell me that he doesn't want to go on television with this? I mentioned being his agent, and said something flippant about the talk show circuit this morning, but— "

"Relax, Suz," Leslie said chuckling, handing her a head of lettuce. "I was trying to warn you on the phone, but you hung up too fast."

"This should have been the first thing you said to me: 'Hello, Suzanne, Ian and Mike have lost their minds.' That's it." Suzanne paced the kitchen squeezing the head of lettuce while trying to steady her heartbeat.

"I don't know how to give CPR over the phone, hon. So, I figured that I could just wait till you got here and had your coronary in my kitchen. But if you don't stop, I'll have to resuscitate my salad."

The fact that Leslie was gleeful about the whole event didn't make her feel better. Setting the head of iceberg down hard on the counter, Suzanne folded her arms and stiffened. "Okay. Let me have it. What do Fred and Barney propose now, Wilma?"

Leslie threw her head back and laughed. "It's not all that bad, really. Ian is really bright, you know."

"He's an attorney. He ought to be."

"All right, but I'm spoiling his surprise. Don't ruin it, Suz. He's so excited. You should have seen him when he came in here today. He looked like a little kid who had skipped all the way home from school, waving an A paper in his hands."

Suzanne let her breath out slowly. "So, what did they do?"

"*They* didn't do anything. Ian did all the legwork."

Frustration overtook Suzanne, and she felt like she could grab her friend up by the lapels at that moment. The problem was all Leslie ever wore was big tee shirts and oversized sweaters. However, she might just decide to grab Leslie by her crystal pendant, and hang her from the highest kitchen cabinet. "Do you have any idea of how much trouble he could be in if the authorities found out that he was running a business illegally? They could deport him to some foreign country or something."

Leslie's smile was all knowing. "Ah, so that's it. You were worried to death about him. Admit it. You thought that he had left the house today, and you'd never see him again. Now you're worried that something awful could happen to him, like . . . someone taking him away, maybe?"

Suzanne snatched up the lettuce and flung open the cutlery drawer. "Don't be silly. He's a pest, a problem, a pain in my a—"

"Suzanne, wait till you see how this guy can use his hands! He's great at this stuff."

Mike's voice startled her so badly, that she spun around, flinging the lettuce across the counter. Ian watched calmly as it ricocheted off the wall and spun to a stop at his feet. All she could do was stare at him wide-eyed, brandishing a large kitchen knife.

"Ah, the memories, Michael. This is how Miss Suzanne and I met. I even think she had the same pose. Lovely, isn't she?"

Mike looked at Ian and punched his shoulder. "You must've really shaken the little lady up."

Suzanne was almost sure that she did growl this time, and she dared Ian with her gaze to laugh.

"Well, you fellas go wash up and get the kids. Salad is out, but I can nuke some broccoli." And just as though nothing out of the ordinary had happened, Leslie began chopping up a new vegetable and telling her about some customer at the bookstore.

Suzanne felt disoriented. Somehow she had landed among a group of aliens, and she was the weird one for being sane. Yet, her friend had come extremely close to a kernel of truth. When she had put the key in the door and called out, she was expecting to hear Ian's voice. When she didn't, there was such a sense of loss that engulfed her that she actually had to fight back the tears. She thought he had gone, had abandoned her because of the fight. Now that she found him, and in high spirits at that, she just wanted to wring his neck.

Rather than give Leslie any further fuel to

needle her with, Suzanne opted to listen to her friend's idle chatter. She could be patient for another half hour, until the men scoffed down their food and the kids ran up to take their baths. Fine. She'd let him draw her curiosity out like a wisdom tooth extraction. Because, once they got home . . .

Home?

Did she say home in the we, collective, sense? Now it was confirmed. She had definitely lost her mind.

Twelve

Ian folded his arms across his chest, and stood firmly before the door. "Remove yourself this instant, Suzanne. We have said all that will be said on the subject. I am not a child, and do not need your permission to go to work!"

"But you can't go and try to fake it in a deli! What happens when the teenagers get there? They mob that place for lunch, and after school. They could ask you questions, or something? How are you going to pull it off?"

"I'll pretend to be on drugs."

Suzanne groaned. "C'mon, be serious."

"I am serious."

She looked at him hard and thrust her chin forward. "Why are you being so stubborn?"

"This subject is closed. After you've railed at me all night long on the issue, now you are going to make me late on my first full day to work. I won't have it. Your behavior is intolerable. To think that I was foolish enough to believe that you'd be happy. You couldn't even support my *business* idea. Yet, a man— my friend, whom I've only engaged twice— has the vision and the courage to become my partner. Please remove yourself from my path, madame. I have nothing further to say."

She could tell that he was more than angry. He was hurt, and there were no words at this point that would mollify him. All she could do was stand aside, and let him pass. If he got into trouble, well . . .

"Do you want a lift over there?" It was a half-hearted peace offering, albeit a little late.

"No. Thank you very much. I could use the exercise."

Suzanne cringed as the door slammed shut. He was furious. He seemed almost as angry as he had been when she found him, wet, ornery, and hopping mad. But this time, she was the direct cause. Maybe Leslie had been right. Maybe if she had not played devil's advocate so hard when they got home, or had shown a little more enthusiasm when he and Mike unveiled their crazy, artists' colony, antique store idea. How was she supposed to know that he had gone to the library? How did she know that he had done research by watching almost a week of MTV, and knew teen fashion trends better than she? Okay, so he had a point: the biggest spenders in this sagging economy were teens.

But how did he expect her to be all giddy and encouraging about refurbished, not-quite antiques, safety pins to hold together turn-of-the-century clothes, amid old books and trunks, with a stage plunked in the middle for poetry readings, and cappucino machines on the side for a coffeehouse. It was wild! Create a village meetinghouse, where artists could sell their wares on consignment, people could sell props from one-act plays, and Ian and Mike would get a merchandising cut to go with their herbal tea sales? Silkscreened tee shirts, love beads . . . on commission? And, her turncoat girlfriend had gone right along with them, even down to suggesting locations, and recommending a loft!

She had to get out of the house before the walls closed in on her. They had even talked about using the local media to promote their beatnik scheme . . . Damn!

Too rattled to think as the phone rang, she headed back up the stairs to find her shoes. "What now?" she muttered, allowing the answering machine to pick up the call. What else could go wrong?

As the message ended and Suzanne slipped on her heels, she heard the first few chords of Leslie's voice. Snatching the receiver from the hook, she sighed. "Hi, Les. I was almost gone, just couldn't find my shoes."

Her friend jumped right in, oblivious to Suzanne's distress. "Great. Glad I caught you. Listen, Suz, I got a call from Rahmin this morning, and he won't be able to get over until Saturday. It was a sketchy message, but he said something about extending his spiritual retreat for another day, and—"

"Oh, that's just great!" She had had it. Suzanne flopped down on the bed and stared at her feet. "You know, Les, I just can't take any more of this B.S. I really don't care where Ian

Chandler came from, how he got here, or his cosmic destiny. My business is falling apart, my life has been in upheaval now for more than a week, and I'm tired."

Leslie didn't respond immediately. When she finally spoke, her voice was low and soothing. "I know this transition into awareness has been very strange and very difficult. It turns a person's life upside down. The whole thing is unsettling. Look, why don't you get away for a minute, just a few hours . . . without me, without Ian, without the hassles at work. Just a breather, okay?"

Suzanne shook her head and fought the urge to scream. "See, that's just it," she said, keeping her voice even. "You two can afford to be irresponsible. I can't. Ian doesn't exist, for all intentional purposes. He doesn't pay people's salaries, keep the lights on, pay rent for office space, or a mortgage. You at least have Mike to rely on. He may sit at the kitchen table and scheme up a million dollars with Ian, but I bet he went into work today, didn't he?" She didn't wait for Leslie to reply before railing on. "And this is just great for your New Age Bookstore job. They don't have a problem with your calling in to take off a few hours to *ohmmm* to the universe! For you, that's like career development."

Disgusted, Suzanne stood and picked up her briefcase. "Listen, I don't mean to be rude, but I have to go to work. I'll talk to you later, when I'm in a better frame of mind. Rahmin can come whenever. I really don't care."

She ignored her friend's deflated goodbye and

hung up. Today, she had decided to take back control of her own life. These people had no concept. They were energy bandits who sucked the rational side of her brain out through her ear. She would not have it! No. She would go to work, efficiently manage her business, then come home. Ian could get thrown into an insane asylum for all she cared. Mike could second mortgage his house, run his family into bankruptcy on a whim. Leslie could dematerialize and Zen out, and Rahmin could be the one to house her interesting guest, if he needed to do more research. That was it. The breaking point. She would not let her mental, physical, or psychic space be invaded any longer by these strange concepts or people. Finité.

Thankful that the drive to work was uneventful, Suzanne walked into her office and shut the door. She had barely said good morning to her staff, and didn't care. Everybody always had a problem. Everybody always needed her to do something. Who cleaned up her messes? Who fixed her snafus? Who took the weight of the world off of her shoulders? She did. So, that's who she would rely on for now. Herself.

Working through lunch with her door shut, she began to feel better as she brought order to her surrounding chaos. By one o'clock, she had handled eight placements, rescheduled the Blue Cross meeting for follow up, gotten the pile on her desk to a manageable level, and could see a light at the end of the tunnel for the week. Order. She had brought some semblance of order to her environment. At least she hadn't lost her basic skills in the process of redefining her reality, as Leslie had called it.

Hunger suddenly tugged at her as her stomach began to signal her to take a break. She really hadn't been hungry for days, not since everything began. Of course, she ate, but it was merely a perfunctory exercise. She hadn't tasted the food, or enjoyed the meals in a relaxing way. Today, she decided that she would.

Maybe she'd get out and walk to her favorite downtown deli. Or she might get a sandwich and sit in Rittenhouse Square and watch the people walk by. She owed herself the break and the solitude. Yes. That was it. Leslie had been right about one thing. She needed to get away from them all.

Rolling up a few bills, she crammed the money into her suit pocket, and locked her purse in her desk drawer. Today she didn't even want to be burdened with carrying a bag. With her luck, it would be the day that someone snatched her purse.

"I'm going out for a couple of hours," she said flatly, when her receptionist looked up. "Let everybody know. I need the air."

It was as though everyone in the office instinctively knew that The Boss was in a bad mood. No one had knocked on her door all morning, as if her frowning entry had warded them off. Her secretary had held all calls, simply taking the messages and piling up the pink slips of paper in her bin. It was wonderful. Liberating. She was setting boundaries, and forcing those around her to respect her space. Perhaps this day wouldn't be so bad after all.

Suzanne turned her face up to the spring sun as she exited the building. People were everywhere, rushing about in a sea of humanity. But she paced slowly, going nowhere in particular. For once, she was not in a hurry. She was at peace. She could decide what she wanted to eat, and where.

Choosing a small take-out deli, she entered the store, and ordered a tuna on rye to go, with juice. As the squat deli clerk made her sandwich, her mind reflexively went to Ian. The thought made her smile. She couldn't imagine him taking thirty orders amongst the hubbub of teenagers, crowded into a tiny shop. He would probably be wonderful at it, though. Like Leslie, he seemed to thrive on chaos.

She could just see him creating the orders, asking a hundred questions while he did it, and personably offering old world charm. He did get along well with people. Everyone who met the man took an instant liking to him. It was Ian's way that affected people so strangely . . .

"Tuna on rye, to go!"

Snapping out of her reverie, Suzanne stepped up to the counter and paid for the bag of lunch. Unable to stop herself, she smiled and nodded at the deli clerk. "Thanks. You have a nice day."

Appearing surprised, the man hesitated for a moment and returned her smile. "You do the same, ma'am. Boy, I wish everybody would pass on a little sunshine every once and a while. Have a good day."

Oddly buoyant, Suzanne nearly skipped to the park. It actually was turning out to be a pretty good day. When she reached the park, she found an empty bench. Old people were out feeding pigeons, kids were lacing through the walkways on rollerblades, couples walked hand in hand, artists were out sketching in the grass, and old men fought over checkers. Center City. It was wonderful.

Spreading her brown bag lunch on her lap, she bit into the three inch thick half of her sandwich, breaking off the crust and tossing it to the birds and squirrels. Before long, a street person gingerly took one edge of the bench, looking at her for permission. When she smiled, he sat down and leaned back, enjoying the same sun rays that fell upon her. As she watched him from her peripheral vision, she noticed that the man's demeanor had a certain peacefulness. Despite his circumstances, he seemed more at ease with himself and his environment than the busy executives who cut through the park, frowning and arguing with each other, in a hurry to go somewhere. But here, this man just leaned back, soaked in the sun, and went with the flow of his environment.

Suddenly feeling guilty for her abundance, Suzanne looked down at the other half of her sandwich. She had thrown much of the first half to the birds . . .

"I don't want to insult you, but I'm not going

to finish the other half of this. If you'd like it, you can have it."

Offering the man the food, she held it out cautiously. Yet, she was not prepared for his humble smile or his delicate refusal.

"No, ma'am. Thank you. It's real nice, but, you haven't eaten that much of it. I'll live."

She was astounded. Here a person who looked as if he were literally starving, yet had some regard for his fellow man. From what she had heard or seen on the news, she assumed that these people were all crack addicts and degenerates. Why else would they be on the street? Adjusting her seat, along with her thinking, she tried again. "No, really. I'm just going to toss it, and I hate to see good food go to waste. If you want it, you may have it."

The man looked at her a long time, and spoke softly. "Much appreciated, ma'am. You know, not a lot of people appreciate what they got. If it don't come all wrapped up in a pretty bow, then they don't say 'Thank you, God, for givin' it to me.' I ain't too proud to say thank you."

He reached out his hand tentatively, and accepted the food from her, but held it between them. "Now, you sure?" he asked while politely waiting for her response.

"Absolutely."

What else could she say to this quiet man of dignity? She watched how he devoured the sandwich, almost choking as he finished it in four bites. Another wave of guilt swept through her. She had never known hunger. She had never been pushed to this level of degradation. Nothing in her reality would have made her just give up and drop out of life And this man was fairly articulate. At one time, he was somebody's child. He must have had dreams, aspirations . . . a life, other than this.

Suzanne just stared at the man before her, who was wiping his mouth with the back of one hand, while crumpling up the paper in the other. When he stood and staggered over to a trash can, she was speechless.

"Gotta keep the parks clean, you know," he said sitting back down on the bench. "Thanks again, lady. God bless you."

Never in her wildest dreams would she have imagined that a vagrant would care about trash in the streets. It just didn't make sense. Digging in her pockets, she produced her lunch change. "Here, I want you to have this," she said motioning for him to accept the money. "You have a good day, all right?"

The man took the two single bills and coins, and nodded several times. "Today you'll get something special, cause you've been kind to somebody who you didn't have to care about. It all comes back, is what I say. Thank you, miss."

Almost in a daze, Suzanne rose and walked back to her office building. The man's words rang in her brain, as did those of the deli clerk. What was going on? It seemed as though strange people, and odd little messages were coming her way— things that she usually would have dismissed. Was that it? That in this new awareness, she was just paying attention now? Was Leslie right, or Rahmin . . . ? They believed that this stuff is all around us everyday, if we just open our eyes to see it and our ears to hear it.

Mellowed, Suzanne entered her suite and greeted her staff warmly. "Hey guys, look . . . I was having a bad morning, and I'm sorry that I took it out on everybody."

The more they protested and joked with her, the more guilty she felt for having been so surly. Her behavior had been inexcusable, just as Ian had said. A rush of emotion swept through her. She wanted to see him, to apologize and to re-affirm his dreams. What had given her the right to dash them, or to take away his joy of getting a job? Was it because he had done it without her help? It had been so narrow-sighted, all because she couldn't see the gift in it for him.

Retreating to her office and closing the door again, shame washed over her. Gift. The word congealed into a pang in her heart. She had to call Gran. Suzanne dialed the number and closed her eyes. Hadn't her grandmother given her a precious gift? Something so personal and so helpful to her own chaotic life. An unex-pected present, with no strings attached. And all the old woman wanted was a little company and a little laughter. Surely, Suzanne thought to herself, spending more time with her elderly grandmother would be like a crust of bread. Something one didn't have to think about. Something genuinely offered from the heart, and hungrily accepted by someone who would deeply appreciate it. Something she could give back . . .

On the fifth ring, Suzanne almost gave up, but was stopped in the process of disconnecting the call by her grandmother's familiar salutation.

"Gran, it's me, Suzie."

"Oh, my Suzanne! I'm so glad you called. I'm always glad to hear your precious voice. How are you, my dear?"

"This time I called to see how you were doing. To see if you had a little time for us to spend the afternoon alone. Would you like a surprise visit? That is, if you don't have plans with your new beau?"

The sound of the old woman's chuckle made Suzanne smile.

"Of course I have time for you, my sweet. Always. Come as soon as you can. Have you eaten?"

"I have, so don't go to any trouble. But I will join you in a cup of tea. How about in forty-five minutes?"

Gran laughed, sounding like an excited school girl. "That will be perfect! It is such a pleasant surprise. Oh, my Suzie, you do find such ways to brighten one's day. I'll look for you about half past three. Drive safely."

Exchanging merry goodbyes, Suzanne hung up and collected her belongings. It took so very little to make people happy, that she wondered why it seemed to be such a hard thing to do. As she left the office, she thought about the state of the world around her. If everyone just took a little time— just

extended a kindness, a smile, a pleasant word—
what a difference that would make.

She almost chuckled out loud. She was starting to sound just like those New Age wackos.
Les would love it!

This time when Suzanne wrapped her arms
around her grandmother a chill ran through her
body. For some reason, Gran didn't seem like
her old vivacious self. Suzanne couldn't put her
finger on it, but something was definitely different. Gran seemed older, more tired, in spite
of her lively conversation. As they entered the
house, Gran joking and giving instructions all
the way into the parlor, fear gripped Suzanne.
A new reality hit her. Gran was eighty-four years
old. Although she seemed to be timeless, there
would come a day when she'd miss her mirth,
her laughter, her special hugs.

"What in heaven's name is wrong with you,
child? You've come to perk me up, but you look
as though you've lost your best friend." The old
woman's face held a gentle expression, one of
knowing.

"Oh, Gran," Suzanne protested, trying to ward
off her grandmother's accuracy. "Don't be silly.
I'm here to visit you. I just missed you, is all."

Pouring tea into the delicate china before
them, Gran looked at her and smiled. "I saw
you earlier this week."

Suzanne didn't answer, and Gran sighed.

"Some days, child, the cup is half full. Other

days, it's half empty. Same portion, but different perspectives. Now, have out with it. What's wrong?"

Tears formed in Suzanne's eyes, and her will to remain stoic was instantly shattered by her grandmother's warm wisdom. "Oh, Gran," she nearly wailed, "I have made such a mess of things. I've been so selfish, and haven't counted my blessings, and I've hurt people, and haven't appreciated what was given to me . . ." Large splotches of tears dotted her crisp linen skirt. She didn't try to stop them now, just hung her head with shame.

"All you've been is human, dear. Your cup is still half full."

Gran handed Suzanne the tea, and she warmed her palms around it.

"You know, dear heart, everyone comes to this realization, sooner or later. Just be thankful that you weren't my age before it dawned on you." Her smile captured Suzanne's soul. "Ah, yes, youth," Gran chuckled softly. "Such a painful time. And I take it that this new lover of yours has been hurt, or hurt you . . . so now you want to erase that pain, and wipe it away to start fresh?"

Startled, Suzanne sipped her tea quickly. "We are just friends, Gran. It hasn't progressed to that point. I doubt that it ever will. It's just that— "

"Just that it needs to, now. It's time."

Wide-eyed, Suzanne merely stared at the woman before her. She knew Gran was eccentric, but this? This was embarrassing.

"Oh, come now, Suzie. Don't be such a prude.

I've seen the way you two look at each other. And, my God, the man is handsome. He is a gentleman, and respectful, and seems to have such a kind heart. What could be wrong with getting to know him better?"

"Well, for one thing," Suzanne stammered, trying to hash out the reasons for herself as she spoke, "he's going through a career crisis. And for another, he's angry at me, and is still grieving for his fiancée who died."

"Oh, that," her grandmother scoffed, waving her hand to dismiss it. "Please, darling, if I waited until each man in my life was as financially solvent as myself, I would have joined a convent. Women are far better at money management than most men. As for the other issues, well," she said and then released another chuckle, "Darling, anger fuels passion, and grief creates a need for contact. Nothing comes in a neat bow, you know."

Again, Suzanne could only stare at the woman. "Gran, someone just said that to me today. About packages and bows . . . gifts."

This time, Gran set down her teacup and leaned forward, taking Suzanne's hand in her own. "Look into my eyes, child, and tell me what you see?"

Confused, Suzanne did as requested, but nothing registered. "I don't understand?"

"That's because you're too young to understand, yet."

"But what was I supposed to see?" Craning her neck even more, Suzanne tried hard to focus on some hidden truth that might be hidden in her grandmother's eyes.

"That, first of all, you're trying too hard." The old woman laughed. "And, that life is so simple, if you just look at it that way. Second, that everything you are seeing now has been seen by someone else before. There's nothing new—just different stages for the same play."

Suzanne sat back and pondered her grandmother's words. "Nothing's new?" she said in almost a whisper.

"Hardly."

Waiting a moment before she spoke again, Suzanne leaned forward and kissed her grandmother. "What am I going to do when you're gone? I can't imagine it."

"Oh, child, I'll never leave you. That's why you've got to look into my eyes. You'll see me again, somewhere . . . in someone else."

The concept took Suzanne aback. "What are you saying?"

Gran only smiled and refilled the tea cups.

"Gran?"

Offering a deep sigh, Gran sat back in her chair. "I'm saying that life is eternal, with no beginning and no end. Love is like life, and doesn't wisp away with dust to dust or ashes to ashes. And that my love for you will glimmer in someone else's eyes one day. And you'll reflect that to someone else . . . and on and on it goes. Forever. So, what's to worry if this old lady is gone? I'll never stop loving you."

New tears formed in Suzanne's eyes. "Are you

feeling well, Gran? I noticed you seemed a little under the weather today."

Gran scoffed and bit into a tea biscuit. "We all have our good days and our bad days. I can't complain. I've lived a full life."

"You're scaring me, Gran. I don't want to talk about this. Okay?"

Without saying another word, Gran rose and came around to Suzanne's chair, and hugged her. "Come out to the garden with me, Suzie. The roses are beginning to bud."

Thankful for the transition, Suzanne looped her arm through her grandmother's elbow. As they passed neat rows of rose bushes, Gran pointed out her most cherished possessions with pride. Nearing the gazebo, they stopped a while to look at the pines, then Gran pulled her along to the remote gravesite in the far corner of the property.

"Suzie, when I saw that young man weeping against the headstones, my heart almost broke."

Speechless, Suzanne looked at her grandmother. She hadn't thought Gran was paying attention, and had assumed that the elderly woman was engrossed in the light after-dinner conversation with Leslie, or her search for her diary.

"It broke my heart too," Suzanne finally said, giving Gran's hand a gentle squeeze.

"Yes, well, we all have loss to contend with. That's how we know we've lived. Sooner or later you'll lose a cherished one, some position, some money, some special trinket or gift, maybe even a child. But, there is always something that is returned after such a grievous loss."

"But . . ." Suzanne couldn't even form the words to go along with her objection. It just seemed too hard, and so unfair.

"But," Gran said calmly, "some people are so consumed for so long about the loss that they never get to see the roses come up again. They only see the dead withered bushes and the thorns. They never realize that within each of those nubs, there's new life inside, waiting to burst forth with spring. Or that the thorns were put there to protect the new, delicate flowers just like the hearty branches support all of that wonder when it does bloom. Just look for the buds," she said heading back to the house. "Water it, prune it back when it gets too wild . . . talk to it everyday. Give it love, attention, and be so proud of it when it flowers. That's the gift, Suzanne. It's perennial. It doesn't die."

The two went back into the house without speaking, and Suzanne lowered her nose to the small bunch of flowers on the coffee table as they sat down. Gran smiled again, and winked at her.

"But one thing I forgot to tell you, my sweet. They may be lovely in the house, but they die quickly there. They need their own soil in order to grow. Even if you change the water daily, and give them plenty of light from the window, they must put down roots. Cut flowers don't last long."

"Never cut anyone's dreams," Suzanne said softly, locking into her grandmother's gaze.

"No, dear. Never do that. That's the real beauty, you know."

Thirteen

Suzanne entered the house, calling once for Ian then giving up. Only the timer lights were on and it was so quiet that she could only assume he wasn't there. Slowly taking the stairs, she went into her bedroom, kicked off her shoes, and cleared her sporadic messages from the answering machine. Leslie hadn't called. Ian wasn't home. The only message of note was a quick thank you from Gran requesting that Suzanne bring her friends back to visit on the weekend if they had time.

Depression crushed in on her, and the weight of it made her sprawl across the bed. There was so much to think about . . . so many wrongs to right. So many things she needed to say to people. People who had been her friends.

Nervous about the response she would get, Suzanne reached for the telephone and dialed Leslie's number. When the tape machine picked up, she placed the receiver back onto the phone without leaving a message. What could she say? She had hurt Leslie's feelings, when all her friend was trying to do was help her.

Suzanne's body hurt. Tension had wound its

way through her neck and pulled at her shoulders. Slipping out of her suit jacket and skirt, she let the articles drop to the floor. It was unlike her customary neat way of hanging up every item, but she just let everything fall where it may. What did it matter? Lying down in just her blouse and half slip, she pondered her life. Had she been too consumed with order? Making little issues seem like they were monumental while discarding those that were really important?

Suzanne looked out of the window as she lay across the bed. Dusk was settling over the sky, turning everything a rosy orange. It was beautiful. How had she missed this sight? How many spring evenings had she neglected to enjoy it? How many laughs had she taken for granted, how many acts of kindness had she whisked by, unthinking, unappreciative of the moment? She missed the sound of her friend's voice. She also missed Ian, who in a brief time had become a dear friend as well. Now what? How did one reverse a hurt, or take back angry words? She had never considered that question before. She had always been nice to people, always accommodating. She had never consciously hurt anyone, but now, in one fell swoop, she had hurt two people who were very dear to her.

Confusion tore at her brain. Where was the fine line that stood between standing up for oneself and marking boundaries, and hurting people? No one had taught her that. There was never a guideline or roadmap to follow for that problem. She had been so good at understanding business. So good at negotiating and efficiently handling everyone else's issues except her own.

"I thought I heard you come in."

The voice startled her, and she turned her head quickly, causing a muscle in her neck to throb. "I didn't know that you were in the house. You scared me."

Suzanne looked at Ian, who stood in the arch of the bedroom door with his cardboard box of clothes.

"I seem to be doing that consistently. I was going to leave you a note, but I guess it's best that I do this in person." He set the box down on the floor, and looked away from her. "I have caused you nothing but aggravation since I arrived, and I am sorry for that. I wanted to leave these things, since you bought them . . . I have no right to take them. I'd only ask that you allow me one working outfit. When I receive my pay, I can begin to reimburse you for all the clothing, food and—"

"Please," Suzanne exclaimed, standing quickly and moving toward him while using her blouse to cover her bra. "I owe you an apology. Ian, we just had a minor difference. One that I started." Panic coursed through her, as her mind snapped back to the homeless man on the bench.

"No, it is I that should beg your forgiveness. I have intruded upon your life and caused chaos. I have behaved as though the pittance of a job that I managed to secure would be enough. It was foolish . . . prideful. No grown man can subsist on that—"

"But, you had the gumption to try," she insisted. "With all the odds against you, you went out and did something positive. That says a whole lot, Ian Stewart Chandler. A whole lot in my book."

He still didn't look at her, but cast his gaze downward. "It's just like before, Suzanne. You're a woman of means, and I have nothing that could come close. What could I hope to offer? Not even a seventeen-year-old girl would be so foolish—"

"I'm not a seventeen-year-old girl. I am not looking at the job you have now, or the surface of your circumstances. I can see much more than that. Please take these things into the guest bedroom, and at least give me a chance to explain myself to you. If you owe me anything, it's that."

Ian merely stared at her before picking up his box and walking down the hall. Grabbing a pair of sweat pants, she ripped off her hose and half slip, and pulled the pants on quickly. She met him in the hallway before he could get back to her room.

"Would you build a fire?" she asked nervously, "And let me make dinner?"

Nodding, Ian responded quietly, his voice very distant. "I am weary beyond words, Suzanne. It's as though I've been searching so long for peace that, even in my sleep, there is no respite. Do you know what that feels like?"

Touching his face, she looked deeply into his eyes. "Yes. I am too familiar with what you describe. Lost souls, Ian. We're both lost souls."

For a moment they stood facing each other without words. This time, she was determined not to turn away. This time, she wanted to see whatever gift there was in the depths of his eyes. This time, she wouldn't be afraid.

"I have wanted to kiss you so many times," he said quietly, still not moving toward her. "But by what right did I assume to display any affection toward you? Especially when I can't even support myself."

Standing on tiptoes, she brushed his mouth gently, then stood back to stare into his eyes. "Some gifts require no payment. Isn't that what we had agreed upon earlier? If nothing else, I have a dear friend. I wouldn't give that up for the world."

Ian's shy smile threatened to shatter her heart. She had never witnessed a soul returning to life, yet she recognized the emotion of hope that lay within it.

"I have another gift for you. Something that you can have as we eat our dinner. Are you hungry?"

Appearing a little embarrassed, Ian shook his head. "I can have my fill at the deli. And, since I thought that I was leaving tonight, I tried to eat as much as I could."

"Good, then," she said cheerfully, returning his smile. "We can have some hot tea by the fire, while I find your present. Okay?"

Accepting her offer, he went down the stairs and she collected her briefcase. Once she was sure that Ian was in the living room building a fire, and wasn't going to leave, she spun the combination locks to open the case. In the center of it lay her journal, and she carefully took the small book out, clutching it to her chest. "Dear God," she whispered, "don't make me out to be a fool." Closing her eyes briefly, she took a deep breath, then hurried to join Ian. When she arrived in the living room, he was poking at the logs and had started the flame.

"Tea?" she asked softly, concealing the book as she left the room.

Without waiting for his answer, she began the task of heating the water. What in the world was she going to do if he laughed? Or worse, if he was offended or didn't feel the same way? Fear nearly paralyzed her, but she managed to prepare a tray, adjusting the tiny book in the center of it before reentering the room.

Placing the tray on the coffee table, she motioned for him to join her on the floor. Easily sliding beside her, Ian busied himself with fixing his mug of tea, making no mention of the book that lay in the midst of bowls and spoons. The fact that he also seemed nervous didn't help stem her own jitters. It was as though they had just met, and a new anxiety made their once easy banter impossible.

"Well," she finally said, unable to take the strain any longer. "Aren't you going to ask?"

Ian kept his gaze steady on the sugar bowl, as he dumped an extra teaspoonful into his mug. "I don't know if I have the right, at this point."

Suzanne sighed, and picked up her journal, setting it in her lap. "Maybe you're right. I don't know if I have the right to ask you to read something so personal. I don't want you to think badly of me, or that I'm pressuring you, or anything."

"Too sweet," he said putting down his mug quickly.

"What?"

"The tea— I made it too sweet. My fault."

Suzanne had to smile. "This is awkward, isn't it? What's happened to us? We were going along so well, then poof. The comfort level just disappeared. Why?"

Ian studied his mug, making a face as he took another sip. "It's always difficult," he said in a logical tone. "Nothing worth having comes easy."

She just stared at the man without responding.

"They said it's going to rain," he said abruptly, breaking her train of thought. "I heard it on the radio in the shop. Better close the windows."

Suzanne laughed. "Yeah. That's just what Les and I said that night you fell in from out of nowhere."

She watched as Ian ran about, closing all the windows downstairs and dashing up the stairs to shut the others. Standing, she went to the kitchen, dumped his tea, and poured him a fresh cup of hot water with a new bag. Not giving it a second thought, she prepared it the way he normally took it. One sugar, and just a spot of milk.

"That's better," he said out of breath and taking a seat before her again. "So is this. What happened?" he asked, quizzically looking into his mug.

"Things change. Sometimes for the worse,

sometimes for the better. The trick is, you never know till you try."

They exchanged a knowing glance, and turned their attention to the light drops of rain that had begun to form on the window panes.

"That's just the question, isn't it, Suzanne? We are always afraid, because we just never know."

She could feel his gaze burning against her cheek, but she could not turn around to face him yet. Indeed, she was afraid. Afraid of what she might see in his eyes. Perhaps afraid of what she wouldn't.

"I wanted you to have my journal," she said quietly, still not looking in his direction, "because I thought it would make you see that— I don't know what, actually. But, ever since you came here, at night . . . It was what you said about not getting respite, even in your sleep."

"You don't have to explain, Suzanne. In fact, I may just understand better than you could imagine. That's why I have something for you."

This time she did look at him. And, when he handed her a neatly folded stack of papers that he withdrew from the back pockets of his jeans, she didn't reach for them. She just stared at them in awe.

"You did this?" she asked in a quiet voice. "All of this since you've been here?"

"It's a compilation of my thoughts, my fears, my research, my dreams, and I wanted to share it with you, Suzanne. I wanted you to understand my erratic behavior— the frustration— the grief, as well as what you've meant to me. I was going to leave this for you, because I thought you deserved to know. It's the not knowing that robs one of peace."

Gingerly reaching her hand out to accept the papers, she offered Ian her journal with the other. "I want you to know too, then. Would you take this?"

As they exchanged the items, each held the other's writings in their lap without looking down.

"Scary, huh?" Suzanne said, forcing a smile.

Ian nodded. "It's like disrobing."

His words sent a tremor through her body that almost made her close her eyes.

"Then, perhaps we'd better wait to read these when we're alone? Maybe, it will be less embarrassing that way. We can talk about what we've read at breakfast tomorrow, only if we want to. Okay?"

"Yes," he said, sounding relieved. "I think that would be a much better idea."

Somehow the decision to postpone reading the intimate writings seemed to lift the tension between them. Soon their old camaraderie returned, and they could talk again. Suzanne nearly rolled on the floor with laughter as Ian described the antics that went on in the shop during his first full day of work. He was amazed at the wisdom she had gained from such unexpected sources, and made her promise to take him to Gran's house again, just for the sheer joy of the old woman's company. They were back. Their friendship was back.

And as the rain splattered against the windows, it was as though the heavens had opened up to cleanse their world.

Yawning, despite the good time they were having, Suzanne finally begged fatigue. Ian gave in as well, collecting the tray and returning it to the kitchen. They both admitted to long days ahead of them, and together turned out the lights and went upstairs. It felt comfortable . . . natural.

When he stopped at her door, there was an awkward moment, but it passed quickly as he bade her goodnight and she heard him go into the guest bedroom. There was no pressure, no stress, no words to get in the way of their happy reconciliation. Tonight, she was sure that she'd sleep peacefully.

Slipping out of her clothes, she picked up the scattered items that were on the floor and dumped them into the chair. She chose a soft white cotton gown and spread it out on the bed as she prepared to take a hot shower. She had made the choice as much for emotional comfort as she had for the physical comfort it brought. The light garment had a pretty lace border and a small satin ribbon that graced the scoop neckline. It reminded her of her childhood, when there were no worries, no boys, nothing but her girlish dreams.

Suzanne left the bedroom and turned on the shower, feeling satisfied and relaxed. Allowing the water to pummel her body, she lathered on her special scented gel, and took in its fragrance. The little things . . . just enjoy the little things in life, she told herself, staying until the water became lukewarm.

Enjoying the sheer pleasure of the new texture, she indulged herself in fluffy special towels. The ones that she always saved for company, but neglected to use for herself. Still half wet, she took her time to apply lotion, giving every inch of her body attention. How often had she just jumped out of the shower in a hurry, put on deodorant, spritzed on some perfume, and hustled out of the house? Madness. Pure insanity. Things were going to change from here on out. No more rat-racing.

Dimming the lights, she pulled on the fresh nightgown, and almost groaned with pleasure. It felt so good to be relaxed, clean, fresh . . . with no worries. Her life was good. She'd read Ian's writings by the nightstand light, then go to sleep. What a day! She could hardly wait to begin the next one.

Quickly sliding between the sheets, her body came in contact with the crisp, cool linens. Even the bed felt good, if one just allowed the mind to be free. Pulling his stack of papers to her lap, she fluffed up four big pillows behind her head, and snuggled down into the warmth.

She handled each page delicately, admiring his fine script and his insightful analogies. The detailed account of his capture, as he called it, was riveting. For the first time, she truly saw the twentieth century in all its wonder, simply by looking at the world through Ian's eyes. Then there was the fear, the anger, and the pain. She sat gripped by his heart-rending account of losing all that he had ever been . . . all that he had ever loved. At times, she was forced to stop as the tears in her eyes blurred her vision. Almost unable to go on, she took a deep breath, wondering how she would have survived this trauma had she been in Ian's shoes.

Yet there was an undercurrent that pulled at her. As she read his daily accounts of the events from the past week, there were his nightly dream entries. Each one was marked with a note: ". . . Just prior to dawn, I have again awakened." It was eerie, for each night she would toss and turn and wake just a little after four a.m.

The writings also seemed like they came from two different people. His daytime entries were logical, practical, businesslike— even funny at times. Scattered through them were "to do lists," and things that he didn't want to forget— how the telephone worked, or his encounter with the garbage disposal. But the pre-dawn dream entries were sensual and flowed more like poetic lyrics. Strangely similar to her own.

As she allowed her mind to soak in the words, she could feel her body respond to the raw sensuality contained within each entry. It was as though she could anticipate what he'd written before she even read it. Then, as if they had shared the same dream, she saw it . . . his entry from the night they had driven in the country. Suzanne ran her hand over the letters on the page, allowing her memories of that day to collide with Ian's words.

"*My mind has been overtaken by a tempestuous passion . . . She haunts me till I fear madness. My body betrays me with the Eros of youth . . . her scent fills my nostrils, till she is all that I breathe . . . yet I can only taste her mouth as I drink her in with wine . . . while her soft utterances besiege my ears, until she is all that I hear . . . and her touch . . . pure torture, as it turns my longing to ache . . .*

"*Were I not a man of reason, I would give in to my desire, for I have already felt her warmth in my soul. It wraps itself around me, as I beg for sleep . . . luring me with the false promise of release. She has fully captured my heart, thus my body has followed suit. Raging against this confinement is impossible, and my passions dare not be revealed. For what have I to offer her, other than momentary pleasure?*

"*No. dear Lady, you deserve so much more . . . more than I can ever hope to give. My bondage is my own, my suffering my penance, for daring to fall in love with someone like you. Thus, I will keep my peace, and beg heaven for mercy . . . and each drenched awakening will be my testimony to you.*

"*I can only beckon you with my mind to tell me when . . . just tell me how to capture your heart, as you have taken possession of my own. If only—*"

She had to stop reading. As her gaze had roved over each sentence, she could feel a warmth radiate up her thighs. It was as if his words had ignited long forgotten sensations within her, and she closed her eyes. She had to stop feeling this way. This was not written about her, it was his longing for Marissa. And, oh, how she wished a man could feel that way about her. Just once. Just for a moment in time . . . to want her that way. To have his body ache with longing for her, just as hers now ached for Ian's touch. It was pure agony.

Unable to stand it, Suzanne put the papers on her night stand and turned off the light. She would read the rest in the morning, when her emotions were clearer. When she could be more in control of the way she felt.

Later, remembering the dream she'd had that night, she pulled her body up into a fetal position to ward off the physical discomfort of desire. She had dreamed of him . . . of making torrid love to him, and had awakened damp, out of breath, and nearly out of her mind with need. She had never felt it that strongly in her life before. No matter how hard she tried, the feelings would creep back, pushing her reason away from her.

Suzanne steadied her breathing by concentrating hard on the rain. Convinced that it was merely an issue of mind over matter, she decided not to give in to her urges. She'd been celibate for years now, and she'd had these troublesome stirrings upon occasion. But she was always in control— always able to think her way through them and not give in to them. This time she wasn't sure.

As lightning arched through the sky, she parted her lips and took in a shallow breath. Her eyes had nearly closed to slits and she could feel her heartbeat pounding within her chest.

Just be still, she told herself. It would pass. It had to. Yet when she adjusted her legs for more comfort, a shiver of want coursed through her body. It was bad this time, and she wondered if he had read her journal.

Her cheeks burned with embarrassment of the thought of Ian reading something so private . . . especially when she had described the primal urges that had pulled her from the depths of sleep. She stared at the starless sky and tried to think of something benign. Her mind leaped to the night she and Leslie conjured up Ian Stewart Chandler in the first place. She had felt this way for the week prior to his appearance. That had to have been it. She'd even begun to fantasize about talk show hosts.

But as each bolt of lightning streaked the sky, she could almost feel its powerful current run through her body. Tempting fate, she flipped on the night stand light, and picked up the pages.

"If only you would come to me, my love, and release us both from the agony that binds us. For I have not the right to come to you, even though you have visited my room so many times in my dreams.

"Suzanne, if only you could understand how much I need you. That no mere child could take the place of a woman. Yet, in your eyes, I am but a child. New, and stumbling ineptly, in this strange world of yours."

In a state of shock, she whispered the last paragraph. "He said, 'Suzanne.' " Reading it again quietly, she let her vision settle on the top of the page, and move down slowly. What she saw was incomprehensible, forcing her to read the entire passage over and over again. "Suzanne?" she whispered in awe. "Me?"

Aware that her pulse was racing, she sat on the side of the bed to steady herself. He wanted *her*. Not Marissa. Hundreds of questions immediately attacked her brain. Why did he want her? How could she be attractive enough to compare to a seventeen-year-old? Was this just grief talking, or was it real? What would happen if this was only some fantasy because of their proximity? She needed answers.

Standing quickly, Suzanne snatched the papers from the bed, and opened the door to her room. Halfway down the hall, she stopped short, as Ian came out into the corridor. He didn't speak, but advanced toward her, holding her with his gaze. When he was inches away from her, he stopped, still staring at her with intensity.

"I want this to be real . . . not just a fantasy," she said quietly. "You're still grieving."

She could tell that he held roiling emotions in check while he reached to push a few stray hairs away from her cheek. His hand trembled as he grazed her face with two fingers, and he withdrew it immediately, swallowing hard in the process.

"I know that I have no right to feel this way yet there's no way to describe or define it. I feel like I've already been with you," he murmured, looking down at her and stepping closer. "I am made of but flesh and blood. Forgive me."

"I thought it was just me, that I was feeling this way alone. I felt that I had no right . . ."

Her whisper trailed off as she stared into his eyes. Something so familiar pulled her, that she touched his face to be sure he was real.

Covering her hand with his own, Ian closed his eyes, taking in a deep breath through his nose. "Tell me you are not a dream haunting me yet another night until I cry out."

Lacing his fingers through hers, he lifted her hand from his cheek, passionately kissing the center of it. The contact of his mouth sent a heat down her arm, making the now over-sensitive tips of her breasts sting with anticipation. She wanted that warmth to blanket all of her. She needed him to kiss her lips the way he had just taken her palm. Every inch of her now cried for his attention.

"Please," she whispered, standing on her toes to take his mouth. "Don't be a dream for me."

Immediately their bodies fused to one, devouring each other's mouths frantically, as he ran his fingers through her hair. Tears crept from the corners of her eyes, splashing against the waves of pleasure that overwhelmed her. It had been so long . . . it felt so right. He loved her.

Holding her back a little, Ian's voice nearly broke with emotion. "Suzanne," he breathed raggedly. "I cannot endure."

No longer fearful of the consequences, she took his hand and guided him to her bedroom. He stopped her advance at the side of the bed, pulling her gently to him, again singeing her throat with a trail of soft kisses. Almost in a daze from the exquisite sensations, she untied the satin bow at her neckline and let the soft gown fall away from her shoulders to the floor.

With trembling hands, he traced her body, closing his eyes briefly as he took in her nude form. "I had dreamed . . ." he began haltingly, "but never dared to hope."

Cupping her breasts, he lowered his mouth to them in a slow caress. There was no control as she gasped, inhaling ribbons of pleasure that immediately consumed her with the heat of his mouth. Struggling to free him from his tee shirt and sweat pants, she allowed her hands the luxury of his texture— his shoulders, his arms, his chest, his torso. Each gentle stroke drew a deep moan from his depths, further heightening her desire as she absorbed the sensations.

It was as though they were connected. His pleasure had become hers. Her pleasure had become his. In the dim bedroom light, they stared at each other, exploring the new terrain of their bodies. The acute ecstasy that registered on his face as she bathed her hands with his skin made her arch to accept each gentle stroke that caressed her own.

They had become one.

Nearly unable to stand, she allowed her body to sink to the bed. Timeless moments passed as he looked at her with adoration, before closing his eyes against a new wave of desire that assailed him.

"You are so beautiful that it hurts, Suzanne."

His words took her breath and, as he knelt before her, she almost cried out when his mouth grazed her thighs. New tears formed in her eyes and spilled down her cheeks, his kisses becoming more intense, until finally capturing the core of her.

The groan that escaped her lips began deep within her, exiting her mouth as a plea for mercy. Clutching at his shoulders, she tried to pull him to her, and his gentle refusal created new explosions that shattered her. She cried out his name, becoming oblivious to all but the pleasure he created. She needed him— to connect with him, to join as one and be completed.

"Please," she breathed, the words stopping in the currents of her pleasure. "Ian— I too am made of flesh."

Her tender beckoning broke his resolve, and as he covered her body with his own, he groaned deep within his chest. "For so long, my love. I've needed you this way."

It was as though they were transported, neither able to communicate using words. Now, their skin, their hands, their eyes, their limbs, their touch . . . every caress became the voice that conveyed their emotions.

Instantly, she felt his body join hers . . . and her heart joined his, melting into one as each consumed the other. His head dropped against her shoulder, and she shuddered as she heard him repeatedly gasp her name, blending them in a place not marked by time.

Bound to him by unending waves of pleasure,

she twined her legs with his, never wanting to be free. Ian's grasp now threatened to lift her from the bed. She could feel him quake within her, no longer able to stop her own. Joining her climax, he threw his head back and cried out.

His incarceration had ended with her name.

Spent, they lay together for what felt like a long time. Stroking her damp hair away from her face, he covered her mouth again with his own.

"Suzanne. I have searched the world for you."

Lifting to brush his mouth, she gazed into his eyes. "We've been this way since the beginning, haven't we?"

He allowed his head to drop to her shoulder and caressed her so tenderly that she almost sobbed.

"Oh, dare I even imagine what you have been to me? I cannot fathom the glory of what has happened. All I can be assured of is, my love for you transcends the passage of time. I would drown for you again, Suzanne. I just did."

His words cloaked her in an understanding that she had never known. A rare sense of peace came with his warmth, bringing with it, the need to be his forever. It felt so right, so sure this time. She didn't want to question it. Their magic could not be explained, nor could the feelings she had when she was in Ian's arms. Maybe, this time, she didn't have to.

Fourteen

Dawn crept through the window as Suzanne watched the sun restore the world with light. Never had she felt so complete, so alive. Snuggling against Ian's warmth at her back, she sighed while allowing herself to drift off peacefully again. They had shared a night of splendor, endlessly making love until they were literally spent from exhaustion. Now, the thought of leaving his arms to go to work seemed unbearable. Just one more day . . .

"Good morning, love," she heard him whisper, as he pulled her tighter against him. "I wish I could stay here with you forever, but I must get myself out of bed, sleepyhead."

Suzanne groaned and let her head fall back to his chest. "Do we have to? Can't we sleep in, have a late breakfast, and go for a ride? Maybe visit Gran a little later?"

Ian chuckled deep within his chest, and she could feel his laughter vibrate through her body.

"Suzanne, you are making it hard to keep my word to my new boss. No, one must be on time. I promised him."

The cool air that swept against her when he

rose made her shiver, and she snuggled down deeper in the covers to ward it off. Sadly watching him slip on his shirt and sweat pants, she tried again to stay his leave. "Aww, c'mon, he won't miss you for one day. Will he?"

Ian did not dignify her comment with a verbal response. Pecking her forehead as he tied his pants strings, he turned to leave. "I won't be gone long. I should be home before midnight. Then I'm all yours again."

"Midnight?" she asked, becoming alarmed and raising herself to sit up in bed.

"Yes, darling. Midnight. I must work from eight o'clock a.m. until eight o'clock p.m. Then I am meeting Michael and a few of the fellows to discuss business. I should be home around midnight."

She didn't know whether she was more astonished at his new sense of independence or threatened by it. It was obvious that Ian had somehow begun to create his own circle of friends, his own network of people to interact with, and was no longer solely hers. The rational side of her brain told her that this was a good thing. But the other side of her brain still wanted his undivided time and attention. Too conflicted at the moment to be rational, she opted to let the other side of her brain take over.

"Why do you have to go out with them tonight? I mean, we just found something special between us . . ."

He studied her face from his station across the room, and abruptly dragged his fingers through his hair. She could tell that he was becoming frustrated with her again, but she couldn't help it. She wanted to spend more time with him, and didn't want to share it with *the boys*— not just yet.

"Suzanne, we've been through this. I need to work to be able to finance my business venture. At one time I managed some fairly extensive investment portfolios. The one thing I learned through that experience is that you never allow your client to invest what they cannot afford to lose. Hence, I have no intention of allowing a good man like Mike Peterson to mortgage his house against a risky venture. That would not be ethical. However, we do need capital to begin."

She could only stare at him for a moment. He sounded like a Wall Street maverick, and yet he had no plausible way to make his idea work. The last thing she wanted to do was to dash his hopes, and she certainly didn't want to see him fail, but how in the world was he going to earn enough money, working in a deli, to go into business? Then there was the legalization issue. What about that?

"Listen," she began as respectfully as possible. "It may take a very long time to raise the kind of capital you probably need to start this kind of operation. Why don't you let me talk to some people who could hire you to do research— as a paralegal, maybe? Or— "

"Suzanne," he said firmly, cutting her off. "I have a plan of action. No, I do not intend to use the deli job to fund this business. That job is merely for incidentals and to have money in my pocket. A man should not have to request that a woman buy him shaving supplies or drawers. That is intolerable. And, despite your protests, I will begin to repay you with my first salaried week. Now, let us be done with this conversation."

Unable to let it go, she wrapped the top spread around her body like a robe, and followed him into the hall bathroom. "But, Ian," she persisted, ignoring his hot glare, "how are you going to do all this stuff without getting caught? I couldn't bear it if anything happened to you. Not now."

Obviously struggling with his annoyance, he kissed her briefly, then gently shoved her out of the bathroom. "Go to work, my dear, or sleep in. Please leave a man's business objectives alone. I assure you that I will only use legal and ethical practices. I love you."

She stood on the other side of the hallway bathroom door in total amazement. How could he have made the most tender, exquisite love to her the night before, then get up, bright-eyed and bushy-tailed, telling her about a night out with the boys? Then, to patronize her like she was *the little woman*, when she knew more about modern business than he ever would! Oh, he was most definitely going to hear about this. Who was Ian Stewart Chandler to decide when a conversation would be over? Didn't she have any say in the matter? After all, this wasn't eighteen seventy-two. Men!

Impatiently pacing the hall for him to come out, she waited until the shower stopped running. "Ian, I am getting dressed and going down to make tea. I want to discuss this before you leave."

Not waiting for him to answer, she dashed into her room and let the spread fall to the floor. She'd certainly give him a piece of her mind over breakfast!

Fully dressed in fifteen minutes, a female world record, Suzanne descended the stairs and marched into the kitchen. The light was on, tea cups were out . . . Correction. One tea cup was out, and beside it lay a little slip of folded paper. The other cup was in the sink. Fury made her ears ring. He better not have . . ."

Snatching up the note, she read it carefully. It was brief, but upbeat, in Ian's normal tone.

"My Dearest Suzanne,

Try not to worry yourself over how I conduct my business affairs. I did not have time to discuss differing philosophies at length this morning. I had to go to work. Hopefully, when I arrive home this evening, we can find a more enjoyable way to spend our time. Have a pleasant day.

Yours always, Ian

P.S. Memories of our evening will guide my day."

She didn't know whether to be angry or flattered. He had clearly decided that he was not going to discuss his business, or the crazy way he intended to fund it. Yet, he did make the most tender reference to their lovemaking. Still . . .

Resigned, she opted to skip her morning tea. The ritual didn't seem to have the same significance without Ian sitting at her kitchen table.

How odd, she thought. Just a week ago she would have had her breakfast with just the television to keep her company. She was used to the solitude, and had even come to enjoy the peacefulness associated with it. Now she couldn't bear the sound of emptiness in her own home. When did that happen?

Trying Leslie again, and getting her answering machine, she somberly collected her purse and briefcase. Her hair was still wet, and she pulled her fingers through it to keep it away from her face. *Back to business,* she told herself. *Suzanne, get back to work.*

She didn't have the heart to call her friend Leslie all day. She knew that Leslie really couldn't talk on her job, with customers filing in and out of the bookstore. Plus, she wanted to be considerate of Leslie's hectic Mommy schedule. This time, Suzanne made it a point to put her friend's needs first. She knew Leslie's basic routine. After working her day job, Leslie began shift two. She'd have to shuttle kids from soccer practice and other after school activities. Then, she'd have to rush home and get dinner on the table for Mike and the kids. Then, there was homework, bedtime stories, baths and maybe time for discussions with Mike. Perhaps her girlfriend would even try to fling a load of laundry in the washer between all of that commotion. The only free time to talk to the woman who stayed in perpetual motion was while she was doing the dishes and kitchen clean-up. Ten o'clock K.P. Thank God for cordless phones, or they would probably never talk.

The more Suzanne thought about it, the more she knew she owed Leslie an apology. How did women do it? Work one full-time job with low pay and hassles all day. Then, basically go home to a second job for no pay, no vacations, and most times, no appreciation. In the scheme of things, maybe Gran was right— there was nothing new under the sun. At least not much in terms of women's advancement, no matter how she looked at it.

Bored with the frozen dinner she had microwaved, Suzanne looked at the phone again. Maybe she'd call Les around ten. It was Friday night, and Mike and Ian were out with the boys. In the last year, Leslie had only gotten out with the girls once. It just wasn't fair. And when did her poor friend ever have a chance to sit in a hot, relaxing tub, paint her toe nails, or read a book? New anger captured Suzanne as she thought about it. Romance? When in the world did Leslie find the time to conceive two kids? She could understand how the first one got there, when Mike and Les had time alone. There were possibilities. But, with a wailing infant, still in diapers, and her friend's unrelenting schedule . . . how the hell did any woman make herself desirable?

Smiling at the irony, Suzanne shook her head and tried to picture herself in Leslie's situation. She could see it now. A lusty husband, coming

in from a few beers with the fellas, all in a good
mood, relaxed and wanting to make passionate
love while the haggard housewife tries to offer
up her tired body as a ceremonial sacrifice, ignoring the wails of the two o'clock feeding, and
trying to stay awake long enough for him to get
finished. The movie, *Norma Rae,* instantly
popped into her mind with Sally Field standing
at the kitchen sink preparing dinner, while dirty-
faced, hungry children and an irate husband
clamored for her attention. Suzanne chuckled as
she remembered the scene where Field lifted her
house dress and told her husband to get it while
he could, because she was too tired and too busy
to serve it on a silver platter. She was sure Leslie
could relate.

And pregnant? How did any woman do all of
that, with a toddler, one in a high chair, another
in the oven, and a man . . . ? She'd seen those
poor female P.O.W.'s while standing in the
check-out line in the supermarkets. She'd have
her five items in the express lane, still dressed
in her work clothes. They'd be dragging two
overfilled carts, and looking like they were going
to drop where they stood.

Maybe Leslie was right. What if marriage
wasn't all that it was cracked up to be, at least
not for the woman? She could see the benefits
that men got from the contract . . . yet, they
acted like they were going to prison. Could that
be their ploy? Act like you don't want to do
it, like the other person will get more out of
it than you, just to make the woman want it

even more? Then she's trapped. The old bait
and switch. Too late, the ink on the certificate
is dry. It worked in business negotiations, why
not in relationships? Suzanne thought about it
hard. What if she'd really been pining to go
to an internment camp, mistaking it for paradise?

Maybe that was the curse of not being young
and in love. She had seen and heard too much
to believe in the fairy tales of her youth. She
had seen reality.

But why her mind had taken such a wicked
turn, she couldn't imagine. Perhaps it was because all of a sudden she was feeling married.
Loved and left. It was seven o'clock, and Ian was
out on a Friday night with the boys. She was
washing cups at the sink, albeit a far cry from
Norma Rae's kitchen, and she had worked all
day. What if they had had a family? What if
someday she had to do *his* laundry, food shopping for a group, instead of her easy single-life-
ten-item lane purchases? And what if she were
the one who had to clean up the beer cans after
the boys left? The thought was frightening.
Maybe she was too old to change. What if she
really couldn't get used to the new role? Clearly,
she didn't have a lot of hope that Ian would
make any dramatic changes. Men born in this
century were finding that difficult enough. It
seemed to take too much energy to turn a man
into a suitable house partner. Most women she
knew gave up after the first five years. In five
years, she'd be forty-six. No. She definitely

wouldn't be able to battle over funky socks and toilet seats for five years. Only youth had that much endurance.

Turning off the kitchen light, Suzanne went upstairs to lie down. She decided to take a little nap, and get a second wind for the big fight when Ian got home. She knew how to pace herself. If she called Leslie around ten, she could talk with her for an hour or so, and have her strategy together by the time Ian hit the door. She'd turn off the ringer and let the machine pick up nuisance business calls. Perfect. All she needed now was some rest.

"Suz, wake up!"

Suzanne tried to switch her brain on to pick up the telephone. The urgency of Leslie's voice had awakened her out of a sound sleep with a start. She had been dreaming heavily, and the sudden change was disorienting. Snatching the receiver from the hook, as soon as she recognized Leslie's voice, she pressed her ear to the phone.

"Les, what's the matter?" she asked, still groggy, "Are Mike and the kids all right? What time is it?"

"Yes. Mike is home now, and the kids are fine. But, he called from the station and had to leave Ian."

"What? The station?" Suzanne's brain refused to work.

"They were out at a bar," Leslie said, sounding near hysteria, "and Ian insisted that he drive home, since Mike was drunk. Something about some commercial— 'Friends don't let friends drive drunk'— and— "

"What!"

"Listen, we've got to act fast. They were both stinking, okay, Suz. And when the cops pulled Ian over, and he didn't have any identification, they started arguing, and— "

"What!"

"Listen, listen. Then, Mike vouched for Ian, okay? Saying that they were best friends, and he wasn't letting any cops take his friend in for bullsh— "

"What?" Suzanne's voice had reached a pitch that she hadn't been able to hit since puberty.

"So, there was a scuffle, and— "

"What!"

"Shut up, this is serious, Suz. Ian started quoting law, and Mike got pushed, so Ian jumped in it to defend Mike, and— "

"What!" Suzanne was standing as she screamed the question.

"The girl that was with them was under age, but— "

"What!"

"She said she would testify, since the fellas were nice enough to try to drive her home, and— "

"Testify?" The blood rushing to Suzanne's brain made her dizzy, and she had to sit down again.

"Yeah, at the bail hearing. We've gotta go get him tomorrow morning."

Suzanne was numb. She had left the man for

a few hours, and now he was in jail. Her worst nightmare rose like a specter before her. How the hell was she going to get a man from the past, with no I.D., out of the slammer?

"I called over to your grandmother's, because I kept getting your machine. There should be at least four messages on there from me, starting at one-thirty a.m."

"What? You called Gran's house at one-thirty in the morning? Why in the world would you— "

"Because Ian told Mike that you were worried about her, and wanted to go visit her today. I thought that since he was out with the boys, you had gone alone. And, since I hadn't talked to you— "

"Does Gran know?"

Leslie didn't answer immediately, and that was all it took for Suzanne to read between the lines.

"Oh, my God, Les. She'll have a heart attack for sure, now."

"No," Leslie said more calmly, "actually, she took it pretty well."

"Took it pretty well?" Suzanne was incredulous.

"Yeah," Leslie said in a nonchalant tone. "She was up anyway, said she could never sleep when her arthritis was bothering her. She was rooting through her papers and said, 'Boys will be boys. A little fracas shouldn't be too terribly problematic.' "

"A little fracas? This isn't a Friday night bar fight. Ian is from another *century!* He, I take it, assaulted a Jersey State trooper!"

"No. It was the local yokels."

"Is that supposed to make me feel better, Les? Why didn't you call me?"

"I did. Look at your machine. You must have been really sleeping hard, because I kept calling, and Ian couldn't use his one phone call, because he doesn't know how to dial out. He can only answer the phone."

Suzanne looked at the machine, and indeed, the red message light was blinking away. "Maybe I should call Gran and let her know everything is all right, so she doesn't have to worry. But, how are we going to get him out? Is Mike up on charges?" Hundreds of questions flew through her mind at once. "What are we going to do, Les?"

"Okay. Here's the plan," Leslie said confidently. "First, call Gran. Let's not have an eighty-four-year-old woman worry about this mess. Mike is okay. He wasn't driving, and he didn't push the cop. He got pushed, so they let him go. They just took him because he refused to leave Ian. Next, we call this girl who lives close by. Let's get her info, so she can go with us in the morning. You'll need to take some cash though, Suz. I don't know anything about this bail stuff. Hopefully they'll release him on his own recognizance and in your care. I saw that on "L.A. Law." But we'll probably have to get him a lawyer. Plus they won't give him over to us until after ten o'clock. So we need to get the wheel turning first thing in the morning."

Suzanne could not speak. As she absorbed Leslie's plan, which for once made sense, she was still numb.

"Suz. You got it?"

"Yes," she said in a daze, still absorbing Leslie's words.

"Good, then I'll pick you up at eight-thirty And— oh, my God!"

"What? What? What's wrong, Les?" New fear sent another adrenaline rush through Suzanne's veins.

"Rahmin. He was coming over on Saturday, and— "

"Are you crazy? Who cares! Unless he can make people walk through walls like the old Hindus were supposed to, then it doesn't matter, Les! This is real life, present day drama! You can't *Ohmm* Ian out of prison. Jesus!"

"Okay. Okay. You're right," Leslie said while chuckling. "I'll postpone Rahmin until this mess is settled."

Again, Suzanne was incredulous, but she didn't have the energy to argue the point. "Let's just get him free, then we'll go from there. All right?" she said evenly, now pacing the floor.

"Okay, kiddo. I'll beep at the door in the morning. 'Bye."

Suzanne just stared at the phone after Leslie hung up. It was all too much to take in at once. Ian in jail? A fight with the police? And, now, she had to call Gran?

Slowly reaching for the phone again, Suzanne took a deep breath and punched in her grandmother's number. This time, Gran answered on the second ring.

"Hi, Gran," she said, filled with humiliation. "I'm sorry that we've disturbed you so late. Everything is going to be all right. It was just a little misunderstanding, but Ian will be fine. I'll call you in— "

"Now, Suzanne," her grandmother cut in with irritation. "Do not try to patronize an old woman. If it was just a little thing, then they would have let him go. I detest the authorities. It reminds me of what happened in France after World War I, there was so much brouhaha with the French Resistance— "

"Gran, please." Suzanne's frazzled nerves couldn't take it. "It will be fine."

"That nice young man needs a good attorney. We Hamiltons have had them for years. It's the only way your rights and money are protected, darling. Do not be so naive. Now it's settled. I will make a few calls— "

"Gran, really, don't." Suzanne's mind raced and slammed from one problem to the next. "Mr. Barnes can't help Ian."

"And why not?" her grandmother asked with a trace of indignation. "Barnes is a Yale graduate, and has represented some of the most grievous cases out here on the Main Line. Do you remember the Winstons, and their tax evasion problem? Well, Barnes— "

"Gran. This isn't a white collar crime situation. Okay? Ian doesn't have papers to be in the U.S., and he's in deep water." Suzanne almost blanched as the words fell from her mouth. She had no intention of telling Gran that tidbit of information, but she also knew how head-strong her grandmother could be. Especially, when the woman thought there was some injustice to battle.

"Well," her grandmother said after a moment. "That does change things a bit."

"Good," Suzanne sighed. "Then it's settled."

"What jail is he in, and what are the charges?"

Suzanne gave her grandmother the information to humor her. She knew it was the only way to end the call.

"Ah, well, that should do it, I would imagine," Gran said calmly. "Well, you children take care, and try, dear Suzanne, to get some rest. Won't you, darling?

Suzanne had to laugh at the irony, as she made her goodbyes to her grandmother. "I will, Gran. You, too, despite all the excitement."

Her grandmother had one last parry to make before she hung up the phone. "I always sleep well. *I* have a clear conscience. Now, don't you dare to keep me away from the rest of the excitement. You know how I love theater."

Suzanne put the receiver in its cradle and stared at her telephone. Last night, she'd slept like the dead for seven straight hours, recovering from an evening of passion with Ian and a full day of work. It had been the first night she'd gotten any real rest since he'd erupted into her life. And now, according to her grandmother, she was supposed to just slip off to sleep, while Ian suffered alone in a cell overnight?

It was incredible. There were just no words.

Fifteen

Suzanne had been standing on her front steps since eight-fifteen, waiting for Leslie to arrive. When she saw the beat-up Pontiac pull into her driveway, she rushed out to meet the car. Peering into the window, she shot Leslie a quizzical look before getting in the back and sitting behind the pretty young blonde who occupied the front passenger's seat.

"Morning, Suz. This is Opal."

Suzanne reached over the seat and extended her hand. "Hi." She was too stunned to force a smile, and sleep deprivation was again tormenting her brain.

"Real bummer," the girl said lightly, as Leslie pulled off. "They're really nice guys, and so what if he didn't know how to drive? I was helping him learn."

A wave of nausea stopped Suzanne from commenting.

"Opal's going to graduate from high school this year. Ian met her in the deli."

She could see Leslie smiling at her from the rear-view mirror, and she looked out of the window to ignore her friend. "Delightful."

"I'm going to be an artist. Or, maybe a model-actress. I haven't decided yet. I'd love to do a music video. But those guys really have a neat idea about the coffee house. You know, like, where do people really have to hang? Especially out here in the 'burbs. It sounds cool. And I, for one, would go. You know? Artists need a place to express themselves without all that hassle from the establishment."

Suzanne refused to say a word. Her knuckles were turning white as her nails dug into her palms.

"Hey, do you think it was a conspiracy, or something? You know, like, the cops got the word that those guys were going to do something controversial, like open a coffee house. Wow, man. I never thought about that. When I told my friends, they said, hey, they'd support the old dude, you know? So, when he opens his place, we'll be there in force. It's too, too radical."

Suzanne rolled down the window to get some air, and she could see Leslie's shoulders shaking from repressed laughter.

"Well, Opal, you have to stand up for your rights," Leslie said, still chuckling.

"You are so right, Lady," the girl exclaimed, raising her hand and waiting for a high five from Leslie. "Hey, they did it at Woodstock, you know?"

"Yes," Suzanne said in a controlled voice. "Even the clothes are back."

The young woman turned around in her seat

and gaped at Suzanne. "You wore bell bottoms and platforms? Get out of town!"

Leslie gave in to a full belly laugh, and responded for Suzanne. "No. My friend Suzanne never did bell bottoms, hipsters, or clogs. I did that."

Spinning in her seat, the girl gazed at Leslie with awe. "Wow. You must be a real cool mom. Were you a real live beatnik? Wild!"

"Beatnik was before my time. A . . . ahh, a hippie was more like it."

"Cool."

Suzanne prayed that her tolerance would hold up long enough for them to reach the Court House. She didn't want to do a jump and roll from a car that was moving at sixty-five miles an hour. But if the girl didn't shut up . . .

"Hey, that cute one, is he your old man?"

Leslie reached her hand over the back seat while still driving, and patted Suzanne's knee. "Now, we just have a few more minutes to go, kiddo."

"I mean, for an old dude, he's pretty sexy. If you two aren't hooked up, or anything . . ."

Suzanne forced a smile and answered the girl through her teeth. "He's just a friend."

Heading off a disaster, Leslie jumped in. "Well, really, my girlfriend is sort of shy. They just started going together last week." Leslie ignored her glare and giggled. "It's been sort of an ill-fated match. The jail thing really put a strain on the relationship."

"Wow, I can dig it. Too bad. That's really

heavy karma, the lost love thing and all. Wait'll I tell the gang. They'll really come out now, with this Romeo and Juliet thing going on. Deep."

Suzanne leaned her head back on the seat and closed her eyes. Something was happening to her. Visions of satisfied retribution flitted through her tired brain. She'd get every last one of them. First Leslie, since she was in closest proximity to her hands. Death by strangulation. Then, she'd take an ink pen into Ian's cell and stab him to death. Then Mike, for encouraging them both. She'd have to contemplate his demise. And Opal. She could get pushed from a fast-moving vehicle on I295. Perfect.

When was this going to end? What in the name of God had happened to her normal, ordinary life?

"What do you mean, he's been released already?" Suzanne leaned across the desk and glared at the administrative officer.

"Like I said, lady, his attorney came in here, produced his I.D., and we let him go."

Suzanne looked at Leslie and Opal, then back to the officer. "Are you sure you released Ian Stewart Chandler?"

"Look," the man said impatiently, "I don't have time for this today. Here's his exit paperwork. Do you recognize the signature?"

Suzanne took the stack of papers that were attached to a clipboard and studied them carefully. It was indeed Ian's distinctive, aristocratic penmanship. But, how in the world . . . ?

"Satisfied?" the man asked in a huff, snatching the board back from her. "Look, a lot of guys have more than one old lady, okay? Or money their wife doesn't know about. The shit hits the fan in here everyday, when the wife or girlfriend number one comes to get him, and he's been sprung. That's not my business. That's a domestic problem. So, take the complaint to family court, lady. Otherwise, step out of line and go home."

It was destined to be the longest car ride home that she had ever had to endure. Once they had let Opal off at her door, Suzanne spun on Leslie.

"Do you believe this? Do you absolutely believe this!"

Leslie tried to calm her as she shifted the car into gear. "Now, Suz, I know you're upset, but—"

"Upset? Upset! I'm going to have a brain hematoma! Upset!"

Leslie tried unsuccessfully to stifle a giggle. "You've gotta get used to it, Suz. Men always—"

"What?"

"Suz, you've gotta go with the flow. Chill out."

"Chill out! Chill out?" She could only fling her hands in the air and scream. "I'm having a nervous breakdown, is all. Just losing my mind! And it started with you!"

The rest of the ride home, Leslie tried to give her examples of male madness, which was badly designed to make her feel better. Then she had tried to come up with a million different plausible excuses for the inexcusable. Without realizing it, Leslie was sealing Ian's fate. Her legal defense was not helping him.

Quickly exiting the car, she thanked Leslie and promised to call her later in the day. She ignored Leslie's admonishment to hear the man out. Hear him out! She'd throw him out! Her hands were shaking so badly with rage, that she could barely get the key in the locks to open the door. When she finally got past the barricade, she barreled in the house like whirling dervish.

"Ian Stewart Chandler! I'm home, and you'd better be!"

Noticing the kitchen light on, she headed straight toward the back of the house. He was calmly making a pot of tea, and had set out two cups.

"I thought you might need something to calm your nerves. I imagine that you've— "

"Calm my nerves? Have you lost what is left of your mind?"

"I don't want to discuss this until you're rational," he said in an irritatingly even voice while pouring hot water into the mugs.

"Rational? Do you call what happened last night rational? Do you presume to tell me that picking up a minor, *in a bar*, driving . . . *DRIVING!* Getting drunk . . . fighting with the police . . ." Fury took her speech as she began to repeat words. "The *police!*"

"Sit down, Suzanne, before you work yourself up into a lather. All is well. I'm fine now."

"All is well?" She was incredulous, but did take a seat before she passed out.

"Yes, well, Mike did say that the young lady would create the vast majority of your hysteria. But I assure you, it was purely market research, to understand the young minds of your day."

Seething, she spoke to him with nearly a sarcastic snarl. "Up close and personal, I assume."

"Oh, surely you aren't concerned about Miss Opal. She's just a child. A rather interesting commentary on modern society, however."

Suzanne ignored the tea that was placed before her and continued to glare at Ian.

"Now, as for the driving, Mike is going to show me how to do that task. Although, when he's sober, this time."

She could feel her eyes narrow down to slits. "YOU DO NOT HAVE A LICENSE! Not even a damn permit!"

"Correction, Madame. Fate has deemed to smile upon me. I am thoroughly legal these days, and I have not implicated myself by asking unnecessary questions."

Suzanne stared at Ian's new wallet wide-eyed as he produced a social security card, a driver's license, a Visa Card, and a passport.

"What did you do?" she whispered, terror making her blood run cold.

"*I* did not do anything. This very nice, and apparently well connected, gentleman collected me from prison today, and presented me with these. He said he was a *very special* friend of your grandmother's, and had come to my aid in her behalf. He also said the fewer questions I asked, the better. So, we shook on it, and he drove me home. Very pleasant man."

Suzanne sat quietly stunned for a moment. One of her grandmother's lovers. No.

"Gran? Did you say Gran?"

"Yes, Cecilia Hamilton. We must get by this weekend, so that I may extend my deepest appreciation in person. I wouldn't have it any other way."

Pushing her chair back from the table, Suzanne rose and walked over to the phone. Dialing her grandmother, she kept her gaze steady on Ian.

"Gran," she said in a slow, even voice. "It's me, Suzie."

"Oh, my pet. Did Mr. Tatarglioni clear up your little problem? He's so nice, has sat on several charity boards with me for years. Did you meet him, darling?"

Suzanne chose her words carefully. "Did Mr. Tatarglioni provide Ian with false papers? Tell me that you did not involve yourself with something like this, Gran? Please."

She could hear her grandmother sigh with impatience.

"Oh, now, Suzanne. Let us be realistic. The man had a little problem, and we could solve it. No harm done."

Suzanne was almost speechless. Almost.

"Gran? This is a *felony*. People do ten to twenty for this kind of thing."

"Oh, Suzie. Listen, darling, my dear Sicilian

friend and I have been very close, ever since we met in Rome, and—"

"Sicilian? Are you crazy?"

"Oh my, yes. I'm absolutely mad about Italian men, but you mustn't tell my current friend. He's just British. Not quite the fire, but a dear man nonetheless."

Suzanne held the phone away from her ear, and screamed.

"Suzie, are you all right, pet?"

She couldn't respond to her grandmother, for she had sunk to the floor and had begun laughing.

"Suzie, you're scaring me. Put Ian on the phone."

Wiping her eyes, Suzanne held the receiver to her ear. "I'm just fine, Gran. I don't know what to say or think anymore. Everything, everybody's crazy! I'm the only sane person I know. I just had to hear myself scream before I jumped over the precipice along with the others."

"Good. You gave me quite a scare there for a moment," the old woman said irritably. "Now everything should be settled. Let's not go on and on beating a dead horse, Suzanne. That nice Mr. Chandler doesn't have to worry about any more nasty little legal problems. It was justice, with a small twist. That's all. And, when others aren't playing by the rules . . . well, you simply have to learn how to play. And, anyway, the wealthy all have skeletons in their closet. A crazy nephew here, a debauching uncle there, inheritances built up from prohibition income, smuggling during the Revolutionary War—so why quibble over getting a poor, honest fellow some necessary papers? The man was, after all, an attorney in his heyday. He should not be working at a deli."

Suzanne stood slowly, and spoke in a low tone. "What did you say, Gran? About Ian being an attorney?"

Cecilia Hamilton laughed deeply. "Oh, now, Suzanne. Surely, you young girls didn't think you could keep it from me forever, did you? I *knew* something terribly exciting was amiss, and you were keeping me out of it. I should be extremely perturbed. But then the challenge of figuring it all out was the best part. So, I forgive you. Now, do bring that handsome man over to see me soon. Won't you, my dear? I have so many things to ask him. But let's not discuss any of this in front of poor Mrs. McDonnell. When I told her, she crossed herself and threatened to leave my employ, and I couldn't possibly replace her. She's been with us for years and is like family."

Starting again, Suzanne spoke to her grandmother calmly. "Did Leslie tell you all of those insane things when she called last night? You can't— "

"Suzie, I will try to overlook the fact that you have just insulted me. It's not like you, and not very becoming. Of course dear Leslie wouldn't let the cat out of the bag and ruin the surprise of it all without telling you. You can be so disagreeable sometimes, Suzie. You'll have to work on that. No. I was up rummaging around when she called. It just helped me to piece the clues together, is all. I've known about such phenomena since my old Rosicrucianist days. And my second husband was a Mason, you know. A very high level one, at that."

It was more than she could comprehend and Suzanne issued a weary sigh. She mouthed her goodbyes and a promise to visit on Sunday without allowing any additional information to penetrate her brain. Enough had besieged that gray organ already. She just couldn't take any more. Not now.

When she hung up, she filed past Ian, and waved away his questions. No more. Enough. She was going to lie down. She didn't want to discuss the interesting people he'd met in jail, how he was going to finance his business, or what he planned to do next. She just wanted to get her body somewhere prone, not think, and close her eyes until Rahmin came.

"But aren't you hungry?" Ian protested as she dragged herself up the stairs.

"No. I'll eat when Leslie and Rahmin get here."

"What about Cecilia? Are we definitely set to visit her tomorrow?" he went on while following behind her.

"Yup, and you can all discuss the mysteries of the universe while I go outside and look at the roses."

Looking worried, he touched her shoulder. "Suzanne, I am really sorry. Look, I know last night gave you quite a scare. But you don't look well. I'd feel better if you were still angry. But this defeat that you have about you . . ."

Removing his hand, she walked into the bedroom. "I'm sorry if my *aura* is cloudy, or some such nonsense. Maybe Rahmin can fix it."

She didn't even look at him as she kicked off her shoes and flopped on the bed face down.

"Can I bring you anything?" he asked, still standing in the doorway.

"Yes," she intoned flatly, without lifting her head. "A bottle of Scotch, at least fifty barbiturates, and a priest."

She groaned as she heard him rush to her side.

"You cannot be serious. Things have been chaotic, strained, but, Suzanne . . ."

Waving him away again, she spoke into the pillow. "I was just joking."

"Well, it is certainly not a joke. Suicide is never funny."

"No," she said, letting out a deep breath with the word. "With my luck, and the way this karma crap works, I'd probably just get to come back and do it all again, anyway."

Ian shifted restlessly from foot to foot before leaving. "I will check on you in a couple of hours. I won't be a bother, but I will peep in to be sure that you are resting and haven't become distraught again. When Rahmin comes over, I will notify you."

"Fine."

"I would like to learn to use the phone. Could I attempt it on the gadget downstairs?"

All she could do was nod.

"You took the restaurant's numbers from a big yellow book. Does everyone have a number?"

"Yes," she said without enthusiasm. "Look up their name alphabetically, punch in the number next to their name, and wait for them to answer. Their addresses are under their name. Don't put that in. It won't work."

"Great. Thank you, Suzanne," he said cheerfully, shutting her door. "I'll be up in a couple of hours. Sleep well, my love."

"Yeah, right."

She merely closed her eyes, and closed him out.

Sixteen

How had she allowed these people to take over her life? Suzanne stared blankly out of the window, as Rahmin went on with his astrological litany.

". . . So, you see, your charts are all in a fantastically unique alignment. Suzanne is a Capricorn, which means she's industrious, ambitious, yet extremely rigid. Leslie, Ian, and Michael are all Sagittarians, which should make things fairly unsettling for the outnumbered Capricorn."

"You might say that," Suzanne answered with no small measure of sarcasm while turning her focus to their small group.

Leslie just grinned while Ian knit his brows as though in deep analysis of the concept. She wanted to run screaming into the night. The entire week had been a travesty. Why end it now, she thought, mentally re-joining the discussion against her will.

"Oh, you must be reeling," Rahmin added with a smile. "This is a terribly stressful configuration, but one that promises growth for all."

"How did we all come together like this?"

Leslie asked in an awe-struck tone. "This is so bizarre."

"Well," Rahmin began again slowly, "there are several factors to consider. First of all, we cannot just look at the sun sign in any natal chart. We must look at the positions that the other planets hold, as well as the planetary positions of the Heavenly bodies as they shift astronomically."

When everyone, except Leslie, looked confused, Rahmin tried again.

"You see," he said, taking out a piece of notebook paper and a pen. "The next planet to consider is The Moon, the inner person. The sun tells us how someone appears outwardly, the moon, inwardly. Sagittarians, by their sun, or outward nature, are pleasant, gregarious, love animals and nature, are fairly disorganized . . . but extremely intelligent and articulate. They make good teachers, attorneys, and so on. And they will fight an injustice for the underdog with vigilance— sometimes to the point of the ridiculous. Most importantly, their sense of adventure will get them into scrapes from time to time, but being the luckiest sign in the zodiac, they always manage to bounce back. This explains, Leslie, Ian, and Michael's personalities well, don't you think?"

"Curiosity killed the cat," Ian said, looking first at Leslie, then Suzanne.

"But satisfaction brought him back," Leslie chimed in with a chuckle.

Suzanne just groaned and shook her head.

"This is precisely it," Rahmin exclaimed, clapping his hands. "Look at how the three of you just processed my small comment. Ian took the dark approach, but had a comment. Leslie had an optimistic comeback. Suzanne was annoyed, because this disrupts her previous concept of order."

All three students glanced at one another, then back to Rahmin. It was eerie, but without knowing any of the participants beyond Leslie, he had accurately described a significant chunk of each individual's persona.

"But if Leslie and I are in the same constellation," Ian asked in a serious voice, "why did we have differing reactions?"

"Ah, well . . ." Rahmin said stretching, "aside from different environmentals, like parents, gender, age, you all have different birth times, which gets back to different planets."

Ian's puzzled look drew Suzanne's curiosity to the fore. She couldn't believe that he was actually considering these off-beat theories. Not Mr. Straight-laced Attorney.

"Ian, you have a Scorpio moon. Which means you have a dark side, and awful temper. Jealousy is no stranger to you, nor is the concept of revenge, or using slightly devious methods to right the perceived wrong. Let us just say that I am glad the ethical Sagittarian sun balances this aspect of your chart. A Scorpio influence can be good and bad when it comes to business ventures and love. In business, you can be ruthless, successful, but very loyal. However, if a partner ever deceives you, you will not rest until the wrong has been righted. That is both a Sagittarian and a Scorpio trait. The difference is, Sag is fire— burns hot, blows his stack, and is done with it. Scorpio is water, and will nurse the issue for an eternity, plotting the revenge along the way."

Suzanne blanched, and she looked at Ian, then Rahmin. Now she was worried.

"So how does such a person respond in a personal relationship?"

Rahmin smiled. "Very passionately. Scorpios love deeply, love possessively, and secretively. Once they let you into their nether regions, they are hard pressed to turn you loose without a fight."

Suzanne swallowed hard. "Oh, well, I guess that answers my question."

"You, too, have a Scorpio moon. Both of you have a Scorpio moon, *and* a Scorpio Venus. It could be a deadly, or powerful, combination. The sparks should fly in all directions!"

Leslie laughed, and Suzanne kicked her under the coffee table.

"Now, our Leslie has a dear, Aquarian moon under her Sagittarian exterior. Flighty, creative, intelligent . . . will join groups to save the world before saving her own family. Aquarius is an expansive sign. The sign of humanity."

"But what about, Mike?" Leslie chimed in excitedly. "How does he fit in?"

Rahmin reshuffled his papers and leaned forward to look at them more closely. "Ah, very interesting. You see here? Michael has a Cancer moon, opposing your Aquarius one."

"Which means?" Suzanne asked cautiously, monitoring her friend's expression.

"Which means that they have very differing perceptions of happiness. While Aquarius loves everyone, and no one person in particular, Cancer's center focus is hearth and home. So, while my dear Leslie is longing to save the whales, Michael is redesigning kitchen space for maximum efficiency. Both partners are deflated when the other isn't ecstatic about their discoveries. Yet their overall Sagittarian sun is probably what makes them respect the freedom that their mate needs. It had to be what drew these two together in the first place."

Leslie sat back. "Wow, that is what every fight is about. Take Ian's business idea, for example. All three of us thought it was a wonderful idea. Mike and I were happy as clams. I said, "Throw caution to the wind. You're forty-three and have always wanted your own business. So, let's take a second mortgage, and make it work. Besides, it was for starving artists and young people, who need a place to commune and get inspired. He said, 'Great business idea, but hell will freeze over before we ever mortgage the house for anything, even college tuitions.' Then we got into a whole blow up about it. Just like we did about Suzanne."

Suzanne looked at Leslie and guilt gripped her. "Me? I didn't know I was causing problems between you two."

"Sagittarians must not be known for their diplomacy," Ian grunted under his breath.

"Actually, tact is the one thing that Sagittarians most assuredly lack," Rahmin commented with a smile.

Appearing embarrassed, Leslie tried to explain, digging herself in deeper along the way. "No, really, Suz. It wasn't a big fight. It was one of those how-come-you-have-to-babysit-your-girlfriend arguments, when you've got your own family, type of thing. He just didn't understand that there was this cosmic stuff going on, is all."

Rahmin chuckled, "The altruist versus the paternalist. The world at large, versus the nuclear family. You know, Leslie, like Ian and Suzanne, you and Michael are double positioned."

This time even Leslie looked confused.

"In essence, you have an Aquarius moon, and Aquarius is also in the position of your love planet, Venus. Which means you tend to love and befriend the same way. Open, free, adventurous, and hate non-creative confinement. Michael has a Cancer Venus to go along with his Cancer Moon. Meaning that, home is where his heart is, and rows don't blow over without his sensitive Cancer feelings getting hurt. He is loyal, and takes a friendship or a romantic involvement very, very seriously."

"I can vouch for his friendship," Ian said in a protective manner. "He would not be moved, not even for the authorities."

"Oh, absolutely!" Rahmin said excitedly. "A perfect fit."

"So, where does that leave me?" Suzanne asked defensively. "The stuffy, odd man out?"

"No. No," Rahmin crooned softly, as though to mollify her hurt feelings. "You, my dear earth sign, bring grounding and balance. You see, Suzanne, your role is to be the stabilizing force in this melée of eccentric personalities. Your purpose is definitely a good one. Ian brings fire, but must temper his Scorpio nature. Leslie brings a thirst for adventure, and optimism beyond all imagination. Michael offers the supportive character and enthusiasm with his Sagittarian spirit, but it is well focused on that which is most important, the home. And, Suzanne brings access through her Capricorn ambition, work ethic, and resources. Yet all of you Sagittarians bring her out of her brooding, subterranean Scorpio self. Or make her enjoy life, when the Capricorn in her gets too bogged down with working hard. It all plays very well together, if you can remember the strengths and weakness of each other."

The group fell quiet for a moment, looking at each other with a new awareness.

"I'd love to have you do Gran's chart. Now, she's a piece of work," Suzanne chuckled.

"When was she born? Do you know time of day and location?"

Suzanne stared at Rahmin before answering. "Her birthday is August twelfth, but I couldn't tell you the rest. That was eighty-four years ago."

"I knew it!" Leslie nearly yelled. "A Leo. That fits perfectly. The *grande*, Gran."

"What?" Suzanne asked becoming totally confused. "A Leo? What does that mean."

Rahmin sat back and watched as Leslie began, obviously enjoying his student's performance with pride.

"She loves everything done on a grand scale, Suz. She loves large, insists on spending her money on only the best, has servants and a lifestyle like royalty. Her entertainment budget must be the Gross National Product of small nations, and she sits on every high visibility charity board in the city of Philadelphia! Simply grand!"

Suzanne had to smile, and even Ian chuckled.

"She is just that, and more, Leslie." Suzanne's heart warmed at the description of her eccentric grandmother. "They broke the mold when they made Gran."

"Old world aristocracy at its finest," Ian chimed in with respect. "I marvel at the woman."

"Well, then, I must certainly do her chart."

Suzanne murmured under her breath as Rahmin rose and walked over to the windows. "How much do you want to bet he'll end up as her lover?"

Ian turned his head and nodded as though to avoid looking at her, but not before she saw his broad smile. She knew he wanted to laugh, and she enjoyed nudging him close to an outburst in a situation where he couldn't respond.

"So," Ian said abruptly, attempting to change the subject and ward off her secret humor. "What about these other influences that have affected us?"

Rahmin stretched and lolled his neck from side to side before returning to his seat. "Ah, yes . . . the other aspects. Well, we have accounted for the individual astrological impact. The next issue is the universal impact."

Suzanne leaned back and tried to get comfortable, settling in for another lecture.

"You see," he began in his customary style, "we are coming into a new age of awareness as Uranus enters. That planet will hold the position for at least another year. Which means everybody will go through startling perspective changes. It is a time for deep introspection and preparation."

Again, the threesome glanced at each other in confusion.

"Which means that strange occurrences will happen on a fairly regular basis, making the strange seem normal and the normal seem strange."

"I can vouch for that," Suzanne said dryly, looking at her counterparts.

"The other consideration that we must factor in," Rahmin said, staring at Ian, "is karma."

The questioning glances that went around the room seemed to make the old man smile broadly.

"Yes, karma," he said triumphantly. "We have our personal astrological influences to consider. That affects the way we react to our environment. The astronomical position of planets, which defines the way our environment pushes or pulls us along, much like the tide. That one creates market fluctuations in the economy, sets the tone for wars amongst nations, etcetera. And, karma, which determines who will come into our personal space, at any given time, to teach lessons still unlearned from a previous existence. So one must ask several diagnostic questions about all three in order to determine the answer to why something may be happening to them. Very simple."

"I beg to differ with you, sir. It all seems extremely complex to me."

Again, Ian's customary thinking frown returned. Although his eyes were steady on his subject, Rahmin, one could tell that his mind was racing to another question a million miles away.

Rahmin nodded, looking at Ian with an empathetic expression. "I would daresay this must be very difficult for you."

Becoming defensive, Ian stiffened and glanced at Leslie. "What do you know of my circumstances? Have I been discussed?"

"Easy, Scorp," Suzanne said, chiding him. "Let the man finish."

"I haven't had a chance to tell him the whole story, Ian. Honest." Leslie looked from Suzanne to Ian, her voice pleading for understanding. "Just bits and pieces, since he was already gone on the retreat. We've been trading answering machine messages, just to confirm this meeting. All we really discussed is the stuff on the first day . . . about the spell, and everything."

Ian's shoulders relaxed, and Suzanne let out a silent breath. The last thing she wanted was a

misunderstanding between Ian and her best
friend. They were both important to her, but it
was difficult to manage these two live wires. She
wanted to ask Rahmin if the ground wire ever
got a break, or did it always have to get struck
by lightning?

"Mr. Chandler," Rahmin began slowly, but
never losing his peaceful smile, "your secret is
safe with us. We are all your friends. You must
learn to trust."

Ian cast a skeptical glance in Suzanne's direction, but when she nodded, he relaxed. "What
secret would that be?" he hedged, his attorney
personality taking over.

Rahmin just shook his head and chuckled.
"Still a skeptic. Ah, well, to be expected."

Suzanne patted Leslie's hand. Her friend still
seemed upset that Ian had challenged her loy-
alty. In the back of her mind, Suzanne knew
that she'd have to clean up that mess too, before
they all left.

"I am not a skeptic. Just a man of reason."

The smile on Rahmin's face broadened. "Is it
reasonable to find yourself displaced in another
time, in another reality, but feeling as though
you've known all the participants in this drama
for a lifetime?"

No one breathed for a moment.

"What draws you to the conclusion that I have
any frame of reference for such a situation?"

Ian's cool response was riveting. She had
seen him angry, drunk, passionate . . . but

never predatory. It was electrifying, like watching a courtroom drama unfold.

Rahmin's peaceful expression changed slowly. It was as though his face was becoming older as they sat there staring at him. Nothing actually changed, per se, but his eyes aged . . . Where they once held a curious merriment, they now looked very wise and quiet, all mirth from his face dissipating. His new demeanor was unnerving, but there was something about it that signaled the group not to speak.

"What was the argument in the garden about?"

Rahmin's statement made both Suzanne and Ian draw a simultaneous gasp.

"What did she conceal from you . . . Marissa?"

Ian leaned forward and looked at the old man squarely. "I have told no one of an argument. Not even Suzanne. But she dreamed it."

Standing quickly, Suzanne stepped away from the sofa and headed for the door. "Ian, the journals. Where are they?"

"In the guest room night stand," he called out in the otherwise silent room. "Bring all of it."

When she returned, she could tell that no one had spoken while she was gone. Producing her journal and Ian's papers for Rahmin, she handed them to the elderly man and sat down.

"I don't need to read it," he said mildly. "I just need to feel it."

Again, no one spoke or exchanged glances. Their focus remained on Rahmin.

"Betrayal. Deep and haunting betrayal exists

with passion and love. You were never sure, though. You could not rest until you found out what it was. She died with the secret buried within her."

"The pregnancy?" Ian whispered. "I didn't know. I just found out . . ."

"No," Rahmin intoned distantly. "That she didn't know until it was too late. But, the other . . . you questioned her, and she couldn't tell you. Wouldn't tell you."

"We fought about her parents— about their strong feelings against our union."

"But," Rahmin went on, "in your soul, you sensed more. When you got close to it, she fled."

"I apologized because I brought her to tears. Then, I kissed her hard, and we were done with it. *They* abducted her. She didn't flee." Ian stood and paced, raking his fingers through his hair with frustration. "What else could there be?"

Blinking hard, Rahmin yawned, his old demeanor slowly returning. "I just know there's more. Her soul fled, not her body. She allowed them to take her, but knew that would not be enough to stop you. Eventually you'd find her, and find out about this secret, and confront her. Then your love would be severed once and for all. She knew that you'd never forgive her if you became aware that she had a dark secret that she didn't share. The most secretive sign of the zodiac, ironically, demands the greatest disclosure from their lovers. Therefore, she died. It was an easier alternative than losing you. Trust.

Forgiveness, Ian. You have come to a cross-roads."

Suzanne stared at the old man, tears surprisingly coming to her eyes for no reason. "She slipped away in her sleep, Gran said. She died young, of influenza."

"One just doesn't decide to get a plague, then die from it! This has gone beyond the pale. It is a ludicrous theory."

Walking toward the door, Ian turned around once to face the group. "I am tired. I need to take my leave to rest. I am sorry for the abrupt departure."

For a while, no one spoke after Ian left the room. Finally, Rahmin cleared his throat, leaning forward and clasping his hands around Suzanne's.

"Dear restless soul . . . this time, you must tell him. His lessons are trust and forgiveness. Yours are faith and hope. It is very simple, yet so very hard."

The old man removed the documents from his lap, and placed them on the coffee table. "I am tired now, as well. So much energy to absorb . . . so very exhilarating."

That wasn't exactly the description she would have used, but Suzanne politely nodded anyway. "Thank you," she said in a quiet voice. "We really appreciate your help."

Rahmin touched her face and smiled knowingly. "Your lover will be fine, as soon as he stops this denial. He cannot accept that his Marissa was anything but pure and good, which, ironically, is what she wanted him to believe for eternity. We must be very careful of what we pray for, for the wheels that we may set into motion. Because we just might get what we think we want. Herein lies karma, and karmic debt. There is always a price . . . always a consequence.''

They walked Rahmin to the door, and Leslie looped her arm around Suzanne's waist as they stood on the porch. She had been unusually silent, which Suzanne hadn't noticed until Rahmin drove off.

"You're her, Suzanne," Leslie said quietly, touching her face as they stood in the moonlight. "And you love him . . . and have made love to him, haven't you?"

Suzanne let the tears fall in the darkness without wiping them away. The multiple realities of Leslie's questions had washed over her as soon as Rahmin had implied them. She did love Ian. She had made love to him. Was she also Marissa?

Closing her eyes, she swallowed down a sob and reached for Leslie. "Yes," she whispered against her friend's shoulder. "Oh, God . . . yes."

Seventeen

Fatigue continued to weigh heavily upon her as they drove to Gran's. Last night, Ian had been so upset that she had just left him alone to think. She understood all too well what it meant to require space. Time to hash out a problem in one's own mind, before having to confront others. Hadn't she demanded as much of Leslie and Ian the day before? So how could she impose her need for human contact on him now?

Breakfast had been almost painful, each of them moving about like ghosts sharing the same space. Ian had been polite, as had she. But neither seemed to want to discuss trivia, even at the cost of isolation.

As Suzanne pulled into Gran's drive, she cringed inwardly. Knowing Gran, she would become immediately suspicious. Then again, maybe her blunt, cheerful comments might draw them both out. At this point, Suzanne was beyond careful, planned behavior. She had been beaten into submission and forced to accept the unpredictable flow of things. All she wanted now was, for the comfort between them to return. She didn't care about zodiacs, stars,

or karma. She wanted to hear Ian's easy laugh,
see his broad, confident smile, and to feel the
warmth of his arms encircling her again.

She missed him, what they had become. Before Ian came into her life, she could readily
accept her isolation. In fact, she had become
used to it. He brought chaos, excitement, and
passion. New emotions that she'd wished for, but
hadn't a clue about how to handle when they
presented themselves to her. She fought those
changes vigilantly, begging God to return her to
her old, staid life. He did. Now what? How was
she going to go back? How could she stand the
silence of her own space? How in the world was
she going to go back to a celibate life, devoid
of passion?

Perhaps that's what made her weary. Constantly fighting against her own emotions, which
constantly exploded within her. It had taken
every ounce of strength not to get out of bed,
walk down the hall, and climb into bed next to
Ian. She wanted to take in his scent, to feel his
warm body next to hers, hear him breathe as he
slept. But she didn't, when maybe she should
have.

"Are you ready?" she asked quietly, bringing
the car to a stop.

Ian only nodded and opened his door.

It was going to be a tough night.

This time, when Gran answered the door,
hugging them both and dragging them over the
threshold, the old woman looked worried. Her
face did not have the same cheerfulness that al-

ways made one feel welcome. Gran was withdrawn, just ever so slightly. But enough that Suzanne could see something was wrong.

"Gran," Suzanne whispered, leaning down to kiss the old woman again. "Do you feel okay today? Have we come at a bad time?"

Unexpected tears filled Gran's eyes, and she hastily blinked them back. "Oh, and I promised that I wouldn't be so silly when I saw you two. This is ridiculous," she fussed, scolding herself as she wiped her eyes. "Just old age. Getting sentimental in my years."

Ian took Gran's hand and leaned forward, issuing one of his warmest smiles. "Dear lady, you will never age, and tears are quite appropriate for any occasion you desire. I just hope that we haven't upset you too badly in the last few days. I begged Suzanne to bring me to you, that I might thank you for your kindness in person, from the bottom of my heart."

Gran covered her mouth with her free hand as new tears spilled down her wrinkled cheeks. Struggling with emotion, she took a few short breaths before speaking. "This is why I adored him when I met him, Suzanne. A consummate gentleman, your Mr. Chandler. Kind enough to flatter and tolerate an old woman . . . even after all we've done to him."

Suzanne and Ian exchanged glances, and he leaned forward again to kiss Gran's forehead.

"Whatever slight you may perceive, all is forgiven. It is not even remembered."

Reaching out her hand, Gran stroked Ian's

face tenderly. "Oh, dear man . . . how can I ever repay you? And, you don't even know, do you?"

Appearing confused, Ian shook his head and cast a questioning glance at Suzanne, who said nothing.

"I must go call Mrs. McDonnell, and freshen my face. I wanted this to be a fun visit for you two, not so gloomy. I promise that I will have collected myself when I return."

Gran rose on shaky legs, allowing Ian to help her up. Then, as though she could bear their company no longer, she hurried out of the room, clutching her hands to her waist.

"What was that all about?" Suzanne asked, her heart pounding fast. "She was so upset. I've never seen her like this before. Do you think I should call a doctor?"

Ian shook his head. "I don't know what came over her, but she seems to feel like there has been some wrong done. I can't imagine what Cecilia Hamilton could have done to either of us. I don't think her problem is physical."

"Maybe she's worried about the false papers?" Suzanne said nervously. "Knowing Gran, she'd feel guilty if anything went wrong with the transaction. Or, maybe she feels somehow responsible for this time travel stuff, but that doesn't make sense. She wasn't even there when Leslie and I did it."

"You're probably right about the papers, Suzanne. That's what I thought too. So, I just wanted her to know that, whatever the outcome, I appreciated the effort."

In that instant, she knew he understood. Somehow he had crossed over the very fine boundary
into female logic. It was the same way she felt
when she saw the burned food in the microwave,
and the ragged bunch of flowers he'd picked and
set on the kitchen table. It was the effort, not the
result. And, it was also startling that she had
crossed the boundary of male thinking when
he'd described his business idea. She hadn't
given him credit for the effort, or his courage to
try. She had been singularly focused on the probable results.

"Oh, Suzanne, Ian, it's so good to see you!
Please, don't stand up for me."

Mrs. McDonnell had come into the room, cus-
tomarily sweeping them into a warm embrace.
Yet her rosy, efficient expression held fear,
something Suzanne had never seen in the
woman's eyes before.

"Dear heart, give me your hand," she whispered, pulling Suzanne to her. "I hate to talk
to you about these things in such a way, but I
must be brief. Your grandmother will have my
head if she finds out that I've confided in you."

Suzanne searched the woman's face, and in
her heart she understood before Mrs. McDonnell said a word.

"It's Gran's health, isn't it? She's failing?"

Mrs. McDonnell's eyes filled with tears. "Oh,
child. She's eighty-four years old, and promises
us to live forever. But her kidneys . . . and her
heart . . . Oh, dear girl, every morning when I
go up to wake her, I say a prayer. It has been

answered so far, but I know, there will come a day . . ."

Suzanne covered her mouth and fought back a sob. "Why now, though? She seemed in perfect health last week. And— "

"I know. I know," the older woman said, patting her face. "But that was the most energy I've seen her have in a long while. She was so excited that you were coming . . . but, she's starting to scare me. She's been putting her effects in order . . . giving things away . . . making me write lists, and calling Mr. Barnes, the attorney. They say, with old people, that their mind is half the battle. If they no longer want to be here, that's when they leave us."

"But Mrs. Hamilton seemed to have such a rich and happy life. Her granddaughter obviously loves her, she has a full social calendar— it's not as though she were abandoned, without a soul to care for her?"

Mrs. McDonnell looked at Ian and shook her head sadly. "That's just the thing. I don't know what's come over her lately. She's happier than I've seen her, but also getting sicker. She's not what I'd call depressed, but she seems to be making preparations. Try, dear hearts, to cheer her up. I don't know what else to do . . ." Mrs. McDonnell's voice trailed off in almost a sob. "She's like my own mother. And I couldn't bear it."

Both Ian and Suzanne gave Mrs. McDonnell a reassuring hug, vowing to do whatever they could to lift Gran's spirits. But that was the strange part. Gran didn't seem to be particularly sad. She just seemed to be having a bout of sentimentality . . . something everyone experienced from time to time.

"Well, that's better. I do thrive on the theatrical," Gran exclaimed, sweeping into the room and appearing quite revived. "Poor Mrs. McDonnell. She must tolerate my mood swings. Why, I can remember when I went through the change," Gran chuckled, giving Ian a wink, "that poor woman had to endure such angst, till I thought she'd take her leave of me. Perhaps I'm just going through a second phase of it."

Suzanne had to smile. Gran always had a way of springing back to life, just like the new blooms of her rose bushes. To Gran, depression was intolerable. Self-pity was strictly forbidden. High drama was always the order of the day.

"Well, Gran," Suzanne said, giving her a sly smile, "it would serve you right to go through it twice. Especially since it never seemed to affect your social life." Instinctively, Suzanne knew that a little game of wits always cheered Gran.

"Are you talking about sex, Suzanne, in your own cryptic way?"

Ian muffled an embarrassed laugh, and looked down. Suzanne's cheeks burned in only the way Gran could make them. She'd thrown her grandmother a veiled challenge, one designed to get her talking about her many exploits . . . but she had never expected an open debate on the subject.

"I was just saying that— "

"That I never became a dried up, menopausal old woman? Humph," Gran scoffed. "Who in the world would ever want to do that? Give up men? Oh, not on your life."

Forced to chuckle, Suzanne pecked her grandmother on her cheek. "That's what keeps you so young, and lovable. Is that your secret?"

Flattered, Gran smiled. "Absolutely. It is better than any youth supplements or face creams you can buy. It— well, perhaps this is not a conversation for mixed company," she added with another laugh, casting a knowing look toward Ian. "So, how are you two lovebirds getting along?"

This time Ian's face flushed, and he looked away quickly before answering. "My friendship with Suzanne has been most fulfilling. Your granddaughter is a very kind person."

Gran smiled and winked at Suzanne. *"Fulfilling?* That's nice."

"Gran, please! You're incorrigible," Suzanne protested, standing to accept a tray of finger sandwiches from Mrs. McDonnell.

"Well, I just wanted to know if things were going along as they should. You can't blame an old woman for her curiosity."

Ian coughed, and picked up the tea pot. Focusing on the obvious diversion, he busied himself with his task.

"Gran, now don't pull that 'I'm a poor, old woman' routine. You selectively use your age to get what you want, and you know it." Suzanne laughed as the elderly lady wrinkled her nose and made a face.

"Oh, drats! Caught again, by my clever grand-daughter. Father used to always say, if you want a straight answer, ask a straight question."

Suzanne's body tensed. One never knew how far Gran would go. Anything was possible.

"So, Mr. Chandler, what do you want?"

Ian almost spit out his tea, and he looked at Suzanne nervously before setting down his cup.

"Me?" he asked in an unsure voice.

"Just like an attorney," Gran said smiling, adding sugar to the hot liquid in her cup. "They always hedge, and get you to be specific first. That way, they only address the question at hand, not the possibilities at large."

"How did you know that I used to be an attorney?"

"Oh, we needn't go over the obvious," Gran said, dismissing the subject with a wave of her hand.

Ian smiled. "Then let me rephrase my question. When you ask me what I want, in what area of my life do you mean?"

"Perfect!" Gran exclaimed, winking at Suzanne again.

"Gran, can we just visit today? It's been an eventful week, and—"

"Oh, I was hoping that it would be," she said knowingly. "Now, back to your question, Mr. Chandler. Let me consider it." Gran stirred her tea slowly, and looked at him hard. "How was it?"

Suzanne nearly dropped her plate.

"Fantastic!" Ian's smile had a wicked charm about it, and he sipped his tea calmly.

Gran looked at him with a newfound respect. "I'm impressed. This man won't scare off. Gets right to the point."

Aghast, Suzanne looked at both of them, still gaping.

Ian closed his eyes, and leaned his head back. "Mrs. Hamilton, it was the most interesting, fulfilling . . . mind boggling . . . creative . . . experience in all my days. The feeling I had was positively indescribable."

Suzanne's mouth went dry, and she swallowed hard to moisten it. Gran sat back in her chair, and cleared her throat. For the first time in Suzanne's life, she thought that she might actually be witnessing her grandmother blush. For once, Gran was more embarrassed than she.

"Well," Gran said, fidgeting with her cup. "I am certainly at a loss for words."

Ian smiled harder. "Dear lady, it was the most exhilarating week of discovery— "

"You needn't go on," Gran protested.

"But, I have needed to tell someone who would listen," Ian insisted, ignoring Suzanne as she vigorously shook her head.

"But, that is so personal, so, uh, er— "

"Mrs. Hamilton, I must. Pray, let me continue. Your granddaughter is simply amazing. First she opened my— "

"Oh, dear God." Gran set her tea cup down and clasped her hands in her lap.

"Let me just say that Suzanne showed me things I've never known."

"Ian, please," Suzanne whispered, her voice catching in her throat. "A little respect for my—"

"You are correct," he said calmly, not bothering to hide a chuckle. "I shouldn't go on and on, to hog the conversation. Forgive my passion, dear. Your grandmother wouldn't be interested in my boyish excitement over finding a job, and starting a business. Now, would she?"

"You rat!" Gran laughed, leaning forward to slap Ian's knee. "You scoundrel! You cad! You positively wicked man!"

Suzanne let out her breath and joined Gran's laughter. "He is *terrible,* Gran. I assure you. This is what I have had to endure all week!"

Ian sat back, his smile one of smug triumph.

"I deserved every bit of it, sir. Point well made," Gran said still chuckling. "Oh, Suzanne, he is precious. Now, do tell me, *specifically,* about this business idea."

Their afternoon was spent sharing stories, philosophies, and friendship. As their visit wore on into the evening, it was finally Mrs. McDonnell's urging that broke up their little party, amid protests. Ian had kept Gran in stitches of laughter, and occasionally Mrs. McDonnell would peek her head into the room and join in, casting a thankful glance before disappearing again.

"Ian, thank you so much for cheering Gran up. I couldn't have done it. Leslie couldn't have done it. And I know that Mrs. McDonnell or any of Gran's stuffy bridge partners couldn't have done it. She needed a little male flattery and attention."

Ian leaned back in the passenger seat and chuckled. "She's quite a lady, Suzanne. I love teasing her and the sound of her laugh. She's so much fun to be around, and misbehaves so badly."

Suzanne laughed. "Can you imagine what she must have been like at sixteen? Or at twenty-five? Especially, in *her* day? Oh! Her parents must have literally pulled their hair out."

Agreeing with a chuckle, Ian slapped his leg. "Suzanne, she would have been considered a complete outrage, but loved and adored by everybody. They would have talked behind her back, and insured that she had an invitation to every ball."

"Just like Les said. The grand Gran! Belle of the ball, Mistress of Ceremonies."

"The question is, which ceremonies?"

Suzanne looked at Ian for a second, and giggled again. As he joined her laughter, she could feel their old connection return. It was a slow and subtle change. Gran had returned their gift of company with a gift of her own. High spirits.

"She really likes you, you know," Suzanne said quietly as the mirth began to dissipate.

"I truly can say, Suzanne, that I like her as well. She is a special woman, and you've been fortunate to have someone like Gran in your life. I never did."

She looked at him for a moment, as a silent understanding passed between them. She had never asked him about his family or his friends or his life prior to Marissa. Suddenly she wanted to know everything about this man. Who was Ian Stewart Chandler, deep down inside?

As they crossed the threshold of her home, she turned to him and touched his face. "Ian, sleep in my room tonight. I've missed you."

His eyes held a quiet intensity, but within the depths of them, she also saw a new openness. No longer needing words, he led her up the stairs. The isolation had been banished. The fear had been conquered.

Dare she hope for tomorrow . . .

Eighteen

The weeks had flown by as though they were days. It was already the middle of May, and it seemed like they had met just yesterday. Yet it also seemed like they had spent a lifetime together . . . enjoying mornings before going to work, looking forward to homecomings and arguing over philosophical differences. Without realizing it, they had fallen into a comfortable routine. Only tiny ups and downs patterned the landscape of their lives. What others might have called boring was for her a wonderful normalcy to be appreciated.

Plunking down the hamper, Suzanne pulled the colored clothes away from the whites, and began a new wash cycle. She didn't even mind that Ian and Mike had piled up junk, which they called collectibles, in her basement and laundry room. Nor did she mind that they dirtied up her kitchen at least three days per week. When the fellas came over to hash out the latest way to drywall the small abandoned garage Ian had found, she didn't care. At this point, it was all still theoretical and fun.

But, when Mike plunked down a thousand

dollars, along with Ian's five hundred, to begin a lease . . . she worried.

No matter how much she protested, her three friends outnumbered her on any vote, yet, she still felt like an exciting part of it all. Though they had dubbed her with the responsibility to keep them all on track, she didn't really mind. Somehow, she had been included as the little group's fiscal manager. That was her second job. The behavior police. Not always fun, rarely appreciated, but at least she was involved.

Leslie was the group's cheerleader. Ian was the market developer and researcher. Mike was the nuts and bolts guy. It truly amazed Suzanne how talented each of them were in their roles. It didn't take long for them to appreciate the need for each position. When one of them would go off on a tangent, another member of the group would pull in the reins.

Suzanne smiled as she thought about Mike's reaction to not having two bathrooms installed, especially when Ian suggested that they save money with an outhouse. Leslie, who cheered anything, had said, "Great idea. We could rent Port-O-Potties, like at parades, and save a bundle." Mike had been appalled, his sense of aesthetics traumatized.

Suzanne chuckled to herself as she folded a dry load of Ian's work clothes. Most of the time the arguments around her kitchen table had gotten so heated that she had been the only voice of reason. Yet, Ian always had new ideas that were useful. Like getting the high school kids and local artists to help paint the godforsaken facility with murals. Actually, when they were finished, it did look pretty good.

But, Mike . . . They did have to get a hold on him, and slow some of that enthusiasm. Leslie had begged them to make him stop picking up every old sofa, broken chair, and three-legged table he saw on the trash piles. Their garage looked like a furniture store, and Leslie could barely drive the Pontiac for the way Mike had loaded it up with knickknacks in the trunk.

But, despite the chaos, even she had to admit that the guys had cleaned up a good deal of the refuse . . . sanding it down, polishing it up, or adding a coat of paint and polyurethane. To see the once abandoned garage turned into an eclectic paradise had been inspiring. It really didn't matter to her any longer whether their crazy idea would work. If all they had gotten out of the exercise was a deeper friendship, a lot of laughs, and company, it was well worth the fifteen hundred dollars the guys plunked down. It was the effort, not the result, that counted.

Pulling more clothes from the dryer, Suzanne stopped and looked at the already folded pile. Each day, she had become farther and farther removed from the hustle of Center City. She had found herself looking very hard at trash, and wanting to get home and into jeans. The sleek, orderly office space that had once been her haven no longer had the same gravitational pull on her. Unconsciously, she had found herself

haggling with street vendors for cheap plants,
bringing them home as a token contribution to
the business. When she stumbled upon an old,
beat up, antique cash register in a South Street
junk store window, she'd felt like she had discovered the pyramids.

How had a transition like this taken place? If
she didn't get her mind back to work, she knew
she'd be poorer. But, somehow she also knew
that she was experiencing a wealth of spirit that
could not be compared. Maybe this was what
Leslie had found? Peace amongst the chaos.
Suzanne considered her friend's noisy children,
dirty kitchen, and big, lovable teddy bear of a
husband. They had problems, they had fights,
but they had a way of looking at life as though
their cup was half full.

In the last six weeks, Suzanne could admit that
her cup was half full. She didn't even care if
she had to work in that crazy coffee house, serving espresso and pasta salad to wacky artists.
Her spirit was buoyant. She didn't even care if
she had PMS . . .

Suzanne stopped, and stood still. When was
the last time she had gotten her period?

Quickly leaving the laundry room, she went
into the kitchen and flipped the calendar. This
was mid-May. No. Before that, was April. No.
Before that, was March . . . Yes. God would not
do this to her. No. Not at forty-one years old!

She turned around and around in the same
spot on the floor, trying to get her bearings.
Okay. Calm down, she told herself. Logic it out.

She'd been under severe stress. Sure, they hadn't used condoms. He was from eighteen-seventy-two— they didn't have AIDS. But she wasn't stupid. She'd used a sponge. That device had a ninety-eight percent coverage ratio. She'd sue the manufacturers if she was one of the two percent! No. She had to be rational.

Taking a deep breath, she walked more slowly to the counter and collected her purse. She could just make herself feel better for about ten bucks. Any drugstore carried those little tests. She'd buy one and in five minutes go back to sorting clothes. She would not ruin a perfectly good weekend by becoming unnecessarily hysterical. Any—

The sound of the phone ringing stopped her train of thought. Annoyed with the intrusion, she picked it up quickly and answered the call.

"Suzanne," a familiar woman's voice said through tears. "Dear girl, she's gone."

"Mrs. McDonnell?" Suzanne didn't want to acknowledge the voice.

"Child, yes. Your grandmother," she said with a sniffle, "passed peacefully in her sleep last night."

Suzanne let her body slump against the refrigerator. No! her brain screamed, yet her voice said the words. "Was she in pain? Was it a heart attack? Dear God, what happened?"

Mrs. McDonnell let a small sob escape. "No, love. The doctor's said she just died of old age. Natural causes. We had tea together, earlier that night. We'd laughed and talked about old times.

Then she told me to go to bed, and to kiss you when I saw you. But, she always talked like that. After your last visit, she seemed so much better."

Suzanne let the tears fall, and she covered her face with one hand. "She called me last night, too. We stayed on the phone for nearly an hour. She had asked about the little business, and had spoken to Ian briefly. Then she wished us good luck. There was nothing in her voice that would tell you she wasn't feeling well."

"But that's just the thing, love. I think she might have been feeling just fine." Mrs. McDonnell paused to blow her nose. "Maybe, my dear friend Cecilia wanted to go when all was well. It was not her style to leave loose ends. She detested unfinished business or clutter. Everything had its place, she would always say, but she was one of the worst offenders of her own rules."

Suzanne held the phone to her ear, and numbly took down the balance of the information from Mrs. McDonnell. Gran had indeed been thorough. She had left no aspect of her own funeral to chance.

"Always giving directions," Suzanne whispered affectionately, when Mrs. McDonnell was done. "Always."

Suzanne stood at the small gravesite with her friends surrounding her. She was oblivious to the two hundred and fifty other mourners that clustered behind her. How did one ever begin to come to terms with such a searing loss? Gran was Gran. There was no replacement possible.

Casting the first rose, she waited for the ceremony to conclude. The sky was flawless, and large fluffy clouds dotted the blue like cotton balls. A perfect day for the grande, Gran, she thought. Picturing the old woman's kind face, Suzanne smiled. "You do have a flair for the dramatic," she whispered, casting her gaze at the crowd behind her, and hoping that Gran might hear her.

Ian squeezed her hand and pulled her closer. She was blessed. There were trusted friends beside her, and Gran had lived a full life. Yet she felt guilty for not being able to accept that Gran was gone. The intellectual side of her brain told her that the woman was, after all, eighty-four years old. But, the emotional side of her, the side that cried, and laughed, and got angry, could never process this reality. She felt crippled. It would be impossible to imagine seeing Gran's mansion with new owners, or not receiving her weekly, outrageous telephone calls. Worse, how would she manage without Gran's hugs, or the way she touched your face when you pleased her? No. There was no replacing Gran.

Filing back to the house, Suzanne walked without seeing the faces of the crowd. She just nodded and stopped as people walked up to hug her, but she couldn't concentrate on what they were saying. It all sounded the same, anyway. Just like at the wake. Everyone had a warm, memorable story to tell about Gran. Perhaps that's the way it should be, she thought. People remembering your light, your laugh, your non-material gifts. If that were Gran's only legacy, then she had shared it abundantly.

"Suzanne, I know this is an awkward time, but I didn't just want to mail you correspondence, or call on the phone. Your grandmother and I were very dear friends, and she made me promise to check on you personally."

Blinking away her daze, Suzanne made her mind focus on the man standing in front of her. "Mr. Barnes. Oh, yes, Gran was very fond of you. Always. Thank you for handling everything so well."

"It was the least I could do," he said shyly, taking her hand. "But, if I could have a private moment with you?"

Ian let her elbow go, and nodded to Mr. Barnes. "I promise to have her back in a moment. Thank you," he said.

The older man led her into the study, obviously familiar with her grandmother's house.

"Please, Suzanne . . . have a seat. This is an awful time, but I had no way to know when I could speak freely to you alone."

Suzanne took the Queen Anne chair next to him and stared at him blankly. "I don't understand what this is about. Is everything all right with Gran's affairs? Don't they normally hold a reading of the will, later, or something?"

The old man reached into his breast pocket and pulled out a pair of half-reading glasses, placing them on the delicate bridge of his nose. As he dug into his breast pocket again, he sighed, and Suzanne could see moisture begin to fill his eyes.

"This is difficult, Suzanne. Yes, you are correct. Under normal circumstances, there is a formal reading. And there will be. But as an attorney, I advise you to challenge it, and will give you all the documentation you need to fight it."

Shock sent a wave of adrenaline through her body. "Why on earth would I challenge Gran's will? I loved her, and wouldn't do anything to go against her wishes. I'm appalled that you'd even consider advising me to do so."

"Please, hear me out," the old man said firmly, unfolding the paper in the process. "As I said, this is difficult. I can't bear this. I loved her too much, and have known your family too long."

Suzanne could see the old attorney battling with his composure. Something inside told her to remain quiet, to hear the man out.

"She has always been a tad eccentric," he began softly. "Anyone who really knew Cecilia understood this. However, lately, she was taken with this notion of reincarnation . . . or time travelers. I don't know what you call it. But we all assumed that this was just another one of her zany phases, and that when she had exhausted her curiosity, she would drop it like so many other things."

"Mr. Barnes," Suzanne said evenly, "my grandmother may have been many things, but she was neither senile nor crazy. I cannot argue her beliefs now."

"Wait," he said quickly, placing his hand on her wrist to stop her from rising. "She thought she owed someone a debt. A substantial family debt. To the tune of three million dollars, Suzanne."

Suzanne blanched and settled back into the chair. "What?"

"This is precisely my dilemma. Now, by law, I cannot show anyone the will before it is read in front of all the beneficiaries at the same time. However, I am in no way held accountable for a personal letter sent from one lover to another," he said dropping his eyes. "You may have my correspondence. You may need this in court."

Suzanne took the note and read it slowly. When she looked up, Mr. Barnes was still holding her in a steady gaze.

"Do you understand the implications of this?"

"I think so," she said quietly, as she folded his letter.

"Let me be plain about what this means. I have had innumerable arguments about this with Cecilia. In fact, we practically fell out of each other's favor because of it. I refused to draft this insanity into a will, and she went so far as to go to another attorney to have it done. However, she did keep me listed as her executor."

Too stunned to respond, she just nodded.

"You see, somehow, she believed that she accurately researched some horrific melodrama that took place over a hundred years ago. Cecilia had

it in her mind that the Hamilton family de-
frauded their attorney out of his investment portfolio with Franklin Savings Fund— an old fund
that survived the bank crashes of that era. The
reason they took his money was dubious at best,
even if they did steal it. According to Cecilia, it
had to do with repayment for their daughter's
lost virginity and the stain on her reputation. She
believed that the Hamiltons planned to use this
money to *bring out* one Marissa Hamilton in the
London social scene, then use the attorney's money
as an inducement and dowry for a wealthy, gen-
teel husband. I argued with Cecilia until I was
blue in the face . . .

"Then," the old man continued emphatically,
"she said that Marissa's father thought that it
was his right to make the attorney suffer such a
loss, with the knowledge that another man had
the legal right to the girl *and* the money."

The old man snatched off his glasses, and put
them back in his jacket. "She claimed that had
it not been for this three million dollar investment, in a bank that didn't fail, the Hamiltons
would have been financially bankrupted. Susan,
she even believed that her ancestors went so far
as to try to have the man killed in some drowning
accident!"

Suzanne didn't say a word as she handed the
letter back to Mr. Barnes. "My grandmother
said that she had researched this?"

"Yes!" he said standing and pacing toward the
windows. "And that's why she was willing to give
your inheritance to a complete stranger. But,

we're not just talking about three million dollars, Suzanne. There would have been a way to manipulate that outrageous sum, and pay the bastard off. But, no. Cecilia, with her misdirected sense of justice, insisted that we had to give him all of the furnishings, stocks, bonds, liquid assets— she even went to Sydney, her accountant, who called me with questions, asking him to compute the time value of money on three million from eighteen seventy-two! This is madness, and I won't allow it! You must fight this, dear child. You must propose that your grandmother was insane, and had been conned, or you'll lose everything but the house. That's all she's left you, Suzanne. The house!"

Suzanne stood slowly, trying to re-orient herself. She felt as though she might pass out. The sudden change of position made her dizzy and nauseated. "I need some air," she stammered. "Please, just some air."

Leslie looked down at the plastic strip and handed it to Suzanne. "What are you going to do? Jesus, Suz. Have you told him?"

Suzanne curled her head down to her knees and wrapped her arms around them. Sobs tore through her, and she didn't bother to try to quiet herself. "How?" she sputtered. "How did this happen to me?"

Pacing in the tiny bathroom, Leslie's voice bounced off the walls as she continued to walk back and forth. "Geeze. Did you use a sponge every single time? Think back. Hard. Every time?"

"I haven't had a chance to think about it," she wailed. "They just buried Gran this morning! When was I supposed to think about it?"

Leslie squatted down next to her by the toilet, and put her arm around her shoulders. "Listen to me. We can get through this. Maybe it's a blessing, you know?"

Suzanne threw off Leslie's arm. "A blessing! Three days ago, Gran was alive . . . and I just thought that I was a little late, from stress. Okay. Then, before I can go to find out, Mrs. McDonnell tells me Gran passed. In the space of three minutes, my life changed. I was too upset about Gran to even worry about what I was sure was just my own miscalculation. Then, as I'm leaving her grave, her attorney comes up to me and tells me that my grandmother has left *Ian Stewart Chandler* my family's entire inheritance! And, as we're driving home, Ian thinks I'm just grieving about Gran, but *nooooo!* Now, I have three things to worry about. Because, Les, I didn't use anything that first night we made love. I remembered! So now I'm pregnant, my last living relative is dead, and a man I don't even really know stands to wipe out my family's entire legacy! Wake up, Leslie! This is not a blessing. It's a freaking nightmare!"

Nineteen

"Will you explain this sudden meeting in Philadelphia, and why I had to take a day off from work?"

She refused to answer Ian, and she looked at the traffic ahead of her with disgust. "We're going to be late. Damn! Of all days."

"Listen, you haven't seemed well since the funeral. Maybe we should have just postponed this junket?"

Turning in her seat to face him, amid the stalled traffic, Suzanne's eyes narrowed. "Oh," she muttered, not able to keep the sarcasm out of her voice, "You'll want to go to this meeting."

Ian stared back at her and shrugged. "As you wish. But, in my opinion, you do not look well."

She swung her body away from him and gripped the steering wheel tightly. Fear continued to pump adrenaline through her veins. It was as though everything around her was moving in slow motion, getting in her way, and blocking her final destination. She had planned this for days. All she had to do was keep her cool until she got there. Once they got to the office, she'd know.

Now more than her own life hung in the balance. This venture was far from theoretical.

Thankful that Ian had fallen silent for the balance of the ride, she turned her car into the lot and parked. Just a few more minutes, she told herself as she paced while the lot attendant tore off the stub and gave it to her. She didn't even wait for Ian when the man was done. Turning on her heels, she hurried up the street, and went into the high-rise.

From the chrome pane of the elevator, she could monitor his worried expression without directly acknowledging him. She was many things, but a stupid woman, she was not.

An eternity seemed to pass as she waited for the doors to open. Pressing the button for the seventeenth floor, she stepped into the car and kept her eyes on the slowly ascending numbers. Again, she silently cursed her luck, as the doors opened and closed slowly, letting people on and off each floor. She had taken the local.

When her floor came, she didn't even signal him. She just brushed past the other passengers and bolted for the free space of the hall. Who cared how he felt? Who cared if he had ever seen or ridden on an elevator? There was something more important to attend to than that. The past, and his eighteen seventy-two understanding was not reality. The future. That was now her reality.

"Suzanne, it's good to see you again." The receptionist smiled and looked from Suzanne to

Ian with a cautious expression. "Have you discussed everything?"

Suzanne just nodded, and gave Ian a warning glare to be quiet. She certainly didn't need him to begin pummeling her with questions again. Her nerves were rattled enough.

"Good, then you can go back now. They're waiting for you."

The walk down the corridor seemed as though it would take forever. She had to force herself not to run to her destination, by counting each footstep along the way.

"Suzanne. Mr. Chandler. Thank you for coming today."

Mr. Barnes held Ian in a fixed glare, and his knuckles were white as he gripped the edges of his desk.

She ignored Ian, as Mr. Barnes introduced the others in the room. They had come too far for her to give Ian any indication of what might happen next. No, the element of surprise would be all hers. *Trust?* Did Rahmin say that Ian Chandler was to learn trust? She almost laughed at the irony. He's going to *get* a trust, not learn it. And, yes, she would have to *hope* that he hadn't swindled Gran somehow.

Opening with the customary legal rhetoric, her grandmother's attorney rattled off a list of charities and foundations that Cecilia Hamilton's money would fund. Turning his attention to the small group, he looked up from his papers as he addressed each participant, awarding them their share of the will. When he got to Mrs. McDonnell, his expression warmed.

"I know this has been hard for you. You two were so very close."

"Yes," she said wiping her nose with a tissue and shoving it up her sleeve, "there was no one like her."

"Well, she obviously felt the same way about you, Mrs. McDonnell. She thought you should have the property in London, fully furnished, with a three hundred thousand dollar stipend for your many years of faithful service and friendship. In her own words, Cecilia Hamilton wrote . . . 'She was like a sister to me, one that I never had. At other times, like a daughter, or mother . . . much kinder than my very own, whom I lost early.' "

Mr. Barnes stopped as Mrs. McDonnell dissolved into tears, hiding her face in her hands.

"She was like me Mum. None like 'er, God rest her soul." Looking upward, Mrs. McDonnell crossed herself and blew a heaven-ward kiss. "Dear Ceci, thank you, love, for all you've given me. Where could an old housekeeper with no education go? And you even thought to shower such kindness down on me before you left us. God bless ye."

Suzanne swallowed hard, and leaned over to hug Mrs. McDonnell. It was nearly impossible not to cry as the old woman wailed with a mixture of grief and happiness. She wished she could be that free. Open enough to release all of the tears within her, not caring who saw, or what they might think. Once the older woman had settled down, apologizing profusely for the outburst, Mr. Barnes continued.

"We are almost finished," he said tightly, glaring at Suzanne. "Are you sure about your decision not to contest?"

She didn't look at the others as she nodded. There was nothing to say. It had been done. Her grandmother had made her decision, and there was no way to explain that Cecilia Hamilton wasn't mad. In that instant, Suzanne wasn't sure who was crazier— her grandmother for giving away a fortune to a stranger, or herself, for deciding not to challenge it.

This was the ultimate acid test. She knew that she had to know for sure in her heart, beyond a shadow of a doubt. It was all planned. She'd look in Ian's eyes as the will was read. If even a flicker of a scam registered . . . if anything he said, did, or thought, came across as opportunism, then she'd never carry to term.

He could have the money. She had grown up around it, and saw that money alone couldn't make one happy. Despite what people said, it didn't make things easier unless you earned it. Her affection for Gran had nothing to do with putting in time until her dotty old grandmother died. No, she'd seen kids and grandchildren who behaved this way. She saw the unholy alliances that families made for the sake of money. That's why she had gone off on her own years ago.

But she was also not foolish enough to want to

be a forty-one-year-old, working, single mother. Never! She didn't care what the popular views were, she didn't want that. If she had, she could have found a sperm donor long ago. She wanted a unit. A loving partnership for her child. Money, child support, or inheritance couldn't buy that.

Mr. Barnes just shook his head, and she could see him holding back his words as he fought for propriety.

"Very well," he said dryly after a long pause, not looking at her as he read the document to himself. "But, Suzanne . . . this breaks my heart."

Mrs. McDonnell cast a confused glance in her direction, but Suzanne just patted the woman's arm for reassurance.

"And to my dearest, Suzanne, I offer you new life. One devoid of old debts, one wiped clean of an ugly past. I bequeath you my house, without the contents. May you fill it with laughter and love, not furniture. May you hang on to your memories, rather than hang them on the wall. And may you always have roses, my love. For the thorns of life are many, but so are the blooms."

"Dear Lord!" Mrs. McDonnell exclaimed. "She could not have turned that poor child out into the world without a penny?" she said, her expression wild-eyed. "Surely not, Suzanne. I know for a fact that the girl was everything in the world to her. There must be some mistake?"

"I assure you, Mrs. McDonnell," the attorney

said in a near whisper, "I was as shocked as you were when I read this."

"Please," Suzanne said, battling tears. "I know what she meant. She was not crazy. We'd talked about it at length . . . one day in the garden alone."

Shaking her head, Mrs. McDonnell wiped her eyes. "Merciful heavens."

"Well, and here we have our last portion."

The attorney held Ian in a glare so filled with hatred that Suzanne could only turn away. Instead of looking at Mr. Barnes, she focused on Ian as the balance of the will was read.

"And, to Mr. Ian Stewart Chandler, I first apologize for his inconvenience. My family owes him more than his life, since they tried to break his soul. I attempted to figure out how much a man's heart was worth. Or, for that matter, his dignity, or his future, all of which the Hamiltons stripped away. There seemed to be no number large enough to cover the damages. Thus, I had to make it up, as best I could imagine.

"For our grievous family debt, I leave you thirty-seven million dollars in liquid and capital assets. This will be issued in the form of investment instruments and cash, the balance of which will be furniture from the original Hamilton property. Spend it well, with only my best wishes for your future. You were a friend to me and my family, Ian Stewart Chandler, and I am sorry that they treated you so badly. You were a man of honor, even to the end. Thank you for offering your forgiveness, without ever remembering the transgression."

Suzanne had watched Ian's face during the reading. His expression had never changed. Not once. She wasn't even sure that he'd blinked. A cool terror held her in its grips. She was dealing with a vampire, and now carried its spawn within her. The chilling reality made her ill, and she stood without speaking and fled the room.

As she ran down the long corridor, it felt like the walls of the narrow space were closing in on her. She was vaguely aware of voices behind her, but everything was so distant, so far away now. Her only objective was fresh air. To be out, and free, and away from this madness. All of it. Spells, time travel, karma, zodiacs, ghosts. She'd run and run, until her legs couldn't carry her.

Bolting past the secretary, she felt like a trapped animal. There was no time to wait for the elevator doors— she had to get out. The fire escape offered her only hope before they caught her. In two easy moves she had opened it, slamming her shoulder against the thick steel to get it to move. Freedom. The dimly lit stairwell provided an exit, and she hung onto the rail as she rounded landing after landing, trying to get away, to put the madness behind her.

Voices carried down from the stairs above her. The faster she ran, the more distant they sounded, the lighter she felt, until there was nothing . . .

* * *

"Dear God, man. What are they doing to her back there?"

Leslie held his hand, as Mike paced in front of the doors marked Emergency.

"Mrs. McDonnell called," Leslie said quickly, squeezing his hand in the process. "But she was hysterical. She said that Suzanne had probably flung herself down two flights of stairs. Oh, Ian. She wouldn't have tried to kill herself, would she?"

Ian stared at the doors and spoke without looking at his distraught friends. "I don't know. I was trying to take it all in, trying to figure out what debt Cecilia Hamilton spoke of, when Suzanne bolted. She just began running, and crying, and she wouldn't heed my calls. When I got to the bottom, she had fallen."

Mike looked at him, the fear registered clearly on his face. "They have to be able to do something, you know. All this fancy equipment. All this modern medicine. They can practically bring people back from the dead."

All three friends looked at each other, exchanging the unspoken horror with their eyes.

"It's happening again, isn't it?" Leslie said quietly. "She's running. That's why she's still unconscious."

Ian pulled his hand away from Leslie's, and dragged his fingers through his hair. "I can't bear to lose her again. Make her come back. Leslie, do whatever you do. The doctors lost her the first time. Their medicine didn't work. Use your magic, your spells. I beg you, make her come back to me." His voice broke with emotion, and he turned away from them to hide his face. What had he ever done in his life to deserve to twice witness the loss of his heart? If God wanted payment, he could have all of Cecilia Hamilton's inheritance. If He required penance, he'd give up his dreams. If He required blood, he'd offer up his life.

"Ian," Leslie said tearfully, touching his shoulder. "I don't have any magic, just faith. God wouldn't take a pregnant woman like this, would he?"

Ian turned to face her, and held her upper arms tightly. "Say it again? I am not hearing this."

"He doesn't know, Les? You mean, she didn't tell him yet?" Michael came over to Leslie and stood before her. "The man has a damned right to know! How could she not tell him?"

Ian released Leslie's arms, and allowed the tears to fall without censure. "Because, she never respected me, and never will. I had nothing to give her but false hopes and dreams. Cecilia's inheritance means nothing. It was a lottery, not earned. I'll never be what she wants."

Leslie grabbed him, stepping around Mike, but he twisted out of her hold and began walking down the hall toward the exit.

"It's not true," she yelled behind him. "You were owed it this time. That's not what it's about. She doesn't believe— she's not sure you would still love her."

The last part of Leslie's sentence made him

stop and turn around. When she caught up to him, Mike was right behind her.

"The drowning— you don't remember the argument with Marissa before you went over, do you? She knew that they were going to take your accounts from Franklin Savings. She knew that they were going to send her to London. But she couldn't bear to tell you, because that would mean a total break from them. It was you or them, Ian. She wanted to keep you both. You were asking a seventeen-year-old girl to divorce her family, social circle, everything she had ever known, to be with you. They wanted her to give up the most precious gift to her soul to be with them. You all tore her apart. Then they found out about the baby— and it ruined everything. Her father was so angry that the money didn't matter any longer. There was no price to be had but your life."

"What *are* you babbling about? Can't you see the man is in pain. This is no time . . ." Michael's words trailed off as Ian walked toward the double Emergency Room doors.

He stood to the side, allowing a team of doctors to whisk in another patient, then he entered.

"I need to see her," he said evenly to the nurse by Suzanne's bed. "I will not be moved."

Ignoring the woman's protest, he bent over and kissed Suzanne gently. "Madame, if she dies in your care . . . at least give me the opportunity to say goodbye."

"Are you her husband? Or closest relative?" the woman asked irritably.

"Yes. I am."

"All right, sir. You can stay. But, let's not be too dramatic. She's taken a tumble and has banged her head pretty good, but she's not in danger of dying." Opening the chart, the woman read from the information without looking up. "We have her scheduled for an MRI. The X-rays didn't show any broken bones. We'll probably keep her for at least twenty-four hours for observation, because she came in unconscious. And— "

"She's pregnant."

The nurse looked at Ian closely. "Why in the hell didn't anyone tell us when we took her back for X-rays? Damn it! We asked the question when she was admitted. This hospital is not liable for any results, based on the faulty intake information we received from you."

"Nurse— you said liable?"

"Doctor," the woman corrected.

"Doctor, I wasn't even aware, until her friends arrived, that she was pregnant. What liability is there? What damage? As her husband, and her attorney— "

The woman paced out of the curtained area, and Ian could hear her yelling instructions.

"We've got a serious problem in D. The lady's husband didn't tell us that she was pregnant before we did the series. Call administration and legal, and get somebody down here. She's already in a high-risk category because of her age, and we just nuked an attorney's wife."

Ian wasn't even looking at the woman when she came back in. His sole focus was Suzanne's bruised face, and he allowed his fingers to gingerly graze the surface of her skin. A knot of anguish tore at his stomach, and he let out his breath in small, regulated increments. How had he been so foolish— so possessive not to understand? Was he so arrogant in his past that she couldn't trust that he'd still love her no matter what her family had planned? Did she think he'd blame her for the money? Didn't she know that she was worth much more than that to him?

"Please, come back to me," he whispered. "I understand. I'm not who you think I am."

"Sir, we need to work on her. We're concerned about her lack of response, and the unconsciousness. We've got to get some head shots and find out if the brain is swelling or if there are any contusions and hematomas. If you'll have a seat outside, we'll come and bring you back in when we're finished."

Ian stared at the doctor, and the two other medical team members that had joined them, without releasing Suzanne's hand. "Don't ask me to leave her. I cannot."

Letting out a slow breath, the doctor conceded with a warning. "Okay. Just don't get in our way."

Ian sat in the hallway chair, watching Suzanne take slow even breaths through the window. He had witnessed the marvel of modern medicine first hand. Yet, with all of the awe-inspiring devices, all of the breakthroughs, they still couldn't get her to respond. As the doctors had conferred, speaking to each other in low tones, he could tell that they weren't sure of what was wrong.

Not much had changed since his time, really. At least not the way people reacted to things. The learned men were thought of as gods, able to correct any situation. He knew the games professionals played, he had play acted as a great one himself . . . where the facade of all-knowingness was given to the masses, while the truth came out behind closed doors. When it was all said and done, even the play gods had to pray for a solution.

He had been there for so long, sitting in the same position, that the distraction of the nurses filing in and out of the Intensive Care Unit no longer irritated him. They seemed like uniformed phantoms, checking their little machines, writing notes, adjusting tubes. Busy work. None of their ministrations had even caused Suzanne to stir.

By eleven o'clock he had forced Leslie and Michael to leave. What was the purpose of making them hold a vigil in the hallway? They had a family, children to tuck in bed . . . The harsh reality of Suzanne's condition sent another wave of remorse through him. What if she didn't pull through? What if she lost the baby? What if there had been some horrible damage to the child?

He needed to move, but feared being thrown

out of his makeshift post. Instinctively, he knew that it had only been tolerated by the hospital staff due to guilt. Fine. If some hospital regulation had been breached, and they feared liability, then he'd use that to his advantage to stay as close to Suzanne as possible.

Cautiously monitoring the nurse who sat at the unit's center, Ian stood and stretched, slipping behind the glass enclosure. Just one more kiss . . . He would remind her again how much he loved her. It wasn't scientific, it wasn't medicine, but he hoped it would be magic.

Peering down at her, he touched the soft strands of her hair gently. The bruise on her cheek had darkened to a deep crimson and, as he looked at it, a stabbing ache went through his chest. How had this all happened so fast? One moment she was sitting safely beside him and they shared a future. The next moment everything had shattered. She had run from him as though she were afraid of him. And nothing that his mind could fathom explained it.

As he leaned over and brushed her mouth, he whispered, "If you leave me now, Suzanne, I'll only come looking for you." He wasn't sure where the comment had come from. It just seemed familiar. Since he'd arrived, he'd had difficulty with keeping his old life separated from this new one. Conversations, people's names, faces . . . everything had started blending together the longer he stayed. "Cecilia will never forgive you for this, darling, even though she thrives on theater."

Ian straightened himself, and looked down at her. Nothing. Not even a flutter of her pretty lashes. Defeated, he turned to go back to his post, when a sound stopped him.

Almost afraid to move, he turned slowly and stopped, listening closely for any sign of movement from Suzanne's body. Something deep inside of him pulled at his reason. It didn't make sense, but he had to follow the gut hunch. What if Leslie was right? What if Mrs. McDonnell's theory had been right, about people willing themselves to die?

Moving back to Suzanne's bed, he tested the theory. "Gran, I'm sure, would be appalled."

He waited, holding his breath, watching Suzanne's face for any sign of life. Then, he saw it. An infinitesimal flutter of her lashes, a fraction of movement beneath her lids. Squatting immediately, he brought his face close to her ear. "Gran loved life. She will be angry with you for letting go."

When Suzanne's brow knit into a frown, he stood immediately and called for the nurse. Causing a commotion, he yelled until three station attendants were at his side.

"She moved!" he said excitedly. "I saw her. She's alive!"

Their blasé responses shook him. "Did you hear what I said? She needs help."

"Sir, if you don't calm down, you'll have to leave," one of the nurses said, gripping his arm tightly. "This is an Intensive Care Unit, and all of the patients on this ward are either critical, or here for highly monitored observation. We cannot tolerate this level of disturbance on the ward."

"But she moved," Ian pleaded in a lower, more controlled voice. "Do something."

"Sir," another one of them said firmly. "Coma patients can have a wide range of movement without actual consciousness. It is often upsetting to loved ones, who are hopeful. Why don't you go home and come back tomorrow when we've moved her to a normal room? We just wanted to keep her in I.C.U. until we can properly evaluate the head injury."

Ian stood firm, and moved closer to the bed. "Look, I'll show you." Leaning in to Suzanne, he spoke to her in a normal volume. "Suzanne, are you taking over Gran's role? She thrived on theater."

All of the staff looked down for a moment, then shook their heads. "Sir . . ."

"Audrey, look," one said, motioning excitedly. "She's smiling!"

"Call Doctor Wainsford. Tell her the patient is coming around. Good work, sir. Keep talking to her."

Ian knelt by the bed, stroking the hair away from Suzanne's forehead. The sounds of people walking about, giving orders, and checking her vital signs didn't stop his flurry of words.

"And, I am indeed going to tell Gran how badly you behaved. Then I'm going to suggest that she come to dinner at your house, and I'll show her your journal."

"Uhmmm, Ummm."

Ian fought the urge to gasp, kissing her forehead instead.

"This time I'm going to tell her everything. Especially about the baby."

"No."

Suzanne's mouth had mumbled the word. It was garbled, barely coherent, but it was magic.

In that small interval, when they revived her, and began rushing about her bedside again, he understood. Having lost her twice, but being given another chance, it became clear to him how precious the commodity of time was to man. To waste it on angry words, vengeful acts, and despair was to throw away diamonds. Every moment that he had left to cherish her, would be appreciated as though it were a diamond. And, he would mark his realization with one for her finger.

Twenty

"You gave us quite a scare, lady." Leslie leaned down, kissed her, and smiled.

Her head hurt. Bad. Almost too much to talk. But, as Suzanne gazed up to Leslie's face, she forced herself to smile. "I was taking the short-cut to the parking lot."

Leslie's smile vanished, and she squeezed Suzanne's hand hard. "You weren't trying to hurt yourself, were you? I mean, I know it's been rough, and I know you have a lot of decisions in front of you . . . but, you've gotta have faith, kiddo."

Suzanne shut her eyes briefly to the harsh overhead lights. "No, Les. Believe me. This was not intentional. There are a few more clinical ways to take care of my problem. I just needed air, and had to throw up, when my heel caught the last— "

Dropping her hand, Leslie stepped back from the bed. "You cannot be still thinking of— I can't believe it. He'll be crushed!"

Suzanne stared at her friend for a moment. "What do you mean, he'll be crushed? Ian doesn't know anything about this. He's happy.

He's gotten whatever he came back from the past for. I'm done."

"What?" Leslie didn't lower her voice, even after the nurse came in and scolded her.

"I don't care if everybody hears this," she nearly yelled, pacing at the side of the bed. "Well, Suzanne, you've finally found my limit. We are through. That's it, you're on your own."

Confusion slammed the words around in her brain, bouncing them off of Leslie's volume. "What are you talking about, Les? I'm in no condition to argue with you about the realit— "

"Just shut up, Suzanne! Put a muzzle on it. Do you think that all Ian wanted was some inheritance? Do you think that the cosmos would allow a man to come through the vortex just to pick up a check from some eighty-four-year-old woman before she died!"

"Shhh," Suzanne winced, rubbing her temple. "Look, I don't know how this works, but— "

"But the man went out of his mind when he thought you were going to die. He didn't tell you that, did he? Don't believe me? Ask the nurses or the doctors. He threatened to sue the whole damned hospital if they didn't put a chair outside of I.C.U. where he could see you. He made Michael call Mr. Barnes and Mrs. McDonnell, and promise to have papers here the next morning so he could sign them with a witness."

"Papers? For what?"

"To give you back the entire cut from Gran's money. What else? Do you think he's been to Vegas or to Disney World while you've been in

here? Mike finally got him to change his clothes
in the men's room after two days, and go with
him for coffee in the cafeteria. He's been sta-
tioned at your bedside like an armed guard, just
watching you sleep. And when he found out you
were pregnant, he flipped!"

"What? Who told him? Mike? He wasn't supposed to know either."

Leslie folded her arms across her chest, and
glared at her. "*I* told Ian. The man had a right
to know."

"You thought he had a right to know?"
Suzanne pulled herself up to a sitting position,
cringing as a pain shot through her skull and
shoulder blade. "That was for me to tell him."

"Yes it was, wasn't it? But we thought you were
a goner. Remember? So, we told the poor man,
okay? And, he cried like a damned baby in the
hospital hallway, begging me to work some magic
to bring your ungrateful butt back here. Then
he stood by you and kept talking to you, while
the nurses ignored you. That's love, Suzanne.
Unconditional. Free of Charge. Real. So don't
you dare give me this righteous my-business-has-
been-violated crap!"

Leslie stalked to the far side of the room taking deep breaths. Again, it seemed as though so
much was happening around her, and she
couldn't make heads or tails of it. She vaguely
remembered having a conversation with Ian
about Gran. Something about theater. It was all
so fuzzy, but she could recall seeing his face as
she faded in and out of sleep. Her head hurt

too much now, to even consider an argument. But, she'd never seen Leslie this angry with anyone, other than Mike. And papers? Had Ian actually given away thirty-seven million dollars? Impossible. Not as much as he wanted the business. Not as important as money and status and prestige were to his male code of honor.

"Look," Suzanne said quietly, lying back down and closing her eyes. "Let's talk about this when I get out of here. I can't think right now."

"No."

Suzanne opened her eyes and stared at Leslie. Her jaw was set firm and her hands were on her hips.

"In a few moments that wonderful guy will be back. He'll see you awake, and want to tell you how much he loves you . . . and maybe talk about the baby."

"I don't want to discuss it now."

"Well you're *gonna!*" Leslie yelled, bringing the nurse back again. "And, you are *not* going to upset him. You are *not* going to hurt him. You are *not* going to send him away, feeling like he's lost you again. If you treat my brother like this, I'll *never* forgive you!"

Both women fell silent and just stared at each other for a long time, until Leslie's breathing had normalized.

"Did you hear what you just said?" Suzanne whispered.

"Yeah," Leslie said quietly. "Where did that come from?"

Suzanne closed her eyes and inhaled. "It's happening again, isn't it?"

Leslie didn't respond immediately, but came over to the bedside. "Look, Suz. All I know is that the man is honest, and he loves you. Nothing comes in a neat little package, you know?"

Suzanne opened her eyes and swallowed again. "You are the third person to tell me that. I can't take it any more. Really."

Leslie shook her head. "No, *I'm* the one who can't take it any more, Suz. You've got it all right under your nose, and can't even see it. You'll wind up a rich, frustrated, wrinkled old woman. Gran was trying to save you from that. She knew if she gave it all to you, you'd be so afraid that some guy just wanted you for the cash that you wouldn't take the risk to live. *She* had courage. *She* lived. The least you can do is honor her memory with an attempt."

Moving from her side, Leslie headed for the door. "I want you to lie here and think about what I've said. And I mean it, Suzanne—you mess this up, and we're done. Don't call me. Don't write me. It's over."

She watched Leslie's form as it passed through the door into the busy hallway. In all of their years of friendship, Leslie had never turned her back on her this way. They'd had spats, disagreements, of course. But this was serious. There was a disheartened quality about her friend's tone that caused shame to wash over Suzanne.

How could she have known that Ian loved her this much? The last thing that she clearly remembered was the stoic way he accepted Mr. Barnes' pronouncement. The man didn't even flinch when his section of the will was read. To her, that signaled a level of calculating cool that only predators possessed. How was she to interpret Ian's behavior? Unlike Leslie, she wasn't up on reading people's minds, figuring out their karmic consequences, or their zodiac alignment. She was a pragmatist, and could only take her cues from the vast reservoir of business experience that she had accumulated. It was the only skill that never failed her, even while this madness was swirling around her. Now Leslie was telling her that rational deduction couldn't help her.

Everything was falling apart. And a baby? Ian hadn't asked her to get married. She couldn't assume that he would, especially after getting a windfall from Gran. Maybe he'd want to buy a cadre of Playboy Bunnies and tour the modern world. Or become a music video producer, and have fawning teenage groupies, like Opal, at his beck and call. Not be stuck at home, married to a pregnant, not-so-Barbie, feminist. Money did weird things to people, especially men. She'd seen how power had corrupted. Her own father was the best example.

Leslie wasn't being fair. She didn't know how Ian would react. How could Leslie guarantee that he wouldn't change? And what if Ian did ask her to marry him? She was forty-one years old! A baby? She was in a high-risk category. That meant she might have to stop working in order to carry to term, if she could. She didn't have anyone to take over the business for her. Gran had left her with a white elephant— a mansion that could take up to two years to sell, with a heavy real estate tax burden, not to mention inheritance taxes. If Ian got bored and ran off, where would that leave her? Jobless, with no money until she could sell Gran's house, and with a newborn baby. It was just too risky.

Suzanne pulled the thin hospital spread up to her neck as a shiver ran through her body. Who was Leslie to guilt trip her? She'd already thought about this from every angle before the will disposition meeting. She would have loved to believe that everything would go right, that Ian would be faithful, and not lose his mind with his new bankroll. She'd love to consider a normal life, with him working out his business venture from the ground up. It would be the best of all possibilities if she and Ian could love, and raise a family, and grow old together . . . just like the elderly couple they'd seen walking by The Pretzel Hut in Rancocas Woods.

But, how many women started off with those dreams just to have them shattered? She didn't think that there was ever one bride who had walked down the aisle in her white dress, thinking that she'd be left, or beaten, or divorced. Every one of them probably started off with such hope and belief in a happy ending. What happened fifty percent of the time? The statistics of failure were printed in the newspaper regularly. She had never been a gambling woman, and these odds were pretty grim. Then, to bring a new life into the middle of it? One that could be born with birth defects because she'd waited so late . . .

Suzanne closed her lids as the tears slipped from the corners of her eyes. Why, now? When she had no defense . . . when she didn't have Gran. And, now, not even her best friend.

"How's our favorite patient doing?"

Suzanne tried to force a smile as Ian and Michael came into the room.

"Oh, Mike, I'm getting there. But, I'm still pretty tired."

"I told them that I only want you to have the best care," Ian said in a soothing voice while coming to her side. "Only the best for both of you."

Suzanne cringed, but did not allow her expression to change.

"Where's Les?" Mike asked, looking around as though it were an afterthought. "We told her to stay with you till we got back."

"Probably just had to run to the ladies' room. Guard duty is tiring. You all look like you need a break," she said, patting Ian's cheek, and closing her eyes again to escape his loving gaze. "Try to convince him to go home tonight. The poor man needs his rest."

"I will not abandon you to this place," Ian said, kissing her forehead. "That is out of the question."

"I'm going to be fine, you can check with the doctor." She returned his kiss and pushed a stray hair from his forehead. "Now, if you want to really make me happy, you will go home and get a good night's sleep. If I'm worried about you, then I won't rest."

Ian kissed her again. "If anything happened during the night, I'd never forgive myself."

"It won't," she reassured him, gazing at Mike for support. "Look at him, Michael. He hasn't slept in three days, and he's literally swaying on his feet. Please make him go home and put him to bed."

Ian hesitated, and cast his gaze from Suzanne to Mike, then back again. She could see the conflict in his expression, and she nudged him as he fought her suggestion.

"Just for one night. You can come back in the morning. Maybe you can fix yourself a decent meal . . ."

Her words trailed off with the look on his face.

"Suzanne," he said quietly, "it's just not the same there with you gone. I mean, I'm unused to not having you to enjoy meals with, or to just sit and talk . . ."

"Listen, why don't you come home with Leslie and me. We'll fix you a good dinner, and either the kids can double up, or you can have the pull-out sofa. That way, we can keep an eye on you for Suzanne, and the doctors can keep an eye on Suzanne for you. I can drop you by the hospital on my way to work tomorrow, and pick you up when I get home. Les can help you call, if you just want to tell her goodnight. Deal?"

Grudgingly, Ian conceded, looking at her once more for permission to leave.

"I'll be fine. Go. Mike, thanks. You're a gem."

"Suz, you two guys are my favorite people. Any time. No trouble at all."

She watched them file out of the room, and her heart ached. Why couldn't it all be as simple as Mike and Les made it out to be? Their view of the world seemed so basic, so uncomplicated . . . and they seemed totally fulfilled. She had missed the window of opportunity to be a blushing, twenty-year-old bride. The clock had ticked well past the hour of having kids, running to PTA meetings, and roughing it with a new husband. There was no way to go back— to cheat the clock and steal a few treasured hours when you'd missed something important.

Forcing herself to face reality, she refused to hope. Hope meant that you got hurt. Badly. Hope meant that your dreams got devastated, and after enough times, you lost faith. That's what had sent her tearing down the hall before she'd fallen. She had hoped that Ian was a man with integrity. That every one of his soft murmurs, and protestations of love, had been true. But when she saw him coldly accept the inheritance without emotion, it had only taken a moment to dash all of her dreams. So much had been riding on his reaction and when the dream vanished, so did her last shred of faith.

Twenty-one

Suzanne tried to take in the doctor's words, as she held the hospital release paperwork in her hands. No one had discussed this with her, not even Leslie.

"I'll go over it again, to be sure that you can make your OB/GYN aware of the potential added risks. When you were admitted, you were unconscious. We asked your husband—"

"My husband?"

The doctor stared back at her and frowned. "Are you having any trouble remembering dates, times, telephone numbers? Maybe we need to run some additional tests, since we never could find out why you stayed out for nearly twelve hours?"

"No, it's just that . . . Please, go on. I'm sorry I interrupted you."

"Anyway," the doctor went on, sounding a little defensive, "when we asked him the standard questions upon admittance, and again, prior to taking you up to x-ray—"

"You took x-rays?" Suzanne let the papers fall to her lap.

"We know that this has to be upsetting, but we had no indication from your husband that pregnancy could be an issue. Plus, with your age, and—"

"What does this mean? Does this mean that there will definitely be something wrong? Does Ian know about this?"

"Calm down, Mrs. Hamilton-Chandler. This does *not* mean that birth defects are a guaranteed outcome. In your age bracket, however, it might be hard to make a determination between what was x-ray related, or age related."

She could not believe what she was hearing, or cope with the conflicting emotions that pulled her in two directions at once. Tears filled her eyes suddenly, and she didn't bother to hide them from the doctor. "Does he know," she asked while battling for composure, "that something could be wrong with the baby?"

The doctor looked down and nodded. "Yes, we discussed this with your husband. Extensively. We hate to deliver this kind of news. The vague, not quite concrete maybes. It only frightens patients, and doesn't help much because there's nothing to do, but wait and see what happens. Your husband has been aware of the situation from the first day of your stay. But we had a hunch, based upon the way he performed in here, that he might not tell you out of concern that you'd worry. However, to hide from a problem, to not deal with it, is not a solution. That only creates a spiral of more issues. That's why it's best for you *both* to know. You should be under an obstetrician's care, one who specializes in high-risk pregnancies, anyway. They should be looking for any damage when they run the ultrasounds, do amniocentesis, etcetera . . . and can advise you on your options, whether you carry to term or, therapeutically abort."

Suzanne stared at the doctor blankly. She had thought these things herself, but, to hear someone else say it? To hear her name changed to Mrs. Hamilton-Chandler and, in the same sentence, the doctor clinically discussing abortion? The collision of concepts, feelings, and emotions, again tore her in two separate directions. "You can't give me a guarantee, can you? A way to be a hundred percent sure? You just don't know?"

Shaking her head no, the doctor leaned against the bed and looked at Suzanne squarely. "You know, Mrs. Hamilton-Chandler, this was the hardest thing for me to accept as a medical student. We all had dreams and aspirations of becoming physicians, so that we could heal the world and eradicate disease in our lifetime. And we studied hard under the masters, especially those of us who went on to intern at the university teaching hospitals. In institutions like these, my colleagues and I get to see the newest technology come down the pike. At one point, I was sure that almost anything could be solved through modern medicine. I thought that it was just a matter of time and research dollars. But, in every doctor's life, there comes the 'out of the ordinary' case. The stumper. Where the odds are stacked against the patient, none of the standard treatments work, and we throw up our hands. Sometimes we get hit with something where we have to admit that it's a crap shoot. That's all odds are . . . fifty-fifty, eighty-twenty, who knows?"

"But what are the odds in my case that something could be wrong?"

Dr. Wainsworth sighed. "Suzanne, who knows? I could tell you five percent, and you could be the unlucky five percenter. I could tell you eighty percent, and you could be the luckiest twenty percenter in the world. Like I said, who knows?"

Choking back a sob, Suzanne pressed on. She had to know, even if she was pretty sure about her decision. "But then, how do you guarantee anything at all?"

"We don't," she said plainly. "In this profession, we hedge. We call it medical science, but, it's more like an art. So, we say, 'in most cases, the probable outcome will be XYZ percent.' We don't give anybody a five year, fifty thousand mile, warranty. And, with pregnancies you *never* know what's going to happen. There are so many variables that the most sophisticated computer couldn't calculate them— like gene pool from the time both of your families began, environmentals, stress factors, diet, predisposition and exposure to certain diseases . . . That's why I never wanted to go into obstetrics. Too many hopes, dreams, and lives are riding on those cells splitting correctly, and approximately seven healthy pounds of humanity coming into the world. If you ask me, you'd have to be half shaman, half doctor, to predict the outcome."

Suzanne wiped her face and blew out a breath. "So, this baby could be healthy, despite my age, the x-rays, and anything else?

"Possibly. And if you were a twenty-year-old woman, with no health problems or drug dependencies, with no exposure to x-rays, who ate only healthy food and walked two miles a day . . . I'd still tell you the same thing. Possibly. That you had the *probability* of delivering a healthy baby. I would never say that I *guarantee* that you'll have no problems. Pregnancy is like many things in life— it's fun getting into the predicament, it's tough to go through the process of getting out of it, and you don't know what you've got until it's in your hands. Understand? Roulette. No guarantees, red or black. We're not gods, we're just humans."

Still in a state of shock, Suzanne could only nod in agreement as Dr. Wainsworth signed her out of the hospital. A doctor, a medical doctor, had told her that nothing was guaranteed. The woman had pulled back the curtains and told her that even the scientists gamble. What it seemed to boil down to was hoping that your choice was the correct one. After that, it was up to some higher powers that be.

"She said I could come back in, after she had a private exit consultation with you. Do you need more time?"

Suzanne looked down at her feet, hoping that Ian would not discover she'd been upset. There was no need to worry him. He'd been through enough over the last couple of days. "Yes," she said quietly. "I promise to hurry along. It'll just take me a minute to get my things."

Her home had been restored to its original silence, no longer the headquarters of frenetic entrepreneurial activity. Ever since she had returned two days ago, Ian had practically converted it into a rest home. He'd removed the answering machine from her room, only leaving the telephone with its ringer turned off for emergencies. He forbade her to come up and down the stairs, and had plugged the little kitchen television into the bedroom wall jack. Each morning he made breakfast, and brought it upstairs to her, coming home for a late lunch to check on her, and again at dinner time.

When she had asked about the progress of the coffee house, he refused to talk about it, insisting that any business conversation might upset her. All of the hammering, painting, and sandblasting of furniture was done at Mike and Leslie's house once she was tucked in bed for the night. So were the fun dinners, great laughs, and stimulating debates. Those activities were no longer held at her kitchen table. She felt like an invalid, oddly disconnected, and locked out of everything exciting.

Did she say, exciting? Suzanne flung the magazine she'd been holding across the bed. Since when did she crave excitement, constant interaction, and change? This was not her normal reaction to things. Too much commotion and mess used to get on her nerves. Stability was her watchword. Consistency. Predictability.

Then, again, what had been predictable in her life over the last two months? Nothing. And, hadn't she fought tooth and nail to get things back to what used to be *considered* normal? It was odd how traditional normalcy had been where she started, then wild changes came to be normal, almost expected, and now, she was back to square one. It felt strange.

Everything was so different. Even her relationship with Leslie had changed. It was strained, and Leslie only spoke to her politely, in a calm civil tone that bordered on cool. She knew that her friend didn't approve of the fact that she hadn't made up her mind about the baby yet— and hadn't told Ian that she hadn't made up her mind. Leslie had looked at her, shook her head, and walked out of the bedroom when she declared that she needed more time to think. At first they had debated the subject. Leslie felt that she shouldn't allow Ian to assume any longer that they were a couple having a baby. Guilt wore on her. She didn't want to make him hope, if there was none to be had. But she also didn't want to dash his hope, if there was some.

"Oh!" Suzanne yelled, clutching her head with both hands, then shaking her arms as she looked up. "What do you want from me," she cried out to the empty room. "I'm only human! How do you expect our pea brains to figure all of this cosmic stuff out? If you guys up there had just simply written it down! But signs, messages, and mumbo jumbo? Who can accept it?"

Standing quickly, Suzanne went into the bathroom and washed her face. She had to put an end to this. She had to make an appointment, go to an OB/GYN, find out what her options were, and make a decision. She couldn't take another day of this silent worrying, deciding, hashing it out. She didn't care what the hospital had said about taking it easy for a couple of more days and not driving. She had to get out of the house before she lost her mind. The silence was deafening, and Ian's kindness was destined to kill her, if nothing else did.

After showering and pulling on her sweats, Suzanne went to the Yellow Pages. If her own doctor was booked, surely someone else could take her this morning. It was only nine o'clock, which meant she had four hours before Ian came back home to check on her. If she could get a ten o'clock appointment, then she could be back at home by eleven-thirty or twelve. That would give her an ample window of time to return, and hop in bed, before Ian got there at two. Thank God he couldn't leave during the middle of the lunch rush, she thought, thumbing through the pages and reaching for the phone. Maybe, someone up there was on her side, after all.

She hated doctor's lobbies. No matter what time one arrived, or what time your appointment was, you always had to wait. Naturally, her own doctor was booked a week in advance, and she now had to endure a clinic on the other side of town. Whatever. Just as long as she got some answer from a professional in the specialty.

Suzanne looked around at the women who sat waiting with her. Some where pregnant, some were not, and others had babies with them. Bored, having already read every magazine published during her confinement, Suzanne began to look at the people around the room. Curiosity tugged at her as she tried to imagine why each woman was there. She marveled at the patient expressions of the mothers who were handling incorrigible children. The more she watched them, the firmer she became in her resolve. She was definitely not cut out for this motherhood thing. No way.

"Are you finished reading that one?" a pleasant woman seated next to her asked softly.

Suzanne looked down at her hands, and offered the magazine. "Oh, sure. I was just stalling for time, and not really reading it. Be my guest."

The woman smiled and accepted the magazine. She had a kind face, and looked to be about Suzanne's own age. Like most of the other women around them, she was older, well dressed, and had a professional air about her. If they hadn't met in the waiting room, they could've bumped into each other in Center City.

"Thanks. I hate waiting too. I must have already read every issue that they have in here. Actually, I'm just going through them all again for a second time, since I'm in here so much."

Her comment startled Suzanne. What possible ailment could have a woman in her doctor's office enough that she could have read this stack of literature twice? Not wanting to pry, Suzanne just smiled.

"Are you here to see the fertility specialist, too?" the woman asked calmly, pushing her efficient brunette bob behind her ear.

Suzanne looked at the woman's pearl earring briefly, then cast her gaze back to the woman's face. "Ah, uh, no . . . not exactly. I'm already pregnant."

The woman just sighed and closed her eyes for a moment. "Congratulations. I know how hard it is. Every time I come in here, I say a little prayer . . . but nothing."

Suzanne could see the woman's eyes misting over as she tried to smile and look down at the magazine. Her pain tore at Suzanne, and she felt that she had to tell the woman something positive. If only as a courtesy.

"It'll happen for you, I'm sure. They can do things today that were never dreamed of."

When the woman looked up, pools of tears had formed in her eyes, and Suzanne reached into her purse quickly to produce a tissue.

"That's what we keep hoping. But John is getting so frustrated. The entire process is so humiliating for him . . . and it's eating away at his masculinity every time he has to go back there . . . and, well, you know. It's causing fights at home, like you wouldn't believe."

Suzanne was speechless. What was there to

say? She had heard about this stuff on the news, seen it on talk shows, but never had to personally deal with it, since pregnancy was never her objective. "Listen, when you guys have a healthy, happy, baby in your arms, all will be forgotten. You'll see."

Shaking her head in agreement, the woman dotted her face, obviously trying not to smudge her immaculately applied eye shadow. She had that flawless, I'm-not-wearing make-up, finish. The one that the Cover Girls got away with in cosmetic adds. To look at this woman, she initially gave one the impression of confidence, success, of having it all. But, as the tears streaked her face, Suzanne was drawn to the familiarity of the woman's disguise. She had been that woman for a long time. The type that people envied, without ever knowing the hidden pain within her.

"Thanks," she finally said, accepting another tissue from Suzanne. "You didn't come here to listen to my problems. Everybody that comes into the high-risk office has something to worry about. I mean, we really shouldn't complain about our lives. John and I have a lovely house, good jobs . . . take vacations from time to time. I guess we should be thankful."

Suzanne stared at the woman. Suddenly something made her reach over, and cover the woman's fists which were clasped tightly in her lap. "But you two want a child. And there's nothing wrong with feeling angry or sad because you don't have one. All you're asking for is a complete family, and just because you have the other material things, doesn't mean that those things can take the place of the greatest gift in the world. Go easy on yourself, okay? I've been where you are. I know what that feels like."

The woman looked up at her, and allowed the tears to streak her face without dotting them away. "Oh, yes. You understand. How everybody makes you feel so guilty for trying to pursue a career and waiting until you've chosen the right man. And, when you're like us, and have waited too late sometimes, they almost laugh at you. You can see it in their eyes. That haughty, 'See what you get for waiting so long— told you so.' "

As the woman's bottom lip trembled, righteous anger coursed through Suzanne's body. Gripping the woman's hands tighter, she leveled her gaze at her. "Damned right, it's not fair. Just because you wanted to live a little bit of your life first, and try to provide a decent home for your family? And so what if your Mr. Right took a little longer to find you, than everyone else's did? Does that mean you're supposed to be denied the very basic fundamentals of a family unit? It's an outrage how insensitive people can be."

Suzanne looked around and lowered her voice. "I'm sorry. I guess I'm just passionate about the issue. Listen, I'm forty-one. How old are you?"

"Thirty-five," the woman said softly. "We've been trying for four years now."

"Well, my Mr. Right didn't come along until

this year. I had been to at least fifteen baby showers by then, been everybody's bridesmaid, and have cried myself to sleep on more nights than you can imagine. I stopped going to the park on Sundays, because seeing all of the young mothers out with strollers would make me depressed. And, I hated being *Aunt Suzanne*. Hated it. Because, no matter how excited the kids were with the toys I brought them, or places I took them, nobody came running up to me to kiss their boo boos when they fell down, or called me Mommy. I know the pain, and I'm so sorry that this is happening to you. Really, I am."

Grasping Suzanne's hands tightly, the woman looked deeply into her eyes. "It only took you guys a year?"

Immediately, guilt washed over Suzanne. How could she tell this desperate woman that they hadn't even tried? How could she admit that, in a moment of glorious, unplanned passion, she and Ian had created a life? The realization made her heart race. *They had created a life*. The way it was originally designed to be created. Without doctors and technology, during love and passion. The old fashioned way.

"Yes," Suzanne finally whispered. "But, have faith and don't give up hope. I'll pray for you."

Smiling, the woman gave Suzanne's hands another squeeze. "Thank you so much for your support, and talking to me this morning. I'm glad you didn't say things like, 'oh, maybe you two just weren't meant to have children,' or 'you can adopt,' you know? I understand that nothing is guaranteed, and that even if I do get pregnant, there will be risks. But, I just want to feel that life growing inside of me. One that we made together. It sounds so corny . . . but I really want to be a Mom."

Suzanne's heart broke as she looked at the hopeful expression on the other woman's face. Just a few kind words, an intimate sharing of herself, had changed a complete stranger's day. Immediately, she understood how wealthy the simple act of giving made you. There was no way to describe the feeling that ran through her body, when the once tense and depressed woman, smiled again. There was no amount of money that could buy that feeling. No drug in the world could reproduce it. And, yet, the woman had given her something priceless in the exchange. A deeper appreciation for what she already had.

"Listen," Suzanne said in a cheerful whisper. "I'm going to be coming in here regularly, to get my check-ups. Is this when you normally come in?"

Perking up more, the woman nodded yes.

"Then I'll try to schedule my visits at the same time. Maybe you and I can have coffee, or herbal tea after our appointments, if you have time?"

The woman beamed. "Oh, yes. I'd love to, and will make the time. I need a little support when I come out of my doctor's visits. Most of the time the news is so disappointing."

"Well, then, it's settled," Suzanne said confidently. "We have a weekly date to support each other."

"But what did I do?" the woman asked, appearing surprised. "You were the one holding my hands, keeping me from falling apart. I just sat here and blubbered like a fool in this waiting room," she added with a shy giggle. "I promise not to, next time."

Suzanne smiled back at the woman warmly. "Oh, no . . . never promise not to show how much you care, or how human you are. That's never foolish. And, as for what you gave me, I'll explain the next time we get together," she said looking up as they called her name.

Standing, Suzanne turned to her new friend, held up her right hand and crossed her fingers. "Do you believe in magic, or a little luck?"

The woman laughed. "At this point, I'll believe in anything, as long as it gets me pregnant."

"Then, on the next stormy night . . . set up a romantic dinner for two. Have a good bottle of wine, and light a fire. Then let nature take its course. I promise we'll laugh about all of this one day over coffee when the kids are driving us nuts."

Raising her right hand and crossing her fingers, the woman laughed. "To magic, a little luck, and good friends. Suzanne, my name is Melinda. Melinda Krantz. And I promise to pray for you, if you'll pray for me."

Suzanne bent down and gave Melinda a hug.

"Here's to good luck. Good friends. And magic.
Keep the faith and never give up."

"And, you're sure? They said that they'd
monitor you, and everything?"

Suzanne smiled as Leslie paced before her.
"Yup. They won't be able to tell for a little
while— nothing's guaranteed, you know?"

"Did they say for you to stay off your feet?
Did they give you any special instructions?"

Chuckling, Suzanne leaned back on the rack
of books behind her. "No. So, for now, I'm
just going to take it a little slower, but not really change anything special about my routine
until they tell me to. I just wanted to share
this with you first. Oh, Les. I'm so happy!"
Suzanne opened her arms and went over toward Leslie to hug her. "You were so right.
Just have faith."

Returning the hug, Leslie held her back. "Suz,
listen to me. I don't want to see you hurt, or
disappointed. If something goes wrong— and I
pray that it doesn't, but— "

Suzanne stopped Leslie's words with another
tight hug. "Is that what I used to sound like?
Always doom and gloom and worst case scenarios? Aw, Les. I'm so sorry. Please, don't turn into
me. Don't stop being your optimistic, lovable,
Sagittarian self. I can change. It took some doing, but really, I can."

Leslie's eyes filled and she walked back to the
register, ringing a customer's order without

looking up. When the patron left, she gazed back at Suzanne.

"Suz, listen. I've been doing a lot of soul searching myself, lately. I didn't have the right to impose my belief systems on you, or to change your life. Mine didn't turn out so hot, you know. Like, I'm working in a bookstore for five bucks an hour. My kids don't have a sure way to go to college. And Mike has taken a second job on weekends to finance his dream. All because I was this flower child, got pregnant without a plan, and we had to get married. If I had been more like you, and had gotten my act together, maybe Mike wouldn't be forty-two, frustrated, and— "

"No. Don't." Suzanne said quietly, stemming Leslie's self-lacerations. "Oh, honey . . . why is it that we all want what we don't have? Each of us brings something to the table. Your zany humor and ideas have kept everyone going for years. But, who cheers up the cheerleader when she's down? We've all dumped on you, blamed you, and fussed at you for your crazy schemes. We've fought you as you've dragged us into them, and cursed you when they didn't go quite as planned. But when have we ever stopped to say thank you? Thanks for the great time, Les? Thanks, for picking us up when no one else would, Les? Thanks for being the cruise director and taking us on an adventure, Les?"

"I didn't take Mike on an adventure, I trapped him. Not on purpose, but accidentally. But, that doesn't matter. That's how he feels. Trapped. I mess things up pretty bad sometimes, Suz. I just don't want to do the same to you. If something's wrong with the baby, God forbid . . . I couldn't face you, knowing that I might have— "

"Don't even go there, Les. Please."

Suzanne pulled her friend into another embrace and petted her hair. "You give your good wishes from the most open place in your heart. You just try to make others see that the cup *could* be half filled. If it isn't, you will always look for another cup somewhere, or turn the glass to the side to get a better angle."

"Yeah, that's why my sink is full of dirty dishes," Leslie said, chuckling through her sniffles.

Suzanne had to laugh, and she held Leslie back to look at her face again. Even through the tears, her friend could find something funny to say, something to lighten the mood. It was indeed a gift that Leslie possessed. One that she'd always cherish.

"Which of us does this for you, Leslie? And all that you ever ask in return is that we be happy. It isn't fair, and you had every right to call me on it. That's your problem, though. You never set boundaries for any of us. Not for me, not for Mike, not for the kids. My problem is, I set too many. For *everybody!* Myself included. And, by the way, you didn't get pregnant by yourself— unless you have some real magic up your sleeve that I don't know about. Mike helped. And, if he got you pregnant, he had to *enjoy* helping— you know what I mean?"

Leslie looked shocked that she had spoken to her that way. "Yeah, he sure enjoyed it all right," Leslie said giggling. "I think that was the night he asked me to move in with him."

"See, there you go!" Suzanne exclaimed. "And he is also responsible for pursuing his own dreams and making them happen. You've never begrudged him that, or tried to take that away from him. If anything, you've always encouraged him to try out new business ideas. Right? But you've been the convenient excuse until now. Look, until his clock started running out, and the reality of time set in, he was just happy as a clam to go out bowling and chugging beer with the boys on Friday nights. Now that the kids are half grown, and the bills are piling up, you are the sudden cause of his downfall? Don't buy it."

Leslie just looked at the counter and bit her lip.

"When was the last time you guys went away alone for the weekend?"

Leslie just shrugged and didn't look up.

"Would you like to do another magic spell? I've been learning about magic while I was trapped in the hospital and in the house. Wanna try?"

This time, Leslie did look up. A combination of confusion and amazement crossed her face. "You've been studying magic? Alone?"

"Yup," Suzanne said with a giggle. "Sure

have. I just so happen to have some fairy dust in my purse. But don't burn it in the fireplace, though. It's plastic."

Twenty-two

She couldn't understand it. What was wrong with him? It seemed that the better she felt, the more elusive Ian became. Late nights, gone all day, and half the evening on the weekends, refusing to sleep in her room, shrugging away caresses. Something was definitely wrong.

As she stared down at the candlelit table in the dining room, the pattern on the plates began to blur. Maybe she had just been fooling herself. It was so comforting to believe that just by being optimistic, good things would happen to her. Leslie had never explained how she handled the multiple disappointments in her life. What did one do, when the cup really was half empty?

By ten o'clock, Suzanne began covering the meal. He'd probably eaten already anyway, and her stupid attempt to surprise him had backfired. What a waste. Roast duck, baby carrots, wild rice . . . It was romantically silly. She had had this great idea to make old fashioned recipes to snap Ian out of the doldrums. She had thought maybe he was homesick— maybe he was tired of the nineties rat race, and craved a little touch of the good old days. That's why she had bought that stupid corset-looking thing at Victoria's Secret.

Flinging a silver spoon into the sink, Suzanne forbade herself to cry. It had been over a month. What was wrong with him? She wasn't even showing yet, and already he didn't want her. Okay, so her breasts were sore. But how would he know? Dotting the corners of her eyes with a tea towel, she tried not to mess up her make-up. Make-up! She had spent a small fortune on the stuff, trying to change her look, trying to look younger, prettier—as though she wasn't wearing any.

Then, there were the dress and the shoes . . . the kind of Laura Ashley feminine stuff she never wore!

Tears streamed down her face against her will. Forgetting about the mascara, she wiped it with the back of her hand, coming away with a big, black smudge. When she saw it, she could begin to feel her bottom lip tremble. That was it. The dam broke. Who cared anyway? He didn't. Holding onto the edge of the kitchen sink for support, Suzanne just let the sobs come. She was trying so hard to be Miss Cheerful. Trying so hard to think of everyone else first. Feeling guilty when she had to go to work. Trying to be considerate, and always ask how his day went . . .

"Suzanne?"

Suzanne spun around at the sound of Ian's voice. "It's ten o'clock at night, I fixed a special dinner, and you ruined it, and where the *hell* have you been?" The words just poured forth like the tears, in one long sentence.

Ian blinked twice and stared at her for a moment. "What happened to your face?" he asked nervously, walking toward her and touching her cheek.

When he brought his hand away, the tips of his fingers were stained with a black, inky substance.

Suzanne could feel her lip tremble again, and she took a deep breath before speaking. She would not cry. "It's— it's— mascara! It's ruined! Everything is ruined! And, I hope you're satisfied!" She left the room, heading upstairs to hide herself in the bathroom.

What a disaster. A supposedly romantic evening gone bust. He'd never want her now. For, that matter, she didn't want him.

"Suzanne, love . . . open the door. I am sorry about the meal. But, in your condition, you must eat. Let me bring you a tray."

His attempt insulted her. He was still treating her like an invalid, not a woman. She'd never come out. She'd starve first.

"Please. Open the door so we can talk."

Waiting a few moments, until she was ready, Suzanne stood and opened the door, wiping at her make-up in the process. Brushing past him, she went over to the closet and kicked off her new shoes.

"I do apologize for being late, without advance notice," he began tentatively, "but— "

"No problem," she said in a falsely upbeat voice. "No problemo."

"Really, something came up, and I—"

"And you didn't bother to call me. Like I said, no problem."

To ignore him, she used the exercise of fishing through her closet for a nightgown. If the cold shoulder was what he wanted, then the cold shoulder would be what he got. *No problem.* Finding the oldest, raggediest, flannel pajamas that she could excavate, Suzanne went into the bathroom to change into them. He'd never see her body again, since he didn't want it. Fine. He didn't have to see her pregnant, forty-one-year-old pear shape. Fine. He could do whatever he wanted to do. Talk to whomever he wanted. Fine. Fine. Fine!

She almost hurt her shoulder when she flung open the bathroom door, and stopped short to see Ian sitting in the chair holding the new corset.

"What is this?" he asked with a knowing smile, and shaking his head at her ridiculous flannel outfit.

A combination of embarrassment and anger coursed through her as she snatched it from his hands, and stuffed it in a drawer. It was bad enough that he had rejected her. Now, he knew that she had been waiting for him, not just to come home, but to make love! Worse, he was smiling at her as she stood before him in old Christmas pajamas.

Her dignity in shreds, she snatched up a pillow with the top blanket, and hurled it at him. "Out!"

Ian allowed the jumble of covers to hit him and fall to the floor, but he didn't move. He just stared at her, and continued to smile harder. Again, tears blurred her vision, and she stiffened herself to dig in her heels for the stand off.

"Well, you don't want to sleep here normally," she said in a shaky voice. "You apparently have lost interest . . . you don't talk to me, you stay out late, I never see you anymore . . . now, that you have so many friends . . ." Fighting back a sob, she continued. "And, so, if I bore you . . . and I'm not what you want . . . then, you can go elsewhere. We're not married."

"Is that what this is about, Suzanne? Getting married?"

Ian's smile infuriated her.

"No. It's about respect. You didn't respect me enough to even call me. So you can just leave."

"I see," he said mildly, standing and picking up the pillow and spread.

But when he threw the tangled covers back on the bed and walked in her direction, she wasn't prepared for his serious expression. He'd been laughing at her up till now, so what had changed in three seconds? Fear paralyzed her. This was it. She had known it would come, since the beginning. Dear God . . . and she was pregnant!

"Who is she?" she whispered, backing away but getting stopped by the bed. "I knew it would happen, so I'm not surprised. I just want to know— to hear you admit it. You owe me that."

She would not cry.

"You are correct," he said slowly. "I owe you that."

Before she could think about it, her hand had moved on its own. It had become another entity, unhinged itself from her body, and slapped his face. Covering her mouth, she stood motionless, not sure of how he would respond.

"I am in love with her. She's beautiful, Suzanne."

That was all he had to say. The slap had been deserved. She was karmically correct. Now, she could kill him without guilt. Any woman judge in the world would understand.

"I don't need to hear any more. I've heard enough," she said quickly, trying to pass around to the other side of him and out the door. "Get out of my way. I'm leaving."

"Her eyes are hazel," he said looking at her intensely, while holding onto her wrist. "She has auburn hair, that gives sunlight a new brilliance, and a smile more intoxicating than wine. Her laughter is warm and genuine, just like her heart . . . But, I haven't been giving her enough attention lately. You see, other obligations have kept me from her. She's pregnant, you know," he said moving closer to her face. "And I can't allow her to continue this madness of driving about, and going up and down elevators . . . or stairs. She might fall

and hurt herself. Yes, Suzanne, there is someone special in my life. I confess."

Shame forced her to look down, but Ian lifted
her chin with two fingers and brushed her lips.

"So I have hidden the fact that I've needed to
get a second job . . . lifting boxes on the docks,
where my good friend, Michael, works on the
weekend. And, because I love this woman, Suzanne, I must marry her in the appropriate
manner. I am sorry that I am so old fashioned,
and too old to change. So, I must make her an
honest woman. I must get down on my knees,"
he said, kneeling before her and kissing her
waist. "I must go into my pocket . . . and present her with my promise to love her always."

Suzanne covered her face and cried. What
could she say to the man who knelt before her?
All of the nights when he dragged in tired and
smelly, all of the mornings that he had left notes
under tea cups, all of the weekends that he left
her alone . . .

"I don't deserve this," she wailed, refusing to
take his hand. "I thought the worst things about
you, Ian. I didn't understand why you didn't
want me . . ."

"I did not want to disturb your rest, by leaving
and entering your bed so late," he whispered.
"Not while you are fashioning within you that
precious gift."

New sobs made her sit down on the edge of
the bed.

"Now, dinner will not be so ruined, will it?"

he asked, kissing her again and slipping the ring on her finger.

She didn't even look at it, but hugged him and hid her face in his shoulder. "I'm so sorry," she sniffed, trying not to smear even more make-up on his shirt.

"No apology necessary. It is already forgotten."

"But will you talk to me again . . . include me in with the gang again? I miss everybody so much."

Ian brushed the wet hair from her face. "We miss you too, Suzanne. Everybody does. But I haven't wanted to discuss business with you until I was really sure that you felt better."

Nodding her head, she touched his face. "I'm not made out of glass. I won't shatter if there's a problem. I want to be in on things— like before, when we first started."

Ian smiled and took a seat next to her on the bed. "You are already in on things, darling."

He chuckled at her puzzled expression.

"Remember the papers I handed you from Mr. Barnes?" he asked while patting her hand as though to reassure her.

Becoming nervous, she nodded her head but took her time to form a question. She didn't want to hear anything ugly. Not now. What had he done? Was he going to confess that he never went through with the transfer, or something else less ethical? Suzanne closed her eyes and braced herself. "Let me have it. What now?"

"I transferred all but three million back to

you. I decided to let bygones be bygones, since I'm not sure about this time value of money calculation, anyway."

Suzanne looked down at her new oval diamond, and slipped it from her finger. She studied the beautiful antique filigreed setting, and closed her eyes as she placed it in Ian's palm. "I cannot accept this."

"Before you turn me away, hear me out," he said, still sounding cheerful. "I decided to gamble with my three million, not the whole amount."

"Is that supposed to make this—"

"Hear me out, madame," he said, forcing her to look at him again. "I have a vast repertoire of rationalizations, excuses, and hedging techniques at my disposal. But none are required here. Just the truth.

"The truth," she repeated, looking at him hard.

"I sank a portion of it into a college fund for our children, based upon the sweat equity that all four of us had originally invested in scraping down that Godforsaken garage. Not one of the parents can touch it. That way, not one of the mothers have to worry about the errant proclivities of men. That should be settled. Now, next issue— Mike and I donated the garage to the local artists and kids, as a community center. It should help keep them out of trouble, and generate just enough to break even with a couple of part-time, minimum wage positions available."

When he hesitated, she smiled. "I suppose Opal got a job out of this? Should I be jealous?"

"Please. Trust me, Suzanne. I would lose my mind within the hour. Have you heard that child's chatter?"

She had to laugh.

"And, as for the rest of it . . . I invested equal shares in a real coffee house franchise. You own a chain of four in the Delaware Valley. Barnes did the paperwork since I'm not barred yet in this state."

She stared at the man in amazement. "Yet?"

"Well," he chuckled, "I do have identification, and suppose I could get into my old Alma Mater again, if I want."

"You are not serious?" she gasped, covering her mouth.

"Mike and I will run the franchises. We'll have a good income, and stock to shore us up. Leslie has no interest in business, per se. She just enjoys contemplating the universe and helping people. We must respect the individual talents of others, Suzanne."

"But, what about me?" She was still in a state of shock.

"Your placement agency should be able to keep Mike and me staffed . . . and I heard about all of these gadgets that let a person work from home. Would you go with me to a store one day, and help me familiarize myself?"

She could only shake her head. Things were definitely not what they seemed on the surface. But two questions still nagged at her, and she decided to clear the air, once and for all.

"Okay," she said, taking a deep breath. "Why are you still working at the docks, then?"

Ian laughed, slipping the ring back onto her finger. "Because I'm building credit."

"What?"

"A man must buy his woman's ring from the fruits of his labor, not a windfall. That is the traditional way. I only used the Visa to reserve it, because my pay is so low and I wanted you to have it immediately. We do have a delicate time issue, you know. There is no need for unnecessary public scrutiny. So, I paid for half of it with my earnings, and the other half I still owe. But, I'm afraid you'll have to tell me where to send the merchant his money." Ian furrowed his brow. "Michael never fully explained this, and there is no address for the claimant on that little card. How on earth do you send them your payments? Do you use those money machines, Suzanne?"

"You are adorable," she said kissing his face. "I'll show you. Don't worry."

"Now," he said, standing, "Is this row over?"

"Yes . . . but— never mind."

"Suzanne?" Ian sat back down and looked at her. "What else have I neglected?"

She couldn't tell him. She had already put him through enough. "It's nothing. I love you."

Ian swallowed hard and stood quickly. "I should go to bed."

Crestfallen, she just nodded. "I guess you're tired. I haven't been very considerate . . . I thought that it was just because you didn't want to."

He stared at her, and inhaled deeply through his nose. "Never, ever believe that of me. Ever."

She didn't understand. His gaze held an intensity that bored right through her, making her want him in the worst way, but he never moved in her direction.

"Well, with work, and everything . . . I know that you need your sleep."

"I haven't slept much in a month, Suzanne. I must go now, before I lose my perspective and do you harm. I am only flesh and blood, but this is more import— "

"You think that you'll hurt me?" she interrupted, standing and moving toward him. "Oh, Ian. Is that what's been wrong?"

"Since your fall . . . and in your delicate condition. They told me of the risks, and with the x-rays. How could I be so careless as to— "

She cut off his words with a kiss, allowing her body to melt against his.

At first, he didn't respond. But, as she continued to caress him, he enfolded her gently, still treating her as though she might break. His tenderness was so compelling, yet the emotions he fought so severe. She could feel his conflict, and she tried to reassure him without words.

Leading him back to the bed, she pulled him beside her. "There are so many other ways, if you're nervous," she said, kissing his throat and making him draw a ragged breath. "I'll show you how much I've learned, and how much I love you Ian? Just trust me . . ."

Epilogue

Rahmin folded his hands in his lap and looked up to the majestic cathedral ceiling. Inhaling the frankincense as the altar boys went by in the processional, he smiled. "Ah, rituals . . ." he murmured, enjoying the organ music and turning his attention back to the congregation. It was always so hard to remember what one was supposed to do. Some times one was supposed to stand, or kneel, or pray, or intone, or Ohm, or go prostrate . . . The others who came regularly always seemed to know. He travelled so much, and to so many different types of religious dwellings, that it was difficult to sort it all out at times.

What was the Catholic christening ceremony . . . ? "Ah, no matter," he said under his breath, trying to stay focused. The process would be over soon. Unlike the process of living, which took several lifetimes.

Rahmin smiled, for today he saw good works come to a fruitful juncture in the road. His students had learned . . . they had grown, just like the baby in the priest's arms would grow. They had endured, and stayed on the path. Long enough for Leslie to learn how to stand up for herself. Long enough for Michael to learn to take responsibility for his own dreams. Long enough for Ian to give trust and forgiveness a try . . . and long enough for one of his most difficult students, Suzanne, to gain faith and hope.

Chuckling to himself, he spoke in a very soft whisper. "Now, Cecilia. We are in a church. You cannot speak ill of people, that is not karmically correct. You know better. No, just because what you said about Mrs. Scott was funny doesn't make it nice. I know, I know . . . but she'll just have to come back again to correct her debt. That is not your affair, now, stop it. No, I'm not being cross with you, my darling. How could I ever resist you? You have been my weakness for centuries. Isn't that how I was thrown out of the Sistine Chapel? Do you remember the year? Oh, I'm flattered. And I thought you had forgotten."

He cleared his throat as one of the parishioners gave him a nasty glance. "You must contain yourself, my love. Yes . . . she is beautiful. A perfectly, healthy little replica of you. Oh, and did I tell you, they're naming her Cecilia?"

Afterword

Minds are like flowers: they function best
when opened.

"Whatever you can do
or believe you can, begin it.
Boldness has genius, power and magic."
— Goethe (1749-1843)

EVERY DAY WILL FEEL LIKE FEBRUARY 14TH!

Zebra Historical Romances
by Terri Valentine